The Owl of the Durotriges

Yassmin Sanders

Published in 2012 by FeedARead.com Publishing – Arts Council funded

Acknowledgements

I would like to thank Gloria Morris for her archaeological input, Jill Petts for her painstaking editing and apposite comments, Jennie Johnson and Lucy Rutter for their valuable suggestions and Ian Sanders for his his help with continuity, horsey bits, and fight re-enactments in the kitchen.

Map of Central and Southern Iron Age Britain

List of Characters by Tribe

Durotriges
Chela, a young healer
Hanu, King of the Durotriges
Gowell and Ivor, Hanu's sons
Erea and Cinea, Hanu's daughters
Elanor, Chela's foster-mother and a healer
Annan, a young noble
Lughaid, Hanu's Chief Procurer of Slaves
Yarrow, Chela's wolfhound

Atres
Irven and Briona, King and Queen of the Atres
Kendra, only child of the King and Queen
Fionn, a noble of the Clan of Morffryn and Kendra's betrothed
Caradwg, Fionn's father
Cator, a swineherd
Kelwin, an Elder of the Atres
Ferehar, Briona's servant
Pedwar, Kendra's wolfhound
Malvina, Huel and Morvyn, Atres children

Vellani
Bryn, ailing King of the Vellani
Doran, Bryn's heir
Canogus, a noble and Doran's cousin
Brendan and Mylor, Vellani warriors
Taral and Carod, guards
Lann, adopted into the Vellani tribe
Cerid, Lann's mother
Liam, a healer

The Canti and Regni
Engus, King of the Canti
Wil, a Canti noble
Berris the Small, King of the Regni

The Veneti
Bearcban, King of the Veneti
Armelle, Bearcban's daughter
Riana, Armelle's escort and companion

The Druids
Deryn, Chief Druid at the Isle of Lynd
Bari, a young Druid Priest
Druce, Chief Druid from the Isle of Mona
Eryr Fawr, Durotriges resident Druid

Other Characters
Keary, a wandering musician and poet
Grypsos, an Alexandrian Greek sailor

Places
Viper's Fort, the Durotriges seat of power (Hengistbury Head)
Awelfryn, centre of the Atres kingdom, a hill fort in modern-day Wiltshire
Ravensroost, the Vellani powerbase, a defended settlement in modern-day Bedfordshire
Buzzardstone, home of the Clan of Morffryn, at the western edge of the Atres territory
Lynd, an Island off the north-eastern coast, on the Humber Estuary
Mona, a Druidic base (Anglesey)
Saramis (the Isle of Wight)
Armorica, the Land of the Veneti (Brittany)

ONE

Vipers' Fort, Southern Britain, 82 BC.

The Voice of Chela, a Healer of the Durotriges

It is only bone, I tell myself. Just another bone. Ignore it. But I cannot. As though drawn by some dread force, my gaze rests on the tangle of hair, skin and sinew clinging to a tiny skull. It takes a moment for the shock to echo through my body but there is no avoiding the truth; the decaying mess once shaped a living child. Perhaps I helped birth it. I may even know its name.

The infant's skull has been placed deliberately, even tenderly, at the base of one of the oaks. It glows against the darkness of the tree's hollow heart and though the stench of decay speaks eloquently enough of its death, the child's spirit lingers on. I can feel its gaze upon me.

I reach for Yarrow's shaggy grey head and dig my fingers into the fur at his neck. He responds with a warm lick and I notice how the cold air turns his breath to vapour. I do not wish to linger here; the lightening sky tells me that dawn is nearly upon us, and so I shrug the basket off my back and place it at my feet. Blood has soaked through the wicker into my woollen cloak and I can feel its sticky wetness between my shoulder blades.

I shiver and rub my arms. I know this place, of course. I've been here many times before, at Samhain, to mark the passing of the dead, when we light torches and sing, but this is the first time I have dared venture into the Druids' nemeton alone. The silence is total, devoid even of a blackbird's song and I can hear my own blood rushing in my ears.

I look around and compare the items littering the ground with my own offering. There are some coins and a dagger, but mainly there are bones, human, animal, all jumbled together, food for the Druids' blood-thirsty deity, Dis. In my mind's eye I see Him pointing his finger, wanting to know what I have brought to appease Him. What am I doing here, I wonder, talking to this male god? I am here, I remind myself, to bind Gowell's heart, so that he does not leave me, and for that I need a God who thinks like a man.

I squat and pull my meagre sacrifice out of the basket. The odour of flesh wafts up in the still morning air and hits my stomach. Yarrow, dribbling, thrusts his nose at the meat.

'Down!' My voice is a harsh whisper but I have trained him well, and he moves away, gazing at the piglet. I too stare at the dead creature before I stand awkwardly then carry it to the Bloodstone, a boulder reddened by the iron in its veins. It sits solidly at the centre of the clearing, emanating a malevolent power. The smiths have a magical way with such stones, breathing fire into their beings, transforming them into a new life-form, but the Bloodstone serves an altogether different purpose, its story oft spoken by the weavers of words. Nature placed it here, they say, not man, when the world was born, a silent demand from the twilight gods and upon which the offerings are placed. I stroke the stone, seeing how the dried brown liquid of dreams and prayers has stained its already dull red surface.

I set my piglet on the shallow dip of its uppermost edge and kneel. Out of reverence to Dis, I pull at the hood of my birris, baring my head, but glad also that my hair falls to screen my face. A shard of golden sunlight breaks through the gloom and turns my hair blood red. How apt.

I speak my prayer out loud, asking Dis to change the course of my life, and my voice sounds strange to my own ears. I finish the rehearsed words and though I sense there is more to give, I am at a loss to understand what is required of me.

My gaze is drawn once more to the infant's skull, with its baleful stare. I realise then that my piglet cannot compete with such an offering, even though I spent many hours tending the ailing pig farmer's wife. Dis will laugh at my gesture, and I begin to wonder if I might even have given offence. A new wave of despondency settles over me. In any case, is it right, this desire to control another's will? I know the answer, and the iniquity of my act sickens me. I move away from the stone, my head bowed. Yarrow follows, throwing backward glances at the abandoned meat.

The grove grows ever more oppressive and I am anxious to leave. I sling the empty basket onto my back and quicken my pace, striding away from the Nemeton. As I pass through the ring of ancient oaks and leave the Great God's domain, it is as though my mind is floating some distance from my leaden limbs. Icy leaves yield under my doeskin boots, filling the silence with a crunch. Pink and gold sunbeams slide through skeletal branches, touching my skin, but their warmth is just a promise. The raw morning numbs my cheeks and stings my eyes. Ordinarily I would feel exhilaration at nature's cold beauty, but today I barely notice the shimmering dawn.

I pause at the edge of the wood, where the ground rises high enough to offer a view over Viper's Fort, the Durotriges' centre of power. I can see my home from here and note that my fern-mother, Elanor, is awake, as the tell-tale smoke from our freshly-kindled hearth seeps through the thatch. Beyond the settlement, the deep-water harbour sparkles, calm as a marsh pond, protected by the spit of land that curls around it before rising up into towering cliffs. I think of the headland as a fist, raised in defiance against the encroaching sea.

The harbour is astir and I watch as the crews of two Veneti trading ships load their cargoes, readying themselves for their journey home. There are no slaves at the dock this morning, and I am glad to be spared the sight of their misery, but I know there is a consignment of hunting dogs below deck, because I can hear their anguished whines skimming across the still water.

My hatred for the Veneti builds again, just as I was beginning to think I have my emotions in check. It is probably the misery of the hounds that has stirred me, but I surprise myself with the depth of my loathing for the powerful Veneti with their mighty ships, controlling as they do the entire coastline of Armorica. No trader, it is said, can enter their harbours without paying their crippling tariffs and those who sail further out to sea, in an attempt to avoid their greedy grasp, fall prey to the wrath of the capricious sea Goddess Eluna whose hunting ground is Morhiban Bay itself.

Of course it's not just the misery of the dogs that has upset me. I am a practical woman, a healer, not a faint-hearted sop. The presence of the Veneti ships means I am forced to acknowledge the reality of Gowell's voyage tomorrow. Despite my pleas, my rages and my cajoling, his mind is set and I know deep down that my offering to Dis will have no effect. On the morrow Gowell will be journeying to Armorica to fetch his bride, a princess of the Veneti. Their union, they say, is designed to cement relations between our two peoples. Yes, I understand the politics and the need for the alliance but even so, I feel my stomach tighten at the prospect of losing him, whether to the Goddess Eluna, or the woman who waits for him at Morhiban Bay. As a final insult, Gowell has denied my request to spend our last night together. This evening there will be a feast to celebrate his voyage. He is, after all, the Durotriges heir, and his father will ensure he has a good sending off. It will be a night for the men.

So lost am I in thought, that it is only Yarrow's throaty growl that brings me to my senses. I turn and face the trees, my hand curling around the cold handle of my dagger. I peer through the sea of brown bark, trying to make out what has caused the dog's hackles to rise.

Then I see the Druid, Eryr Fawr, his linen robe shining in the gloom, dragging a youth into the nemeton. The boy's arms are bound behind his back. He is so bony and small; he can only be a slave. I watch as the priest presses him down until he is kneeling in front of the Bloodstone, his face mere inches from my own sacrifice which is brushed aside without a thought.

I lift a finger in warning to Yarrow, who stands stock-still, awaiting my command. I pray I have not been seen, but the priest looks up, riveting me with his eyes, scrutinising my soul. I know him, of course, for he is our Dream Teller. He does as he pleases and no-one dares question him, but there are those among us who believe he is overly fond of the streaming of blood. A wave of fear courses through me but the priest turns away, ignoring my presence. In my mind's eye I walk up to him and stab him through the neck. I untie the boy and lead him to safety.

But in truth, I am powerless, for even here amongst the irreligious Durotriges, it is unthinkable to cross one of the priestly caste. Instead, a numbness creeps over me and I back away, reality more dreamlike than my imaginings. Even before I reach the last of the trees, a scream rips through the quiet woodland.

I run, Yarrow at my heels, wanting to distance myself from the stench and misery of death. I know now that Dis is too potent a God for me. I hear his mocking laugh at every turn, as his dark-winged ravens chase me down the twisting path, cawing in derision at my awkward flight.

TWO

The Voice of Lann, a Warrior of the Vellani, and a guest of the Durotriges

Tonight I sit at Hanu's table, an honoured guest of the 'King' himself. King of this dung heap they call Viper's Fort. The table is piled high with treasures, enough to buy the loyalty of the numerous tribes they now call the 'Durotriges'. What a joke! Opposite me sits the heir apparent, Gowell. He is already drunk and wears a self-satisfied smile on his face. What I wouldn't give to wipe that smile away. But I must be patient. My Lord Doran has a plan, and I, and my kin, will be avenged. And so I bite down my disgust and pretend to be enjoying myself. It is two years since Doran sent me here and if I have not learned to conceal my contempt by now, I never will.

Gowell's father, the 'King', has invited every chieftain in the vicinity, and true to form, each and every one of them has turned up, no doubt hoping for a boon. At least there are no women here tonight to belittle me with their sly comments, and for that I am grateful. The feast is meant to be in celebration of Gowell's voyage to collect his Veneti woman, but if you ask me, it's just an excuse to show off their wealth. No wonder Gowell looks so smug. It must please him to know his father commands such loyalty, only because it will ease the way for him, when the time comes. But Gowell will never be King. Doran will see to that.

I have to concede, however, that Hanu knows how to lay on a feast. There is wine, mead and beer for all and the roasting pig is hissing and smoking over the hearth, filling the room with a mouth-watering aroma. Slaves have been commanded to ensure no-one goes without and they are as attentive as ever, carrying jugs of wine and platters of meat and bread to the revellers.

The table at which I sit dominates the area behind the hearth, facing the door. Swords; horse adornments; ceremonial shields and a huge pile of newly minted Durotriges coins occupy one end of the table whilst we 'honoured guests' crowd together at the other end. I notice the coins are stamped with the new Durotriges emblem, a horse rather than their traditional owl. The horse belongs to the Atres tribe, in the west, who carve its image on their hillsides. The Durotriges are showing their contempt for the Atres by stealing their emblem. But what do I care? I loathe the Atres as much as I detest the Durotriges.

My eyes rove around the room. Smaller tables, around which the lesser guests are arranged, radiate outwards, forming an arc around the hearth. Amphorae full of the finest Roman wine line the walls, all for the giving. I might ask if I can take one for my lord Doran, who appreciates such things, and I feel myself brightening at the thought of home, even though it will be a short visit. I am here as part of an exchange, ostensibly to foster good relations between the Durotriges and the Vellani, as is the custom. Hanu is my 'nutritor', and is therefore honour-bound to treat me as his son whilst I am with him. I cannot help wondering, however, how he would treat me if he knew the depths of my hatred for him and all his kin.

The room is getting noisier as the men get drunk. Bawdy ballads fill the air and as they sing, they bang the tables with their fists. It is not to my liking, but I know better than to protest.

Gowell is trying to talk to his brother, Ivor, and has to raise his voice. I can hear his words quite clearly. Ivor seems marginally more sober than Gowell and I wonder, not for the first time, how different they are to each other. Gowell's physique and bearing single him out from all other men, but it is Ivor who has all the brains.

'Our father has done us proud,' says Gowell.

I follow his eyes as he watches his father, Hanu, walk amongst his people, endowing those he favours with gifts and ordering the slaves to bring them the choicest cuts of meat. The display of wealth is impressive, and as everyone present knows, a blood alliance with the Veneti will guarantee continuing prosperity for those in favour. No-one wishes to be left out and they grovel like worms to be part of Hanu's newly formed 'Durotriges'.

I turn my attention to the others at our table. Next to Ivor sits Eryr Fawr, the resident Druid. I see how the priest's avaricious eyes caress the gifts and how his hands fidget to touch the precious metal. I stifle the urge to spit at him. I was taught by the Druids and know how they should behave, and it is not thus. Eryr Fawr sickens me, for it is his kind who has brought the name of the Brotherhood into disrepute.

There was a time when every Druid would command respect, and though Eryr Fawr may read the omens and observe the rituals, his power has fled. One only has to look at him to realise as much. Once a true Druid, the easy life amongst the Durotriges has corrupted him, making him lazy and complacent. It is common knowledge that Hanu's regard for the Brotherhood is as shallow as a winterbourne at midsummer's eve, though he pays lip service to Eryr Fawr. The Druids

14

are aware of Hanu's feelings, of course, for nothing escapes them. They will not tolerate such disrespect for long and it is time Hanu realised that the Druids are powerful in the land and only the reckless would consider crossing them.

'Eryr Fawr,' Gowell is shouting again. 'Are the omens good?'

'They are indeed,' replies the priest, and I notice that he is sober. 'I made a sacrifice this very morning that I am sure will please the gods.'

'Then I too am well pleased,' says Gowell, running his fingers through his dark curls. He really is very vain, for a man.

Hanu returns to the table and takes his place between his two sons. The first round of giving complete, he nods at his guests and sets about eating. Lughaid, Hanu's Chief Procurer of slaves, is beckoned to join us and takes his place next to me. Lughaid is another loathsome individual, one who thinks only of his belly and his gonads. He and Eryr Fawr stuff their mouths with food, and so I feel obliged to make polite conversation.

'Is the Twrch ready?' I ask, raising my voice.

'She is,' replies Ivor. 'Our gifts for the Veneti are well secured and our crew are making the final checks as we speak. We sail at dawn.'

'I still think it a bad idea to send both your sons on this journey,' says Eryr Fawr, addressing Hanu. Food falls out of his mouth as he speaks. He is truly disgusting. 'Would it not be better to leave one at home? Just in case?'

'You forget,' says Hanu, his eyebrows knitting into a frown, 'my sons here know these seas as they knew their own mother.'

I notice how Hanu's eyes mist over as he finishes speaking. The death of his wife is still raw and the strong wine has unseated his emotions. Gowell looks at his father, hoping, no doubt, that he will not embarrass them all by weeping. I find myself rather wishing that he would burst into tears.

'And anyway,' joins in Ivor, 'you'll be coming with us as our Elder, won't you Eryr Fawr? No harm will befall us, especially as you've observed the rituals.'

Eryr Fawr remains silent. It is obvious he does not relish the prospect of the forthcoming voyage one bit, rituals or not. I wonder if the Priest detected the scorn in Ivor's tone. If I had someone to wager with, I would bet that by morning, Eryr Fawr will be stricken with some mysterious 'illness', forcing him to remain ashore.

'Lann, will you accompany us too?' asks Gowell.

It is not often that Gowell speaks to me and I am slightly taken aback. I am perfectly aware that he and his brother harbour a dislike for me and I know he asks out of politeness, fully expecting me to decline his offer, for although I have sailed with him and Ivor on occasion, I have no great love for the sea. There is a mischief inside me, however, that urges me to accept, but I have other plans.

'Thank you, but with Lord Hanu's permission, I would like to leave for a short while to visit my mother.'

'She is no better?' asks Hanu.

'I'm afraid not.' I speak the truth here, my mother is ailing.

'Then go with my blessing. And give my greetings to Bryn, even though he may no longer know my name. And his son, Doran, of course.'

I love King Bryn as the father I never had, and it pains me to hear his name on Hanu's vile tongue, especially as he denies him the honour of his true title. It is no secret, however, that my master, the Vellani King, has been stricken with a grave illness and recognises no-one. I will lose a part of me when Bryn dies, but I am happy in my allegiance to his heir, Doran, who will soon take the Vellani throne.

I nod my thanks, not trusting myself to speak.

'And you, Ivor, isn't it time you found yourself a woman?' It is Lughaid, who, as he speaks, winks at the young man. Lughaid, a big man, is clearly drunk and as he talks, he gestures wildly with his arms. Ivor has turned bright red. I have been here long enough to know that Ivor hates Lughaid, and would not wish to talk of such things in his company, nor in mine, for that matter.

'No, I have not put my mind to it yet,' says Ivor, after a pause, drawing his finger through a puddle of spilt wine.

'I hear King Irven of the Atres has a pretty young daughter, ripe for marriage,' says Lughaid, making squeezing gestures with his hands. A leer spreads from under his greying moustache but he is too drunk to notice the effect of his words until Hanu explodes with a sudden rage.

'That monster, Irven's, flesh and blood? With a son of mine?' He shouts, bringing his fist down onto the table with a crash, sending the new Roman tableware skittering to the floor. His face darkens and his eyes narrow. The room quietens. Ivor puts a hand on his father's arm. Gowell looks worried. I manage to conceal my mirth.

'Lughaid here speaks from ignorance,' says Ivor. 'Don't worry, father, you know I wouldn't consider it for a moment.'

16

To the relief of the guests, Hanu relaxes and the carousing resumes. The King takes another swig of wine, but glares at Lughaid before leaving the table.

'You oaf, Lughaid,' says Gowell. 'See how you have angered my father.'

'I'm sorry,' says Lughaid, 'I was only jesting. Your father's enmity with the Atres is no secret. I shouldn't have mentioned Irven's name on such an auspicious day.'

'It's the wine,' says Ivor, taking another slurp from his drinking horn. 'It addles the senses.'

For once I find myself in full agreement with the younger brother.

'It is King Irven who quarrels with us, not the other way around,' says Gowell after a while, and his voice sounds wheedling. I wonder sometimes if he has any principles, but I also know that the toad, Lughaid, is valuable to the Durotriges for his knowledge of the slave market and Gowell does not want to alienate him entirely. It all comes down to wealth and power in the end.

Ivor suddenly looks tired and turns to his brother.

'I weary of these revelries,' he says. 'We have an early start and a hard day's sailing ahead of us. We should think of retiring.'

Gowell nods and downs the rest of his wine in one gulp, as though preparing to leave. I am relieved for I too wish to retire. I have had enough of their company for one night.

'What of Chela?' asks Ivor, as he stands, leaning onto the table for support.

Of course, the woman Gowell has been bedding since they were childhood sweethearts. I'd forgotten about her. And so has Gowell, it would seem.

'What of her?' says Gowell, and I see that I was right.

'Have you said farewell?' Ivor persists, and I wonder if he has a soft spot for the flame-haired healer.

Gowell merely shrugs. Just then Hanu returns, his good humour restored.

'More wine,' he shouts, and a slave comes immediately to do his bidding. A grin of resignation passes between the two brothers as they sit down once more and hold their horns out to be filled to the brim. I groan inwardly. It's going to be a long night, I can tell.

THREE

Chela

It is two full days since Gowell left and I am miserable. It will not do for Elanor to see me like this. She will only worry, and she has looked so tired and drawn lately.

I calm myself with deep breaths before walking through the doorway of our roundhouse. Yarrow settles himself in the porch; he is a big dog but his large frame barely fills the wide space.

The sturdy wooden door has been left ajar and the light streams in, illuminating Elanor who is standing over the black iron cooking pot, stirring its contents. The cauldron is suspended just above the fire and the single chain that holds it quivers as it disappears into the sooty rafters.

'You're back early,' she says, glancing up, meeting my eyes.

'The child has died. There was no more I could do.'

I am referring to the little girl I've been trying to heal for the past week. The sickly infant finally succumbed to the cough that wracked her body and though her death was no surprise, it nonetheless saddens those of us who tried to save her.

Elanor gives me a sympathetic look but remains silent. I am grateful. Words will not bring the girl back. Instead, she holds out a spoonful of the brew for me to taste.

'What do you think?' she asks.

Elanor laughs and I realise I am wrinkling my nose as my tongue seeks to recognise the bitter-tasting mess of leaves and herbs. There, I have it: nettle tops, dried fennel and dill seeds form the main part of the concoction. Fresh herbs would have been better but it is still too early in the year to collect them from the wild or grow them in our sheltered garden.

'Let me guess, it's for Megan - to give her energy and plentiful milk?'

'Well done,' beams Elanor. 'And barley, for goodness.'

Elanor turns back to her cooking pot.

'By the way,' she says, 'what happened to that piglet you were promised from the farmer?'

I feel myself reddening. I have not told Elanor about the sacrifice, but I know that my fern-mother is not one to be lied to. I swallow hard.

'I took it to the Bloodstone, for all the good it will do me,' I say.

Elanor stops stirring.

'We could have used the meat,' she says, and I feel the reprimand in her tone. 'What did you think – one word to the gods and Gowell will change his mind and come running to you?'

'Something like that,' I say, avoiding her scrutiny.

'No-one understands the true meaning of sacrifice these days. They think they can kill something and the world will do their bidding.'

I flinch at Elanor's harsh words, but I know I deserve them.

'You're right, as ever. It was a futile gesture in any case, even supposing the gods were listening,' I say. 'Eryr Fawr was there. He brushed my offering aside as though it were a mere spider's web. He had a juicer morsel for his work.'

Elanor raises an eyebrow, prompting me to continue.

'A young boy. His screams still echo in my mind.'

She shakes her head, muttering a curse under her breath.

I squat next to the fire and grasp the wrought-iron poker in one hand, my fingers curling around the boar's head handle. I prod the logs, sending a shower of sparks into the air. I know how much Elanor hates the Brothers and the fear they wield over the people. I change the subject.

'Shall I take the brew over to Megan?'

'Yes. That would be good,' replies Elanor, and I think she has regained her even temperament. But there is more to come. She studies my face before sitting down heavily on the low bench next to the hearth.

'I'm sorry it hasn't worked out for you Chela,' she says. 'I sometimes wonder if I did the right thing by you.'

'What are you saying, Elanor?'

I am truly sorry about the piglet, and wish to appease my fern-mother, but right now I am not minded to have a deep conversation of this nature. Elanor, however, wants to talk.

'Perhaps I should have found a noble's family to foster you.'

'Oh Elanor, please don't talk this way,' I say, swallowing hard. 'A noble's family could not have cared for me as well as you.'

Elanor laughs and her soft nature shows through.

'None could have resisted your infant charms, believe me! And if I had found a noble family, you would have been assured status and a dowry, and could have made a good marriage.'

'I do not want a 'good' marriage, Elanor. I want Gowell, and I cannot have him.' I look down, because I am close to tears again and I don't want her to see. 'And he would not have married me, in any

20

case, regardless of my dowry or status. This Veneti alliance is far too important to him.'

Elanor nods. I know she will not argue that particular point.

'You have taught me the plant-lore, Elanor, and thanks to you, I will always have a place amongst the Durotriges. So don't worry yourself that you did or did not do the right thing. I'll have to take what I can, and if Gowell comes to me, despite his bride, I won't turn him away.'

'Chela, for the love of the Great Mother, isn't it time you started putting Gowell out of your mind? You could marry an ordinary man! A good farmer who would not expect a large dowry.'

'And suffer a loveless union? I don't think so. Anyway, marriage isn't everything. *You* didn't suffer for the lack of a husband, did you?'

I had not meant to set my words loose, but they are out, and it's too late to call them back. Elanor turns away sharply.

'I just don't want you to become embittered,' she says, after what seems a long while.

Despite myself, I laugh harshly, and regret it immediately because I can see I have upset Elanor again, for she has squeezed her eyes shut. But I have underestimated my fern-mother, who is tougher than I think.

'Well, at least you took the silverweed,' she says. Her voice is spiky. 'If you had fallen with child you would be in a right mess by now.'

I look up, surprised at her tone. I want to lash out with hard words, and then I remember that she has been unwell. Feeling guilty, I soften my voice.

'I'm sorry,' I say, 'I didn't mean..'

Elanor cuts me short.

'It's alright,' she says, struggling to her feet. 'Here. You finish this off. I haven't sown the seeds yet and the heavens are right today.'

I nod and begin to stir the concoction. The liquid just covers the cauldron's base, enough to fill one jug.

'Don't let it burn,' warns Elanor. She tries to sound cross, but a gentleness has begun to suffuse her face, reaching her eyes. I smile back. All will be well. The quarrel has been averted.

If anyone deserves the title 'fern-mother' it is Elanor. Ever since I can remember she has curled around me, like a fern in early summer, protecting and nurturing me, even though I am not her kin. I would be wise to remind myself of this more often.

I watch as she leaves the roundhouse, relieved to be left alone. As ever these days, it is Gowell who dominates my thinking, a fact that irritates me beyond reason. I wonder, not for the first time, that had I carried his child, would he have married me? I cannot be sure, and in any case, such conjecture is futile; the silverweed has guarded against that eventuality.

The herb was brought as a gift from Elanor's man, Grypsos. Some twelve summers ago Elanor nursed the sailor's ulcerated leg and let him stay in our home for the time it took to heal. It did not take long for a romance to blossom between Elanor and the swarthy Alexandrian. I remember, as a little girl, finding them kissing one day when I barged in through the doorway. I was upset at first, thinking he would replace me in Elanor's affections, but I soon realised that Elanor had more than enough love for the both of us.

It was not long before I began to think of Grypsos as the father I never had. I would curl up in his lap and play with his shaggy grey-streaked beard as I listened to his tales of exotic beasts from the shores of Africana and the easy life of those who dwell in the lands of olives and grapes. In his heavy accent and faltering language, he would describe his homeland, with its mighty buildings, palaces and tombs. We would listen with rapt attention, trying to imagine the warm countries to the south and the way of life that so differs from ours. The distances Grypsos traverses are unimaginable, but his tales were enough to sow the seeds of restlessness in my young heart. But of course that sort of life is unthinkable for one such as I, and I must dwell in reality, not dreams.

Every year Elanor and I wait for his ship to arrive, laden with olive oil and wine, but above all Elanor waits, with mounting excitement, for the exotic herbs and spices that Grypsos keeps especially for her. I remember the year he brought the seeds of the silverweed plant all the way from its homeland, Cyrene, on the northern shores of Africana. Such was the demand for this plant amongst the Roman women that its numbers had dwindled until there was virtually none left. Elanor's prowess as a gardener enabled her to cultivate the seeds in our little garden, where they flourish. We dry the herb and have sufficient to let Grypsos take some back with him to Rome where, he tells me, he turns a good profit.

It is rare that the married women need the silverweed; children die more often than they thrive, but those who have not yet sworn their fidelity, or whose wombs have suffered through repeated births, ask for Elanor's ministrations.

As soon as the brew is ready, I wrap a piece of sacking around my hands and lift the heavy pot off the hook before placing it on the flagstone. I drape the cloth over one of the dragon-headed fire-dogs, and then ladle the concoction into a wooden jug.

Setting the jug down to cool, I walk over to the oak ladder that leans against one of the internal supports. Climbing up, I reach the wooden ledge that runs around the interior of the thatched roof, its planked flooring warm against my bare feet. I dodge the curing hams and drying fish and head for a corner of the loft where I store my personal belongings. My eyes sting from the accumulated smoke that seeps upwards through the thatch, but I ignore the discomfort. Kneeling, I pause for a moment to look at the lid of a carved wooden casket, on which the almost imperceptible face of a hound winds in and out of flowing tendrils and interweaving leaves. The box was a present from Hanu. Opening the lid, I delve inside and pull out a golden wrist torc, the only link to my past.

I wipe my stinging eyes with the sleeve of my tunic as I finger the slender piece of solid gold. I was two days old, so the story goes, when my Atres mother was taken by the spirits and my father not long after killed in a raid. The pure gold band, with the swirling pattern of the Durotriges owl inscribed on its inside, belonged to my mother.

For reasons best known to her, when I was orphaned, Elanor brought me south to start a new life at Viper's Fort and we have lived here ever since. I often wonder why the bracelet displays the Durotriges symbol if my parents were of Atres stock. It should, by rights, be a horse. Elanor claims not to know the answer. In fact, Elanor refuses to talk about my parents at all and I have long since stopped asking questions, especially as the Durotriges and Atres are sworn enemies. I do not wear the bracelet, for fear of losing it, but sometimes I pull it out and close my eyes, hoping to attract a dream of my mother. Today the bracelet provides scant comfort so I fold it in its cloth, put it away and climb back down to ground level. I feel guilty. My simple act feels like a betrayal of the woman who has raised me, even though I know Elanor would not have considered it so.

As my thoughts return to my fern-mother, I decide that before I take the brew over to Megan, I will prepare a tonic. Elanor's energy seems to wax and wane like the moon. And there is more, I am sure of it. I often catch her lost in thought, chewing her lip, a worried frown deepening the lines on her forehead. She dismisses my concern with a wave of her hand, and I know her well enough not to press the matter.

I crush the imported sage and thyme with a pestle, then add the dried rose hips, muttering a healing prayer to the Great Mother as I work. I add a measure of cold water from the pitcher, then carefully wielding the iron tongs, drop in a red hot stone from the fire. The pot-boiler releases its heat, causing the water to bubble.

I contemplate my world as I let the herbs steep. It could be a great deal worse. Elanor is good to me and every day brings fresh knowledge of the plants and their uses. I have a lovely home, I never go hungry, I have a fresh water spring not twenty paces from my abode, and I enjoy my labours. I have friends, Cinea and Erea, Gowell's sisters, and Ivor too. Perhaps even Gowell and I might be friends again. We were all raised in a tumble together since we were babes. Hanu, I know, has a soft spot for me, even if he doesn't consider me a worthy daughter-in-law. He took me and Elanor in when we were in need; gave us shelter and a place in the community. Perhaps I should be grateful for my lot and stop complaining.

Yet there remains a persistent pain that crouches like a toad in the middle of my chest, heavy and dull. And it refuses to budge, no matter how I reason with it.

FOUR

Awelfryn, the Kingdom of the Atres, three days journey north-west of Viper's Fort.

Lann

I slow my horse to a standstill and gaze at the hill fort that rises up in front of me, dominating the landscape. So, this is the famous Awelfryn, is it? The ancient stronghold of the Atres tribe, from whence its Kings have ruled since the time of my ancestors' ancestors. Perched atop a natural hill, its shining chalk banks reflect the sunlight and dazzle my eyes so that I have to shield them from the glare.

I urge my mount closer until I am able to observe in detail the tortuous pathway and towering gateway that guard its entrance. I am conscious that the approach to the hill fort offers no cover of trees and I feel exposed. I am dressed as a simple farmer, and I should not arouse the suspicions of Awelfryn's guards, unless I loiter too long in full view. Even so, it occurs to me that if the alarm were raised, an intruder would be easy prey, to be picked off at will by the sentries. Then I remind myself that these defences were built in times of turmoil, before the Atres were forced to accede their land to the Durotriges in the south and the Dobunni in the west, before the Druids' Peace was set upon the land and before the Atres warriors lost heart and became idle in their beds.

My schooling with the Druids comes in useful as I remember that 'Awelfryn', in the old tongue, means 'Windy Ridge' and by all accounts the hill fort lives up to its name. Many have moved away, I am told, preferring to dwell at Larksfield, in the valley below, amongst their workshops, smithies and industries. But King Irven and his retinue remain at Awelfryn, a sense of place and tradition running strong in their blood. What a joke!

When I am satisfied I can glean no more information from my observations, I direct my horse towards the sprawling town. I have left the other men on the borderlands, with express instructions to meet me on the morrow on the scrubland that fringes the Greenway. There is no guarantee we will complete our mission tomorrow, or even the next day, but we need to be ready, should the opportunity present itself. Doran has placed a great deal of faith in me, and I do not want to disappoint him. He is a strange one, right enough, educated in Rome with foreign ways, but he is Bryn's son and therefore my master. I mean what I say when I swear I would lay down my life for either one of them.

I stop short of hailing distance of Larksfield, remove the Vellani terrets and ornaments from my horse, and replace them instead with ones carrying the traditional design of the Durotriges owl.

It is market day and Larksfield is crowded with farmers and traders bartering their goods and hoping for a bargain. As I near the gateway, my senses are accosted by the noise of industry, the banging and hammering of the smithies and carpentry workshops and the din of the leather-workers tooling designs onto bags, saddles and clothing. By the time I walk past the jewellers and wheelwrights, my ears have become accustomed to the racket. The smell too, is notable and although I know the tannery will be located at the farthest edge of the town, the stench of urine, dog faeces and discarded carcasses permeates the entire area, catching me at the back of my throat.

I dismount and guide my horse through the newly constructed jumble of buildings, in search of food. Sure enough, near the centre of the town, an old man, whose back curls like a scythe, has set up a rudimentary spit on which he roasts a small pig. His wrinkled complexion speaks of many years in the open air. I guess he was probably once a farmer. Now, beyond his useful years on the land, he has been given the job of selling slices of cooked meat in exchange for dried apples, dairy produce or whatever else might be suitable for barter. Next to his stall I notice a woman working a clay oven from which the sweet smell of warm bread emanates, fighting for dominance over the less attractive odours of the town. I secure my horse to a hitching post next to a water trough, then exchange a wooden spoon for a small loaf of bread, before turning my attention to the meat vendor.

'Hail stranger,' says the old man in a quivery voice. My stomach is rumbling as I approach his stall.

'A good day to you,' I reply. 'A slice of your pork would be most welcome.'

As I speak, I produce a small wooden whistle from my bag. The old man turns the whistle over in his shaky hands, sniffs it then blows a note. It is sharp and clear. He nods his head and carves a slice of meat from the pig's haunches. I place the meat inside the loaf and, leaning against a redundant hitching-post, begin to chew. I am surprised at how hungry I am.

'Travelled far?' enquires the aged farmer, glancing at the Durotriges designs on my horse's bridle. He has already taken me for a farmer, by the way I am dressed.

'The south,' I say, between mouthfuls. 'Just passing through. The strap of my bag is broken, I need to replace it.'

'And to where do you journey?'

I had, of course, anticipated the old man's questions. The age-old enmity between the Atres and the Durotriges means they do not enter each other's lands in any number that could be seen as provocative. Lone travellers, on the other hand, are not considered a threat but are, nonetheless, a curiosity.

'West, to help my kin with the sowing this spring,' I say. 'My sister is widowed and struggles to manage.'

The old man gives a stiff nod of his head.

'The lateness of spring has been bad for all,' he says. 'Everyone who can be spared is in the fields, now that the ground has thawed.'

'Your King, does he send his warriors to help?'

The farmer cackles, his rheumy eyes fill with moisture.

'You jest! Irven couldn't care less, and the nobles are just as bad. Yet they expect us to pay our dues. There was a time when they would protect us from the cattle raiders but no more. They do nothing but eat, drink and lord it over us!'

He lowers his head and I lean in closer to listen, catching, as I do so, a whiff of sour breath.

'I'll tell you this. The only person at Awelfryn who cares about us at all is King Irven's daughter, Kendra.'

'I hear she is pleasing on the eye too,' I say.

'Her body is yet that of a girl, though she is of marriageable age. But her hair is the copper of beech leaves in the autumn sun. When she matures, she will be a true beauty, have no doubt.'

'Does she venture out? I would treasure a glimpse of such rare loveliness,' I say, hoping my words do not arouse the old man's suspicions. He may be aged, but he is not stupid, even though the Atres are famous for their lack of brains. I needn't have worried, however, for the farmer is happy to have someone to complain to.

'She is in the fields as we speak and will be there every day until the sowing is complete. You can't miss her. If it wasn't for the fact that she and Fionn of the House of Caradwg are to wed and take over from Irven when he dies......well...'

The old man stops talking and begins to look around, fearing he has said too much.

'Here, stranger,' he says, changing his tone. 'Have another slice of meat.'

'Thank you,' I say, helping myself. 'I have no interest in the politics of this land, but I can sympathise with your lot. 'Tis the same in the south.'

The farmer looks relieved. We talk of mundane matters for a while until I take my leave, heading towards the leather workshops. It has been a simple matter to glean the information I need. The gods look upon me kindly today.

There is one more task to complete and for that I need to leave my horse behind and enter Awelfryn, unnoticed. There must be some part of the defences through which I can sneak without attracting attention. Then I will return to Larksfield, collect my horse, and find somewhere to wait until it is time to meet my men. I smile. My plans are coming together well. Very well.

FIVE

Awelfryn, the Kingdom of the Atres

The Voice of Fionn, a Noble of the Atres

So deep is my concentration that when I first hear the scream I banish it to the recesses of my mind, thinking it a bird call or perhaps a fox. Then I hear it again, the cry of a woman, high pitched, but this time it is cut off abruptly. It sounds far away, carried by gusts of wind around the hill to the forge in which I labour.

I am irritated and curse out loud. It is not often I get the opportunity to use the forge these days and my time here is precious. If this is just children fooling around there will be trouble. I try to ignore the scream, but I cannot. I curse again and put down my beeswax carving, just as I hear the unmistakable thunder of horses' hooves.

The enclosing earthen banks of Awelfryn hug the contours of the hill, so that its summit rises to a plateau at the centre of the settlement. The forge is at its western edge, and the commotion is coming from the south-west. I run up the steep bank and look across the fields to where the villagers were sowing seeds this morning. Even at this distance I can make out Kendra, in her red cloak, her unmistakable auburn hair swirling around her face, Pedwar at her side, snarling and baring his teeth.

She and the farm-workers are at the mercy of six warriors who are rounding them up, armed with powerful swords that I know can slice through flesh with one blow. Children, women and men flee in all directions, trying to confuse the horsemen, but Kendra and a handful of others have been penned in, encircled by the warriors. I witness one of our men being decapitated as he tries to square up to the strangers and my blood runs cold.

All this I see in an instant but I am too far away to be of any use. I know that by the time I reach my horse the raiders will have fled, but I must try. I break into a run and head for the south-eastern edge of Awelfryn where the Folk meet is situated and where the nobles and warriors will be sitting. I doubt they will have heard the commotion from there; such is the direction of the wind. But why, by Esu, haven't the watchers raised the alarm?

'Intruders!' I shout, and as I approach the royal house, I spot the Queen's servant, Ferehar.

'Ready my horse!' I scream, then run on towards the Folk meet.

The warriors, who have been entertaining the visiting Canti envoy's men, hear my shouts and emerge from the feasting hut. They look groggy and ill-prepared and even though I know they could not have heard the screams nor the horses' thunder, I feel my anger rising.

'Raiders!' I shout. They look at me as though I have lost my mind. 'The King's daughter has been taken. MOVE!'

My words penetrate their foggy brains and they begin to organise themselves but I cannot wait for them. I dash into my own quarters, grab my sword and shield, then sprint to the horse enclosure, take the reins from Ferehar's grasp, mount Gwilym in one leap and ride through the open gates, in the direction of the fields. I can hear the Atres warriors behind me, riding hard to catch up and I am glad I am not alone.

Although I am one of the younger of King Irven's warriors, my status as Kendra's betrothed confers upon me a certain authority. I have been groomed to lead and I am glad to say, the men do not balk at my commands. Whether this is because I passed all the tests required of a warrior well before my time, and thus the men respect me, or because Irven has told them to listen to me, I know not. What matters is that they obey me, even though my tattooing ceremony, marking me as a man, is yet four moons away. I lead them in the direction of the raiding party, hooves thudding on grass, but after three hours of tracking, we are forced to admit defeat.

The torrential rain slows our progress. Mud churns beneath our horses' hooves and mist envelopes the hilltops. The raiders soon outdistance us and are, in a few moments, entirely out of sight, despite their cargo of captives. I order the Atres warriors to split up and continue their search in different directions, but when we regroup on the borderland at twilight, I can tell even before I speak to them that they too have failed.

Before I face the King and Queen or indeed my own father, I break away from the dejected band and head to the fields in search of some clue to the identity of Kendra's abductors. The area is deserted, the wounded long gone and the body of the brave farmer carried home. I dismount and stand looking at the ground, not wanting to believe what I have witnessed today. But darkness is fast descending and I realise that to search any longer would be futile. Then I hear a whimper. The sound comes from the long grass at the edge of the field. It is Pedwar, lying on his side and licking a bleeding sword wound. He is in a sorry state, weakening by the minute. I should end the hound's suffering and raise my sword to finish him off, but I cannot go through with the act. Pedwar is my link to Kendra, and I cannot bear to end his life. I wrap the dog in my rain-soaked cloak, lift the almost dead weight onto my horse, and take him back to the roundhouse I share with the other warriors.

The house is empty and I learn from Howell, the servant who tends to our needs, that the entire settlement is congregated at the Folk meet, waiting for me to give my account of the chase. Before I leave the house, my stomach churning, I command Howell to tend the dog as best he can.

The frantic downpour has settled into a steady drizzle, soaking the thatched roofs of the roundhouses and dripping off the eaves. Even though the rain has eased, water runs in a mini-torrent down Awelfryn's central track way, gouging out pebbles and mud as it flows down the hillside. I jump across the newly-created stream and enter the meeting house.

Word has obviously travelled fast, for I see that the Folk meet is crowded. Some have travelled from afar, for their clothes are soaked through, their woollen garments giving off a musty vapour. I nod to the crowd through the smoky haze of the central fire, before glancing at my father, Caradwg, who sits hunched on the bench nearest the hearth. He acknowledges my presence with a terse smile, but remains silent. I can tell he is displeased, for our family's one chance to wield true power has just been snatched away from under our noses.

The visiting dignitary, Wil of the Canti, sits on Caradwg's left, whispering to his Elder. King Irven and his wife, Briona, occupy a raised bench in front of the hearth. The fire has been banked up with fresh logs and blazes, adding to the light from the imported oil lamps that cast long shadows against the lime-washed walls. I take my place on my father's right side, facing the King and Queen, the fire playing between us. A sturdy oak table to my right is heaped with weaponry. I add my sword to the pile, as is the custom. Irven's eyes are red and his face, as usual, is slack from too much wine. Briona, my future mother-in-law, sits stony-faced, her back rigid.

The Elders are here, as is right, and they, along with Atres nobility, take the best seats, whilst the rest of the onlookers stand, packed together, craning to see the proceedings. The room quietens without prompting and all eyes settle on me, expectantly.

31

SIX

The Woods of Rhiw

The Voice of Kendra, heiress to the Atres throne

I grit my teeth and close my eyes. I try to remain calm, to think, but it is difficult to do either, for my abductor has placed me face down and wedged me tight between the wooden pommel of his saddle and the horse's withers. My arms are pinioned to my side and with every motion I bang hard against the saddle. I will be black and blue by the time we stop. If that is not bad enough, a leather bag, uncured and stinking of putrefaction, has been placed over my head, forcing me to endure this journey blind. I think I will suffocate from a lack of air and the foul odour. I bite down the reflex to gag, for to be sick right now would not be a good thing. Escape is out of the question, and the best I can do is to concentrate on catching my breath.

I have no idea who has been taken with me, but I do remember that Cator was by my side when I was snatched. I cannot quite believe what has happened; that I, the King's daughter, have been taken by raiders in broad daylight, so close to Awelfryn. I am too incensed and too uncomfortable to be frightened, and just want this nightmare journey to stop. This must be a stupid mistake, for who in their right mind would attempt something so audacious? Once my father realises I am gone, there will be trouble and my abductors will pay with their lives, of that I am sure.

The journey seems to go on for ever until at last the horseman slows his pace to a walk. I can hear birdsong and the gentle trickle of a stream. Eventually he stops and I am lifted off the horse and dumped on the ground.

I wrench off the sack and blink. Everything is a blur, then I realise that I am in a small clearing in a wood and the sun is low in the sky. I recognise my companions and I am flooded in equal measure with relief and anxiety. Cator is here, and for entirely selfish reasons, I am glad to see him, but the others are going to prove a nuisance, if we have to attempt an escape. Standing next to me and looking petrified, is Morvyn. He is aged around twelve, thin and wiry and known for his quiet nature. It is not Morvyn, however, who causes my heart to sink, but the sight of the twins, Huel and Malvina, barely six summers old, who now stand shivering silently together. I let out a sigh and exchange a worried look with Cator.

Cator slides his eyes to the edge of the clearing, making me aware of a large man standing to one side. Behind him is parked a wagon, a slave-carrier, whose sides are raised in wooden poles topped by a slatted roof, so that whoever is carried inside cannot escape. I look at the slave-wagon in dismay. Slavery is an anathema to the Atres. My father's refusal to deal in human cargo has contributed in no small part to the Atres' decline and there are many, even amongst our own kind, who think him foolish, my mother included. But not I. My father has many faults, but for this one stance, I feel only pride.

We huddle together, tired, hungry and confused. I am looking for an opportunity to speak, but the men keep their distance and I cannot yet be sure who leads them. We are all battered from the ride and each of us sports a purple bruise from the constant banging against the saddles. Before long one of the men approaches.

'Go, drink from the stream,' he says, his tall form towering over us. 'But do not think of running off, do you hear!'

He needn't have worried; the idea of the forest at dusk, with its blood-sucking demons, fills even grown men with fear. The prospect of escaping into these woods in the dark, with Esu knows what beasts abroad, is not to be considered and our kidnappers are the lesser of two evils. We obey without question as we are all thirsty, and when we have drunk our fill, we stand around fidgeting, wondering what is expected of us. I realise that we look like a disconsolate rabble and so I straighten my back and raise my chin. Perhaps I can reason with them; if it is gold they want, I will guarantee payment but before that, I must see to the children.

Malvina is crying. Huel stands next to her, clenching his teeth, but his face is pale. I feel sorry for the two children and put an arm around each of them. They must be exhausted. I lead then to one side of the clearing and settle them down under a hawthorn that, despite its spikes, seems to offer protection from the gloomy forest.

Before long one of the men approaches and doles out a hunk of bread each and some cheese. We are hungry and even the stale bread is polished off without a murmur. I find my courage and address him.

'Which one of you is in charge here?' I ask, but the man does not even acknowledge that I have spoken. He ignores me and joins his comrades at the other side of the clearing. I feel my anger building, but Cator places his hand on my arm to calm me. He is right, I suppose. There is little that can be accomplished this night and it will not do to antagonise them.

It does not look as though the men are going to light a fire and so Cator takes Malvina in his arms to warm her, and I do the same with Huel. All our clothes are soaking wet, but to take them off is out of the question. Morvyn huddles close and I see that he is shivering violently.

'Sleep now,' I say to the children. 'We will be found soon, don't worry and then we can all go home.'

The twins are asleep almost instantly, despite the trauma of the day and their dread of what lurks beyond the clearing. Morvyn, Cator and I whisper our fears to each other, and watch our captors. The men sit around in a circle; one is polishing his blade, another whittling a piece of wood, whilst the rest talk amongst themselves in low voices.

I use the time before darkness descends completely to observe the men and I can now be certain of their leader. I have heard his name called by the others: Lann, meaning 'peaceful'. His horse is bedecked in bronze terrets that speak of wealth but what is more interesting about the finery is the Durotriges owl whose form can be discerned dancing in and out of the designs. I have heard much about the Durotriges. They are the most powerful tribe in the land, and when my father utters the name of their leader, Hanu, he without fail spits, as though it were poison in his mouth.

'I think we should do as they say,' I whisper to the two boys, whose faces are so close I can feel their breath on my cheek. 'At least until we know where we are.'

'I agree,' says Cator. 'And then we can plan our escape. We would soon be dead if we tried to run now.'

When the darkness becomes impenetrable, the men settle down for the night. I and the others lie down too, but just as I am about to drop off, the forest comes alive with sounds. Owls hoot and something, Esu knows what, makes a wretched screaming noise that reverberates around the trees, until it is finally killed by whatever beast stalked it. Then a wolf howls in the distance. I find myself staring into the blackness, my eyes wide open.

'Cator,' I whisper. 'Are you awake?'

'Yes.' He finds my hand and squeezes it.

'Did you see what happened to Pedwar?'

Cator does not answer immediately and I begin to think he has drifted off to sleep. Then I hear him take a deep breath before answering.

'I'm so sorry Kendra, but I think I saw him killed. He was trying to protect you.'

'Oh.'

It is hard to absorb such news. I am grateful to Cator for being honest with me, but that is the way of our friendship, no lies, no matter how painful the truth. A tear slides down my face. I raised Pedwar from a pup. I miss him already and I will never see him again.

I wonder what my parents, and especially Fionn, are doing to try to find us. They cannot be far. I conjure Fionn's face in my mind's eye but his features are elusive and I am too upset to hold the image.

Since my betrothal, I have struggled to come to terms with the prospect of marriage, less than one year away. I would rather spend time with Cator, finding birds' eggs or badgers' dens, or helping him tend his pigs. My mother, who tries to forbid my friendship with Cator, keeps reminding me that I am nearly fifteen summers old and no longer a child. But when Fionn tries to kiss me I am overcome with embarrassment. I know he is considered handsome by the other girls, with his thick black hair and dark eyes, but somehow I cannot see him in that way. I am so ill-prepared for marriage and all that entails, but now, as I lie on this forest floor, I find myself wishing I had tried harder and shown him a little more love.

SEVEN

Awelfryn

Fionn

Every single person in the room is staring at me but I resist the urge to grasp the corner of the table for support. I take a deep breath and clasp my hands together behind my back before launching into my story. After all, I remind myself, if I am to be King one day, I must get used to speaking thus.

'We chased them over the fields, through the bogs of Brihar, and across the Dewi,' I say. 'We could see the prints of their horses' hooves in the soft ground, but,' I lower my head in shame, 'they had such a head start, we lost sight of them and only had their tracks to follow. Eventually we lost even their traces in the cloud atop Broch Hill. They could have taken any route from there.'

'And did you not think to split up and go in different directions?' demands Irven.

'Let the boy finish!' It is Briona who speaks, glowering at her husband as she does so.

'Of course we did,' I say, meeting the King's gaze, though my legs feel weak. 'But the weather was against us all. We could not see the way.'

Irven rises to his feet and surveys the room. His face is red and his eyes glint in the firelight.

'This very act is an outrage! We will have redress,' he says. 'Mark my words. But we cannot act until we know the perpetrators.' He shoots an accusatory look at me. 'And the trail grows cold as we speak!'

Before I can respond, a woman of middle years, a commoner, judging by her clothes, pushes her way through the crowd and stands in front of the King. I do not recognise her but the crowd hush, waiting for her to speak.

'I know who did this,' she says.

I jump as a log crackles in the grate. No-one dares breathe.

'It was the Durotriges.' The name writhes in her mouth.

'You have proof?' demands Irven. 'This is a serious matter. You know what is at stake.'

I notice a strange fire in the King's eyes and how his voice sounds starved of breath.

The woman's eyes narrow.

'Oh I understand well enough the seriousness of this matter. Is not the death of my husband serious enough? Twenty summers we were wed!'

Irven averts his eyes though his cheeks are flushed.

'The man who killed Geraint, as he fought to save *your* daughter, Irven, - left this behind.'

I lean forward to see what she holds, and I am ashamed that I have not given a second thought to the man whose beheading I witnessed, nor to his widow, who now stands in front of me.

She uncurls her hand. At the centre of her palm she holds a delicate brooch made up of interlocking lines ending in two round eyes. The Owl of the Durotriges. The information is whispered through the room until the noise grows to a deafening crescendo.

'Silence!' roars Irven.

The audience quietens, waiting for their King to speak. I look at the royal couple, and note the Queen appears to be agitated and that Irven is staring at her, not in empathy, but with something approximating hatred. After an uncomfortably long a pause, Irven draws his eyes away from Briona and addresses the gathering.

'This is an act of war!' he says, his eyes shining.

'War!' comes a cry from the back of the room.

'War! War! War!' The rally is taken up by a number of voices, accompanied by foot stamping, until the entire Folk meet reverberates with sound. It is only the Elders and I who refrain.

Irven takes a step forward, swaying slightly. He raises his hand and the room quietens.

'We will strike our enemy and avenge this act, do not fear,' he says. Before he can continue, Morgana, a respected Elder, stands.

'And what of the Peace of the Land?' she demands. 'How can you talk of redress when we are bound by oath to the will of the Druids?'

'Perhaps, Morgana, it is time to turn our backs on the Brothers,' says Irven, and his words draw a murmur from the audience. I too am shocked.

'Their so-called 'Peace',' he continues, 'was meant to serve all of the tribes. Instead we see the likes of the Durotriges grow fat whilst we are obliged to sit idly by watching our power diminish.'

Another of the Elders, a wizened old man by the name of Kelwin, stands.

'The Brotherhood of Druids set the laws of the land,' he says, wringing his hands and glancing nervously around the room. 'To disobey them is unthinkable. Is it not the Brothers who have ensured that the Tribes of the South do not raid in each other's territories for slaves? Have we not the Brothers to thank for the absence of warfare?'

The audience begin to talk amongst themselves, some agreeing with Kelwin, others wanting immediate action. I watch their faces, trying to gauge their mood.

'And see how soft we have grown,' says the King.

'It is well known, Irven, that you have no respect for the Druids and some would believe that our misfortune stems from your disdain for their rule. But the Brothers are not the only issue here. Now listen to me.' Kelwin pauses for effect then continues in a low voice. 'I do not need to tell you that this is the emblem of the Durotriges. But we cannot be absolutely sure it is the Durotriges who are the perpetrators. This taking of Kendra *must* be a mistake! At the last reckoning Hanu had two thousand chariots at his command, twice our number. Not to mention his horsemen and foot soldiers. Why do we not settle this in the normal manner, pitting our greatest warrior against theirs?'

'Old man,' says Irven, 'you utter the words of a fool. This is no trivial matter that can be settled by a mere show of strength! By Esu, they have taken my daughter! And what's more, the Durotriges have bled us dry and the Brothers have stood by and watched them do it. Hanu's kin have grown greedy for slaves. It is they who have broken the Peace of the Land. The time has come to take back what is ours and for that we need a proper war!'

Irven is in full spate, his voice rising as he speaks. He is a formidable sight.

'But if we go after him in force now,' insists Kelwin, standing his ground, 'he would show no mercy and we would be wiped out without a trace. If Hanu's hand is in this, we will seek redress, but we need the Brothers on our side, not to mention the help of our allies, the Canti and the Regni.'

As Kelwin finishes speaking, I see Irven glance at Wil of the Canti, hoping for support. Wil tries to remain non-committal, but it is clear a response is required.

'If it is proven that this is Hanu's work,' says Wil, weighing his words like a merchant at the dockside, 'and the Brothers agree to action, we will help you, have no doubt.'

It is not the answer Irven seeks and I see him struggle to remain calm. I wonder that he expects the Canti to ignore the rule of the Brotherhood. As far as I know, they have no quarrel with the Druids.

'Very well,' says the King, after he regains control of his anger. 'We will send an envoy to the Brothers to inform them of this sacrilege. We will see what they have to say on the matter. And I will call for a meeting of our clans three days hence. We should have had word from the Brothers by then.'

Morgana and Kelwin sit down, clearly relieved. I have a burning question that cannot wait.

'What were our guards doing?' I ask, staring at the King. Awelfryn's guards should have seen the approaching band of horsemen from afar, yet they had not raised the alarm. The omission has niggled away at me all day.

'Given a sleeping draught in their beer, so it seems,' says Irven. 'We have been caught unawares. We have no option but to show those vile Durotriges that they cannot just march into our stronghold and steal our children!'

Another murmur ripples through the crowd. Awelfryn is large and many people come and go through its gates daily to ply their trade, but the idea that an enemy could so easily render our guards impotent makes me feel uneasy.

'Then it *was* planned,' I say, and I can feel my anger rising. 'Not simply a chance raid for slaves nor,' I look pointedly at Kelwin, 'a mistake, as some would have us believe. If we do not act quickly, we will lose Kendra. Esu alone knows what they have in store for her. We must go after them. If we delay, she will be lost.'

'Not so fast, my son.' It is Caradwg who speaks. 'Kelwin is right in one respect. We cannot just march against the Durotriges. Not without more proof or help. We will be crushed. Perhaps they took Kendra by mistake and did not realize who she was. If we ask Hanu for her back, he may well be willing to let her go.'

Irven laughs and its bitter edge takes me by surprise.

'Are you a worthless old fool too, Caradwg? Is your son, Fionn, the only one with any brains in your family? Is not the drugging of our guards enough to convince you that this abduction has been planned to the minutest detail? Pah! Besides, you don't know the man Hanu, as

40

do I. He has been plotting against me, mark my words. He thinks to strike at my very heart by taking my only daughter.'

A woman stands to speak. Her fists are clenched and her jaw tight. She reminds me of lightening before it strikes.

'And what of the other children?' she demands. Her voice is low and charged with emotion. 'You have not even spoken their names! Shame on you all. Just because they are not of noble blood, does this mean they are worthless?   All we have heard is of your daughter, Irven.'

The crowd becomes noisy again and the woman is forced to raise her voice. 'It was my twins, Malvina and Huel, that were taken. And my cousin's son Cator, and also young Morvyn. Are their lives so insignificant that you neglect even to mention them?'

'Be calm, woman,' says Irven. 'Do not worry, we will have revenge, I promise you that.'

'Words, words, and more words!' Her tone changes from hysterical to mocking. An uneasy hush settles on the room. 'You talk of war, but perhaps you too prefer to hide behind incontinent old men and women who quake at the very mention of the Brothers! Yes you, Irven, who have sat still, doing nothing while the Atres, once the greatest tribe in the land, suffer impoverishment and disgrace!'

'Take the woman out!' Irven explodes in rage, and I see how my King shakes with anger and I understand that despite the woman's sorrows, he cannot afford to show weakness. Such disrespect cannot be allowed to continue unchecked, especially in the presence of the Canti envoy.

Two warriors carry out Irven's command and the grieving mother is ejected from the roundhouse, shouting all the while. Irven addresses the assembly, taking pains to show no weakness, though those of us who know him well see that he struggles.

'The meeting is over. In three days we will gather again when the clan leaders arrive.'

Irven storms out of the Folk meet, leaving his important visitor in the hands of the lesser Atres nobles. I seek out Briona, who appears to have regained her composure.

'May I speak to you and the King in private?' I ask. I can scarce believe Irven plans to let the trail grow cold for three whole days.

Briona nods and so I take her arm and escort her to the Royal house, Caradwg following on. By the time the three of us enter the sumptuous roundhouse we find Irven already seated in his leather chair, a gold edged drinking horn full of wine in his hand. He looks up as we enter his domain.

'What is it Fionn?' he asks and I can tell he is in a foul mood. 'Do you fear that you will not be King? Is that all you care about?'

I ignore his jibe.

'My Lord, I would ask that I be allowed to search for Kendra and the others in Hanu's lands, if indeed they are there. If I cannot free them myself, I'll return for help. Before they are sold to the Veneti.'

The King says nothing, a faraway look on his face. It is my father, Caradwg who breaks the silence.

'Fionn, this is sheer folly,' he says. 'How do you think you can enter Hanu's lands as an unknown? He has control of more hill forts than any tribe. You will not pass undetected into Vipers' Fort.'

But I have my answer ready.

'I will travel as a smith, of course.'

My father looks at me in astonishment.

'What is your view, Caradwg?' asks Irven. 'Is there any point to this?'

Caradwg takes some time to gather his thoughts.

'We have to be sure it is the Durotriges,' he says speaking slowly and deliberately. 'Fionn has yet to receive his tribal tattoos. By all accounts he is an accomplished smith and could pass for one. I do not wish to endanger my only son, but ...'

'But without Kendra, there will be no throne for the Clan of Morffryn,' says Irven. 'Is that not so?'

'My lord, any inaction would be perceived as weakness,' says Caradwg, ignoring the King's taunt. 'But you know as well as I that we cannot march on the Durotriges without help from our allies and they will not aid us without the blessing of the Brothers.'

Irven nods, a sour expression pulling his lips down at the corners.

'All this will take time,' continues my father, 'but something needs to be done now. This way we can appease our people and Fionn can establish exactly what Hanu is up to, if indeed it is Hanu who is behind this.'

'And if it is not Hanu,' I say, interrupting my father's speech, 'but another of the Durotriges who has done this, then Hanu may lend us men to mount a search, for surely he would not want one of his own to commit an act of war without his knowledge.'

Irven laughs again, sending a shiver down my spine.

'You can be assured that it is Hanu who is behind this. I would wager my best horse on it.'

'You know for certain?' asks Caradwg.

'I know in here,' says Irven. He points to his chest and takes a swig of wine before settling further into his chair.

Then Briona speaks, her voice wrought with the emotions she has been suppressing all day.

'Fionn is right. The Brothers may ignore the matter, and we cannot wait for them to make their decisions. I cannot, nay *will not*, lose another daughter.'

At the sound of Briona's words, Irven seems to soften. He stands unsteadily and walks towards his wife. Stopping in front of her, he caresses her cheek. Briona stands stock still, her expression giving nothing away. She touches Irven's hand with her own and I realise the effort has cost her a great deal.

'Very well,' says Irven, addressing me but not taking his eyes off Briona's face. 'Find Kendra if you can. If she is not already dead. But in my own mind I need no further proof of Hanu's involvement. This is an act of war, a war that has been a long time coming.'

'Take some men with you, at least,' says Briona, snapping her eyes away from Irven and looking at me.

'No.' It is Caradwg who speaks. 'If Fionn is to do this, he must go alone. Only when we have the backing of the Brothers and our allies can we show our hand. To send warriors into the Durotriges' heartland would be provocative.'

'My Lord,' I say, turning to the King. 'What I don't understand is why Hanu would risk the Peace and the goodwill of the Brothers to do this. The Durotriges have already taken most of our land and bar us from their southern ports. What is it we have that he could possibly want?'

Irven sighs and looks at his wife for a long time. When he meets my gaze, his eyes glisten with moisture.

'Just go, Fionn. There is no more to be said.' As he speaks, the King returns to his chair, seeming to recede into himself and cutting all others off from his heart.

EIGHT

The Woods of Rhiw

Kendra

I sit up with a start, wondering why I cannot shake off this horrible dream. Then I remember, and my stomach churns as I face the reality of our predicament. I feel terrible. My eyes are swollen and my clothes still damp from yesterday's downpour. I pull twigs out of my hair and peel away a leaf that has stuck to the side of my face. I must look a sight, but it is not the time to be worrying about my appearance. Cator looks dreadful too. Some insect or other has bitten his cheek and one side of his face is swollen. Somehow he manages a lop-sided smile and I remember why I like him so much.

Even though the sun has barely risen, five of the men have already left, leaving only Lann and the wagon driver, who is called Huw, a short man with pig-like eyes and a belly to match. Huw comes over and boots the twins awake, causing Malvina to cry out from the pain. Before I can reach them, Huel rushes up and kicks Huw on the shin. The fat man curses and strikes the boy.

'Savages!' he mutters.

I am livid. How dare he treat the children that way? We are not savages, but from the civilized tribes of the south. I swallow my fear and address the two men.

'Do you know who I am?' I demand, pulling myself up to my full height.

Lann turns to face me, his eyes glittering, a sneer forming on his lips. I note absently that he has different coloured eyes, one green, the other brown.

'Oh, indeed I do,' he says, stepping close and caressing my face. I stifle the desire to lash out and merely step backwards. He is terrifying. 'But it will serve you ill,' he continues, 'if you utter a single word about your origins to anyone. Do you understand?'

I do not understand.

'My father will pay whatever you want,' I say, trying not to sound too pleading. 'I will guarantee it. Just let us go.'

My words seem to amuse Lann.

'What a joke!' he says, more to himself than anyone else, 'You are all the same, aren't you? You think you can buy everything in this world. You filthy Atres whore!'

45

As he speaks, he raises his hand as though to strike me, but then changes his mind. I am grateful, as I can feel Cator tensing at my side and I do not want him to be hurt. Lann fixes me with an icy stare and I find myself recoiling at the sheer hatred emanating from him.

I decide to obey him until we reach our destination. I can tell he is of Durotriges stock from his horse's ornamentation and even though the Durotriges are our sworn enemies, they, like us, adhere to the terms of the 'Peace' brought about by the Druids. We have sworn not to raid for slaves in each other's territories, and to go against the Priesthood is unthinkable. I will speak to someone in authority and this misunderstanding will be cleared up. And so when Lann gestures for us to climb up onto the slave wagon, it is with grudging acceptance that I acquiesce, the others following my lead.

The wagon is larger than a war chariot and sturdier, pulled by two horses. At least we will be together, but even so, we are all subdued with little to say, as we cling onto the wooden bars for balance.

Fionn

'Three days hard riding to Vipers' Fort,' says Kelwin, as I prepare to set off the next morning. 'Bear in mind that all the clans south of the Great Horse Plain are beholden to the Durotriges. They are wary of strangers and you would do well to keep yourself to yourself.'

Kelwin's rheumy eyes take on a faraway look as he plays with his long plait of white hair. He has been around a long time, travelled far and has a strong memory. His directions are thorough and detailed but he treats me as though I know nothing. I am nevertheless polite, as he is an Elder and worthy of respect.

'Stick to the drove ways and beware the Woods of the Rhiw,' he continues, telling me what I already know. I am impatient to be on my way and try not to fidget.

'The forest is at the centre of three chiefdoms, ours to the northwest, the Vellani to the north and east and the Durotriges to the south. But it is not the people you need fear there. There are evil spirits that roam amongst the trees and the Brothers have a sacred nemeton at its heart. Any who would trespass on their shrine will be cursed.'

Does he think I do not already know all of this, I wonder. I have lived at Awelfryn for two summers now, as a warrior and hunter and I am more than familiar with the surrounding landscape. But Queen

Briona herself requested Kelwin talk to me and I must therefore humour them both.

'I doubt the raiders would have stuck to the drove ways,' I say. 'Not if they wish to remain concealed.'

'That may be the case,' says Kelwin, 'at first at any rate, but before long they would have to adhere to the roads. Any other route would be impassable.'

I nod. Kelwin has a point. In any case, attempting to track the raiders off the beaten track would be futile, their trail cold. My best plan would be to head directly to Vipers' Fort, if Irven's hunch about Hanu is correct.

'The most disturbing thing, Fionn,' says Kelwin, who appears to want to talk, 'is that spies have been watching us. I curse the laxity of the Atres warriors who should have been more vigilant.'

I nod. I want to be on my way, but Kelwin is in full flow.

'The very fact that the guards were so easily duped demonstrates how low the Atres have fallen. A sleeping draught in their beer! Can you believe it! We were a power to contend with, young Fionn, but now we have to rely on our allies for access to trade routes, all the while paying their taxes, and the warriors we can call to battle is reduced to half that of the Durotriges.'

I remain silent, not sure what to say to Kelwin who appears to be criticizing the way of things. He is right though. All the King seemed to concern himself with these days is the wine that flows from the warm lands of the south. The Atres people quarrel amongst themselves and there is distrust and a lack of leadership. But it will not do to voice dissent, for if we are disloyal to our King, then our descent into chaos will be swift.

'It is the Brothers, Kelwin, who do this to us,' I say.

Kelwin sniffs. He clearly disagrees.

'Your own father, Caradwg, who gives the Brothers their due respect, holds a claim to the throne from generations past when the Atres were strong and powerful. You, Fionn, can change the fortune of the Atres.'

I am alarmed. Kelwin's words sound like treachery.

'Well,' I reply, 'this is what the King has in mind. It is why he has arranged for me to marry his daughter.'

'But without Kendra,' says Kelwin, 'there will be no union and our tribe will disintegrate into petty warfare as the clans scrabble for power and control. This is why the Durotriges have taken Kendra. To prevent the Atres becoming strong again.'

'You put much store by my future actions, old man,' I say, feeling flustered. 'But how can we be sure it was the Durotriges who have done this?'

'There is, shall we say, a certain history between our King and Hanu of the Durotriges. They were once friends, true friends, but Hanu transgressed in a way that brooked no forgiveness.'

'What did he do?' I ask. 'I have heard about the horse deal, but that seems too trivial a matter for such a deep rift.'

Kelwin looks down before answering in a voice so low that I have to stoop to hear him.

'The story goes that when Irven was betrothed to Briona, they visited Hanu's lands. Hanu became inflamed with drink and tried to force himself on the young maiden.'

'Irven was within his rights to kill him on the spot.'

'Life is not so simple, young man,' says Kelwin. 'They were best friends. Like brothers. Worst of all, it is rumoured that the Queen had feelings for Hanu and that she has kept these feelings alive to this day. There is also the matter of the sacrifice..'

Suddenly Kelwin looks behind him, fear etching his face. 'But I have said too much, young Fionn, and my head would be paraded on the ramparts for less.'

'Thank you, Kelwin, I will ask no more,' I say, as I chew over the revelations. Certain behaviours and actions are falling into place. But what did Kelwin mean about the sacrifice? I can demand no more from the old man who is wringing his hands in anxiety and so I search out Briona, who has asked that I see her before I leave.

I find her threading wool through the central holes of her stone spindle whorls. She sits in her favourite spot, just inside the porch of her roundhouse, where she can keep an eye on the comings and goings of the settlement. She was famous for her beauty when she first married Irven and she still holds herself proud and straight, though that thief, time, has stolen the gold from her hair and a sourness has thinned her lips, causing them to droop downwards at the corners.

Today I am struck by her demeanour for she seems to have withdrawn into herself and welcomes me with a distant smile. As she sees me approaching she dismisses Ferehar, who sits at her feet.

'Fionn.' She looks at me for a long while before continuing. 'You are like a son to me. I already think of you as part of my family. Am I to lose you as well as Kendra?'

I avert my eyes. I feel embarrassed, afraid my Queen is losing control. I have always admired her strength and I do not wish to witness her weakness. Today her voice has an edge, an otherworldly quality to it. I shiver, remembering how my own mother's voice sounded when the evil spirits took her mind, a long time ago.

'No my Lady,' I say, as firmly as I can. 'I will return, with our beloved Kendra, who will be as brazen as ever after her exploits.'

Briona's smile is weak.

'Ah that she were as mature as you, Fionn. You are ready for marriage. I fear my daughter is yet unripe in the ways of the world. She behaves like such a child. I should have been firmer with her, stopped her associating with the likes of Cator, a mere swineherd.'

As she speaks, Briona reaches down and rummages for a moment in the leather bag that hangs from a cord around her waist, in which she keeps her valuables; the tinderbox for the hearth; a lump of frankincense from faraway Araby and a bar of scented beeswax. Finally she finds what she is looking for and pulls from her bag a shining golden wrist torc, the like of which I have not seen before, and presses it into my hand.

'Take it,' she says. 'It is one of three. Do not let Irven see it, whatever you do.'

I take the torc and prize open the rounded terminal ends so that the bangle fits around my wrist but before I put in on, I examine it carefully. To my amazement, the tiny imprint of the Durotriges owl is visible on the inside of the torc, where it cannot readily be seen. I look at the Queen, hoping for an explanation.

'I don't believe for a moment that the Lord Hanu took our Kendra,' she says. 'If he gives you a hard time, show him this bracelet, for it was he who gave them to me, but do not breathe a word about it to anyone else, I beg you. And.. and if you are able to enter Vipers' Fort and you should meet an old healer by the name of Elanor, give her my good wishes.'

'My Lady, what does all this mean?'

'Hush now. There is nothing more you need know. May Esu be with you.'

I make good progress and by midday I have reached the top of an escarpment overlooking the Great Horse Plain. I can see the Greenway, the road to the south, winding its way through the countryside. The road is set some distance from the woods, and is the safest means of travel, frequented by traders, itinerant craftsmen and such like. Common sense prompts me to follow the road - in truth no more than a rutted track way - but I ought at least to check the edge of the great forest for any sign of the raiding party who, I am sure, would have camped amongst the trees overnight.

Though Kelwin's words echo in my mind, I dismiss my concerns and approach the trees. I am rewarded almost immediately by the tell-tale signs of trampled bracken and horse droppings that speak of the recent movements of a group of horsemen. I hesitate. Would I be wiser sticking to the road, or should I follow the trail?

I take a deep breath and chastise myself for my cowardly nature. I direct Gwilym through the trees and into the forest, following what seems to be a path of sorts that leads through the oaks, though I have to duck my head to avoid the low branches overhead.

Gwilym senses my unease. He is skittish and I stroke his neck to reassure him. We meander through the forest, following a trail of broken vegetation. I lose track of time but eventually I enter a clearing through which flows a small stream. I lead Gwilym to drink, and cupping the cold water in my own hands, slake my thirst before refilling my water skin. As I examine the undergrowth, I notice that much of the ground has been disturbed, and under a hawthorn tree, a strand of wool has been caught in the thorns. It is red, the colour of Kendra's cloak.

Then I notice the grooves of a wagon. This raid has been well planned, that's for sure, but I am encouraged because I know that a wagon would be much slower than horses, easier to follow, and would require the use of the Greenway. I am sure to catch up with them before long and can follow them covertly, from a distance, while I plan my rescue. There is something strange, though. Judging by the track, there are fewer horses than before. Some of the raiders must have taken a different route but I am sure Kendra and the others will have been put in the wagon. I relax a little as I become accustomed to the woodland and begin to enjoy my solitude.

As I negotiate the trees, I contemplate my life and how it has changed. As long as I can remember, I wanted to be a smith. My father only grudgingly permitted my apprenticeship but I learned much in a short time. Being a smith endowed me with an aura of mystery, which I have to confess, I enjoyed. And then my older brother died and that was the end of that. I was sent to learn to ways of the court and to prepare for the day when I will rule the Atres alongside Kendra.

I like Kendra, but I am not sure if I love her. She is a spoilt, untamed child who does as she pleases, roaming the wild places with her swineherd friend, Cator and if her parents can't control her, how will I fare as her husband? But I am a fine one to talk. Both my father and Irven have tried to dissuade me from spending time at the forge, but like Kendra, I do as I please. I smile at the thought and it occurs to me that Kendra and I are not so ill-suited. A shaft of sunlight penetrates the woodland and I feel my spirits lifting.

'Perhaps these trees are not so evil after all,' I say to Gwilym. 'It's only the Brothers who breed a fear into us to ensure we do their bidding.'

Little do I know how much I will come to rue those words. A brown and white blur, the size of a dog, darts out in front of Gwilym, who is already jumpy. Taken by surprise, he rears up in fear. I am in no danger of falling off and grip Gwilym with my thighs, but how could I know that my skull would connect so soundly with the solid oak bough hanging just behind me? The back of my head smashes into the wood and as I fall, I see blood spurting from my mouth and nose in a fine spray, before a darkness overwhelms the knife-like pain that judders through me.

NINE

Kendra

We journey deep into the lands of the Durotriges, now entirely on the tree-lined Greenway, stopping only to rest the horses. Travellers pass us here and there, greetings are exchanged, but no-one pays any attention to the slave-wagon nor its occupants. Such sights are commonplace these days.

Eventually the scrubland gives way to rolling hills and meandering streams edged by meadows. The farmsteads dotting the landscape become more frequent and I find myself yearning for the comforts of home: a hearth and some furs in which to curl up. At the end of the second day we make camp at the edge of a lazy river whose rocks shine bright in the evening light. Lann lights a fire and doles out the same stale cheese and bread, which we eat in silence.

The next morning we are loaded onto the wagon again. We are cold, cramped and still bruised from the horse ride. After what seems an eternity of discomfort, the air takes on a salty tang and the land flattens into reed-fringed marshes beyond which glitters an endless stretch of water. None of us have seen the sea, and its enormity takes our breath away. We cling to each other, wide-eyed, for a moment forgetting our plight.

'What is it?' asks Malvina, curiosity and awe overcoming her fear. 'Is it a lake? I can't see the other side!'

'It must be the sea,' I say. 'By Esu, it is vast!'

The wagon trundles on towards a piece of land that curls out into the sea and then curves back again to enclose a natural harbour, a perfect crescent of calm water, dotted with mighty vessels. I have never seen the like, being used only to the smaller boats that navigate our inland rivers. Beyond the land's embrace swells the vast expanse of sea, white tipped and untamed. The protective spit of land ends in a knot that rises up into a hill, from whence a view could be had of any who approached from sea or land alike.

All this I take in at a glance, but what causes me to groan inwardly is the massive earthwork that rises up in front of us. It consists of a ditch the depth of two men stood one on top of the other. Beyond the ditch is a bank, as tall as the ditch is deep and topping the bank is a palisade fence. Not only is the barrier tall, but it is also wide, stretching from the sea to the harbour. The only means of entry or exit is the causeway that bridges the ditch and leads to a massive central gateway, bristling with guards.

'Behold Vipers' Fort,' says Huw, and I can hear the pride in his voice.

Vipers' Fort. I recognise the name straightaway and know it for the stronghold of the Durotriges King himself.

The earthen road leading up to the settlement is wide enough for two wagons to ride next to each other but on the seaward side, the path disappears into a sandy beach and scrub with no prospect of cover. The landward side is marshland, treacherous and deadly, no doubt. Escape will be difficult. As we approach the gateway we stare open-mouthed at the sheer scale of the edifice. If the Durotriges have set out to impress, they have certainly succeeded.

'Don't worry,' I say to the little ones, trying to make my voice bold. 'This is where the Lord Hanu lives. He will release us, just as soon as he knows who we are.'

Huel and Malvina smile a little, but despite my brave words, I cannot expel the tight knot of fear that lurks in my gut. Cator senses my mood and reaches for my hand, but I withdraw from him, refusing to look him in the eye, lest I weaken under his kindness.

As the wagon trundles through the massive gate, I noticed that on the leeward side of the headland, next to the harbour, there is a sprawling settlement of eighty or so buildings. Some are roundhouses where people must live; others appear to be workshops, granaries and warehouses.

People gather around to stare at us, but seeing only a handful of children, soon lose interest and wander off. I look through the wooden slats of our mobile prison. So this is the famous Vipers' Fort, is it? Granted, its layout is very different to Awelfryn, but there are similarities. Dogs, cats, and geese wander at will, grain storage pits are everywhere, some open, some sealed, and scattered amongst the buildings are chicken houses and the odd family granary. A westerly wind brings the unmistakable aroma of night soil and rotting vegetation from the midden to my nostrils. It smells just like the one at home.

The wagon meanders around the houses before coming to a halt at the far eastern edge of the settlement, where two roundhouses, set apart from the rest, lie side by side. We are allowed off the wagon and stand around disconsolately, wondering what is in store for us.

We do not have to wait over long. A large man, with greying hair and a shaggy moustache, emerges from of the houses and greets Lann and Huw before striding over to us.

'What have we here?' he says. 'These two are not much use, but the older three will fetch a reasonable price.'

'Sorry Lughaid, but I want them for myself,' says Lann, 'for the time being at least.'

Lughaid's wife, a portly middle-aged woman, appears from the shadows and hands Lann and then Huw a wooden tankard of ale each before disappearing without a word. She does not think to offer us any refreshment. Lann, his hair stiff with grime, spits the dust out of his mouth before swallowing the beer in one gulp.

'All of them? What for?' asks Lughaid. 'I could get you a good deal, especially on the two boys.'

'They will be useful in the quarry. Hanu is keen to increase the metal yield from the ironstones.'

Lughaid shrugs and walks over to me. He grabs me by the chin and turns my face this way and that, as though he is looking for flaws. I struggle free and square my shoulders. I am about to spit in the man's face, when I notice that Lann has hold of Huel with one hand and in his other, a dagger glints. He glowers at me meaningfully, his eyes dark with menace.

'What about this frisky young thing,' asks Lughaid, a lewd grin spreading across his face. He thrusts his hand under my cloak, searching for flesh. 'For you?'

I try to move away, but Lughaid is holding me fast by one arm whilst his free hand probes my clothing. Cator moves to my side, ready to strike, but I shoot him a warning look. He restrains himself, but I can feel anger emanating from him in waves.

'I thought she would make a gift for the young Veneti princess, when she arrives,' says Lann.

'A good idea,' replies Lughaid, burrowing deeper into my clothing. I don't know how much more of this I can stand and I finch as his rough hand cups the curve of my stomach. 'You can present her to Gowell's betrothed yourself. That will please the Lord Hanu, at least.'

Cator's fists are clenched and I fear he will not be able to control his anger. Just then Lughaid's wife appears, causing the slave trader to withdraw his hand guiltily. Cator relaxes a fraction and I let out my pent-up breath.

'Where do you plan to keep the others?' asks Lughaid.

'I wondered if they could stay in your slave quarters tonight, until I have sorted out where to house them.'

Lughaid grunts his agreement and follows his wife out of the dwelling, slapping her backside as she screeches in pleasure.

As soon as the slave trader has gone, Lann ushers us into the slave house, the second of the two roundhouses. Cator picks Malvina up and carries her indoors. She wraps her arms around his neck and clings to him for comfort.

After my eyes adjust to the gloomy interior, I find myself in a sparsely furnished abode. There are no chairs, nor mats, just a pile of furs at one end, but there is a simple hearth where at least we might find some comfort. Slatted benches covered with straw line the walls and I notice that the room is divided, as is the custom, into four sections by wattle partitions. As expected, the only exit is through the doorway.

Lann seems pleased with himself. He has let go of Huel and so I decide it is time to speak up.

'I am Kendra. Daughter of King Irven of the Atres.' I make my voice as hard and as authoritative as I can. 'I demand to speak to Lord Hanu immediately. Take me to him now.'

Lann's response is to laugh, but his tone lacks humour.

'What did I say earlier?' he says, menace framing each word.

But I am not yet cowed.

'How dare you speak to me thus?' I shout, hoping my natural authority will make him reconsider his actions. 'It will not go well for you when you are discovered. If you release us immediately I will ask that my father shows mercy.'

Lann's mouth twitches. His hand hovers by his side for a moment, then he raises it and strikes me with such force that my neck jerks sideways and I fall to the floor.

'Do not tell me what to do, girl!' He kicks me in the stomach and I find I am gasping for breath. Then, to my horror, he grabs Malvina by the neck and raises her to the level of his shoulders. It is clear the little girl is choking. Huel rallies and kicks out at Lann but his actions serve to merely inflame the warrior further. He flings Malvina to the floor and draws his knife. Grabbing Huel, he presses the sharp edge of the dagger against the boy's neck. A small cut at Huel's throat starts to bleed. I can take no more.

'Please, no!' I shout, rising to my feet. 'We will do as you ask. Just leave them alone.'

But Lann is consumed by a cold anger. He pulls Huel's head back, exposing the boy's neck and then with one deft action, slices across his throat from ear to ear. Blood sprays across the room then Huel is dropped to the floor. Malvina screams just as Morvyn and Cator rush at the warrior. But he proves too fast for them, tired and weak as they are from their journey. Lann simply grabs Morvyn and holds the knife to his throat.

'Is this one to be the next?' he shouts. 'I will kill you one by one if you dare cross me, do you understand?'

We are stunned into silence.

'Now that's much better, is it not?' Lann smiles a slow smile before letting Morvyn go. But he has not finished. He stoops and grabs me by my wrist, then twists my arm painfully behind my back. He draws me towards him, his face mere inches from mine.

'I have already told you, young lady,' he says, 'not to make up such stories about your background.'

I am incapable of speech, too traumatised even for tears. I think I must be floating, for my entire body feels numb.

'If I, or anyone else for that matter, hear one more word about you being a princess of the Atres, I will chop your companions' heads off one by one and place them on the palisade. Do you understand me girl?'

I nod my assent. Lann, satisfied that he has made his point, releases me.

'Huw!' he shouts through the door. 'Huw! Come and take this worthless slave and throw him into the pit. At least the Goddess can feast on his bones today.'

Huw's large figure appears at the doorway. He looks surprised.

'By Esu, Lann, have you no restraint?'

'Hold your tongue, Huw, and do as I say. And fetch some straw.'

The large man carries Huel's limp body out of the hut and returns with a sheaf of straw, which he scattered on the drying blood. No-one has spoken since the killing. The colour has drained from Malvina's face and silent tears course down her cheeks. Cator pulls her towards him, holding her fast.

Huw puts his head around the door.

'The Lord Hanu approaches!' he warns.

Lann turns to face me, fixing me with his stare. 'Remember what I said,' he whispers. He drags Malvina away from Cator and pushes her towards Huw, then gives Huw his knife.

'If her ladyship here starts her storytelling in front of Hanu, you know what to do,' he says, before shoving me out of the door.

I blink in the light and follow Lann's gaze. A powerful figure is approaching, accompanied by Lughaid. Lann straightens his back and greets Hanu, King of the Durotriges. He is tall and broad-shouldered, his square face delineated by a set of bushy eyebrows under which grey eyes twinkle.

'And just who do we have here?' he says, as he strides over to me. 'Tell me your name, girl, and why you stand so proud?' As he speaks, he tucks a strand of hair behind my ear.

I say nothing, trying not to flinch at his touch.

'A quiet one,' says Hanu. 'Good. She will make a fine slave for the Veneti princess. Is she Silures?'

'I believe so, my Lord,' says Lann. 'I happened upon a trader who was anxious to sell. He gave me a good price. When is the Veneti princess expected?'

'Four or five days' time, all being well,' says Hanu. He looks pleased. 'Go; - take an amphora of wine for the girl. And well done.'

We are given food and some mouldy old furs with which to cover ourselves. Cator sets about lighting a fire in the hearth, using the wood supply that has been stacked outside the roundhouse. We have no oil lamps to illuminate this dreary hut, but the light from the fire is enough to allow us to see each other's faces as night draws in.

The shock of Huel's death has rendered us silent. Tears have created channels down Malvina's grubby face, and I realise how dirty and tired we all are. I find a pitcher of water in the corner of the hut and using an old rag, wipe the little one's face and hands until they are clean. The rest of us tidy ourselves and then we gather around the fire. I can see that Malvina is exhausted. I try to settle her down in a corner of the hut, but she refuses to separate from us and so I let her lie down with her head in my lap, and stroke her hair. After a while she drifts off to sleep.

'I wonder what will become of us,' says Cator, as he pokes the logs with a stick.

'I don't know,' I say. 'But I can't see my father allowing such a thing to go unchecked. I am sure they'll be here before long to rescue us.'

'I fear for her,' whispers Cator, his green eyes glistening in the firelight, just as Malvina whimpers in her sleep. 'Did you know she is one of my kin?'

I nod. I too am worried about her.

'What are we to do?' asks Morvyn. He looks crushed, as I am sure, we all do.

'One thing I have learned,' I say, 'is that we must keep silent, for the moment, at least.'

'Aye,' agrees Morvyn. His voice is harsh. 'Or Malvina will be on our consciences, as well as Huel.' His words wound me, for I know he must blame me.

'Kendra could not possibly have known what Lann would do,' says Cator, leaping to my defence, but I would rather Morvyn's anger than Cator's sympathy for I know that I am responsible for Huel's death.

'I cast no blame, Kendra,' replies Morvyn, but I think he does. I find that I am crying but I do not deserve the luxury of tears. I dash them away angrily.

'You were brave to stand up to him, Kendra,' says Cator, after a while, a catch in his throat.

'I was foolish. But I have learned my lesson,' I say. 'Let us abed.'

The next morning Lann turns up accompanied by a man and a woman. The man wears a creased and weather-beaten face. A farmer, I guess. The woman is of middle years. She looks pleasant enough, and smiles at us.

'The Lord Gowell and his bride will be returning soon,' says Lann, addressing the woman. 'Elanor, you will care for the slave girl until they arrive. Teach her the ways and what is expected of her.'

'Very well,' replies Elanor. 'And what of the little one? Shall I take her too?'

'No,' says Lann, giving me an evil look. 'She will remain with me. I will make use of her.'

'She is a little young to know the secrets of the hearth.'

'That's not your concern, Elanor,' says Lann and with that he commands Malvina to follow him.

The little one clings to my tunic and it breaks my heart to let her go, but I nod my head and push her away gently. She follows Lann reluctantly and I find that I am fighting tears yet again. Cator and Morvyn go off with the farmer and I walk alongside the woman. Not a word is exchanged between us until we reach her house which I note, is situated at the western edge of the settlement, near the midden, whose smell wafts around in the morning air.

As we approach the house I see a big wolf-hound in the porch, barking at the scent of a stranger. I put my hand out for him to sniff and he licks my fingers. Fresh tears spring to my eyes as I remember Pedwar. I bite my lip. I am going to have to do something about all this crying.

I follow Elanor indoors and am surprised to find it pleasantly furnished. The wooden benches are simple but strong and there are furs and skins strewn on the floor and on the seating. Carved designs swirl up and around the pillars, coloured with different shades of ochre and greens through which peek the images of bears, owls, horses and other sacred animals, visible only to those who knew how to look. Bundles of dried herbs and plants, and earthenware pots and jars of every size and shape fill the room. A cauldron, suspended by a long chain, bubbles away over the hearth. Elanor gestures for me to sit but as I am about to take a place on one of the benches, she stops me.

'Not on the furniture,' she says. 'Your place is on the floor.'

I must have looked dismayed for the woman takes my hand.

'It was a dark day when the Durotriges became involved with the taking of slaves,' she says, looking me in the eye. 'And I can see you have not been used to such a life. But there are those who do not care about the rights or wrongs of the matter and will treat you badly if you show your spirit. I am truly sorry, but I have been given the task of preparing you for your mistress.'

A sudden constriction in my throat renders me speechless and so I sit down cross-legged on the floor in front of the hearth and look into the fire. Elanor, still holding onto my hand, squats next to me and runs her fingers through my hair, which I know is caked with dirt. She raises my chin and as she looks into my eyes, a strange expression flits across her face, as though she recognises me.

'They tell me you are Silures. Is that true?'

I hesitate. It would be so easy to tell this kind woman who I really am, but the evil look on Lann's face as he took the knife to Huel's throat, has imprinted itself on my mind. I nod and say nothing. Elanor shrugs. Just then the hound starts barking and whining in excitement as a young woman, perhaps of no more than twenty summers, flounces through the doorway.

'And who do we have here?' she enquires, smiling at me.

'Chela! Come and meet Gowell's bride's new girl,' replies Elanor. 'Just look at her hair and her face. She could be your sister.'

The young woman looks at me long and hard then flashes me a quick smile.

'What's your name, girl and from whence did you spring?'

'Kendra, I am Kendra of the Silures.' I know I sound suitably meek.

'Welcome to our hearth, Kendra. I am Chela. Elanor here is my fern-mother.'

Chela turns and speaks to Elanor. 'So why is she with us, if she is destined for the princess?'

'Lann has asked us to show the girl what is expected of her until Gowell and his betrothed return.'

'I would have thought the Veneti woman will bring her own attendant,' says Chela. I notice she does not use the word 'slave'. 'Though I expect Gowell's household could make use of another pair of hands. When they are married no doubt they will require an entire retinue of servants.'

'So, Kendra, let us begin,' says Elanor as she searches in a corner of the hut for a fine bone needle and some thread. 'Can you sew?'

I nod. Elanor smiles at me before rummaging in a chest from which she pulls a Birris. The felted wool of this particular cloak is torn and obviously needs repair. I have watched the common folk at home do the same work often enough, singing the songs that accompany such tasks. Though we noble women weave wool into intricate patterns, mending and darning are considered the work of servants. My associations with the common folk, so frowned upon by my parents and even Fionn, might prove useful still.

I decide that I like these two women who speak with the soft southern burr. They do not treat me harshly and Chela seems particularly nice. Before long they have set more tasks to occupy me; grinding dried herbs, or fetching water and firewood, and the time passes well enough. They feed me on stew, bread and cheese, and I wonder if the others have fared as well. I only speak when I am spoken to, but I listen to the two women's chatter and watch them closely as they go about preparing salves and potions. But no matter how pleasant these two women are, my predicament here amongst the Durotriges is dire, and in forefront of my thoughts is how little Malvina is coping under Lann's brutal tyranny. As long as I do as he commands, I think Malvina will be safe. It is obvious that the reason he is keeping her hostage is so that I remain quiet about my identity. There is a great deal I do not understand, but I will bide my time and wait for the right moment to act.

TEN

Viper's Fort

Chela

It is the second night of the storm and Elanor, myself and Kendra sit around our hearth, finding comfort in each other's presence. We are lost in thought but each of us is gripped by a dreadful foreboding. Even brave Yarrow hides under the slatted bench in the corner of the roundhouse, whimpering from time to time. The storm has raged continuously for two days and two nights. First came the darkness, brought on the back of a demonic wind, then lightening, tearing apart the sky as it danced to the drumbeat of Taranis himself. Then came rain, rain, and more rain, lashed by the wind, scouring the land as though to scrub it clean of its ills. Trees have been uprooted, fences destroyed and roofs ripped apart. We went out to help rescue the tiny lambs and panic-stricken cattle. The farmers were all cursing the weather, wishing they had prolonged their animals' over-wintering. The people of Viper's Fort shelter in the lee of the headland, close their doors and bank up their fires, and those of us whose loved ones sail the seas, pray to Eluna that they will be spared.

'They should have been back two days ago' I say, not for the first time.

'Don't give up hope,' says Elanor. 'Perhaps they have not left Morhiban Bay yet.'

I nod, glad of Elanor's comfort. I reach for a comb and begin easing out the tangles in Kendra's hair. I feel the slave girl relax against my knees. She has spoken little since moving in with us but she has about her an intelligence that I like. If Gowell and his princess do not return, Kendra will no doubt be sold to the Veneti for a profit. That would be a shame, for I know the girl's spirit is not yet crushed.

I imagine Gowell floating at the bottom of the sea and I shudder. His expected return coincides with the arrival of the storm and all I can hope for is that he and Ivor have delayed or else found shelter. There are many islands on their route where they could have landed. Even the Isle of Saramis, just off our southern shore, has a storm refuge. It is uninhabited now. A sickness scoured the place and it was cursed, but that did not stop Gowell, myself and Ivor from exploring it as children.

63

Saramis is special, full of wild magic. It was where Gowell and I became lovers.

'Eyre Fawr says the storm will be gone by the morrow,' says Elanor, breaking my train of thought.

'Then let us hope he is right,' I say, wondering what offering the priest had to make to glean such information, but I do not voice my thoughts.

Eryr Fawr is proven right. The next day brings white clouds that scoot across a fresh blue sky and the whole world sparkles. I awake early, relieved to be rid of the howling wind that has frayed my nerves and kept me from my sleep. I hurry through my chores then run up to the headland, Yarrow as ever at my heels, to see if there is any sign of Gowell's boat.

By mid-morning I am rewarded by the sight of the Twrch rounding the southern edge of Saramis and heading towards Viper's Fort's harbour. Despite my anxiety at the prospect of seeing Gowell's bride, I find myself grinning from ear to ear in relief. From my vantage point, I can see that others have also noticed their approach. Word must have reached Hanu and his daughters, Erea and Cinea. I watch as Gowell's family mount their best chariots and make their way to the jetty. It will not do for me to be amongst the welcoming party, but I can watch from a distance. Leaving the headland, I make my way towards the harbour which is already humming with activity as merchants and sailors prepare to resume their trade after the inclement weather.

I lean against one of the grain warehouses where I will be able to see and hear everything unnoticed. At one end of the quayside I spot a pathetic group, men and women, with heads hung low, shackled together, shrouded by an aura of subdued sullenness. Slaves, no doubt destined for Rome. I feel ashamed, but there is nothing I can do.

I turn my attention to the growing crowd who have come to see their new princess. Word has travelled fast; there are warriors on horseback, women in long colourful tunics tied at the waist with their best leather gold-trimmed belts. Their children run around playfully. One of Hanu's finest chariots stands ready to transport the Veneti woman to the settlement. I have waited anxiously for this moment and I am nervous at prospect of seeing my rival.

The Twrch comes alongside the jetty and I can see Gowell and Ivor standing together. There are two women on the deck but their heads are covered with shawls so that I cannot make out their features.

There is a sudden flurry of activity as ropes are thrown and caught under a hail of instructions. As soon as the boat is secured a wooden ladder is lowered so that the passengers can disembark with ease. Gowell offers one of the women his hand but I notice she refuses his help. That must be her. Although I crane my neck, she is just too far away for me to see her properly.

Before any greetings can be exchanged, Eryr Fawr must thank Eluna for their safe deliverance. He was meant to travel with them to Armorica, but fell ill at the last moment and so they were forced to journey without the benefit of his wisdom. I doubt they missed him overly. Brandishing a bronze sword the Druid utters his magical words with much ceremony. He takes an age and I can see everyone shifting from foot to foot with impatience. Finally the priest stops his chanting and hurls the sword as far as he can into the harbour.

First to greet her is Hanu. He is in his best attire. Around his shoulders he wears a cloak made from wolves' pelts sewn together. His neck is adorned with a thick golden torc and in his hair he wears a simple crow's feather, to mark that he is still in mourning for his wife, Anwyn, who died in the autumn. He speaks, and I have to strain to hear his words.

'Welcome, Armelle, my daughter, welcome into our land,' he says, smiling. 'Eluna be thanked, you are safe.'

Armelle. I taste the name and find it strange. The Veneti woman's face is still obscured from my view, but I notice that she gives a little bow then raises her head to speak her words. Although her accent is strange, we share a similar language and I can understand her well enough.

'My father, Bearcban, sends his warmest greetings, Lord, and bids you take me into your fold as a token of his love and goodwill.'

Hanu smiles then takes her hand and brings her to the women who wait on the quayside.

The first to greet her is Erea, Hanu's eldest daughter. Though she is a couple of years my junior, we are close friends. Erea stands tall and proud, dressed in the britches and leather tunic of a warrior. In one hand she holds her sword, in the other she carries an ornate golden shield, embossed with gem stones. I remember her fighting to win it and wonder what the Veneti women make of her; for I have heard that in Armorica the women are meek and obey their men in all matters. Gowell will like that.

'Welcome my sister, welcome,' says Erea. 'I feel sure you will be happy in our family.'

Erea introduces her younger sister, Cinea, whose own sword can be seen peeking from the scabbard she wears at her back, but instead of the warriors' attire, she wears a long green woollen robe. Until the day of her wedding, Armelle will live with Gowell's sisters and any unmarried or widowed aunts, and I know it will smooth the way for her if she makes a good impression from the start.

Armelle and her companion are helped onto the chariot. As they set off towards the habitations, I follow on foot. The recent rains have churned up the ground, and straw and stones have been scattered to mop up the worst of the puddles. The chariot meanders along a well-used path that winds through the many pits that litter the ground, until they reach a roundhouse that is set apart from the others whose exterior has been freshly painted in ochre and green, colours of welcome and peace. Throngs of people follow the party, and when they come to a halt, the crowd jostle for a vantage point. Armelle's bride gift, a massive silver wine cauldron, has been loaded onto a separate cart and draws gasps of admiration from the onlookers. By the time I reach the gathering, Hanu is speaking.

'People of Vipers' Fort,' he says, waiting for a hush to descend. 'I bring you Armelle of the Veneti, the beautiful daughter of my friend and ally, Bearcban, to wed, if she is willing, and after the proper time, my son and heir, Gowell.'

A cheer goes up amongst the onlookers.

'At Beltane we will have a grand feast to welcome Gowell's new bride, and to witness their betrothal,' continues Hanu, 'but today please allow young Armelle some peace.'

I break through the crowd in time to see Armelle climbing down from the chariot. The shawl is now around her shoulders and so it is her hair that I notice first, shining in the spring sunlight, like a warrior's polished shield. I have never seen hair like it before. The girl is lovely, even if she does look unhappy. My heart sinks and my elation at finding Gowell alive is replaced by dismay. As I scrutinise my rival, I realise she is unwell. Her eyes are over-bright, her cheeks are flushed and she stumbles as she walks. I'll warrant she has a fever.

I watch Armelle stop for the assembled crowd, Gowell, at her side, and my mood sinks further. His attention is fully on his new woman and he does not once scan the crowd for my face. Has he forgotten me already? I feel the pricking of tears and so I turn my back on the assembly and head towards home.

Elanor is busy with her jars and potions. She looks up and I am shocked to see how tired she looks.

'How do you feel, Elanor? Are you alright?'

'A little tired, but better today than yesterday. Anyway,' she continues, 'What did you make of the young princess?'

'Not much to see. Young, pretty, vacuous. A perfect match for His Lordship,' I reply scornfully.

Elanor chuckles and sits herself down to hear more.

'The Veneti bride is unwell,' I say, trying to make my voice sound bland.

'Oh? What is it that ails her?'

'She looks as though she has a fever. And she is weak. She stumbled as she entered Hanu's hut and had to be nearly carried in.'

'I will make up a tonic and pay her a visit,' says Elanor.

'Of course you will,' I reply and realise how bitter I sound.

Elanor shoots me one of her looks but says nothing. Struggling to her feet, she makes for the door.

'Where are you going now? Can't you rest a while?' I ask.

'Don't fuss so, Chela. I may be tired but I am not dead just yet! I'm going to visit the Grandmothers. They have promised me some honey. If you want to make yourself useful, you can prepare the concoction for the Veneti girl. Use up the feverfew. Oh and put some sage in as well, but not too much. I'll take it to her later.' And with that, Elanor leaves me alone.

The roundhouse is quiet today. There are no sick people to tend to, for a change. The old woman, Tinia, who lives with us and sleeps most of the day behind the partition, is away visiting, and Kendra left this morning to join her new mistress' household. I miss her already.

So engrossed am I in my work that I do not notice that I am being observed from the doorway. It is only when I realise the gloom has intensified that I look up and see Ivor standing there.

'Ivor! It is so good to see you.'

Ivor crushes me in a bear-hug then releases me. He is grinning from ear to ear. He pulls out a folded square of cloth and hands it to me.

'A present,' he says, beaming, his grey eyes shining.

I examine his gift. It is white and of the softest, lightest, finest weave I have ever seen.

'It is called silk,' he tells me.

I am speechless at his generosity. We sit down together, as old friends, and he tells me of their journey; of his experience in Armorica and their return journey in the storm. He tells me how Armelle fell into the sea; and that Gowell dived in after her. They were so close to Saramis they were able to reach the shore before they perished. Ivor and Armelle's companion, who is called Riana, together with the crew of the Twrch, were able to shelter in the unoccupied roundhouses, but Gowell and Armelle were forced to spend the night together in a cave before they were all reunited.

'You mean that for the past two days you have all been on Saramis, virtually within my sight?'

'At the southern tip, but the storm was so bad, we had to stay put.'

I laugh, but I have a burning question.

'And what do you make of her, Ivor?'

A lock of sandy hair has fallen across his face. He tucks it behind his ear then takes my hand, which feels small in his large, square palm.

'She is sullen and rude and it is obvious she does not want this marriage. She thinks she is better than us.'

'How so?'

'Bearcban, her father, let her be educated from the age of five by a Greek tutor. She speaks and can make the symbols of the Latin and Greek languages and knows all manner of useless information. I think she expected to be living in Rome, not here amongst the likes of us.' Ivor laughs. 'She thinks of us as barbarians. In fact I believe she considers herself better even than her own people.'

I am cheered by this.

'No wonder she looks so miserable,' I say. 'But tell me, Ivor, what are Gowell's feelings for her?'

Ivor pauses for a moment, then squeezes my hand.

'If I were you, Chela, I would try to forget all about him.'

We talk a little while longer before he takes his leave. I am grateful to him for visiting me. I busy myself with my work, mulling over what I have been told. Presently there is a knock at the door. I look up, and it is none other than Gowell, standing there, legs astride, hands on his hips.

I run towards him and without even thinking of what I am doing, I fling my arms around his neck.

'You came!' I breathe.

Gowell hugs me for a moment and then prises my arms away from his neck. His one hand encircles both of my wrists, playfully preventing my escape. It is a familiar gesture, one he often uses to tease me. He holds me for a moment and then lets me go. I study him, trying to look beyond his eyes, but though he returns my gaze, he has shut me out.

'How do you find your new woman?' I enquire, and my voice is brittle.

'She is unwell. Is Elanor about?'

There is not even the slightest indication he has missed me.

'I was worried that you had all been devoured by Eluna, in that storm.'

'We nearly were,' says Gowell. 'Armelle fell overboard. She nearly died.'

'She survived though, and so did you.' It is obvious I am angry, but Gowell does not seem to care.

'Yes. I'm sorry, Chela, but I need the ministrations of a healer, now, before Armelle worsens.'

'Elanor is not here.'

'Will you not come then?'

I do not reply. The potion is ready but I do not move.

'Please, Chela!'

Before I can answer, Elanor emerges through the doorway.

'At last,' says Gowell. 'Elanor...'

'Yes, yes I know. Calm yourself, young Gowell. We already know your princess is unwell and has a fever. Chela here has been preparing a remedy. I will come at once.'

'Chela?' says Gowell. He looks surprised. 'You made the remedy?'

'Why? Don't you trust me?' I retort angrily. 'Do you think I might poison your new woman?'

'No, no, you misunderstand. I am grateful. I had hoped you and she might be friends.'

I laugh. 'But of course, Gowell. Of course I will be friends with your new bride, what else? But not today, just not today.'

Elanor throws me a stern look before turning to Gowell.

'Let's go,' she says, 'and see if we can help your young woman.'

ELEVEN

Ravensroost, a Vellani stronghold

Fionn

I lay unconscious for over seven days, struggling to waken from a dream in which a young woman called to me in a troubled voice. She was surrounded by tall fences and her outstretched hands were drenched in blood. I could not make out her features, but her hair is vivid in my mind's eye, a curling auburn mass that shone like burnished gold. When I awake, it is not Kendra's voice I hear, but two men talking, and the content of their conversation disturbs me deeply.

'Do you think he'll recover,' says the first warrior.

Their voices come as though from afar, but I can understand their words well enough.

'He's badly hurt,' says the second man who sounds as though he is chewing something. He spits before continuing. 'Brendan's been nursing him.'

The two men snigger.

'Did Doran pay you, by the way?'

'For the Atres raid?'

A shock travels through me. I am careful not to let them know I am awake.

'No. You?'

'No. And we were promised an amphora of wine each, if we got the girl, if I recall.'

'Doran's not like his father. Bryn would have honoured his word. I don't like him.'

'What became of them?' The warrior, who, I think, must be cleaning his teeth with a twig, spits again.

'Don't know. I expect they were taken away in that wagon. Seemed a bit strange to me, we don't normally raid our neighbours for slaves, do we?'

'Ah well, ask no questions and all that. Pity about the amphora though. Are you going to ask him for it?'

'I might.'

'And stones might roll uphill. Come on, it's stopped raining. We'd better be going before we're missed. If our beloved leader wants to teach us how to fight like Romans, we'd better not keep him waiting, though I can't see the sense in it myself.'

71

The two warriors leave, returning to whatever duties they were evading. I sit up cautiously and look around. I am in a forge, though the place is deserted and the furnace is cold. I am on a straw mattress on a wide wooden bed covered with furs. My head hurts. In fact, every part of me hurts. I try to stand, but as soon as I touch my right leg to the ground, a searing pain tears through me. I groan. I have a serious injury. I also feel weak and dizzy but I fight the desire to lie back down. Where am I? How long have I been here? And, for the love of Esu, what is wrong with my leg? Two things I do know for certain, even if my mind does feel shrouded in fog: I am amongst the very people who kidnapped Kendra, and she has been moved to another location. I will have to be careful.

I try to piece together the events leading up to this. I remember riding through the forest and then Gwilym rising up in fear at something or other. Then nothing. My belongings have been heaped on the floor at the foot of the bed. I wonder whether the gold I was carrying has been taken. A stick is propped up against my bed but before I can reach it, a man puts his head around the forge door.

'Ah! So you are awake! I was beginning to have my doubts!'

I regard my visitor. He is fair-haired, tall, dressed in warrior's clothing and carries a sword but seems friendly enough.

'I am Brendan,' he says, pre-empting my questions. 'And you are at Ravensroost, the home of Bryn, King of the Vellani.' He hands me a wooden tumbler full of water. 'And you?'

I drink deeply, playing for time.

'I'm sorry,' I say. 'I can't remember.'

The warrior looks at me askance. I can tell he is weighing me up and I realise how lame my story must sound. If he does suspect me of lying, he does not say as much.

'Did I have a horse?' I ask. I realise that without Gwilym I will be at a grave disadvantage.

'Stabled, and your gold is intact, do not worry,' says Brendan and sitting himself next to me, begins to tell how he came upon me in the woods and brought me back to be healed.

'I owe you my life,' I say, after he finishes his story. I am lucky to be alive but I also have to acknowledge that there is now a bond between us and an obligation on my part. 'I am in your debt.'

'I will hold you to it, be sure,' says Brendan, and then grinning broadly, slaps me on the back. 'But today I come to offer you the hospitality of my home. You are welcome to come lodge with my family, if you can put up with my parents, grandmother, aunts and sisters who will torment you mercilessly.'

I grin back.

'Thank you,' I say, 'but if it's alright with you, I'd prefer to be here.'

Brendan looks relieved; it is obvious the warrior's home is already overcrowded. I wonder why he still lives at home and not amongst the other warriors, but think better than to ask, for I scarcely know the man.

'What about the forge?' I ask. 'Will I be in the way?'

'Most of the metalwork is done outside the settlement these days. This furnace is more often than not cold.'

I am about to mention that the same is occurring in Awelfryn, but stop myself just in time.

Brendan visits me every day. He has fashioned me some crutches so that I can hobble about, though I cannot go far. He supplies me with a table and a chair with a leather seat, so that the area of the building I come to call 'home' is comfortable enough. When I can put a little weight on my leg, I create a small hearth on the forge floor and am able to cook some rudimentary meals, but I am keenly aware that I am entirely dependent on Brendan. He brings me food to cook, sensing that I need my independence, but more often than not, he turns up with a bowl of stew or some bread that has been baked by his mother or sisters.

One day, he takes me into his confidence and tells me why he does not live amongst the warriors. He is a twilight man, preferring to bed those of his own sex. At first I am shocked, wanting to distance myself from him, but Brendan shows no such inclination towards me, and soon the matter it is of no import. He is sad, however, for he tells me that his one true friend, a man by the name of Mylor, has been sent by Doran to the Druids of Lynd to await his death.

'What will become of him?' I ask.

'They will use him to foresee the future, until the time comes for Doran's Naming as King of the Vellani. Then he will be killed, dismembered and buried at the cardinal points of the Vellani borders.'

I shudder. I have heard of such things, of course, but my own King, Irven, long ago distanced himself from the Brothers, refusing to partake of their rituals. Something happened to sour Irven's attitude to the Druids and although I do not know what caused the rift, I find I agree with Irven's stance. My King has his faults, but he also has many noble attributes. The Elders and my father alike will be in for a surprise if they believe I would join with the Brothers once I become king. *If* I become king, and that depends on finding Kendra wherever she may be. The answer is here at Ravensroost, and I must be vigilant for an opportunity to discover where she has been taken. Every day I test my leg, but I must be careful not to make it worse by using it too soon.

Even though Brendan confides in me, I keep up my deceit. My belongings are those of a traveling smith and as I begin to take on tasks to pay my way, it becomes apparent that I am skilled enough in my art not to raise any suspicions. At first my broken leg means I am limited to carving beeswax for the decorative shield molds. It is enough to earn my keep, but as my bones begin to mend, I take on more and more work.

Doran, I am told, is keen to increase the production of weaponry and to that end, a slave by the name of Cederin is sent to me to work the forge bellows so that I can create more swords, spearheads and the occasional ceremonial shield. I feel ill at ease telling the boy what to do, even though I am used to having servants and issuing orders. But slaves are different. Cederin is quiet and acquiescent, surly even, and I find I am at a loss to know how to treat him. Overtures of friendship are met with polite blankness and eventually I give up. Slavery does not take long to eat at a man's soul, and I am glad my own people have no part in such trade.

Before long Brendan introduces me to his two friends; a young Durotriges noble called Annan and an older man in his twenties, Doran's cousin, who goes by the name Canogus. Annan is lodging with Canogus as part of an exchange to foster good relations between their respective tribes. Canogus is Annan's 'nutritor', and is obliged to treat him as his own kin. I can see, however, that this is no penury, as they are good friends.

Once I am able to leave the forge, hobbling around Ravensroost on crutches, I accept Canogus' regular invitations to sup at his home, but it is Brendan's family who are especially kind and I often grace their hearth with my presence. Mylor's name is never mentioned on such occasions and it is only in the privacy of the forge that Brendan talks of him.

It is a fine spring evening and, as usual, I am still working when others have long since ceased their labours. I do not have much else to occupy me and besides, I enjoy my work. I reach for the tongs. To my right is a mound of fine sand into which I have patted the rough outline of two elongated leaf-shapes. With a steady hand I pick up the glowing bowl of molten metal and pour its contents into the sandy moulds. Another two iron ingots will be ready once they have cooled.

'Not a drop spilt,' encourages Brendan, as he watches from over my shoulder. 'Despite your gammy leg!'

'He must truly be a smith,' adds Annan in his rolling southern accent.

I realise I am something of an enigma to my new friends and I doubt they believe my story. I also know that Brendan must have seen my wrist torc with the tiny imprint of the Durotriges owl, but he has not mentioned it. I feel guilty at the deception, but until I can mount my horse unaided, I am vulnerable, particularly as I know the Vellani are involved in Kendra's abduction.

I lay down the tongs and wipe the sweat from my brow, pleased with the amount I have produced today. The iron belongs to the Vellani and will be used to exchange for goods and as offerings. I do not mind this sort of work, but it is not as rewarding as the delicate artwork that decorates the shields, horse gear and swords that fill the forge in various stages of completion.

'You may go, Cederin,' I say to the young slave. The boy has worked hard all day, pumping the bellows, ensuring the fire does not dim. 'And thank you.'

Cederin says nothing as he slides out of the forge, but there is a glimmer of something there. Perhaps he is beginning to trust me.

Before long Brendan, Annan and I are joined by Canogus, who pops his head around the door to see how the tally of metalwork is progressing.

'What are you two doing here?' he asks Brendan and Annan good-naturedly.

'Trying to persuade No-name to come and sup with my family,' says Brendan, 'but dragging him away from the forge is no easy matter!'

'I've nearly finished,' I say.

'You've done well,' remarks Canogus, as he glances at the weaponry stacked against the walls. 'Doran should be pleased.'

'Is all this for Doran?' asks Brendan. 'None of it to trade?'

'Not as far as I know,' says Canogus.

'What will we do for wine? The Vellani will have nothing to trade. I may have to return home if Ravensroost runs out!' says Annan, showing off in front of the older men. 'Hey, No-name, you like wine, don't you?'

'The wine I've tasted since coming here is good. Though your brewers do produce an excellent drop of ale.'

'Ale is for old men. Only wine is strong enough to slake a warrior's thirst.'

'The last time you had a mouthful of wine, young Annan,' teases Brendan, 'you slid under the table like so much frog spawn.'

We all laugh and I realise I like these men. Without the trappings of rank, I have been free to make true friends, something that has eluded me thus far. Brendan is full of humour, though there lurks a shadow across his face that speaks of loss and sadness. Then there is Canogus, high-born, quiet and thoughtful, already married with a wife and child, and another on the way. And Annan, who, because of his tender years, is constantly on the receiving end of the others' jokes, but bears it all with good grace. In the short time that I have been at Ravensroost, I realise that Annan and Canogus are the only two men amongst the warriors who associate with Brendan, just as they have befriended me.

As we talk of this and that, I pick up my beeswax carving and examine my handiwork for flaws. It is a mould for a scabbard, covered in swirling curves and interlocking designs.

'What news is there?' asks Brendan. Canogus, as a noble and Doran's cousin, is often privy to juicy bits of information.

'The King is much the same,' says Canogus. 'He lies in his bed, death's hand reaching for him, but he will not cross that threshold.'

'It must be hard on Lord Doran,' says Annan. 'This waiting around.'

'Why do you suppose he is demanding all this weaponry?' I ask.

'He's up to something,' whispers Brendan. Since Doran took Mylor away, he loathes him with a passion. 'He's been meeting with Lann, concocting some plot or other.'

'Lann?' asks Canogus. 'I have not seen that twisted individual for a couple of years at least. I thought he was still living with the Durotriges under Hanu's protection, though I suppose he must come back from time to time to visit his mother. Anyway, how do you know such stuff?'

'I keep my ears open.' Brendan leans in a little closer to the group. 'Apparently, it was Lann who carried out the raid on the Atres, under Doran's instructions!'

'That seems a strange way to go about things,' says Canogus.

I can feel myself redden and though I keep my gaze lowered, Canogus has noticed my discomfiture.

'What is it, No-name? What ails you?'

'It's nothing. I thought a memory had stirred, but it has escaped.' I inwardly chastise myself – my reactions will betray me if I am not more alert.

'So what is Doran up to?' asks Brendan, turning to Canogus again. 'You are his cousin and a noble to boot. Surely you must know.'

'What he has told the nobles and Elders,' replies Canogus, lowering his voice, 'is that he plans to march on the Trinovantes, but he will not discuss the details with anyone.'

'But the Trinovantes have been our friends and allies for many a year! I'm surprised the Brothers allow him even to consider such a move,' says Brendan.

Canogus shrugs.

'The man is unfathomable. You know full well we were never close, even though he is my cousin. He has never taken me into his confidence, and keeps his distance. You seem to know more than I, Brendan.'

'I knew nothing of his plans to march on the Trinovantes. All I know is that he has asked the guards to be more vigilant about who comes and goes through the gates,' says Brendan, 'For fear of spies.'

I realise that they are all looking at me.

'You don't think…' I begin, but I falter.

'Well, who's to say you're not a spy, No-name,' says Annan, grinning from ear to ear. His words are meant in jest, but the joke falls flat.

'I told you, I have no idea from whence I hail. You must believe me.'

'Of course we believe you,' says Brendan in an attempt to lighten the atmosphere. 'And what about a certain Durotriges youth who listens to everything we have to say!' he continues, staring at Annan.

'Don't be ridiculous,' protests Annan. 'I am no more a spy…'

'Well there you go,' says Brendan, 'perhaps I should cut out my tongue here and now before I utter another word? No, I have a better idea, Annan. I'll cut out your tongue instead so you don't go tittle-tattling back to your kin!'

Although I join in the mirth, my laughter is insincere, and I wonder if Brendan discerns as much. Whatever the Vellani are up to, I should be more careful. Though I believe these men are my friends, I have deceived them, and I know full well that when the gods of war are summoned, the red haze of bloodlust clouds all judgment.

TWELVE

Awelfryn

The Voice of Briona, Queen of the Atres

I watch with distaste as my husband, Irven, wipes the red wine from his stubbly chin with the back of his hand and belches. He is already slightly drunk and so is his companion, Wil of the Canti. The business of levies and barter concluded, Irven places the silver-edged drinking-horn back into its holder and settles deeper into the goose-down cushion. The fire in the hearth glows and the place feels cosy and snug, belying the unhappiness and tension that is the norm in our home. My husband's large hands, gnarled with the first signs of arthritis, curl around the wolf's claw terminals of his wooden armrests as he stretches his booted legs out straight in front of him. His hound, Artan, snores beneath his chair, his long legs twitching occasionally.

'That was a fine drop indeed, Irven,' says his companion. 'A fine drop indeed.'

I wonder if they know I am here, behind the wattle partition, listening to their conversation. These days, spying on my husband is the only way I can find out what he is up to.

Irven grunts in response to his guest's compliment.

'Last jar of the good stuff,' he says, studying his boots for a moment. 'And that pig Hanu, sitting on a mountain of it.' He spits and I tense at the mention of Hanu's name.

Wil settles further down in his own chair, its leather hammock-seat creaking. He continues to cradle his drinking-horn in his hands, obviously hoping for a refill. Irven makes him wait.

'You and Hanu should have put your differences aside long ago,' says Wil, his voice thin and reedy. He clears his throat and continues in a firmer timbre. 'It would have benefited us all and you wouldn't be in the mess you are in now.'

I cannot see Irven's features clearly, but I am sure he must look displeased at Wil's comments. I doubt, however, that he will cause trouble. Wil is, after all, not only a guest at our hearth, but has just returned from the court of King Engus of the Canti with a promise of warriors and weaponry. He has also been persuading his neighbours, the Regni, to join Irven's cause.

'You don't know the half of it, Wil,' says Irven. I can hear from his voice that the strong alcohol is beginning to tell on his emotions. He

79

summons the servants to bring more wine and both their horns are refilled.

'What news from the Vellani?' asks Irven.

'Old Bryn is nearing his death, they say,' says Wil, after a long drink. 'That young scoundrel Doran is almost willing his father dead. Honest to goodness, it's not decent, I tell you. He has vowed to honour his father's pledges to us ..but .. we'll see. I cannot help but wonder what he really wants.'

'As long as he doesn't ally himself with Hanu and his mob,' says Irven almost to himself.

'The new King will have to be Named,' says Wil, taking another slurp of wine before continuing. 'It's been a good twenty-one summers since the last Chieftain was crowned - and that was you, Irven, I believe.'

'How our lives fly past,' replies my husband, his tone even more melancholy than before. 'The new generation are ready to push the old order out, as is the way of things. Our alliance will be even more important now. The Durotriges grow stronger by the day under Hanu's rule. And Epona alone knows what plans the Vellani might be hatching.'

'And Doran, schooled in the foreign ways,' adds Wil. 'There will be changes, mark my words. I can see only trouble. A great deal will depend on who the Priesthood favour.'

'Bryn and his father before him have had the Brothers at their beck and call for many a year now. The Vellani serve the Druids at the Isle of Lynd well and are repaid for their 'kindness'. I cannot see why Doran would want to change how matters stand,' says Irven.

'Perhaps it would have served the Atres better had you shown the Brothers the same respect.'

'And have them watching over us at all times, interfering in our ways?' says Irven.

I can tell he is angry, struggling to maintain his composure.

'There was once a time when I would do their bidding, willingly and gladly.' He is almost shouting now. 'I adhered to all their rituals and their rules, paid my dues to Lynd and where did it get me? Nowhere!'

My husband's contempt for the Brotherhood of Druids and the power they hold is common knowledge, but I doubt very much if Wil knows the true reason. I can tell our visitor is feeling uncomfortable.

80

'And what of Fionn's mission?' he asks, changing the subject, polite concern edging his voice. 'Is there any news?'

Irven grunts. 'Not a word. I would have expected something by now. If he doesn't find Kendra there will be no marriage, and he'll have no claim to my throne.'

Irven lowers his voice and I have to strain to hear.

'I will have to put Briona aside and take another wife, to ensure an heir from my line will succeed.'

Though his words wound me like a knife in the gut, I hold myself still.

'Caradwg will be disappointed, then.'

Irven laughs. 'Fionn's father? He is no threat, believe me.'

'So what will you do now?'

'I dare not make a move yet. Your warriors and those of the Regni are only just promised, the clans cannot decide on the right course of action, there is no decision from the Brothers and my Elders insist on their approval. They make excuse after excuse to delay their judgement. I am sick of waiting and if we hear nothing by Beltane, we will be forced to take matters into our own hands.'

'Aye,' agrees Wil. 'Otherwise you will appear weak. Have you spoken to the Durotriges?'

'There is no point. This war has been a long time coming. There is no going back now. Even if Fionn does find my daughter, I will avenge this insult, I promise you.'

'Your personal quarrel with Hanu is not my business,' says Wil. 'But my good King Engus longs to curb the Durotriges' power in the south, and for that reason, he will support you, have no fear.'

As Wil falls silent, studying the dregs at the bottom of his goblet, Irven claps his hands and a servant appears out of the shadows to refill their drinking horns yet again. They are now very drunk. I have heard enough and use the movements of the servant to conceal my own footsteps as I sneak out of our home and make my way towards the horse compound. I call for Ferehar to prepare my mount and then head out of Awelfryn, the motion of my stallion helping to soothe the turmoil inside me.

So he would simply put me aside? So be it. A strange relief floods through me. As I ride, my thoughts turn to the past and I recall with sharp clarity the day I began to hate my husband.

It was the young healer, Elanor who alerted me to Irven's pact with the Druid, Deryn, all those years ago. She overheard a conversation between the King and the Priest whilst collecting plants in the woods close to Awelfryn.

'Give me your new-born daughter,' the priest said to Irven, 'and I will make sure you are the greatest ruler the Atres have ever known.'

Elanor had run back to warn me and between us, we hatched a plan to save my little girl.

Two days later, Irven came and stole the baby, thinking none-one had noticed. I followed him and remember how I watched from the shadows, unobserved, as the swirling mist in the nemeton played around the priest's white robe. He appeared spectral and unsubstantial. Droplets of moisture clung to his beard and scrolls of vapour escaped his mouth, shrouding his deathly incantation in a pearlescent mantle. The memory is as vivid as though it were yesterday.

Without looking at the child, Irven unwrapped the shawl and presented the naked new-born to the priest. I marvelled at his coldness, for he knew nothing of the switch, willing to sacrifice his own flesh and blood for glory. The shock of the air caused the child to cry; her sound filled the grove and echoed off the trees that encircled the clearing.

But above all, I recall how Irven and Deryn exchanged a secret smile before the priest lifted the naked, crying child above his head, and how the jewel at the hilt of his dagger glinted in the half-light, its wine-red stone thirsting after infant blood.

THIRTEEN

Viper's Fort

Chela

As I approach Armelle's dwelling, I find my pace has slowed to a dawdle. I have visited the royal women's abode ever since I can remember, growing up alongside Hanu's daughters, my friends. As a child I was fascinated by the carvings of animals that adorn the internal supports, fashioned by the Durotriges' finest carpenters. There are horses, ravens, bears, deer, badgers and wildcats, all coloured in with pigments ground from the earth but only those who know how to look can discern them. The wooden benches have backs to them and are always strewn with luxurious skins and furs, and woven hangings displaying the intertwining symbol of the Durotriges owl brighten the walls. A silver drinking stand with exquisitely carved horns, and a chest, inlaid with silver and bone, said to have come from faraway Africana, make the dwelling feel exotic and foreign.

But today I am nervous. I have had it out with Elanor and, yet again, I am forced to acknowledge her wisdom in these matters. I have decided that I will try my hardest to befriend my rival. As Elanor pointed out only this morning, ours is a small and close-knit community and my role as a healer important. It would not do for me to shun Gowell's bride-to-be.

Summoning my courage, I enter the porch, just in time to see Armelle rise up from the couch on which she had been reclining, and attempt to slap Kendra across the face. Kendra, however, is too quick and manages to dodge the blow.

'You stupid girl!' Armelle shouts, throwing a wooden platter at poor Kendra. 'Don't you even know how to comb hair? Can't you see I'm unwell?'

I look on in amazement. Elanor had told me that Armelle's fever had gone, but she still suffered from a wracking cough. It is obvious, however, that she feels well enough to shout at Kendra who is backing out of the roundhouse. A look of relief crosses Kendra's face as she turns and sees me. I am about to say something in her defence, but she puts her hand on my arm, her eyes pleading with me not to make a fuss.

'I didn't say you could leave!' shouts Armelle, before being overtaken by a coughing fit and lying back amongst the furs and goose-down cushions.

'Easy, Armelle, you need to conserve your strength.'

It is Riana, the other Veneti woman, who speaks. Neither of them has noticed me yet. I raise a finger to my lips, indicating that Kendra is to say nothing. I am about to leave, when Armelle speaks again, causing me to bristle with annoyance.

'These stupid British. They don't know anything. I need a proper slave girl. I knew I should have forced Ranata to come with me. I'm sure she was just feigning illness.'

'This one was brought especially for you, Armelle,' says Riana, who sounds more reasonable than her companion. 'Hanu insisted you have her. You would do well not to spurn your future father-in-law's gift.'

'She is inexperienced and she has an attitude about her that I find annoying,' answers Armelle.

'What truly ails you?' asks Riana.

'These dwellings. Hovels, if you ask me. Why must they be circular? And Gowell's family? Savages, each and every one of them.'

'Shush, Armelle, they could return at any moment, and besides, they are your family now.'

Armelle curls her lip and is about to reply when I stride through the doorway. Just who does she think she is, insulting my friends?

'Good day to you, Princess Armelle and, you I believe, are Riana.'

I keep my voice neutral, hiding my annoyance. I look at Armelle, bedecked in her finery. Even wearing an ugly mood, I have to concede that she is really very beautiful.

Riana smiles and enquires as to my purpose. Armelle says nothing as she looks me up and down.

'I am Chela. Elanor has sent me with a tonic for the Princess Armelle.'

'Oh, so you are the healer!' says Riana, brightening. 'Gowell's sisters have spoken very highly of your talents.'

'You can leave the stuff there,' says Armelle, making it obvious she is not in the mood for visitors.

'Armelle has a bad cough,' says Riana. 'She does not seem to be getting any better.'

I smile as sweetly as I can. The raven-haired one is trying hard to compensate for Armelle's lack of manners.

'Hardly surprising,' I say, attempting to include Armelle in the conversation. 'I hear you nearly drowned. The sea is very cold this time of year. May I examine you?'

Armelle shrugs but does not protest. I lower my head onto her chest and listen to her breathing for a few moments.

'The chill has gone to your lungs. Elanor told me this was the case and so I have prepared a potion of scented mayweed and honey.'

Armelle nods then closes her eyes.

Riana looks embarrassed.

'Please, stay a while and talk to me,' she says, clearly ashamed of her kinswoman's lack of courtesy.

'Thank you. I will not stay long, the Princess is obviously tired, but I hear you spent some time at Saramis. How did you find it?'

I listen to Riana's account of their experience on the island and how Armelle was forced to spend her first night in a cave with Gowell.

'I hope he behaved himself,' I say, before realising what I have said. I feel myself reddening. 'I didn't mean..'

Armelle looks away, but Riana comes to my rescue.

'After we found Armelle and Gowell, we stayed in one of the houses on the island. Ivor told me they are used as storm refuges. They are filled with everything a stranded sailor could possibly want.' Riana laughs and I find myself liking her.

'I know them well,' I say.

'You do?' Armelle suddenly speaks up, curiosity overcoming her mood. 'And how did you come to visit Saramis? Do the British women sail?'

She sounds so rude that Riana gives me an apologetic smile, which infuriates Armelle even further.

'I used to play there with Hanu's children,' I say. 'Gowell and Ivor were good sailors, even as boys and we would often visit the Isle. We had some good times. Have you seen much of Gowell?' I add, trying to sound nonchalant.

'She has been too unwell,' says Riana quickly, answering for Armelle. 'She does not feel able to entertain visitors just yet.'

'You were friends with Gowell?' asks Armelle. She sounds incredulous.

'Oh yes, we go back a long way,' I reply. I cannot resist a little mischief. I wonder whether the young Veneti woman is jealous.

'We used to play the game of split with the dagger - very dangerous and foolhardy, but it taught trust and accuracy.' I say, laughing at the memory. 'I remember how I managed to skin Gowell's big toe once. He howled like a piglet!'

Riana laughs out loud. Armelle scowls.

'In the lands of the Veneti,' she says, 'young girls would not dream of doing such things! And our classes, how can I put it, do not tend to mix.'

The insult is not lost on me. To conceal my anger, I rummage in my basket of potions. If the young princess is intent on making an enemy of me, she is going about it the right way. I slam Armelle's tonic down on the table.

'We Britons prefer to assess a person by their actions and their hearts,' I say. 'Like you, we have our nobility and our common people, and there is a divide, but it is not impossible for a commoner to cross the threshold. And we women are free to choose our destinies. Some are even warriors, especially before they become wives and mothers.'

'I hope you have not formed a bad opinion of the Veneti,' says Riana, who is clearly appalled at her compatriot's behaviour. She looks pointedly at Armelle, 'we too consider the heart above all else.'

I smile at Riana, ignoring Armelle.

'Not at all. I am sure we will have much in common.'

Suddenly there is a crashing sound from the porch. Kendra, who had been hovering in the doorway, drops a clay pot which shatters on the ground. Armelle jumps, startled by the noise.

'You stupid clumsy girl!' she shrieks. Clean the mess up at once and get out of my sight!'

I exchange a sympathetic look with Kendra, who bends down to pick up a broken shard of pottery. Blood oozes from the girl's hand.

'You have cut yourself. Come here Kendra,' I say. 'Let me tend to your cut.'

'Do not think to waste your time on her,' shouts Armelle from her couch. 'She's just a slave and not a very good one at that!'

Kendra keeps her head down. As soon as she finishes clearing up, she withdraws.

I watch as Armelle reaches over and picks up the earthenware jar containing the healing potion. She looks defeated all of a sudden. To my surprise, she looks up. Soft blue eyes meet mine.

'I am sorry,' she says, 'to appear so rude. It is probably my illness that is making me thus. Thank you for bringing me the remedy.'

'Think nothing of it,' I say, smiling sweetly. This young woman changes like the wind. I pick up my basket and bid Armelle farewell.

Riana sees me to the door and as I say goodbye, I know I have a friend, but as for the petulant princess, that is a different matter altogether.

FOURTEEN

Chela

'Ouch,' complains Kendra as I pull out the sharp splinter of pottery from the fleshy part between her fingers and thumb.

'Sorry, but I must get it all out,' I say, in exasperation. 'Keep still. Why didn't you come to me earlier? Why did you wait so long? Five days!'

Kendra does not reply and I must voice my concerns.

'Did Armelle forbid you to come?' I ask.

'No, no,' says Kendra quickly. 'I was only afraid she would tell Lann about me. I did not want her to think I was making a fuss.'

'Why do you fear Lann so much?' I ask. It makes no sense to me, for she is now Armelle's property. Kendra takes her time to reply and I wonder if there is more to this than she is saying.

'He might not let me visit my friends, if he thinks I have been bad,' she says eventually. I look at her in pity. I can see her point. Slaves have few choices and no autonomy.

I shake my head. The splinter has caused Kendra's hand to swell and become hot. I break off a lump from the salt cake, pound it to a powder then add it to a bowl of warm water.

'There. Soak your hand for a while and don't move until I say so.'

'Yes Chela,' answers Kendra. She is clearly in no rush to return to Armelle's household.

'Is the princess any better?' I ask, after a pause.

'She is over her cough, but she behaves oddly.'

'How?'

'She cries for no reason and will not see Gowell, though he comes to pay his respects.'

I digest the news. It seems the betrothal is not proceeding as smoothly as Gowell had anticipated.

'Armelle sounds very unhappy,' I say. 'I would have thought she would be coming around to the idea of marriage. It will soon be Beltane and her welcoming party. Many of the nobles from the surrounding tribes will be invited to bear witness to their betrothal.'

'All the tribes?'

'All except the Atres, of course. Here, give me your hand now.'

'Why not the Atres?' asks Kendra.

'Something to do with an old feud. It is of no matter. Then it will be time for Armelle's house-building. She ought to be looking forward to that.'

Kendra says nothing and so I prattle on about the custom of building a new roundhouse for the married couple, how the entire community will lend a hand and how normally it is an excuse for merriment and celebration.

'But of course, your kin, the Silures, would do the same, wouldn't they?' I say, before realising how tactless is my comment. Her eyes have filled with tears. 'I'm so sorry, Kendra, I didn't mean...'

'It's alright,' says Kendra, blinking away her tears. 'I'm getting used to being here now.'

I shake my head and squeeze what pus I can from Kendra's cut. I then spread a piece of sphagnum moss with honey, before placing it over the wound. Finally I bind Kendra's hand with a strip of the cloth, but not before secreting a flat wooden amulet representing the Goddess Pragana in amongst the layers of bandage.

'There! That's the best I can do. Leave the dressing on for three days then come and see me again.'

'Can I stay here a while longer?' asks Kendra, obviously reluctant to return to Armelle.

'For a little while, but be careful you do not tarry too long,' I say. I feel sorry for the girl, as I watch her stroke Yarrow's head. I wonder why she does not talk of her origins. Perhaps the trauma of being taken is too painful to recall. I wonder if Armelle might sell her, especially if she is dissatisfied with her. That bracelet, sitting in my trinket box doing nothing might go some way towards the price, and then there are always the foreign coins I earn from Grypsos for the dried silverweed. Elanor and I have been so successful in cultivating the rare herb that Grypsos is able to buy it off us to sell on to the women of Rome. I have no need of the coinage and perhaps it could be put to good use. I will say nothing yet, and bide my time, lest I raise the young girl's hopes.

Kendra

By the time I return to my duties, only Hanu's daughters and Riana are inside the main part of the roundhouse. Armelle is reclining on her bed behind the wattle partition. I fill the water pitcher, the heavy work paining my hand, and bring more logs for the fire before sweeping the floor. By the time I finish it is late afternoon. I plucked up the courage earlier to ask Riana if I might visit Malvina and the boys. She said she would ask Lann. I wonder if she has remembered. Lann had expressly forbidden me to visit the others and I have been too frightened to disobey, the memory of Huel's death still fresh in my mind.

I stand in front of Riana with my head bowed.

'What is it girl?'

'I wondered if you had spoken to Lann?'

'Oh yes, I did seek him out. Ivor introduced me to him. He was asking how you were measuring up to Armelle's high expectations.'

I feel weak. I know Armelle is not too pleased with me.

'Do not look so pale!' laughs Riana. 'I told him you were a little unskilled but were a fast learner, so do not worry!'

I breathe a sigh of relief. 'Thank you, Lady Riana. You are very kind indeed. So I may go and visit the others?'

'You may. And do not worry about coming back until bed-time. I will explain everything to Armelle, when she awakes. Off you go!'

I skip out of the roundhouse and run as fast as I can through the settlement towards the workshops near the quayside. Eventually I find a building that shows signs of being occupied. A fire is burning within and as I burst through the door, I see that the room is full of slaves, young men awaiting shipment or others kept behind to toil at the workshops. They stare at me as I enter, then I see Cator and Morvyn coming towards me with arms extended. We hug each other in turn.

'It's so good to see you. It's been over a full moon's journey!'

'How have you been?'

'Morvyn, you look even thinner!'

'What did you do to your hand?'

'Cator, what happened to your eye? Have you been fighting?'

The gabble of questions comes thick and fast. I stop and raise my hand.

'Malvina?' I ask.

Cator looks at the floor, shamefaced, before answering.

'She is forced to stay with Lann. I have only caught a glimpse of her from time to time. I fear he beats her.'

I can feel my anger rising. I look at Cator then spit on the floor.

'I should kill him.'

'Do not think we have not dreamed of doing the same, Kendra,' says Cator, his voice a harsh whisper.

'I must see her,' I reply. 'I have permission to visit you, but I dare not enter Lann's abode unaided. You must help me.'

'Be careful, Kendra, remember Huel,' says Morvyn.

'How could I ever forget him?' I whisper fiercely back in his face. I turn to Cator. 'Show me where Lann lives. There is a gathering tonight of the nobles at the Folk meet and I am sure Lann would not miss such an occasion.'

The other slaves in the hut look up in annoyance at the three of us whispering together, and so we withdraw to the porch. Cator points to a roundhouse a short walk away from where we stand.

'That's where he lives,' he says. 'We can watch from here.'

As we wait, we exchange stories of how we have fared. Cator and Morvyn have been put to work clearing fields of stones. It is hard work, but out in the open, and not a great deal different from what they would have done back home. It could have been worse. At least they are not down a mine. They are supervised at all times, making escape nigh on impossible but both Morvyn and Cator have long since given up the notion of escape for fear of what would happen to Malvina and myself. I explain what I am doing and also that I have been forbidden until now to visit them.

'Now that this new lot have arrived,' says Morvyn, gesturing with his thumb towards the inside of the hut, 'I expect we will be sold off to the Romans any day.'

'Where are our kinsfolk?' asks Cator. 'You were so sure they would come and rescue us, Kendra.'

'I have not given up hope. I am positive they will come soon. I cannot believe my family would simply sit back and let this happen,' I reply, but I realise I do not sound convincing. Where were the Atres?

'Shh!' says Morvyn as he notices Lann's door open and his recognisable bulk stride off in the direction of the nobles' dwellings.

As soon as he rounds the corner, I dart into his sparsely furnished house. My eyes rove around his abode, then I see her, a tiny figure sitting on a couch in one of the alcoves. Her eyes are ringed with dark shadows. She wears a woollen dress that is too big for her and she seems lost and alone, fingering the little hag stone, a pebble with a natural hole in it, which always hangs around her neck.

'Malvina!' I rush up to the girl, folding her in an embrace.

'Where have you been?' she says. 'I thought you'd forgotten me!'

'I'm so sorry, but I was forbidden. It is only today that I have been allowed to visit the boys. Do not breathe a word of my visit to you, do you understand?'

Malvina nods her head as I scrutinise her. She has bruises on her arms, but otherwise seems unhurt and at least she has been fed.

'How is it here with Lann?' I ask, not really wanting to know the answer.

Malvina does not reply, at first, then bursts into tears.

'Tell me, child.'

'He... he.. .....' Malvina cannot go on as sobs wrack her body.

'Shh shh,' I say, controlling my anger for her sake. I draw her towards me and cuddle her tight. I am at a loss for what to say nor how to deal with such a situation.

'I just want to go home,' wails Malvina.

I let her cry, my own tears falling freely, and then when Malvina's tears have subsided, I talk to her about what I and the boys have been doing and how soon, very soon, we will all be rescued.

'There is a dog at the settlement,' I say. 'A little like Pedwar. Very loving, with long grey whiskers. His name is Yarrow.'

'I should like to meet him,' says Malvina.

'I will see if I can arrange it,' I say, wondering how I can accomplish such a thing. Perhaps Chela would help.

Malvina perks up a little and so I dry her eyes. Before long the pre-arranged owl hoot from the boys is heard and I slip from the hut. Cator, who has been standing along the track, pretending to urinate, has seen a figure approaching on the horizon. It is Lann, who has returned early. We watch him from the seclusion of the slave-house porch. I am shaking with anger. Enough is enough. There is no point waiting for a rescue. We will have to take matters into our own hands.

'We have to act,' I say. The boys look at me doubtfully. How quickly their spirits have been crushed.

'But?'

'But nothing, Morvyn. Do you want to go to Rome? Do you want Malvina to suffer at the hands of that monster? Me, I'd rather take a chance with death.'

'I am with you. What did you have in mind?' asks Cator.

I look at him gratefully and raise my hand to caress the bruise under his eye. He meets my gaze steadfastly and a new understanding passes between us. I realise I want his embrace, but in the presence of Morvyn, I draw back.

'I don't know,' I confess, 'but I will think of something. An opportunity is sure to arise and if we are vigilant, we will know when it is time to act.'

FIFTEEN

Lann

By the time my Lord Doran reaches the gates of Viper's Fort, the Beltane celebrations are already underway and the settlement buzzing with excitement. I am pleased to see that his arrival causes a stir, for the horses he and his men ride are the finest to be had, standing a full head above any stallion in the land. Doran was assured by the Gaulish horse trader that they came from fair Araby and I must admit they have a fineness about them, and as they trot through the massive gateway, they draw stares and gasps of admiration from the crowds. Doran looks the part too. He wears a thick golden torc around his neck, in the manner befitting a ruler. He carries a bronze ceremonial shield that reflects the midday sunshine and at his back he wears his sword encased in a golden scabbard, studded with jewels. Even though his garb is that of a Briton, his short hair and clean-shaven face endow him with a foreignness that sets him apart from his own kind.

As I greet him, I am proud to call myself Vellani. My lord is accompanied by five warriors, all of whom I know. They are hard and sinewy and command respect. At Doran's side rides the musician Keary, dressed as ever in his pale linen tunic that covers his britches to his thighs. Strapped to Keary's horse is his kithera, a strange instrument Doran brought back with him from Rome. The group travelled openly on the Greenway and at a leisurely pace, for, Doran tells me, the weather was kind and he wished to familiarise himself with the southern lands.

Gowell breaks through the crowd and leads Doran and his entourage straight to the plateau atop the headland where the festivities are already underway. The area is full of men, women, and children and, enclosed in temporary pens, all manner of livestock. All this is set against the backdrop of the sea, white flecked and continuously moving in the brisk summer breeze.

The area set aside for Hanu and his important guests is sheltered by twisted conifers that cling to the thin soil, and under which tables and benches have been set, so that the visitors can watch the entertainment in comfort. Doran exchanges greetings with Hanu and the nobles from the other tribes, before settling himself down to watch the festivities unfold. I take my place next to him.

'The Atres girl,' he whispers. 'She is hidden?'

'Do not worry,' I say. 'She works as a slave. She will not speak, I promise you that.'

'Good,' says Doran. 'You will be rewarded.'

'I need no reward,' I say. 'Only my place amongst the Vellani.'

'That is assured,' says Doran and smiles at me. I smile back. Doran saved my life once, when I was a small boy, and the memory bubbles up. He dragged me from a bog when I was close to drowning. I remember grasping at something in my panic that turned out to be the hand of a fresh, cold corpse, recently sacrificed to Eluna. I still dream of it. If it had not been for Doran, who saw me and pulled me out, that corpse would have been my eternal companion. To this day I have a dread of such places. Doran has no need to speak of reward. I drag myself back to the present, wiping away the thin bead of sweat that has appeared on my brow at the unbidden memory.

There is wrestling to watch and trials of strength amongst the men, who compete to lift the heaviest boulders. The warrior women join in the horse races, displaying their sword-play and their skill at handling their mounts. Musicians pluck at their lyres and sing, or tell tales, drawing huge crowds, whilst acrobats and jugglers cavort amongst the audience.

Betrothals are arranged, blood ties strengthened, livestock and horses traded and the forthcoming harvest discussed. Young men and women from all the Durotriges clans, bedecked in their finest attire, dance, sing and show off to each other at every opportunity. It is, I suppose, the celebration of fertility but it leaves me cold. I notice that Ivor is preoccupied with the princess' companion, a raven haired woman, but Gowell is alone, his future wife nowhere to be seen.

By the evening, the revelry moves to one of Hanu's large roundhouses where tables creak under the weight of food; cakes and breads, stuffed fowl, eggs, fish, hams, beef, butter and yoghurt aplenty, a cauldron of stewed mutton and a pig, roasting over the hearth. Wine flows freely, as does ale, and there is mead to be had for the nobles. Even the foreign sailors, who normally set up camp on the beaches, are invited to join in. As usual, Hanu wastes no opportunity to show off his wealth. Those who cannot fit into the feasting house occupy the clearing outside, creating their own entertainment. I have no desire to be here, but at least I am close to my master, should he require my services.

Inside the roundhouse, drummers, pipers and singers entertain the guests, until, at Gowell's insistence, the young bard, Keary, takes his turn. I have heard him play at Ravensroost and know what to expect. He soon has the audience enraptured and although I have no time for such sentimental nonsense, I have to admit that he can conjure whatever mood he desires.

When he finally stops, there is first silence and then deafening applause as the guests rise to their feet, stamping the ground and demanding more.

'Where did you find such a melodious lyre?' Gowell asks, stretching out his hand to take the instrument.

'It's a kithara, not a lyre,' says Keary, bowing in the direction of his patron. 'Lord Doran of the Vellani gave it to me.'

As he speaks, he hugs the instrument closer to his chest, a frown spreading across his face. 'It was a gift.'

'Don't worry yourself, young song smith,' laughs Gowell, 'I have no designs on your instrument. Would that I could play as well as you!'

Keary relaxes and offers the kithera to Gowell, who makes a few cursory attempts to create a tune before returning it to the anxious youth.

'Here, have it back - it carries your spirit already,' he says, before turning to speak to Doran. 'You have a rare talent there. How did you come by him?'

'A gift from the Brothers, but he is a free man and I cannot command him to stay with us,' says Doran.

'That is good news for me! Perhaps I will be able to persuade him to perform at my wedding,' says Gowell, as though asking Doran's permission. Doran inclines his head politely and smiles.

'And how is your father?' asks Gowell.

I know that Gowell is merely being polite, for the concern in his voice does not reach his eyes.

'He has been ailing these past few months. His health remains the same, he cannot speak or if he does he utters nonsense, and his face falls to one side. I am not sure if he understands what is going on.'

'It sounds as though an evil spell has been woven over him,' replies Gowell.

'In Rome the physicians would have us believe it is an imbalance of the humours,' says Doran.

I laugh inwardly, because I know that Gowell is at a disadvantage. Doran, however does not wish to alienate his host just yet and so changes the subject, modifying his tone.

'Congratulations on your forthcoming marriage,' he says. As he speaks, he glances across the room and stares, not for the first time, at Armelle. I have noticed there is a definite attraction between my master and the Veneti woman and he is certainly better suited to her than the idiot Gowell. I just hope no-one else has noticed. I glance at Gowell and my fears are allayed. He is already drunk and paying little attention to the women across the room. It will be a miracle if he remembers anything of this evening, let alone be able to discern any subtle signals passing between my lord Doran and the princess Armelle. Content to be at my master's side, I find myself relaxing and listening to the music, and I have to admit, I am rather enjoying myself for once.

Keary continues to perform even over the chatter in the feasting hut but eventually Hanu rises to his feet and addresses the musician. I see that the Durotriges king is swaying. At least Doran knows how to hold his wine.

'Enough young man! Come! Rest, drink and eat your fill,' Hanu commands, through mouthfuls of meat.

Keary bows to the women before sitting on Doran's other side.

'Well played,' says Doran in a low voice. 'I would ask that you stay awhile amongst these people, and act as my ears and eyes.'

'Of course, my Lord,' says Keary. A slave appears at the musician's elbow and a carved whalebone drinking horn from the northern lands, over-filled with wine, is thrust at him, followed by a platter of meat.

I wonder that I am not sufficient for my lord's purposes and feel a twinge of resentment towards the musician, but Doran turns to me, allaying my fears.

'I ask this of Keary, Lann, because I have another mission for you. An important one, to the Druids of Lynd. I will tell you more nearer the time.'

I am delighted, for I was taught by the Druids of Lynd and it will be like going home.

Presently Hanu bangs the table and when the room quietens, proceeds to address the crowd.

'As you can see,' he says, waving a trotter in the air above his head, 'we are preparing for a grand wedding not two moons hence. My son here,' he pauses to take a swig of wine and to slap Gowell on the shoulder, 'and our beautiful Veneti princess over there,' he pauses again to flash his teeth in a friendly leer at Armelle, 'are joining two ancient and noble families together. Their wedding will be a feast to remember!'

All eyes are on Armelle who looks thoroughly miserable. Just then Gowell emits a series of loud burps. The Durotriges heir is grinning from ear to ear, clearly proud of his ability to belch.

'What a waste,' Doran says to me in a quiet voice. 'What a pitiful waste.'

I can only agree.

Kendra

Tonight I must attend my mistress at the Beltane feast, for, I am told, it is fitting that she should have a slave in attendance at all times. I am to ensure her drinking horn is never empty, her platter full, and her every wish met, although once I have seen to these basic requirements, there is not much else for me to do, apart from enjoy the festivities. It is a rare treat for me and although I cannot be seen to eat or drink until after everyone has left, I can still enjoy the music and the storytelling.

Armelle sits on a wooden bench on the women's side of the feasting house. Hanu is speaking and the entire room is staring at her. For once I feel sorry for her. She fidgets uncomfortably until he stops, the music resumes and she is no longer the centre of attention. I stand next to her, ready to do her bidding, but she ignores me. She has no appetite and does not seem interested in drinking, and so there is little for me to do.

In her company are the women of Hanu's household; Cinea, Erea and of course, Riana. Across the room, I can see Gowell, alongside Hanu, Ivor and their guests. I am beginning to know who is who at Vipers' Fort. Sharing a table with Gowell is a strange looking man, clean-shaven with close cropped hair. He sips his wine and adds water to it, unlike the rest of his table. Lann is sitting next to him and the sight of him sends a shudder down my spine. I think he is looking at me, and I feel faint, until I realise he and his master are looking at Armelle. Of course, they would be looking at her, and not at a worthless slave such as I.

'Who are those people?' Armelle ask Cinea. I am curious too and so I lean forward to hear Cinea's reply.

Cinea names each noble, his tribe and clan before she identifies the stranger.

'That is Doran, the Vellani heir,' she says. 'He has spent his youth in Rome, poor boy, and finds it hard adjusting to his father's hearth, so I hear.'

Armelle seems taken with the Vellani. She keeps glancing at him, and I am amazed that people do not notice. He too is being indiscreet. He smiles and I see her returning his smile. Am I the only one to witness these exchanges, I wonder? Then it occurs to me that I am the only one who is simply here to observe; everyone else is joining in the celebrations. The men are already drunk and garrulous. The women too are drinking fast, not bothering to dilute the potent alcohol. All except Armelle and Doran, who seem to be holding back.

'I cannot believe the women drink in the same way as the men,' says Armelle to Riana who seems to be enjoying herself.

'It is harmless enough,' replies Riana, through a mouthful of meat. Pork fat glistens on her chin for a moment before she wipes it away. 'And anyway, they are not so different to our brethren, are they?'

'True,' replies Armelle, and I see her biting the corner of her lip, 'How stupid of me to think they might be any more cultured.'

'There is one thing that intrigues me,' says Riana, ignoring Armelle's sarcasm and turning to Erea for conversation. 'And that is the Owl of the Durotriges. Why do your people adopt it as an emblem? To the Veneti it is a symbol of death.'

'To us it signifies a deadly and silent hunter, a wise animal who cannot be tricked by its adversaries,' explains Erea.

'There's another meaning, though,' says Cinea. 'It symbolizes the crone, the old woman who never marries. One who remains childless and without a man for all of her days. It is said she represents wisdom.'

'I, prefer the first meaning,' says Erea, 'But only because I like to hunt. There is no shame in a woman choosing to remain unmarried, even if the men would have us believe otherwise.'

'I think I prefer the first meaning too.' says Riana, laughing, then pointing to her groin. 'Me, I look for a man who will warm my bed. At the price of wisdom, of course!'

As Erea and Cinea join in the laughter, I can see that Armelle is furious. I think she must believe they joke at her expense.

'Better to remain alone, that to surrender to a life of ignorance,' she says, looking at each of them in turn.

Riana, whose buoyant mood seems unassailable, is quick to reply. I know she has been spending time with Ivor and a romance is blossoming between them.

'Armelle, why don't you try to enjoy yourself?' she says, loudly enough for Cinea and Erea to catch her words. 'You can't tell me you didn't like the music, at least? The worst thing Bearcban could have done for you was to let that Greek Tydeus fill your head with all that foreign nonsense.'

Armelle's face darkens at the mention of Tydeus, her Greek tutor, whom I know from overhearing conversations between the women, she misses enormously. Before she can respond, brass circular trumpets with animal carvings at their mouths herald the arrival of Eryr Fawr.

In the ancient tongue, the name Eryr Fawr means 'Large Eagle', a fitting description when one surveys his hooked nose and claw-like hands. As he strides to the centre of the room, the chatter dies down, for he still commands respect, even amongst the Durotriges, whom, I have learned, are not overly fond of the Priesthood. My father is of the same mind. I cloud at the thought of my father, but try to dismiss my troubles, for tonight I am being entertained.

He is here to tell a story. As the audience shuffle around to get comfortable, I spy Chela and Elanor sitting in a dark alcove. I notice Chela's hair is clean and brushed so that it shines like autumn leaves against the moss green of her tunic.

Riana, who has also seen the healer, turns to Armelle.

'Why don't you invite them to sit with us?' she suggests, a hint of mischief in her voice.

'It would be presumptive of me.'

'Then I will ask Cinea, if you do not object.'

Much to Armelle's annoyance, Riana leans over and whispers into Cinea's ear. Before long Chela and Elanor are winding their way through the crowd towards the dais. Chela squeezes between Riana and Armelle, throwing me a smile as she settles down. Armelle is forced to shuffle along the bench to make room for the healer and makes no attempt to hide her displeasure. The crowd shushes as the Druid, resplendent in his long white robe and matching beard, begins his story.

'The King of the Western Isles had a wondrously beautiful daughter,' he says, his voice filling the room.

Eryr Fawr is an accomplished orator, and I am entranced by his storytelling. I can tell, however that my mistress is bored, for she yawns and fidgets. I look across the room and realise that Doran is staring at her.

Eventually Eryr Fawr stops speaking. People are weeping openly at the tragic tale. There is applause and much foot stamping, before the drumming resumes and the pipers start their tunes, indicating an interlude before the next round of stories and poems.

Just then Gowell, accompanied by Doran and some of the other visiting nobles, rises and heads to where we are sitting. Armelle greets them formally, until she is presented to Doran, who holds back till last.

Doran says something in a foreign tongue which I cannot understand, but I realise Armelle understands the strange language. She answers him and they just stand there, staring at each other.

'Ha!' says Gowell, who is slurring his speech. 'I see you speak the same tongues as my betrothed, here. What is it you are saying?'

'It is Latin,' says Doran quickly. 'The lady Armelle merely enquires if I am enjoying the festivities.'

Gowell seems to accept Doran's words and turns away to talk to one of the Canti nobles. Armelle speaks to Doran again in the strange tongue. This time, Gowell is angered.

'Enough!' he shouts. 'Speak our tongue or do not speak at all!'

Armelle blushes and looks to the ground, but I can see she is beside herself with excitement.

'How long do you intend to honour us with your presence?' she asks.

'I would like to stay for a day or two, if Gowell here permits,' says Doran, placing his arm on his host's shoulder, but not taking his eyes away from Armelle's.

'Stay as long as you wish,' says Gowell, garrulously. 'My home is yours! Come, let's get some more wine.'

'Perhaps we will talk again my lady,' says Doran bowing to Armelle.

'So what do you think of my Veneti acquisition?' asks Gowell not caring that they are still standing in front of Armelle.

I see Doran flinch.

'She is very fine indeed,' he says, talking very slowly. 'I expect you will both be very happy.'

'Happy? Now that's an interesting notion,' replies Gowell, raising his voice.

The noise in the feasting house begins to abate as everyone turns to listen to him. Armelle looks pleadingly at Gowell, but he is too far gone.

'Happy?' He is shouting now. 'Happy, you ask! My beautiful bride-to-be has scarcely smiled since setting foot upon our shores! I fear that she will never be happy again! Eh my sweet?'

'You do me an injustice, Gowell,' says Armelle, looking away. 'You know I have been unwell.'

Gowell raises his eyes to the ceiling then speaks directly to Doran.

'She needs to toughen up, if you ask me, forget all about her homeland and learn to be more like the Durotriges women,' he shouts. 'Then she will be happy.'

As he finishes speaking, Gowell lurches forward and vomits on the floor in front of Armelle. Then he sits down on a bench, holds his head in his hands and calls for more wine.

Standing next to Armelle, I can see she is taut with rage and it is hardly surprising. Gowell has humiliated her in front of the entire community, not to mention the visiting nobles from the major tribes. She heads for the door and runs out of the feasting-house. I have no option but to follow, but I keep my distance. Stumbling in the darkness, she heads towards the woods that rise up into the hillside behind Vipers' Fort. I do not want to venture into the trees, even though they are close to the settlement, but I will be in trouble, I am sure, if I do not follow my mistress to see that she comes to no harm.

Just then, I see a shadow intercepting the princess. She is some distance ahead of me but I hear her cry out. I wonder if she has fallen, but I slow my pace for I know she is no longer alone. I peer from behind a bush and see that she is being held by a man, but try as I might, I cannot make out his identity without betraying my presence. I creep away, not wanting to be privy to such secrets.

Lann

It is mid-morning. Doran and I have been waiting patiently in the roundhouse set aside for visiting dignitaries, and when Gowell does finally turn up, I notice his eyes are red-rimmed and his breath stinks. Doran curls his lip in derision and I know what he is thinking, that this barbarian does not deserve Armelle. Keary and I covered for him last night, and in the mayhem of drunkenness, his absence went unnoticed.

Soon after Doran left to search for Armelle, Gowell drunk himself into a stupor and was oblivious to all around him.

The nobles from the other tribes have already left Vipers' Fort. Only my master and his men remain, on the pretext of wanting to sample the local hunting, and protocol demands they be made welcome.

Doran and I have been talking. He has not wasted his time here and has got to know the measure of the Durotriges' southern neighbours, the Canti and Regni. Attending the feast was a good idea and will help to further his ambitions, but it is not they who command his thoughts this morning.

Doran should have been married years ago, but he has held off finding a bride. He tells me that he finds the local women boring. I know there are those who think his education in Rome was a bad thing, but he is good to me, and if it is an educated bride he wants, it is not for me to gainsay him. He is clearly smitten, for this morning he has talked of little else. He had not thought for a single moment he would meet anyone in this land of Britain who would arouse his interest, but since setting eyes on the Veneti princess, he cannot shake her from his mind. To defeat the southern tribes and take their lands has been his intention but he had thought only in terms of politics and worldly ambition. The fates, however, have seen fit to intervene. Now he has met Armelle, the way ahead is clear. I for my part, want only to see the Durotriges and Atres crushed into oblivion and if I can rub salt into Gowell's wounds by helping Doran steal his bride, then all the better.

He and Armelle have agreed to meet again tonight, in the woods behind the settlement and it is my role to keep Gowell occupied. They should be safe enough, especially at night when no-one cares to walk amongst the trees. Doran will have to be careful though, as such transgressions could cost him his head and the only people he can take into his confidence are myself and of course, Keary who will be staying on at Vipers' Fort for a while.

Doran has no need of his warriors this morning and has commanded them to remain at the settlement. Before long, Doran, Gowell and I set off on horseback to explore the countryside. Gowell, who has never seen a Roman saddle, is fascinated by Doran's. Instead of the single pommel at the front, Doran's saddle has four, one at each corner.

'That is a strange design,' he says.

'I brought it with me from Rome. It's what everyone is using.'

'It looks stable,' says Gowell.

'It works well,' says Doran. 'I will get one made up in my workshop and have it sent to you.'

Gowell thanks his guest and I smile at my master.

'Before we go hunting, would you be interested in seeing our workshop area?' Gowell asks.

Doran, seeing that Gowell has no stomach for hunting, acquiesces and so the three of us ride out of Vipers' Fort's massive gateway and along the roadway until we are clear of the marshland that edges the track. Before long the flat country turns into rolling hills and gentle valleys through which a river meanders. Instead of sweet meadow-land leading away from the water, the banks of the river are covered in piles of slag from the smelting works and the stench of a tannery catches us at the back of our throats. A mass of sprawling buildings and workshops line the river bank, ugly and uninviting. I know this place well, of course, as I spend a great deal of my time here, but this is Doran's first visit.

'We are producing twice as many ingots this year as last,' brags Gowell.

'The silver - is it from the Dumnonii?' asks Doran. He is well aware of the abundance of silver in the mines to be found in the far south west of Britain.

'Aye, and as mighty Rome demands more metal, the Dumnonii are more than happy to let us have their ore in return for wine.'

It is clear that the Dumnonii have no real concept of the value of the exchange. The precious metal is hard to come by. Wine, on the other hand, is as plentiful as water in the Mediterranean lands. This explains the wealth of the Durotriges. They are doing a roaring trade in tin, grain and slaves, and the likes of the Dumnonii are receiving a mere fraction of the value of their ore. It is a similar story with the slaves. A man can be bought for a single amphora and raids are becoming less and less necessary as the northern and far-western tribes select those from amongst their own kin to sell for the ruby liquid. It is as much as can be expected of such savages.

The workshop area is delineated by a low wall and a small unmanned entrance that leads onto the mass of higgledy-piggledy buildings, all surrounded by a miasma of acrid smoke. Outside one of the forges a dozen exquisitely carved shields lie propped against a wall and workmen are busy burnishing their bronze surfaces. No two shields are alike and on each one the central boss holds a unique design.

'The Romans refer to such dedicated manufacturing areas as 'oppida', but ours are small in comparison to yours,' says Doran, flattering his host. He dismounts to have a closer look at the metalwork. 'You have fine craftsmen and of course the Durotriges are famous for their pottery.'

Gowell puffs out his chest. Doran glances at me and I smile back. I know exactly what my master is thinking, that Gowell is easy prey.

'Lann here has taken a special interest in the production, ensuring we have plenty for trade,' says Gowell.

I remain silent.

'This work is truly excellent,' says Doran, picking up a shield covered in a delicately chased image of a human face that seemed to disappear as soon as you looked at it, transforming itself into a vine or a triskel.

'Here,' says Gowell, thrusting the shield into Doran's hands. 'As a mark of our friendship.'

If Doran is taken aback by Gowell's gesture, he hides his reaction well, accepting the gift gracefully. Gowell's skin is taking on a grey tinge, and when he dismounts to vomit into a bush, I speak up, offering to take Doran hunting.

'If you are sure?' Gowell makes no effort to hide his relief.

'We will be fine,' says Doran. 'Lann has come to know your countryside well since he has lived amongst you. He can show me the lie of the land.'

Once we are alone, Doran turns the conversation once more to Armelle.

'I will need you to help me steal her away, when the time is right,' he says.

'Whatever you ask, my Lord,' I reply. 'I am indebted to you and your father. Do not fear, Keary and I will see the Princess Armelle comes to no harm. When do you intend to take her?'

'Soon. Before the raising of the bridal house, for sure.'

I digest this information and nod my head.

'And now,' says Doran, 'about your journey to the Druids of Lynd…'

SIXTEEN

Chela

I am in the meadow beyond the marshes, and as I turn my face to the sun, I acknowledge that the heaviness that has dwelt in my heart has at last, left.

My conversation with Elanor has churned my emotions so that I can barely contain my excitement and for the first time in what seems like an age, Gowell does not dominate my thoughts. I realise he is besotted with the Veneti woman and it is clear there is no room for me in his life. Ivor asked me once what I saw in him, apart from his looks.

'He is stupid, stubborn and vain,' Ivor had said, laughing. 'And he can sometimes be a boorish oaf. He drinks too much and is truly insensitive.'

I remember agreeing with him, and yet I could not say why I loved Gowell, only that when he spoke to me, he made me feel I was the centre of his world and his smile can charm the worms from the ground itself. But that is the past. He has Armelle now, even though the Princess does not seem keen on the liaison. Three days have passed since the Beltane feast and according to Riana, Armelle still shuns his advances.

Good luck to him. She may be beautiful, but her soul is disfigured and when her looks fade, all he will be left with is her ugliness.

Elanor was right, as usual. Time has worked its healing magic and what I heard this morning has given me new hope. It was while we were eating together just after dawn. I was barely awake, but judging by the look on Elanor's face, she had something important to tell me.

'There is something you must know,' she said. 'Something about your past.' Her words come hard, her breathing laboured and I begin to worry.

'What is it, Elanor?'

'I have not been straight with you.'

I stare at her, but say nothing.

'Your mother and father are both still alive.'

I could scarcely believe my own hearing. All these years I have mourned my parents, believing them dead. And now Elanor tells me that it is not so! My first reaction is anger, for I feel I have been deceived.

'Where?' I ask. 'Where are they? You said they were Atres. Was that a lie too?'

'No, my dear I did not lie about that.'

'Where are they now?'

'They are still in the lands of the Atres,' she says.

'And the bracelet? Was that my mother's?'

'Yes. It was given to me by your mother. And no, I don't know why it carries the owl of the Durotriges.'

'Why?' I ask. 'Why did they give me away?'

'To keep you safe,' says Elanor, holding my gaze. 'I should have told you the truth a long time ago.'

'Who are they? What are their names?' I demand, but before Elanor can answer, the door crashes open and young Pari, of of the warrior's sons, dashes in, breathless and clearly troubled.

'Come quick! It is my mother. Please!'

Elanor's eyes do not leave my face.

'We will talk later,' she says.

'Please! Hurry!' Pari is pulling at Elanor's sleeve.

'I am coming, Pari. Be patient.' Then, addressing me, she softens her voice. 'Please don't be angry with me. When you learn the truth you will understand.'

I place my hand on her shoulder, for I know she loves me. Words elude me so I merely nod.

Elanor smiles at me before turning to the young boy.

'And what ails your mother, young man?'

'An evil spirit has entered her body!'

Elanor asks no more questions and quickly gathering her potions, follows Pari out of the door.

'Midday,' she says to me as she leaves. 'I have one or two visits. I should be finished by then.'

I am so excited, it is impossible for me to stay still, and so I decide to go for a walk and collect whatever medicinal plants I might find but despite my buoyant mood and my joy at being out in the spring air, the sun takes a very long time to reach its midday point.

And so it is a cruel blow when I return home at noon and behold Elanor lying on the ground next to the hearth.

I scream, drop my basket on the floor and race towards the fireside. I take in Elanor's blue tinged lips and hear her ragged breath.

I must be calm. I need help. Running to the door, I shout at some children playing nearby. Seeing my panic, they race off to raise the alarm.

I cradle Elanor's head in my lap and feed her drops of the foxglove remedy. She rallies a little and a touch of colour returns to her lips, though her skin feels cold and clammy to the touch. I examine her closely. I notice the pores on her skin and the way a tiny hair sprouts from a mole on her neck. Suddenly she is unbearably precious. I should have seen these little things before, and not taken her for granted. As I hold Elanor in my arms, I feel the closeness of death.

Elanor wants to speak, but I try to make her rest.

'Shh, shh,' I say, rocking her gently. 'Don't tire yourself.'

Elanor struggles to say something, but the effort is beyond her. I hold her close until the women and men of the settlement begin to appear at the door. They help me carry Elanor to her bed then stand around, not knowing what to do. I feed her tiny sips of water, tears running down my face as I watch my fern-mother struggle. Elanor is everything to me. How could I possibly have entertained any thoughts of my real parents when it is she who has looked after me all these years?

Suddenly Elanor's eyes widen as she beholds a form in front of her. She smiles in recognition of her spectral visitor and relaxes into my arms. And then she is gone.

I and the women of Viper's Fort spend the next three days and nights watching over Elanor's body as the last vestiges of her spirit leave her flesh, keening and wailing our songs, helping Elanor's soul to cut its bonds with this earth. Her body is washed, and precious aromatic oils rubbed into her cold skin. Her grey hair is brushed and arranged around her head, on a halo of early summer flowers. She looks at ease, though the blueness has not left her lips nor her eyelids. Herbs are burned; prayers offered and spells of protection cast. Eryr Fawr comes to supervise the rituals, waving his hands mysteriously over Elanor's body. Finaly, we bind her body, ensuring she lies in the position of an unborn child, in readiness for her rebirth.

I sleep fitfully from time to time, as the women of Hanu's household and other noble women, as well as the farmers' wives, take it in turn to watch her. Elanor has helped most of the women in the vicinity with their various births and has tended the sick and dying for many a year. She was much loved and not once is she left unattended. The vigil ensures that neither dark faeries nor demons come to snatch her away whilst she is so vulnerable. I worry that the spirit that had been in Pari's mother might have jumped into Elanor and killed her, but there is nothing I can do apart from conjure a ring of protection around her body and hope the spirit will not impede my fern-mother's journey.

During this time I dream strange dreams filled with regret and longing, indefinable visions of people whose faces are obscured with veils. It is as though Elanor is trying to speak to me, to finish what she wanted to say, but try as I might, I can make no sense of the dreams. Yarrow whines at my side, understanding my loss. I am glad of his company and hug him close.

On the third day, a farmer slaughters a sheep outside the house under Eryr Fawr's meticulous eye. The Brother spreads the entrails over the porch and looks long and hard at the patterns they form on the ground. We all hold our breath as one as the old man scrutinises the purple bloody mass. He mutters strange words and eventually he stands back and addresses us.

'The omens are good,' he announces. 'Her soul has left. There is no residue.'

A cheer goes up, for it means Elanor's soul will be easily re-born. Some prefer to be with the goddess of the earth when they enter the next world but Elanor always said she wanted to fly up to the sky and so we ensure her wishes are honoured. As the sheep is taken away to be prepared for the feast, five warriors carry Elanor to the platform where she is placed, still tightly bound, on a bed of moss, ferns and leaves. Eventually, when the last vestiges of life have disappeared, what remains behind will be gently gathered and burned then placed in the ground.

The platforms for the dead are to be found at the farthest end of the headland, where the land rises up into a hill. The summit affords a clear view of Saramis to the south, with its chalk-white cliffs. Only gorse, heather and the odd tortured shrub grow on the exposed hilltop but there is an outcrop of rock, whittled bare by the incessant wind, which provides shelter for the funeral party.

A fire is prepared, the sheep roasted on a spit next to the platform and offerings of food brought for the living to eat in honour of the dead healer. Hanu himself turns up, his slaves carrying several amphorae of his best wine. Keary attends with his kithera and plays song after song. Some ballads bring tears to everyone's eyes; others celebrate the occasion, and make people laugh. I witness everything as though from a distance, graciously accepting everyone's condolences and gifts. Riana gives me a hug, and brings a tearful Kendra along with her. Gowell and Ivor are there also and Gowell comes over and squeezes my hand. I smile my thanks at him, knowing that he does care a little for me, after all. Ivor is less reserved, crushing me in a powerful embrace, causing fresh tears to spring to my eyes.

'There there, my sister. It is not an occasion to cry, but to celebrate.'

'Thank you, Ivor,' I say. 'But I already miss her so much.'

The only person who is absent is the Veneti princess. I say nothing, but Riana speaks up for her.

'Armelle is still unwell, I fear,' she says, not quite looking me in the eye, 'but she sends her good wishes.'

I know full well that Armelle has no good wishes to send, but today it is a small matter. I brush it from my mind, noting with some pleasure how Riana and Ivor stand next to one another, as though they were one.

As I survey my friends and neighbours, I suddenly make out the form of a man striding through the trees onto the hilltop. His short stature and dark skin are unmistakeable.

'Grypsos!' I shout. 'Over here!'

The Greek sailor, grief etching his normally cheerful face, winds his way through the crowd until he stands in front of me. I run to him and he holds me tight, tears coursing down his face.

'I am too much late,' he says into my hair, a sob escaping his chest as he speaks our tongue in his thick foreign accent. 'Too late.'

'Yes, Grypsos. I am sorry. I am so very sorry.'

We sit together, old friends, Yarrow at our feet. I tell Grypsos of Elanor's ailing health and how every day of late she walked to the hilltop, scanning the horizon for his boat. Grypsos in turn tells me how his vessel had been damaged in the recent storms and how he had been forced to dock in the Veneti ports until he could make some temporary repairs and sail on to the Durotriges harbour.

'I will stay a long while here,' he says. 'There are many more repairs I must commence before I can go again to my home.'

'And your cargo?'

'Not broken, mostly, my thanks go to the gods.'

I nod. I can never quite get used to the way his tongue finds its way around our language. Normally his speech brings a smile to my face, but not today. I am glad he has not suffered too badly with his cargo. Grypsos' life is precarious enough; had he lost his goods he would have been ruined. At least now he can pay for any repairs he might need.

'You must stay with me, now,' I say.

'You sure? Is it, how you say, proper?'

'Tsh! People can think what they like. You are like a father to me and everyone knows that to be so. Besides, you will be company for me. I fear I will miss Elanor more that I can imagine.'

We talk well into the night until the festivities dwindle and people begin to drift homewards. Eventually only Grypsos and I remain, sitting on a fallen tree trunk close to the fire, keeping warm in front of what is left of the smouldering ashes. Yarrow, who has not left my side since Elanor's death, dozes nearby.

'It was a good sending off,' I say, poking at the embers with a stick. 'Elanor would have been pleased at the turnout.'

'It was, my little daughter. I am, how you say, happy for you I was able to be with you on such a day, even if I did not see my dearest Elanor in time.'

I snuggle under Grypsos' arm the way I used to as a child. I like him referring to me as his 'little daughter'.

'I too, Grypsos. And I know Elanor was here today. I could feel her.'

Grypsos does not reply, but as though in answer, an animal, perhaps a fox, gives a cry in the distance, a cry that sounds like laughter.

SEVENTEEN

Kendra

I wince in pain as I edge towards Chela's roundhouse. A bruise is beginning to form on the inside of my arm where Armelle grabbed me, and my little finger aches where she bent it backwards in order to drive home her threats. It has begun to swell around its base, and feels tender. How I had once thought the Veneti princess beautiful is beyond me.

It was shortly after we had eaten this morning that she asked that I accompany her on a walk. I should have been alerted to the fact that something was amiss, for if Armelle goes for a stroll, she usually demands to be left alone.

We walked to the edge of the wood, the same wood wherein I saw her and the man together. Of course, she does not know that I saw her and I would not dare mention it. Once we were out of earshot of any possible eavesdroppers, she grabbed my arm.

'I have heard there is a herb that can rid a woman of an unborn child,' she whispered, her face contorted as though in pain. 'You lived with the healers. Do you know where they keep it?'

I must have looked shocked. A noblewoman of her standing does not need to explain her actions to a mere slave but she must have felt it necessary.

'Don't look at me like that, girl,' she said. 'I know you think I am evil, but know this: whilst I was on Saramis, sheltering from that wretched storm, Gowell raped me and now I am with child. His child. I do not wish to carry such an abomination and I require to rid myself of it. Now answer me. Do you know where they keep the herb?'

It would have been easy for me to have said no, that I had no idea where they kept the silverweed, but instead I nodded, for deep down, and barely registering on my consciousness, I saw how I could use this to my advantage.

'Good. You will get it for me and if you do not do as I ask, I will tell Lann of your worthlessness and have him ship you to Rome.'

As she spoke, she bent my little finger backwards until I cried out in pain.

'Yes, alright!' I said. 'I will get it for you!'

Naturally, I harbour grave misgivings about the Veneti princess' trustworthiness. Once I have carried out her wishes, what is there to stop the evil woman silencing me for good? I am probably the only person who knows of her pregnancy. The wolves are snapping up my choices but what distresses me most is that I am about to betray the one person who has shown me kindness and even worse, it is only eleven days since Elanor's death.

Although Eryr Fawr has proclaimed Elanor's spirit free, I am worried that the healer still lurks in her old home, a silent witness to my treachery, ready to expose my guilt through some supernatural action. But it isn't simply the fear of discovery or the prospect of shipment to Rome that causes me such anguish. Chela still mourns her fern-mother and the betrayal seems so much worse for that.

As Chela's roundhouse comes into view, I spy Yarrow sitting outside the entrance. The hound sniffs the air and wags his tail at my approach. I pause and am taken by surprise at the sudden pang of homesickness that threatens to overwhelm me as I remember Pedwar. I have taken what comfort I can from Chela's hound, who now looks at me from across the path.

Forcing thoughts of home out of my mind, I concentrate on my task. I do not know who, if anyone, is still inside the dwelling and so instead of announcing my arrival at the porch, as is my norm, I hang around behind the granary, just out of sight, and wait.

I know that the old blind woman, Tinia, is staying with Chela and I feel sick at the prospect of having to sneak past her. Tinia is old and infirm and spends most of her days in bed. As I wait, the pain from my finger worsens, coming in waves, making me feel sick and hot. Tears spring to my eyes but I dash them away with the back of my hand. I must be strong!

I wait. The morning is midway to noon and the sun is beginning to warm and bake the muddy pathways that weave through the settlement. I know Chela will soon be leaving to visit the sick, having spent the early part of the morning preparing potions and reciting incantations, and before long she emerges from the porch carrying a basket in her arms.

'Come.'

I can hear her strong voice, addressing Yarrow, from my hiding place. The dog follows. As he passes near the granary behind which I hide, he veers in my direction, causing Chela to follow his gaze. My heart pounds, but Chela does not spot me and whistles Yarrow to heel before setting off on her errands.

When I am sure no-one is about I sneak into the roundhouse and pause near the doorway until my eyes accustom themselves to the gloom. The only indication of Tinia's presence is a gentle snoring from behind one of the wattle partitions. Good. The old woman is asleep.

I can see the pots of healing herbs ranged on a wooden table in an area set aside for the preparation of remedies. I know which of them holds the silverweed, having watched Chela prepare a concoction for a mother who had been ravaged by a succession of failed pregnancies and whose body needed a rest. I also learned from Chela a more sinister use, that of ridding mothers of their unborn children.

I would watch in fascination as she or Elanor spooned the desiccated leaves into a wooden bowl, added hot water, then muttered a charm over the liquid before placing the jar back in its rightful place.

I feel faint as I creep towards the pots. The silence presses around me and the roundhouse, usually so welcoming, feels oppressive. I have not noticed before how the doorway is shaped like a mouth, ready to scream my name out loud. I reach for the jar I believe contains the silverweed and open the lid. Inside is the dried herb, dark green and almost powdery. Pulling out a square of cloth from my pocket, I place two handfuls of the herb onto it, tie up the corners and secrete it back into my clothing.

But there is something else I must do and it is as though Armelle's demands have crystallised a plan that was only half-formed in my mind. After replacing the pot of silverweed, I pull a different jar from the shelf. Inside is another herb, one that can start an ailing heart but, as Chela once told me, if used injudiciously, it can kill. The thought of death reminds me of Elanor, who, I am convinced, is watching. Shuddering, I steel myself to my task and pour half the contents into a pocket of my tunic.

I quickly replace the jar and feeling jumpier than ever, edge towards the roundhouse door. A noise startles me and I freeze in my tracks, unable to breathe. It is Tinia.

'Who is there? Speak!' says the old woman.

Her voice is quivery and old, edged with fright. I decide to keep quiet and creep towards the door. As I reach the porch, I am nearly bowled over by Yarrow who bounds into the roundhouse, barking furiously, closely followed by Chela, who jumps in alarm as she spots me standing stock still in the gloom. As her eyes become accustomed to the dim light, she recognises me and relaxes. Yarrow stops barking and runs up to me, placing his paws on my shoulders and licking my face.

'Kendra! You gave me a fright! What are you doing here?'

'Who is there?' shouts Tinia again.

'Don't worry, Tinia, it's only Kendra. Go back to sleep. Kendra? You look terrible.'

I say nothing in case I give myself away. Instead I hold up my swollen hand as tears begin to course down my face.

'You poor thing. Let me see. Good job I returned for more herbs - I would have missed you otherwise.'

She takes my hand in hers and examines my finger.

'You've sprained it badly. I'll strap it up and give you a remedy for the pain. How in the name of Mafan did you do this, girl?'

I sniff, but remain silent.

'Did someone do this to you? Was it Lann?'

I shake my head vigorously.

'Was it the Veneti woman? It was, wasn't it?'

I shake my head again, but Chela is not convinced. Her face darkens.

'This is no way to treat another human being. I will talk to her.'

'No! Please!' I find my voice at last. 'Please don't say anything.'

I squirm under Chela's scrutiny. I must look a sight, but I can see the sympathy in her eyes

'Very well,' she replies. 'I won't speak directly to Armelle, but perhaps Riana can do something.'

I sit patiently while Chela reassures Tinia that their visitor is not out to murder her in her bed. She then binds my little finger to its neighbour and gives me some willow bark to chew for the pain. The stolen herbs in my pocket seem to want to jump out and proclaim my guilt. I find myself on the verge of confession, but my fear of Armelle and Lann, and the herb I have stolen for my own use prevent me from speaking out. Chela's ministrations, whilst providing comfort, make me feel worthless as a human being, and it is with a low spirit that I leave the healer's presence.

Instead of heading directly back to Armelle, I veer off in the direction of the harbour where the slaves are housed, near to where Lann lives. I am taking a risk, I know, but it is noon and most people will be about their work. With Esu's luck on my side, Lann will be with the warriors or at the workshops and not at home. My blood roaring so loud in my ears that I can barely hear myself think, I sneak around the side of Lann's house and stand stock-still, listening for any sign of the man. Before long, Malvina emerges from the roundhouse with a bucket full of waste.

'Malvina,' I whisper, and as the little girl turns around, the look of alarm on her face is replaced with a smile.

'Kendra! What are you doing here?'

'Is Lann about?'

'No, he won't be back for some time yet. Have you come to see me?'

'I have indeed,' I reply. 'How are you, little one?'

'I'm alright,' she says, avoiding my eyes.

'How is Lann treating you?'

'He scares me. I want to go home to my mother,' she says. 'Is there any news?'

'Let's go inside, where we can talk,' I say.

We scurry inside, where we are in less danger of being seen.

'I have some honey cakes,' whispers Malvina. 'Would you like one?'

'Yes.' I nod. 'Please.'

Whilst Malvina busies herself fetching the cakes, my eyes rove around the dwelling, searching out something that might be suitable for my purpose. Eventually I find what I am looking for and whilst Malvina's back is turned, empty out the herb from my pocket. I smile to myself, knowing that I have him. Just then Malvina returns from the alcove with the cakes, proud of her baking.

'Did you prepare them?' I ask.

'Yes. I'm learning to cook.'

'Listen, little one,' I say after I have eaten. 'I must be off, but if you should need anyone, come and find me. You know where Armelle's house is, don't you?'

Malvina nods. 'But why..'

'Don't worry. Go to bed early tonight, before Lann returns, and I promise you that soon you will be back with your mother.'

'You really promise?' Malvina's eyes open wide.

'I promise.' And with that, I duck out of the austere dwelling and head back towards the royal women's roundhouse where Armelle waits impatiently.

Riana is sitting in the porch talking to Erea, who is busy at the loom. I edge past her and go in search of Armelle who is sitting on her bed, buffing her nails, a faraway look on her face, but as soon as I enter the alcove, she turns her eyes towards me.

'Did you get it, girl?' she whispers.

I hand over the small bundle.

'I see you took your time,' she says, glancing at my bound hand.

'I needed an excuse to be there,' I reply, wishing I could leave now that I have completed my task.

'No one saw you, did they?'

'No.'

'How is it taken? Do you know?'

'I once saw Chela mix it with hot water. I think she made a brew of it. But there is a prayer that goes with it that I don't know.'

'Fetch me some hot water. I'm sure I can do without the prayer.'

I rekindle the fire and set about heating a pail of water. The willow bark has given me some relief, but as soon I use my hand, the ache returns. Chela told me to keep it bound for at least seven days but I cannot see how that will be possible for I know I will not be excused any of my duties.

I take the hot water to Armelle in a wooden beaker and mix the herb into it. Armelle gulps it down in one go, grimacing and fighting to keep the vile concoction in her stomach. She leans back into her pillows and commands me to go. I am only too pleased to obey.

It is early evening when Armelle begins to scream. I am preparing supper, cracking the shells from last year's cobnuts and pulverising the kernels into a paste, ready for baking on the griddle. Riana, Erea and Cinea rush to Armelle's bed. I follow and observe from a distance. Armelle is covered in blood and is screaming in agony.

'Go!' Cinea had shouted at me. 'Fetch Chela at once!'

I run as fast as I can and fling myself through Chela's doorway.

'It's Armelle!' I shout, my breath ragged from the exertion. 'She's bleeding from below and screaming.'

Chela needs no prompting. Grabbing a handful of herbs and potions that she flings into a basket, she runs towards the royal abode. I dawdle behind, my feet leaden, terrified of what might happen. When I arrive at the roundhouse, it is in uproar. Armelle is screaming in pain and the place is full of concerned neighbours who crowd around her bed. Chela is shouting for everyone to leave and gradually the room empties, until only Riana remains at Armelle's bedside. I watch through a wattle partition, just behind Armelle's bed, a cold dread creeping through me.

'She has lost a baby,' says Chela. 'And a great deal of blood. If this bleeding does not stop soon, she may die.'

118

'I had no idea she was with child!' says Riana. 'She tells me nothing!'

To everyone's relief, Armelle's screaming begins to subside. Chela is trying to coax the princess to drink from a small pottery cup.

'Come on Armelle,' she says. 'It will help stop the bleeding and ease the pain. Please drink it!'

There is a sudden commotion as Gowell strides through the doorway.

'Where is she?' he shouts, ripping the curtain aside. He takes one look at Armelle's pale face lying amongst the furs and his voice breaks. 'What ails her?' he asks Chela.

'She has lost her child,' replies Chela calmly.

I see the shock that passes over Gowell's face and I realise he knows nothing of Armelle's pregnancy.

He takes her hand, but Armelle withdraws from his touch. From my vantage point, I can see the hurt cross his face. Then Riana reaches behind Armelle so as to raise her head and as she does so, she discovers the wooden beaker, still stained with the green sludge that clings to its sides and base. She hands it to Chela, who sniffs at it.

'Silverweed,' she breathes, the colour draining from her face.

I want to run from the room, but to do so would mean attracting attention to myself. Just as I am working out how to leave, Gowell turns and grabs Chela by the throat.

'This is your doing,' he snarls. 'Is your jealousy so great that you must meddle in my life?' As he speaks, he digs his fingers into Chela's windpipe. I am trembling, and my bladder threatens to empty of its own accord.

'No,' screams Riana. 'She knew nothing of this, I swear, by the three mothers! Leave her alone!'

But Gowell is in a rage so white, he cannot help himself. Chela's eyes are beginning to bulge. She goes limp and begins to fall to the floor, Gowell's hands still around her throat. Just then, Ivor rushes into the room.

'Ivor,' screams Riana. 'Stop him!'

Ivor leaps on his brother, forcing him to let go of Chela, who slumps to the ground. I want to rush to Chela's side, but I am paralysed with fear. I try to move my limbs but find I cannot. It is Riana who goes to her aid. Chela is coming to, gasping for air, her breath ragged and coarse.

Ivor holds Gowell back, until he is satisfied that his brother has calmed himself.

'Hear her out, brother,' he says. 'She may well be innocent in all of this.'

But it is Erea who speaks.

'Shame on you, brother,' she says. 'This is no place for fighting or violence. Your betrothed is in danger of her life. Let Chela do her job here and then you can get to the bottom of this.'

Gowell glowers at her but says nothing.

'I swear to you, Gowell, that neither Chela nor I gave Armelle the herb,' says Riana. And with that she raises Chela from the floor and makes her sit on the edge of Armelle's bed. 'Now go. We will send for you soon.'

Gowell moves as though in a dream, allowing Ivor to lead him away from the women.

I stand stock still behind the partition, scarcely daring to breathe. I watch as Cinea comforts Chela, wishing I could do the same. Riana turns her attention to Armelle, coaxing her to sip the raspberry-leaf and horsetail brew. After a little while the hollow deathliness leaves Armelle's face. Erea lights a taper of dried sage which she wafts around the room, all the time muttering a prayer to the Three Mothers.

Chela, who remains sitting on the bed, is rubbing her throat, where Gowell's fingers had squeezed the breath out of her. To my astonishment, Armelle reaches over and takes Chela's hand.

'Thank you,' she says in a hoarse voice. 'Thank you for saving me.'

Chela looks shocked but in a moment she finds her words.

'It was not I,' she says, 'but the herbs.'

Armelle's smile is weak but at least she is making an effort.

'You are a great healer. Do not do yourself a disservice. And I am sorry for what Gowell did to you. He is nothing but a lowly brute. I did not mean you to have the blame.'

'Don't worry, I am tough,' says Chela. 'I will survive. Gowell can be rash, as I know to my cost, but he truly loves you Armelle. Perhaps you should give him a chance.'

Armelle says nothing but withdraws her soft hand from Chela's before closing her eyes and drifting off into an easy sleep.

As the sage infuses the room with calm, I begin to contemplate my actions. Even Armelle has shown a decent side to her nature. What have I done? Stolen, then hidden myself away like a coward. I feel as lowly as a slow-worm and despite my best efforts to control myself; hot tears begin to stream down my face. I sniff.

'Who is there?' It is Cinea who speaks. 'Kendra?'

I move out from behind the wicker divide. As Chela raises her head and looks directly into my eyes, I feel the blood ebb from my face. I am light-headed and a strange buzzing sound fills my ears. I know that my guilt must be emblazoned on my face. Chela is about to say something, but before she can utter a single word, I burst into tears and flee into the darkness.

EIGHTEEN

Lann

I am weary today. I have spent the day at the 'oppidum', as Doran calls it, overseeing the production of ingots and keeping those worthless slaves in line. But at least Hanu is impressed with the efforts I am putting in and I need him to believe that I have the best interests of the Durotriges at heart.

I kick off my boots and shrug off my cloak, glad to be able to sit down at my hearth. The girl must be asleep. Let her be. There is no need to disturb her this evening and tonight I do not want to have to look at her miserable face.

I light a couple of oil lamps and stoke up the fire, which cheers up the room. People have called my dwelling 'gloomy' but I have no need for trappings, the sort of trappings a wife might deem necessary. I like it the way it is. Against the wall are stacked a number of amphorae - a token of Hanu's gratitude, a pile of shields and swords and my horse armour. What use have I for luxurious rugs and furnishings? This is not my home and never will be, so there is no point in trying to make it so.

When I was sent to the Durotriges two summers ago as part of the fostering, I lived for a while with the other warriors, at the centre of Vipers' Fort, but I found it hard living amongst the other men. When I asked if I could live in this old house near the harbour, no-one objected and I suspect they were glad to be rid of me. I am aware that I make others feel uneasy. Not that that bothers me. In fact, it has its distinct advantages.

I smile to myself. Hanu values me for the improvements I have made at the oppidum but he has no idea of the hatred I nurture for the Durotriges. And of course there are the Atres. Their turn will come and my mother will be avenged. I wonder how she is, with her grey hair and piercing blue eyes. Though she is getting old, and illness is beginning to claim her, she still holds herself upright and I am proud to be her son. At least she is safe at Ravensroost and well looked after. Not long now, and I will be back home.

I might even take the little slave girl with me. Though she is Atres, she is a quick learner and has the right amount of fear in her to make her obedient and malleable. It is that wilful Kendra I need to watch. As soon as Doran's, plans came to fruition, I will kill her and sell the two boys off to the first trader who comes along. But the little girl, she is learning to cook reasonably well and do the domestic chores that would normally be required of a wife. I have no intention of marrying. I have no desire to sire any heirs and as far as I can see, all marriage ever brings is strife and sorrow, tying a man down. Malvina possesses all the practical attributes of a wife, but without the messiness of love or sex, the thought of which makes me recoil.

I pick up the jug I am whittling out of soft green oak and work at it for a while until my hunger demands attention. The girl has prepared the food for me, exactly as I have taught her and the place is clean enough. Not bad, considering she is an Atres, renowned for their lax habits.

The stew has been taken off the fire and placed to one side. It is lukewarm and so, using the iron tongs, I pick up four of the red hot stones from the fire and drop them into the pot one by one until the liquid begins to warm. Malvina has made some bread and so I tear off a chunk and chew on it while I wait for my food to heat. When it is ready, I ladle some into a wooden bowl and begin to drink the liquid, occasionally skewering a piece of lamb with my knife and placing it into my mouth. The meat is tender from its long cooking and melts on my tongue.

My meal over, I pour myself a tumbler of wine from a lidded earthenware pot, before settling down in my leather hammock-chair in front of the hearth.

A sudden pain shoots through my stomach. Perhaps the lamb has been left too long and has spoiled. Then I find I cannot breathe properly. Sweat prickles at my brow and around my neck, and my tongue is too big for my mouth. I pull at my clothing that seems to want to strangle me but my fingers feel numb and dead. The pain tearing through my stomach is excruciating. I am violently sick; the meal I have not long eaten arcs across the room and lands with a splatter on the earthen floor. I drink more wine, to clear the taste of vomit from my mouth.

Then I try to stand, but as I do so, I feel my legs buckle underneath me and I fall forwards, landing in the hearth, my face in the embers. The pain of the fire sears through me and with a supreme effort I manage to push myself off the glowing coals so that I am lying on the floor next to the fire. Then a blackness begins to envelope me but before I sink into unconsciousness, I fancy I hear the scream of a young girl.

Chela

'Kendra!' I shout, but she runs away and so I decide to let her go. I am in no mood to deal with her right now.

Armelle is asleep. Her apology came as a surprise and I am beginning to wonder whether she is not so bad, after all. It must be hard for her, being forced into a marriage she does not want, a long way from home, and I wonder what really happened at Saramis to make her hate Gowell enough to rid herself of his child. Did he force himself on her? Before tonight, I, who think I know Gowell better than anyone, would have said he is incapable of violence against a woman. But his attack on me has shaken me to the core. I look at Armelle again. Perhaps I have misjudged her.

There is no more I can do here and so I begin to gather my potions when I hear a sound of sobbing outside. Cinea goes to investigate and comes back with a child of no more than six summers, who is crying uncontrollably.

'By the Great Mother, what is going on here?' says Erea. 'Do we not have enough woe this evening?'

The little girl is still crying, but manages to ask for Kendra.

'She's not here. What is it child?' asks Cinea, softening her voice.

'It's Lann,' she says. 'He is ill and has bur.. burned his face.'

I sigh. It has been a traumatic enough day already, and now someone else needs my urgent ministrations.

'Come here girl,' I say and I realise how weary I sound.

The girl is thrust in front of me. I stroke her hair, trying to soothe her and learn that her name is Malvina. I remember then, that Kendra spoke of her and I know who she is.

'Burns, you say? Is he awake?'

'Yes, no, I'm not sure.. but he has been sick and cannot move. I.. I think he fell into the fire.'

I waste no time. I run home and fetch the scented mayweed salve I use for burns then race towards the harbour and Lann's abode, Malvina keeping pace with my long strides. I find the warrior lying on the ground next to the hearth, where he fell, groaning and clutching his stomach. At least he is conscious. The smell of burned flesh and hair mixed with vomit hangs in the air and as I kneel down next to him, I have to force down my own bile. Lann's lips are blue and there is a

125

ruddy rash down one side of his face. The other side us raw from the burn.

'Go fetch some men,' I tell the girl. 'We need to get him to his bed.'

As Malvina runs off to fetch help, I examine my patient. Though his breathing is laboured, at least he is alive. I feel for a pulse at his neck and notice it is very slow. Too slow. I just finish applying the salve onto his burns when three men from the workshops appear at the door with Malvina. They carry Lann onto his bed and leave me to my work.

Suddenly Lann leans over and is sick at my feet and as I recognise the smell, a horrible realisation dawns on me. It is the foxglove remedy; there is no mistaking its signature scent. Lann has been poisoned! Reeling from the shock, I ask Malvina for some salted water and force the half-conscious warrior to drink, causing him to be sick again and again. I need to get the poison out of his system. When there is no more to bring up, he lies back on his furs, exhausted. His pulse beats a little faster now. Perhaps there is hope. The foxglove remedy can rally an ailing heart, but taken in large doses, it can have the opposite effect. I wish, not for the first time this evening, that Elanor was at my side. Making Lann comfortable, I turn to the ashen-faced Malvina.

'Show me what he has eaten today.'

Malvina gestures towards the stew.

'Did you have some?'

She nods. So it could not have been the stew. I cast my eyes around the dwelling until I spot the earthenware bowl containing Lann's wine. Lifting the lid, I recognise the aroma of the foxglove, subtle but unmistakeable. Everything points to Kendra being the perpetrator. It was obvious the girl was forced to steal the silverweed. She must have taken the foxglove remedy at the same time. In the small time Kendra stayed with us, she proved an apt and intelligent student. Too apt! She must have her reasons for wishing Lann dead, and it most probably has something to do with little Malvina, but nevertheless, I find myself marvelling at the extent of Kendra's duplicity.

'Who did this?' I whisper to Malvina.

Malvina does not answer, and looks at the ground. The young girl's silence speaks for her.

I know what I must do. I carry the container outside and empty its contents into the nearest pit. I ask Malvina for water and a rag and scrub the inside before refilling it with more wine from the amphora. Perhaps he will not notice.

'Say nothing to Lann,' I say, though I am sure I do not need to tell her. 'We will blame the stew. Tell him you ate honey cakes instead.'

Malvina nods and then, relief and exhaustion taking their toll, takes to her bed. I stay with the warrior, making sure he does not worsen, until the birds begin to twitter in the trees outside, signalling the arrival of dawn.

I am beginning to nod off when Lann groans and wakens from his drugged sleep. He is weak but able to speak.

'What, what happened?' he whispers, his lips swollen. 'Someone poisoned me?'

'The meat. It was bad,' I say, pointing to the cooking pot. 'I have thrown it away.'

Lann grunts.

'My face? It hurts.' He reaches up to touch his cheek, wincing in pain as his fingertips brush the blisters.

'You fell in the fire. You will be scarred, I'm afraid.'

Lann mumbles something about having a word with the farmer who gave him the lamb, falls silent and then drifts off to sleep. He'll survive.

As I walk home, the events of the night catch up with me and a silent tear slides down my face. It is then that I realise what I must do. There is nothing to keep me here any longer. Gowell does not love me, Elanor is dead, Grypsos will be leaving as soon as his ship is mended, and the young girl Kendra, of whom I have grown fond, has lied and stolen from me. Granted it was Armelle who forced her to steal the silverweed, but the other matter is inexcusable. To think, I had even considered buying her with my gold bracelet! I will not give her up to Lann though. Bad as she is, she does not deserve death and I feel sure she had a good reason for her actions. Nevertheless, I feel betrayed and in no mood for forgiveness.

But worst of all was Gowell's reaction to me when he discovered the silverweed. My neck hurts where he tried to strangle me, but the true hurt is deep inside, a hurt of the soul that I fear will never ease.

NINETEEN

Chela

Two days have passed since the drama of Armelle losing her baby and Lann's illness. Exhausted from all the emotion, and still grieving for Elanor, I first slept, and then kept myself to myself as I sorted out my belongings, trying to decide which to take with me. I do not have many possessions, but if I am to earn my keep as a healer, I will need to take at least some of my salves, a quantity of dried herbs as well as my seeds and a pestle and mortar. I do not possess a horse and so will be limited to what I can carry. I wonder if I can trade some of my belongings for a nag.

Then there is the problem of what to do with the silverweed. Elanor had stockpiled a quantity of the dried herb for which, according to Grypsos, there is always a ready market. It has the potential to earn my keep and to feed me, and if there is none to be had in its native Cyrene, then it is all the more valuable. This year's seedlings will more than likely wither along with all the others growing in my herb garden, but at least I have a good store of seeds that I can take with me. Wherever I end up, I will be able to create a new garden.

I open the wooden casket and as I handle the golden bracelet that had been my mother's, a small hope begins to kindle. If what Elanor said about my parents wanting to keep me safe was true, then it means that they loved me. Love is always a good place to start.

I have not sent for Kendra. The episode has left a bitter taste in my mouth. As for Gowell, it hurts beyond measure that he believes I would scheme to make Armelle lose her baby. Was his opinion of me truly so low? Had it not been for Ivor, I might have died. Gowell has not come to apologise and it grieves me to think that he cannot even accord me the respect our previous friendship demands.

As I busy myself sorting out my belongings, there is a welcoming bark from Yarrow and Kendra's face, framed by those unmistakable auburn curls, appears through the doorway. I notice her eyes are red from crying and she looks pale from lack of sleep. I feel myself softening and beckon her indoors. Yarrow follows her and flings himself at her feet. After an awkward silence, she speaks.

'I am so sorry,' she says, her eyes brimming with tears. 'Armelle swore me to secrecy.'

'I know,' I say. 'It was she who hurt your finger, wasn't it?'

'Yes. I was too frightened to disobey her.'

'You learned well, when you stayed with us. But it is not sufficient to simply know which herb does what. There are words to be spoken over the brew. Words you did not know. Besides which, it takes much more learning to decide the amounts. You were very arrogant to think that you knew what you were doing. You could have killed her.'

'I am sorry,' says Kendra again, 'Can you forgive me? I want only to be your friend again.

'What you did for Armelle is understandable. But what about Lann? I know it could only have been you who stole my foxglove remedy.'

Kendra's eyes widen and she pales even more.

'I know why you did it, you know,' I say.

'You do?' breathes Kendra, looking relieved. 'How?'

'I have eyes in my head, and I see the bruises on Malvina's arms, but unfortunately, such is the life of a slave. He is strange, I grant you, but surely not worthy of poisoning,' I say.

Kendra is about to say something, but I interrupt her. I am not done.

'And because you care for Malvina, it does not excuse the fact that you lied,' I say. 'You stole and you tried to kill him, taking the law of the land into your own hands.'

'No!' Kendra protests. 'There is something you must know.....'.

Just as she is about to speak, there is a knock at the door and Ivor pokes his head through the entrance, followed by Riana. I wave them in. Kendra rises to her feet and stands to one side, looking at the floor, her cheeks flushed.

'What is this nonsense I hear of you leaving?' asks Ivor, trying to make his voice sound jovial, but failing.

'Where will you go?' asks Riana.

'I have kin elsewhere, as it happens,' I say. 'Elanor told me before she died.'

At the mention of Elanor's name, we all fall silent for a while, until Ivor speaks.

'Gowell does not blame you any longer,' he says. 'He knows that it was his fault really.'

'How so?' I enquire, absently rubbing my neck.

'He should have taken better care of Armelle. Especially on Saramis,' he says. His look says more than his words. I wonder if he too suspects his brother of rape.

'As her chaperone, I should have been more vigilant,' says Riana. 'But we could not have foreseen the storm or its consequences. She told me nothing of what occurred and I still don't know what happened, exactly.'

'She obviously doesn't want Gowell's child,' I say. 'Had she come to me I would have helped her. But instead she chose to send Kendra, who had no idea of the correct dosage.'

Kendra shifts from foot to foot as we all turn to look at her.

'Armelle did not want anyone to know that she was with child,' says Riana. 'She thought the loss of the baby would be a gentle affair, some bleeding, nothing more.'

'And so it could have been,' I reply bitterly. 'Instead she nearly lost her life.'

'It would not have solved the problem though,' says Ivor, looking uncomfortable. I can tell he is out of his depth discussing feminine concerns. 'She is still betrothed to Gowell and after this, I doubt if Bearcban would have her back. And she is not like our women, who can look after themselves.'

'But it's better that Gowell knows how she feels,' says Riana. 'At least they can talk about the matter.'

Ivor nods.

'My brother refused to face the truth and wanted to blame someone else for the infant's demise.'

'I thought he knew me well enough. But if he thinks so ill of me, clearly he does not know my heart at all.'

Ivor cannot answer, so changes the subject.

'I hear Lann is up and about. How unfortunate that he should fall so ill on the same day as Armelle.'

At the mention of Lann's name, I see Kendra stiffen.

'It was the meat, so Lann says,' says Riana.

'He will be scarred for life,' I say, as I busy myself folding some clothing.

'Anyway, little sister,' says Ivor. 'Will you not stay? How can we manage without a healer?'

'I have nothing left here, Ivor. My soul yearns to leave this place.'

'Then if I cannot change your mind, please accept my finest horse as a gift.'

I can hardly believe my good fortune and thank Ivor for his generosity with a hug. Then I remember that Kendra is still in the room.

'You may go, Kendra. I think we have spoken as much as we need.'

'When do you plan to go?' she asks.

131

'Early on the morrow,' and then feeling sorry for the girl, I walk over and tousle her hair before adding, 'Go now, and do not fret. You had no choice in the matter. And you need not worry about the other thing. I understand why you acted as you did.'

As Kendra leaves the roundhouse, I turn to Riana.

'She came to apologise. It was not her fault, that she stole the herb. She was frightened to disobey Armelle.'

'I know,' says Riana. 'Don't worry; I will look out for her. I know you are fond of her. Chela, tell me, what are you plans?'

'I intend to travel to the Atres. Apparently my parents are still alive.'

'Atres, you say?' says Ivor, concern edging his voice. 'Irven, their King is making noises about waging war upon us, for some imagined slight.'

'Won't that be resolved in the usual manner?' I ask. 'Warrior against warrior? Does Hanu have cause for concern?'

'No, not really. He doesn't consider the Atres a threat.'

'In any case,' I say, 'I doubt if my parents would be important enough to take part. Elanor died before she could tell me more, but I suspect they are probably simple farmers, not great warriors.'

'Possibly,' says Ivor. 'And it's only full-scale warfare that demands every man fight. We haven't seen such a battle for a generation, at least.'

We chat for some hours as they help me prepare to leave. Ivor arranges for his horse, Tanog, to be brought and also gives me a set of leather bags for all my possessions. Now that I have a horse, I can carry a great deal more. We stand together outside admiring the magnificent black stallion.

'He is truly wonderful,' I say. 'Thank you, Ivor, thank you. Can I ask one more favour of you?'

'Ask away.'

'Will you look after Yarrow?'

Ivor looks at me in disbelief.

'Surely you're not leaving him behind? He will be company for you!'

'I don't know how I will look after him on the journey,' I say. 'I will have trouble feeding him. I fear losing him if he goes off and hunts for food on his own.'

Ivor nods.

'Of course I will take good care of him sister. Don't worry,' he says, hugging me once more. 'I will collect him tomorrow.'

'I will miss you so much,' says Riana, whose turn it is to speak. She hands me a small pouch of Veneti gold coins. 'Take this. Perhaps it will serve you well and remember, you will always be my friend.'

I sigh as I watch Ivor and Riana disappear into the distance. Despite my sorrow at saying goodbye, I have to smile. I feel sure the depth of their relationship will become common knowledge before long. It is a shame that Gowell is not more like his younger brother. He has not come to apologise and deep down I am disappointed, despite what he has done to me.

Cinea and Erea come to say their farewells, after which I eat with Grypsos but I cannot sleep and so decide to leave just before dawn. It is still dark when Grypsos sees me to Vipers' Fort's towering gateway. Holding on to the whimpering Yarrow, he waves as Tanog and I set off along the roadway leading to the north.

TWENTY

Ravensroost

Fionn

My head is throbbing and my tongue is swollen and stuck to the roof of my mouth. I feel a little nauseous and curse myself of drinking too much ale last night with Brendan and the others. I grab my walking stick and hobble outside to the rain butt. The cold water on my face revives me and I drink deeply from the pitcher to quench my thirst. I don't feel hungry so decide to get to work straight away.

Doran has commanded that every smith work hard to produce as much weaponry as he can. No-one knows his plans, but it does seem that the Vellani heir is preparing for battle while his father sleeps the sleep of death. It occurs to me that I might be fashioning weaponry to use against my own kin, but the word is still that Doran plans to attack the Trinovantes, and so I will go along with his requests, until such time as I can leave.

Brendan pokes his head through the doorway. He seems excited.

'I bring news! They have found a woman in the woods,' he announces, clearly pleased with himself.

My head still aches and I am finding it hard to make conversation.

'Why is this newsworthy, Brendan? Does she have three heads?'

'Listen! Apparently she was heading for the Atres people in the west. Instead of sticking to the green lanes, she decided to skirt around the woods but her horse, a fine stallion of fifteen hands, if I might add,' says Brendan, pausing for breath, 'bolted, and she couldn't catch him. She then got lost in the woods and blundered into the Druids' nemeton. Were it not for one of the Brothers who found her, she would surely have perished.'

'I'm surprised they didn't kill her on the spot, for trespassing on their grove,' I reply dryly.

'Anyway,' continues Brendan, impatiently, 'the Brother did not kill her and instead brought her straight to Doran who sent some men out to find her horse. They managed to track the stallion down and retrieve her possessions and that was when they found the wrist torc, packed amongst her belongings.'

'What of this torc?' I ask, struggling to load the kiln with charcoal. Cederin is not here yet.

Brendan drops his voice to a whisper. 'It's exactly the same as yours!'

'You jest!' A frission of excitement travels through me and I stop what I am doing. Brendan is the only other person who has seen the torc and Briona told me it was one of only three.

'If you don't believe me I'll take my news elsewhere,' says Brendan, feigning hurt pride.

'No! Stay! Tell me more. You say it is the same as mine?'

'I haven't seen it, but I was told that it has a tiny Durotriges owl inscribed on the inside!'

'Who told you?' I ask, for I know how words can be twisted through hearsay. But to describe such an unusual pattern, there must be some truth to it.

'The wife of the warrior who fetched her horse, if you must know,' says Brendan in exasperation. 'Why should it matter who told me?'

'Then I must speak with the stranger,' I say. I realise I am trembling and not just through a lack of breakfast.

'She might be able to tell you who you are,' says Brendan, lowering his voice. 'But it might not be so easy to speak to her. Doran seems to think she is a spy, and has her under guard.'

'Then he would do the same to me, if he found out about my torc,' I say.

'He would,' says Brendan. 'In fact, have you tried to leave yet?'

'Not yet, but I was thinking I might try soon,' I say, pointing to my leg.

'Well, were you to try, you might not find it such an easy task. Doran has become, how shall I say, a little more cautious of late and the guards at the gates have orders to interrogate those who try to leave.'

'You don't think I'm a spy, do you?' I ask, hoping my voice does not betray my nervousness.

'Oh, I believe you well enough,' says Brendan, though I think I detect an element of sarcasm in his tone. 'And I am your friend, but what if when you awaken from this spell, you are not able to be my friend any longer?'

I answer without hesitation.

'My friendship to you is sworn. You did save my life, remember? In any case, what is this business about the Durotriges sending spies? I thought Doran was friendly with Hanu's lot? And Annan is still here under the fostering.'

136

'I too thought they were on good terms,' says Brendan. 'Doran even attended the Durotriges' Beltane festivities!'

'He is definitely planning something,' I whisper, 'but it's not for us to know.'

We sit together in silence, each of us steeped in our own thoughts. Above all else, I must find a way to see this woman and ask her about the bracelet. Then as soon as I have solved that mystery, I will find a way to leave. I have wasted far too much time and Kendra is probably half way to Rome by now. I have heard no more about the Atres raid and am afraid to ask questions lest I raise suspicions. All I know is what I overheard on the day I awoke, that Doran is behind the kidnapping, but that Kendra has been taken elsewhere. If it was simply a slave raid, Kendra would more than likely be sold by now, but that does not account for the subterfuge and the more I think on it, the stranger the entire episode seems.

'One more thing,' says Brendan, remembering another morsel of news. 'She maintains she is a healer and has with her a great number of dried herbs and potions.'

'A healer, you say?' I digest the information and know what I must do.

A shadow appears at the forge entrance. It is Canogus. He has already heard Brendan's news.

'I hear this woman is a healer,' I say. 'Perhaps she might be able to help me remember who I am. Do you think Doran might let her try?'

'I will ask him,' says Canogus. 'I cannot see any reason why he would refuse.'

I feel bad about lying to Canogus, but the fact that he is Doran's cousin warns me against taking the Vellani noble into my confidence. Just then Cederin arrives and Brendan and Canogus take their leave.

I greet the boy warmly and believe I am beginning to make some headway with him. He speaks to me now and I have managed to find out a little about him. He is from the North West, near the great mountain Ynys Mon, which, he tells me, is very beautiful, and beyond which lies the Isle of Mona, where Druce, the Chief Druid of the Realm, resides. On hearing of my disdain for the Brotherhood, he is quick to leap to their defence.

'The Brothers of Mona keep the true faith,' he tells me. 'It is the Druids of Lynd who have corrupted the Word and brought the name of the Brotherhood into disrepute.'

'Then why does Druce not stop them?'

'Perhaps he does not know the extent of their corruption, nor their meddling,' he says.

'Perhaps, that is the case,' I answer, unconvinced. 'Perhaps he needs to be told.'

Two days later the stranger visits me. It is evening and I have just finished eating my supper and am about to start polishing one of the newly created swords. A pile of weapons is stacked against the forge wall, their number growing daily. There is a gentle tap at the door and a young woman, perhaps of twenty summers, enters, accompanied by a guard who withdraws to stand outside.

I cannot believe my eyes. It is as though I have seen a ghost.

'Kendra,' I breathe, before I can stop myself. But it is not Kendra. This woman is a good five summers older.

The woman stands stock still, a look of surprise on her face.

'What did you call me?'

'Nothing, I'm sorry.'

'I thought you said the name Kendra. I was told you had lost your memory.'

'I am mistaken,' I say, mentally kicking myself. I really must be more careful. 'My mind plays tricks.'

'My name is Chela,' says the woman. I come from the Durotriges, but I am not a spy, despite what everyone thinks.'

'Such matters are of no interest to me,' I say, and then proceed to tell her how Brendan found me and how I ended up at Ravensroost.

'There is no herb I know of that can help you, young man,' says Chela, when I have finished talking. 'And your leg is healing of its own accord.' She rises to leave, but I grab her arm. Somehow I feel I can trust this woman.

'There is more to my tale,' I say, then present her with the wrist-torc. 'I have been told that you carry an identical one to this.'

Chela gasps and stares at me.

'Mine was given to me at birth by my mother, whom I thought had long since died,' she says. 'I discovered recently that she and my father are still alive, and live amongst the Atres. How did you come upon yours?'

I shrug, not wanting to give too much away just yet. She stamps her foot in frustration.

138

'There is nothing left for me in the lands of the Durotriges and so I decided to go in search of my parents. The one link I had with them, that bracelet, is now with Doran, who believes me to be his enemy. And then I find you, with an identical torc, but still I am no wiser! Can't you remember anything?'

'Our destinies are linked by those pieces of gold,' I whisper, choosing my words carefully. 'We must try to retrieve yours and plan our escape.'

'Are you a prisoner too?'

'I have not been told as much, but I believe Doran is preparing for war, and now he watches whosoever arrives or leaves like a hawk.'

We stare at each other for a long moment. Chela is the first to speak.

'So, have you really lost your memory?'

I hesitate for a split second. My instinct is telling me to trust her.

'No,' I say, relieved that I do not have to keep on lying.

'Then you can tell me how you happen to carry this torc. But first I have something to tell you,' she says.

I find I am holding my breath.

'You mentioned the name Kendra. It is an unusual name. I know of a Kendra.'

'You know her?' I ask in amazement.

'Yes!'

I grab Chela's hand. 'Where is she?'

'With the Durotriges, at Vipers' Fort. But..'

'So Hanu does have a part in her abduction after all,' I say, anger and excitement mounting. 'I have wasted so much time in this place. Is she safe? What does Hanu intend to do with her?' My words tumble out one after the other until Chela puts her hand up to silence me.

'Be still! She is safe, for now at least, and I can assure you, Hanu knows nothing of who she is or why she is at Vipers' Fort. She told us all she was Silures!'

'But why..?'

I watch as the healer bangs her forehead in frustration.

'How stupid of me,' she says. 'She was given to the Veneti princess by a man who has been with the Durotriges for a couple of years now. He is a Vellani, who goes by the name Lann. He is a strange and solitary being. Kendra was very frightened of him.'

'Lann! Yes, I have heard Brendan and Canogus speak of him. He was sent by Bryn under the fostering. He is one of Doran's men!'

139

We tell each other our stories, speaking in hushed tones lest the guard who waits in the porch should hear us. Outside the rain slithers off the tightly-packed thatch and drips off the eaves with a steady and hypnotic rhythm. Inside the building the dying embers of the forge cast a gentle light on the woman's face. She is beautiful, and in the firelight her auburn hair blazes with colour, a golden circle of light framing her oval face.

I tell her everything. Who I am, my mission, my fall from my horse in the forest, Brendan's kindness and my desire to escape.

'Doran is behind Kendra's abduction,' I say. 'We must be very careful.'

'The bracelet,' says Chela, who has been waiting patiently. 'I must know what it means!'

She explains to me what her fern-mother told her and I, in turn, tell her of my last conversation with Briona.

'She said it was one of three. She was keeping the third for Kendra.'

'What of the Durotriges owl on the underside?' asks Chela. 'What does that mean?'

'Briona said that if Hanu gave me a bad time, to show him the torc. *He* must have given them to her! Then there is only one answer to this riddle,' I say, looking at Chela in astonishment.

The young woman returns my gaze. She is scarcely breathing. Then she speaks in a whisper.

'Kendra and I *are* sisters! There is no other explanation.'

'There must have been something between Hanu and Briona,' I say. 'I was told the reason for the bad feeling between the Durotriges and the Atres is that Hanu once violated Briona, but now I am not so sure. I think they must have been lovers.'

A look of alarm spreads across Chela's face, but before I can ask what ails her, we are interrupted by the guard.

'The Lord Doran wishes to speak with the woman. Come,' he says, then, throwing me a cursory glance, asks 'Have you brought No-name's mind back to him?'

'Alas no,' says Chela. 'It will take a while longer.'

The guard shrugs and gestures for Chela to follow him. As she leaves, I can feel my head reeling. So much has happened since my accident. I must plan our escape, but where to go first? Back to the Atres to tell Irven of Doran's meddling, or onwards to the Durotriges to rescue Kendra? Our only hope for escape is through Brendan, but

140

will he betray his own people? I am not sure. But at least my horse is safe and Chela's own horse has been recovered. Plans crowd into my mind, and the more I try to find a means of escape, the more I realise I will need Brendan's help.

Chela

I am so startled by this evening's revelations that I can barely think straight and am finding it hard to digest what I have just heard. My mother, it would seem, none other than Briona, Queen of the Atres, and Kendra, my own flesh and blood! As I follow the guard through Ravensroost towards Doran's quarters, I mull over recent events and know I have done Kendra an injustice. If only she had said something! Then I realise that on my last day at Vipers' Fort, she must have planned to tell me everything but I was too wrapped up in my own problems to sense her distress. I berate myself yet again, barely noticing my progress through the settlement and I am brought up short when we reach Doran's quarters. The guard ushers me in and leaves.

Doran is nowhere to be seen and as I wait for him, I take in my surroundings. How peculiarly he has decorated his abode! Not in the manner befitting a British noble, but in a strange and foreign way. On one wall is a panel, the likeness of which I have not seen in all my born years, depicting a far off mountain with nymphs and animals frolicking in the foreground. The panel is so lifelike, that I am compelled to touch it. Is it magic? A vision into another world? To my disappointment, my fingers find a flat unyielding surface. Realising it has been fashioned by men, I stand back to admire its alien beauty. Doran also has a number of stone figures dotted around his house. I wonder if they are people turned to stone and might spring to life any moment. They remain mute and so, emboldened, I reach out and touch the long curly beard and moustache of a man whose head and shoulders are displayed on a pedestal. I have never seen the like. The fire in the hearth flickers and it is as though the stone man's eyes look straight into mine. I stroke his cold marble lips and wonder if he will awaken and bite my fingers.

'His name is Aristophanes. He is a great Greek poet.'

The voice makes me jump. I snatch my hand away from the statue as though I have indeed been bitten but manage to compose myself before turning around to face Doran. The last time I saw him was at Beltane and I thought him peculiar then, with his short hair and clean-shaven upper lip, but now that I am in his house, I think him odder still.

'It was a gift from my Roman Patron, Lucius Domitius.'

The foreign name sounds strange to my ears but it has a certain ring to it. I resist the urge to ask him about his time in Rome, although I am curious to learn more, for I am conscious that my questions would make me appear naïve.

'You wanted to see me,' I say, hoping I sound calm.

'Yes. Has the smith regained his memory?'

'No, not yet,' I say, 'but I have not given up hope. I need to spend some more time with him.'

'You never did tell my guards what your true purpose was in coming here,' he says. I see he wastes no time in getting to the point.

'Your think me a spy. I am not.'

'Why then, did you stray from the Greenway? A lonely traveller would never consider doing such a stupid thing. What were my guards to think?'

I scrutinise his face, looking for some humanity behind his eyes. He sounds reasonable enough. Perhaps if I tell him the truth, he might believe me.

'I wanted to collect some herbs that grow only at the edge of woodland, and that's the truth.'

'And the journey?'

'To find my real parents. Apparently they are alive and with the Atres. And there is nothing left for me in the lands of the Durotriges.'

Doran gestures for me to sit and I sink gratefully onto a cushioned couch.

'If you must know,' I continue, 'I was disappointed in love and then my fern-mother died, and I found myself alone.'

I can see he is summing me up. He pours some wine into a drinking horn and hands it to me. I accept gratefully.

'Well, I may choose to believe you after all. But tell me, how goes it in the lands of the Durotriges these days?' he asks.

'Their trading continues as ever,' I say. I know nothing of Hanu's politicking and hope Doran does not think I am hiding anything. But it seems his interests lie elsewhere.

'Gowell's wedding? Does it proceed as planned?' he asks and as he speaks, I catch a glint in his eye.

'As far as I know,' I say, not wishing to tell Doran of Armelle's recent experience. 'Their house-raising is due before long, I understand.'

'The bridal house? When?'

'I'm not sure. Before this moon is out, more than likely.'

'And Armelle, what news of her?'

This is a strange line of questioning and I find myself wondering why he is so interested the Veneti woman. I suppose I might as well answer him as honestly as I can, for I cannot see what harm it can do.

'She has not been well of late. She has lost weight and I am afraid she is not very happy.'

Doran's eyebrows shoot upwards. 'She is ill? Is she in danger?'

It is then that I realise that Doran's interest in Armelle is more than simple politeness. Did something occur between them during the Beltane festivities? No wonder Armelle continues to shun Gowell, if her affections lie elsewhere.

'No, I don't believe she is in danger, but I fear she pines for her homeland.'

'So the prospect of marriage to Gowell does not please her?' says Doran, and I cannot help but notice the element of relief in his tone.

'Apparently not. Lord Doran, am I to be kept a prisoner here, or may I leave to continue my journey?'

'I have a favour to ask of you first. You are a healer, are you not?'

'Yes, I have not lied about that or anything else.'

'Then you know about all manner of plants and what they do?'

'I do have a certain amount of knowledge, yes. Is it your father? Do you wish me to try to heal him?'

'It is my father, but I fear he is beyond help. Can you hasten his end?'

I am stunned. I look at Doran and for a moment our eyes lock. I have never been asked to do such a thing before, and it goes against everything I have been taught, not to mention the laws of the land. To kill an incumbent King!

'You ask too much of me,' I whisper.

'Before you answer, come and see him,' says Doran. He is almost pleading.

'You will understand that he has nothing left here. His body clings to life imprisoning his soul, the same soul that yearns for freedom and rebirth.'

143

I nod, speechless. Doran leads me out of his roundhouse and across the settlement to where his father lies. He dismisses the women who keep up their vigil but the Brother who attends the sick man will not leave. I look at Bryn's wizened face, yellow with sickness, sunken into his bones. He can swallow enough food and water to survive, I am told, and sometimes he opens his eyes and looks straight ahead, but he speaks of nothing, neither does he recognize anyone, and his face has fallen to one side. After what seems a very long time, Doran takes me out of the oppressive house and back into his own abode where he pours each of us another drink of wine.

'He has been like that since before Imbolc,' he says, as he hands me a drinking horn.

'I have tried to get the women who tend him to stop feeding him but they refuse, and I cannot insist. He is in pain and the Brothers give him a potion for that, but still he lingers. Will you not help me end it all?'

I swallow down the lump that constricts my throat. Doran seems genuine enough; perhaps I have judged him too hastily.

'Why do you not simply put a pillow over his face? It's easy enough,' I say and I realise my voice is near to breaking.

'You saw how it is. They guard him night and day. But a healing draught, on the other hand? One that might take a few days to work so his death would appear as natural as night following day?'

'The Brothers would have every right to put me to death for such a thing,' I say. 'He is still King!'

'The Brothers need not know,' replies Doran. 'What is your belief in such matters, Chela? What are your thoughts? Do you truly believe he should be kept alive?'

I find I am confounded. I know what I believe, but I do not know if I could do the thing that he asks. The practicalities are not a problem. I know of a mushroom that would work gently away and cause the King to expire three days after the potion is administered. The brothers would make me drink some before allowing me to give it to him, but I could have the antidote at the ready. It carries some risk, but if done carefully, I would be alright. It is the deed itself that bothers me. Could I take the life of a helpless old man?

As I sip my wine, Doran moves over to a chest and rummages inside. Presently he comes and stands in front of me. In his outstretched palm, lies my golden wrist torc.

'If you agree, I will let you on your way,' he says. 'Think on it.'

144

I meet his eyes and without lowering my gaze, take the bracelet from him and put it on.

Doran smiles.

'Then we have an understanding, do we not?'

TWENTY ONE

Viper's Fort

Kendra

Twelve long days have passed since my attempt to kill Lann and I am beginning to believe I have evaded discovery. Chela covered for me, but now what can I do? My plan failed and I do not have another.

I wish I had not left Malvina alone to cope with the consequences of my actions, but I imagined Lann would simply go to bed and never wake up. The last thing I expected was for Malvina to intervene and fetch help. Surely she would have welcomed Lann's death.

How stupid I have been. Malvina is a mere child, of course she couldn't stand by and watch Lann die a painful death, even if he did beat her and she hated him.

Straight after the poisoning, I waited in an agony of expectation, thinking that at any moment he would appear to mete out his punishment. I wanted to confess everything to Chela but by the time I returned to her house at dawn, she had left. The only person around was Gowell who must have come to say his goodbyes too but he was also too late. There is no-one else I feel able to confide in, especially not Armelle or even Riana, who is beholden to Armelle. So I have been waiting, biting my fingernails down to the quick, not daring to seek out Malvina nor Cator or Morvyn. All I know is that the vile man still lives.

I do not dare ask if I can visit the boys, neither is there any word about Malvina. I am simply too frightened of Lann. I sometimes watch his dwelling and the slave house from the hill behind the settlement, but not once have I caught as much as a glimpse of my friends. My observations are carried out in snatched moments and so I cannot form a clear idea of Lann's routine. I so desperately want to see them. They are my only link to a past life that is beginning to take on dreamlike qualities. With each passing day I am more and more inclined to believe I have been abandoned by my father and by Fionn. I am finding it hard to recall Fionn's face. His features are blurred in my memory and when I close my eyes at night, it is Lann who looms vivid in my imagination, with his ugly stare, or in better moments, Cator with his intelligent face and gentle, concerned eyes. Armelle says little these days, too listless even to be rude. Riana is kind enough, but I feel my loneliness keenly, and to my shame, I often cry myself to sleep at night, silently, lest I annoy Armelle.

It is morning, and I am working in the open, sweeping the area outside our roundhouse. The sun caresses my skin and a gentle breeze blows my hair around but I cannot enjoy the fine summer's morning, such is my misery. Suddenly I spot Lann striding towards me. I duck inside, pretending to busy myself at the hearth and keep my eyes down, not wishing to meet his gaze. He bangs hard on the porch, making Riana jump.

'See who that is, Kendra,' she says.

I obey, my stomach lurching in fear. I force myself to look up at him. Down one side of his cheek is a vivid blistering scar that has not yet healed. It makes him look even uglier than usual. He smiles at me but I avert my eyes and bid him follow me indoors.

'Greetings, my Lady,' he says, bowing to Riana. He looks around the room for Armelle, but she is still abed and will not rise for some hours yet.

'Good morning, Lann. Is there something I can do for you?'

'I wish to borrow the slave girl for the morning, if I might,' he replies. 'I need her to show mine how to sew leather.'

I flash Riana a look of pure terror, but she merely laughs. She has no idea how frightened I am.

'Hah! Kendra here is no seamstress, but if you require her assistance, then please feel free. Kendra, go with Lann. And don't look so worried, it'll be an opportunity to see you friends. You would like that, wouldn't you?'

I look at Riana imploringly but seeing this has no effect, follow Lann out of the roundhouse. I must compose myself. Perhaps there is no more to it than he says, and it might indeed prove an opportunity to talk to Malvina and the others.

I do not have to wait long for my worst fears to be realised. As soon as we are outside, he grabs me by the hair and brings his face close to mine. I can see the blisters clearly now, and despite my fear, I feel a certain amount of satisfaction at his disfigurement.

'Did you think me stupid, girl?' he hisses, so close to my face that his spittle lands on my lip. I cannot speak and a strange numbness takes over my body.

'I have something to show you.'

He lets go of my hair and pushes me in front of him. I walk as though on air, in the direction of his roundhouse. As we enter the porch he shoves me in so that I fall and land near the hearth. I struggle to my feet and as my eyes become accustomed to the gloom, I make out the small figure who sits huddled on a fur on the floor. It is Malvina. Though her tear-streaked face shows that she is upset, it is not her face that causes me to gasp in horror. The girl's legs are stretched out in front of her, so that the soles of her feet, covered in blistering sores, are exposed.

'What have you done?' I scream, as I rush over and put my arms around Malvina. 'What have you done?'

'She is a resilient one, I'll give her that much,' says Lann. 'It took a long while to get her to confess, but in the end she told me what I wanted to know. You thought to poison me, did you? Did you think I would not guess at your mischief?'

'So you torture children!' I spit, beside myself with anger. 'You are such a brave warrior! If your quarrel is with me, why do you not kill me instead?'

Lann laughs. 'You are too valuable, for that, my princess, too valuable.'

'I'm sorry, so sorry, Malvina,' I whisper into the little girl's matted hair. This is all my fault. My stupid fault.'

'That's enough,' says Lann, wrenching me painfully away from Malvina by the wrist. 'I have more to show you.'

I am led outside and this time, we walk towards Vipers' Fort's main gateway. I cannot even guess the extent of Lann's evilness until we come to a stop. He says nothing, but points upwards.

I follow the direction of his arm. High up on the palisade fence is a pole, and atop the pole is a head. It does not seem real at first, perhaps an illusion. I look back quizzically at Lann, not registering what I am seeing. Lann waits and a smile spreads across his face. I look up again at the head and then I scream, though my voice sounds distant in my ears.

It is Morvyn's head that gazes out over the landscape. I fall to the floor, my knees buckling under me. No, not another death, please, not another death. I try to speak but my lips feel swollen and useless and I cannot form any words.

Lann seems to be enjoying himself.

'Did you think my threats idle?' he asks. 'Did you not take me seriously?'

I cannot reply.

'I am not finished yet,' he says. 'Come.' He speaks as one would to a child about to receive a gift on their naming day.

My legs refuse to work and so Lann lifts me roughly to my feet. He wraps his hand around my hair and pulls me along. This time we walk past the buildings that cluster near the harbour until we come to a stop in front of a large warehouse used for storing goods ready for export. In front of the warehouse is a clearing devoid of grass, covered in baked and churned mud. A series of totems have been set in the ground and tied to one of these poles is a figure, slumped, his weight supported only by the ropes that bind him.

It is Cator. He has been beaten and his face is covered in bruises but as we approach, he opens his eyes and looks at me. He recognizes me and smiles a bloody smile.

'Here. You can't say I don't ever let you see your friends,' says Lann and as he speaks, he cuts the ropes that bind Cator so that he falls to the ground. I rush to him and cradle him in my arms, rocking backwards and forwards in anguish.

'He's as stupid as you – tried to protect his friends! But he will live,' says Lann. 'As long as you behave, that is, but if there are any more transgressions, I will make you decide who will be the next to pay for your disobedience.'

He spits on the ground.

'Filthy Atres,' he says. 'I am going away soon for a little while, but make no mistake, Huw has orders to kill if you cause any more problems. And I have told him that you are to choose the next victim of your rash disobedience. It is up to you.'

I am beyond words. I hold Cator in my arms, but I cannot think. I am trembling like a leaf and inside my head all I can hear is screaming and all I can see is a vast blackness engulfing me.

After Lann displays the extent of his cruelty, he leaves us alone. Not knowing where to take Cator, I decide to go to Chela's old roundhouse where only Grypsos remains. At least there I can make use of some of the herbs that Chela left behind and try to heal Cator. I am beyond worrying what anyone else will say or do. The only thing that matters now is to help Cator. I wish I could do something for Malvina, but I know I dare not enter Lann's house.

Chela's old house stands empty most days. Grypsos spends a great deal of time working on his boat. Yarrow has gone to live with Ivor and the old woman Tinia lives with another family so the house, formerly so cheerful and pleasant, feels empty and sad. No-one takes any notice of us as we stumble through Viper's Fort, Cator leaning heavily on me for support. When we finally reached the healer's house unchallenged, I breathe a sigh of relief, glad not to have to explain myself to anyone. Slaves, it seems, are invisible, and sometimes that has its advantages.

I light a fire in the cold hearth and set to, washing Cator's cuts and examining his bruises. He has not been mortally hurt, and though it pains him to cough, there is no blood in his spit. His limbs all work and the bruising will fade, if Lann leaves him alone, that is.

'I have brought all this upon you,' I say, my tears splashing his hands.

'How so?' asks Cator, grimacing through his pain.

'I have been so stupid, so rash. Again. How vain I was to think that I could poison Lann and get away with it. It was my fault Huel was killed, and now Morvyn is dead and little Malvina tortured...'

'Listen to me, Kendra,' says Cator. 'Be still.' He takes my hands in his and looks into my eyes.

'You are the bravest of us all. I fear the Atres have forgotten about us and you did what you thought best. This,' he gestures at his bruises, 'This I brought on myself, by trying to defend Morvyn.'

'You stood up to Lann?'

'I had to try, but it did no good,' says Cator.

'I wonder what happened to him to make him so evil,' I say.

Cator cannot answer and I let my tears fall free. He holds me in his arms until I have no more tears to shed. When I am calmed, Cator, despite his discomfort, takes me by the chin, tilting my face towards his then kisses me softly on the lips. I return his kiss and we sit together, talking, our friendship taking on new meaning. I know now that this is the man I love, not Fionn.

It is not long, however, before we are reminded that we are no more than mere slaves. For three days Lann leaves Cator alone. Grypsos has no objection to him being in the hut and every moment I can manage to steal away from Armelle, I rush to his side, to be with him. There is no news of Malvina and I dare not attempt a visit. On the third day, whilst I am occupied with my duties, Lann returns and takes Cator with him, back to work. I do not dare search him out in the workshops and so I make do with dreams of escape, and though my plight is no better than before, the realization that I love Cator and he loves me back, rekindles within me a desire to survive.

TWENTY TWO

Lann

It is the day of Gowell's house-raising and I suppose I ought to show my face, or else they will wonder why I am not celebrating along with everyone else. My one consolation is that on the morrow, I leave for home where I will collect Doran's gifts and messages for the Brothers and then travel onwards to Lynd. I will journey by sea and with Eluna on my side, I will be back well within one moon's journey. Huw has agreed to move into my house until I return and has instructions to keep an eye on things, and if the girl Kendra shows any inclination towards rebellion, he is to damage Cator. Break a limb or two, perhaps. I don't want him dead just yet for I think the girl has feelings for him which I can use to my advantage. I don't think she will cause any trouble though, not after her most recent lesson.

I am walking behind Gowell and Ivor, close enough to be able to hear their words, although they are not aware that I am listening. We, namely myself, the Durotriges heirs and a motley bunch of warriors, are on our way to collect Armelle and take her to the location of their new home, where the entire settlement will be waiting. The warriors are talking amongst themselves, and so I hone in on the brothers' conversation.

'Perhaps I should send her home to her father,' says Gowell.

'I doubt Bearcban would take her back, especially when he finds out that she was with child,' replies Ivor.

I smirk, for I know full well that Ivor's response is not entirely selfless. He has been spending more and more time with raven-haired one called Riana. If Armelle were to be sent home, Riana would have to go with her. Nevertheless, his brother speaks the truth. The scandal about the unborn child is the talk of Viper's Fort.

'You're right, Ivor, as usual,' says Gowell. 'To even broach the subject with Bearcban would irredeemably damage relations between our two Kingdoms.'

'Armelle has no real choice but to marry you,' says Ivor. 'And Bearcban would see it as a sign of weakness - that you had not been able to command his daughter.'

'I know, I know, and yet she does not seem to be able to grasp her situation or to make the best of it. Surely I am not *that* bad!'

I resist the urge to laugh out loud. What an oaf! I see that Ivor does not answer and wonder what he is thinking. Gowell, thick-skinned as ever, does not even register Ivor's silence.

'I wish I had treated Chela better,' says Gowell.

'It's a bit late for that, isn't it?' replies Ivor. I can see what he is thinking, that it is uncharacteristic of Gowell to show remorse or concern, and Gowell's next words simply prove that he is only concerned with himself and Armelle.

'I have driven away the only competent healer we have. Though the old women give Armelle draughts to raise her mood, none of them seem to work.'

'Don't you wonder how Chela is doing?' asks Ivor and I can hear the rising anger in his voice. 'You have treated her ill, brother, she who has been your loyal friend since we were all children together.'

I almost like Ivor. Except that he is a Durotriges, and I am avowed to hate them all.

'You are right there,' says Gowell, and he sounds contrite for once, though I have my doubts for I know him to be a self-seeking boor.

As the two brothers stand together outside the roundhouse, waiting for Armelle and the other women to emerge, I see Ivor place his hand on Gowell's shoulder.

'She will come around,' he says. 'She has no choice. Just give her time.'

'Time is what I lack, brother,' replies Gowell. 'Today marks the beginning of our house-raising and it should be an occasion for joy, and still Armelle will not grace me with so much as a smile. It's only just over two moons to Lamas and our wedding feast!'

I smirk inwardly, knowing Doran's plans in respect of the lady Armelle. I am surprised, however, that he has not yet acted to fetch the Veneti woman for I know that he promised he would have her away before the house-raising and here we are, ready to build the bridal home.

We all fall silent as Armelle emerges from the roundhouse. She looks very fine, if you like that sort of thing, her yellow hair loose about her shoulders, even if she does have a far-away look about her. I see the Atres girl at her side and am gratified to see that she shrinks when she catches sight of me. I don't think I need worry about her in my absence.

Gowell offers Armelle his arm, and after a moment's hesitation, she threads her slim wrist through the crook of his elbow. I notice, however, that she does not look at him.

Presently we arrive at the section of Vipers' Fort that has been set aside for Gowell and Armelle's roundhouse, where it is intended they will live together with their children. It is only the royal family who enjoy such privacy; most people share their homes with their extended families and over-wintering animals. I thank the gods that I have managed to escape such close quarters!

The materials for the construction of the wedding house have been gathered in readiness and Gowell, I am told, has personally chosen the timbers. Thirty-seven felled oaks lay piled up in one long stack. With everyone who can be spared from the fields lending a hand, the house will take three or four days, depending on the weather. The start of the construction is always marked by much feasting and drinking and the festivities will continue until the house is finished. The gifts are piling up, from the most humble hand-carved wooden tumbler, to large earthenware cooking pots. For my part, and on behalf of the Vellani, I have given the couple a fine horse with Arab blood running through its veins, left for me when Doran visited at Beltane. It hurts me to give up the horse, but protocol demands it. Besides, I am sure Doran will let me have another, when all this is over.

Gowell, who is clearly delighted with the horse, insists that I accompany him to examine the reeds for the roof, which are stacked under cover in one of the granaries, and the piles of willow branches that lie to one side ready to be woven into wattle. I make appreciative noises as we skirt past the mountain of lime, manure and horse hair that stands ready to be mixed together for the render. It is the same throughout the land and I wonder why Gowell feels it so necessary to show off.

The weather is kind and I hope it remains so for my journey tomorrow. Everyone is in a festive mood with flowers in their hair and beads around their necks. Those who have gold, wear it. Keary is here, playing on his kithera. I am not sure how to take the Bard, as I think him soft, but Doran tells me he is loyal and so I must trust him.

The older women have constructed a fire on which to roast a large boar and several amphorae of wine lay stacked ready to be opened. The wine is poured into the vast silver cauldron that was Armelle's dowry and every worker is allowed to help themselves to a drink as needed. For the children, a pitcher of ale has been filled and everyone seems ready to have a good time, everyone, that is, except for myself and the Veneti princess. Armelle has been given a seat near the Grandmothers while the rest of the villagers, including Gowell's sisters, join in with the house-raising. I suppose I must play my part and so stand around while the foundations are sorted out, ready to lend a hand.

First, the circle is measured and inscribed in the ground. Then Eryr Fawr checks the porch is aligned towards the east with just a hint of the south in its aspect. This takes an age and after much sucking of teeth, when everyone is satisfied that the orientation is correct, we set to with picks and shovels, digging out the post-holes that are destined to support the porch. It is thirsty work and I gratefully accept a tumbler full of wine proffered by a slave. Why they don't get the slaves to do the whole lot, is beyond me, some nonsense to do with it being an honour and a privilege to lend a hand.

Gowell calls for Armelle and she comes over to partake of the first ritual which entails placing a piece of iron ore and a cow's jaw-bone in the post hole before the post itself is put in place. Armelle does as she is told, flinging the metal where it will lie, whilst the community sing a prayer to Matrea for health and happiness. What a joke!

When all the post holes are ready, the posts - tree trunks no less - are placed within and packed with stones and rubble to secure them in place. Soon a circle of totems stands proud and tall. Beams are fashioned to form a circle that stands atop the poles so that by the early evening the framework is complete. We stand back and appraise our work. It is time to drink and eat. The rest of the building-work can wait until tomorrow. I have to confess I have rather enjoyed the labours for there is something satisfying in the act of creation, even if it is a house for one of the cursed Durotriges.

The entire time, Armelle is compelled to watch, under the beady eyes of the older women, whose respect she has lost since the episode with the unborn child. I see now that she is in deep conversation with Keary and is laughing. I am not the only one who wonders what they are talking about, for I see that Gowell is jealous and is striding towards them. I follow at a discreet distance, curious to find out what is going on.

'You seem happier, my love,' says Gowell, taking Armelle's hand. I notice that for once, she does not withdraw. She must be playing him.

'Keary sang a song at Beltane that I liked very much. He has promised to sing it for us again.'

Gowell seems to accept her excuse. He may be stupid, but I am not, and I know it is just a cover. I can guess what Armelle and Keary are talking about. We are then forced to listen to a song that is unfamiliar to me. If it is Veneti in origin, I wonder how Keary knows it, but then the young Bard is well travelled, so Doran tells me.

'Fair love, your heart lives in the earth
Amongst the roots and stones so dark
You care not for man nor child nor hearth
Our Great Mother mocks me, I hear her laugh.'

'I offer you cattle, I offer you gold
I offer you children, if I might be so bold.
But I know I cannot loosen the chains
That bind you tight, my sweet priestess.
Your role is to worship and tend the flames
Of Our Mother so ancient, our Goddess so great.'

'I offer you cattle, I offer you gold
I offer you children, if I might be so bold.
But I will bide my time 'til Our Mother's asleep
When the brown leaves have fallen
And the hoar frost dost creep.
And though harvests may fail and lakes turn to brine
I will steal you away and make you all mine.'

I cannot help but laugh, for the song is most inappropriate for a house-raising. Keary's impudence is noteworthy! Soon Gowell wanders off and I sidle up to Armelle.

'I need a message sent to Doran,' she says. 'Keary tells me you are going to Ravensroost on the morrow.'

'I am indeed, my Lady.'

'Tell him the house-raising is upon us and that he promised to fetch me before it was complete. Tell him I wither and die here and that Lamas and my wedding day approach fast.'

I nod to indicate the message will be delivered, but I know there is more, for the Veneti woman looks uncomfortable.

'And I would be in your debt, Lann, if you make no mention of recent events concerning my illness. I would not want to worry my Lord Doran.'

'Of course, my Lady. I would not dream of it.' I wonder what Doran would make of the fact that it is common knowledge that she is no longer a virgin and she killed her own unborn child. Probably nothing, for I remind myself that he is besotted with her and would probably dismiss such matters as unimportant. But my loyalty is to him, not her, and it is my duty to tell him. Let him make of it what he will.

I can see that Gowell is watching us. As he approaches, I bow to the princess and move away, but not out of earshot.

'I see Lann came to pay his respects,' says Gowell. His voice is clipped.

'He came to enquire whether I was happy with my slave girl,' says Armelle. 'It was he who gave her to me as a gift.'

I have to admire her guile.

'Of course, I had forgotten. Does our new house meet with your approval,' he asks, sounding hopeful.

'It will do very well,' replies Armelle and I see that as she turns to face him, she is smiling.

'Then let the Great Mother be praised,' he says. His relief is palpable. The poor, ignorant oaf.

'Yes, let us give thanks to Matrea,' says Armelle.

I watch as she carries on smiling at Gowell and I wonder if he has seen what I have, that although her mouth is smiling, there is no warmth whatsoever in her eyes.

TWENTY THREE

Awelfryn

Briona

My husband, the King, has decided this is going to be a gathering to remember. He wants to show our allies how strong we are and that together we are a force to be reckoned with. No expense, therefore, has been spared in feting our guests. Each clan leader is expected to supply a number of pigs, sheep or goats for the roasting fires and the women have been up cooking and baking well into the night. I expect the farmers are grumbling about the unfairness of it all for it is for certain that the lords have simply taken their livestock without so much as a nod to recompense.

The head of each of the twelve clans has contributed half a dozen of their precious amphorae to the feast and warriors have been sent out to hunt deer for the feasting tables. There will be trials of strength and competitions designed to hone the skills of the fighters.

All this leaves me unmoved. I have no stomach for his war; for I do not believe Hanu has taken my daughter. Furthermore, Irven does not know that I overheard his conversation with Wil the last time they were together. If he thinks he can cast me aside without a fight, he is mistaken. I have committed no wrong and the Elders will not permit such a thing, unless I am deemed to be a traitor or have broken my word in some way or other.

The Regni and Canti nobles arrived last night and Awelfryn is full. Deryn, Chief Druid of Lynd, although invited, declined to attend but instead sent an emissary, a short man whose wide face looks as though it has been squashed between two anvils. Irven had not entertained much hope of the Druids backing his bid for revenge. My husband's relationship with the Brothers has been difficult in recent years and so we were all surprised when the emissary let it be known that Deryn would do nothing to intervene if Irven decided to wage war on the Durotriges. They have not even demanded proof and I, for one, am suspicious. Irven, of course, is so bent on war now, that he cannot think straight and will not listen to me. He talks to Caradwg and the Elders and I have to eavesdrop, as usual, in order to glean any information.

The finer details of the alliance were thrashed out last night and now that the Druids have shown no objection, the talks move on at a rapid pace. I made myself as comfortable as I could and prepared to spend the entire evening in my cramped hiding-space, listening.

This is what I heard: The Regni want to employ only a half of their warriors but Wil of the Canti convinced them that in order to win they will need at least two thirds. He has persuaded his lord, King Engus, to pledge his entire army and Irven seems well pleased with this promise. Then the battle was discussed. I learned that the Canti and Regni are to join forces under Engus and march into the Durotriges lands from the east, whilst the Atres attack from the north.

'Hanu's army will be occupied fighting my men. They will not think to look to the east,' says Irven, and although I cannot see him, I imagine him rubbing his hands together. 'It is of the utmost importance that the movements of the Canti and Regni remain a secret.'

'Do not fear,' says Wil. 'Although Hanu is aware of your plans, he has no reason to suspect the Canti and Regni. It will be a surprise.'

'Just make sure it is,' says Irven. 'The outcome will depend on it.'

I wait until my husband and his guests drink themselves into a stupor before retiring to my bed.

The next day dawns glorious and bright, and I have come to take my place beside Irven on our ceremonial chariot. As he surveys the gathering crowds, Irven has to shield his eyes from the morning sun. He is excited for now he has the assurances he requires. My husband does not seem to mourn, as do I, the taking of our child. In fact, rather than brood, he has become ever more focused on war. Seeing my downcast face, he does not try to ease my sorrow, but speaks harshly.

'She is dead or sold by now,' he says. 'All we can hope for is revenge.'

'How can you be so sure?' I ask.

'I know how Hanu thinks,' he replies. 'He would have killed her by now.'

'He will certainly have her killed when he finds that you are planning to march against him!' I shout. 'Why can you not simply send a delegation?'

Irven turns to face me. His eyes narrow and the corner of his mouth twitches in anger.

'All these years, woman, I wanted to believe in you, but I always knew what was truly in your heart,' he says, hissing his words.

I put my hand up to protest but Irven cuts me short.

'That day I caught you in Hanu's embrace? Just how hard did you try to fight him off? Eh?'

'So this is what all this is about, is it? Your jealousy. Well, if you must know the truth, I will tell you. Yes. I loved him, but he was too good a friend of yours to steal me away and so he let you believe he forced himself on me. He was protecting me, and your honour, not that you deserved it!'

I cannot believe I have said these words and it is too late to take them back. A cold rage grips my husband. He lifts his hand and strikes me in the face, in full view of the gathering. I am stunned by the assault, and it takes me a few moments to take in what he has done. When the truth of the situation dawns on me, I dismount from the chariot and run off in the direction of my home.

It is late evening. I am indoors, studying my bruised face in the burnished bronze mirror that was a present from Bryn, the Vellani chief, when the tribes of the land were on good terms. I wonder how Bryn is faring. Rumour has it he is close to death after which that boy of his, the one educated in Rome, will take over. An unknown quantity, but if he is anything like Bryn, then he will be good and just.

My face hurts from Irven's assault. He was wearing a ring and the metal has gouged a cut in my lip which bled and is now swollen. I remind myself that I have lost everything now, my looks matter not at all. I have confessed to Irven what he suspected all along, that I once loved Hanu and he has every right to put me to death. And he probably will too, now that Kendra is gone. He wants an heir and he will take another wife. I have played into his hands and if I want to live, I must flee. I dread his return from the festivities. He will have been drinking all day and will continue well into the night and I thank the gods that he is in the Folk meet this night and not in our home. I doubt he will leave his guests, until they have all gone, but nevertheless I dread his return. He has tasted violence and perhaps yearns for more. My mind made up, I summon my servant.

'Ferehar, I must be away. I have nothing to keep me here any longer and I must make haste if I am to survive. If you would prefer to remain here, that is your choice. I will not force you to accompany me.'

'My place is at your side, Mistress, I will not abandon you. But where can we go?'

'Thank you, Ferehar. We will ride to the Durotriges. Now, tell no-one and whilst I pack my bags, go fetch my horse and another for yourself. We must be away well before the first bird call.'

Ferehar runs to do my bidding and before long, he returns with two horses and enough food to feed us and the horses for several days.

'Well done, Ferehar. I am sorry to put this upon you.'

I cast one last look around the place that has been my home for over twenty years. Since Kendra's disappearance, the place has seemed empty. I pack little of value – the remaining bracelet Hanu gave me, the mirror from Bryn and some gold to buy my way should the need arise. I pack warm clothes and one fine robe. When I am ready to leave, rather than ride out of the main gateway, where the guards are now on a war footing, we sneak over the defences at the unguarded western edge of the settlement. Behind the midden, the palisade fence is broken. How typical of Irven's laxness not to have every inch of Awelfryn fortified. Still, his ineptitude serves me well.

As we wind our way down the hillside, I feel my spirits lift and as we urge or horses southwards, my thoughts turn to Hanu. It has been a long time coming, this reunion.

By the time the sun begins to glimmer in the east, Ferehar and I have crossed the bogs of Brihar and by mid-morning we stand atop Broch Hill, looking down over Bright Valley and onwards towards the Great Horse Plain. It is a long time since I have been this way. It was before I was married to Irven – we were just betrothed. He insisted that I travel with him to the lands of the Durotriges where he could show me off to Hanu. Irven and I made the journey joyfully, just the two of us, disdainful of the well-trodden routes and glad to be travelling together across the ridge-ways and plains and on towards the rolling hills of the south.

Had I known then of the spark that would ignite between myself and Hanu, would I have still gone? True, I experienced love, but it has brought naught but sorrow and bitterness to my life. Now, as I gaze ahead to my future, I wonder if Hanu still cares for me. He married, of course, but I know his wife died and he has not taken another. How will he react to me turning up at his hearth like this? My mind reels at the thought and I realise I have no alternative. My course is set, my choice made.

Although I have traced this journey many times in my head and thought I knew by heart the way to Vipers' Fort, I suddenly feel unsure of myself, the landscape from the top of Broch Hill seeming unfamiliar and hostile. I can just see the trees of Rhiw in the far distance to the east and know my best hope is to head for the forest where we will find shelter if need be. We needn't enter the woods and can just skirt around its edge. By the time we reach southern extremity of the vast forest we will be in Durotriges territory and might ask for help.

By late afternoon we reach the edge of the woodland without any sign of pursuit, but Ferehar cannot relax. He is a simple man and I realise he is most probably worried about venturing near the trees, having heard the tales of fabulous beasts that can fell a man with one blow and eat him on the spot.

'The forest will not harm us, Ferehar,' I say. 'And Irven's men have not caught us up. Perhaps my husband thinks me not worth pursuing.'

Despite my words, I know Irven will do everything in his power to prevent me reaching Hanu. He has no idea how much I know, but he will not take the risk that I might alert the Durotriges to the involvement of the Canti and Regni.

'My Lady,' says Ferehar, 'The King will surely send men to search us out. I fear we must enter the forest and take our chance amongst the tree spirits. Perhaps our pursers will not follow in the dark.'

I nod, grateful for his bravery and companionship, even though he is a commoner. He has been with me since he was a boy and I believe that, whatever the outcome, he will stand by me.

'We'll carry on around the edge a little longer and then we can stop. As you had the foresight to bring water skins, we won't have to search out a stream. I was wise to bring you, Ferehar.'

'It is you, my Queen, who is the wisest and bravest of us, make no mistake.'

We continue on our way, urging our horses onwards throughout the day until the setting sun forces us to enter the oaken forest. Ferehar looks increasingly worried and I begin to understand what it must cost him to enter the woods.

'Don't give in to fear,' I say, in an attempt to ease his anxiety. 'We won't venture too deep into this place, lest we lose our way.'

After a short while we find a small clearing. Once Ferehar sees to the horses, he begins to pile up the dry leaves from last autumn's fall, so that we will have a soft bed each on which to sleep. Once his task is complete, he turns his attention to me.

'Shall we have a small fire, my Lady?' he asks.

'It would be nice,' I reply, 'but dangerous, don't you think?' I see his face and give in.

'If we wait until darkness,' I say, 'the smoke won't be visible. And we have a north-westerly wind, blowing away from the direction we have come.'

And so, as darkness envelopes us, and the trees loom over us, Ferehar brings out his flint stone and strikes a spark onto some dried fungus that he carries in a pouch at his waist. He carefully feeds the flame until we have a small fire to cheer us and once we have eaten some cold meat and bread, our spirits rise. We talk in low voices of recent events until we have no more to say.

'You sleep, my lady,' says Ferehar after a while. 'I will keep watch.'

I lie down on my bed of leaves and despite my worries, fall into a deep slumber.

The next thing I know, there is a commotion and I snap awake. I can dimly make out two struggling shapes in the darkness. Then I hear a groan and the sound of a body slumping to the ground. A man looms over me just as I reach for my dagger. I am still on the ground, supporting myself with one arm, whilst with my free hand, I stab wildly at the air between myself and the warrior. I have no idea if Ferehar is dead or alive, but he is no fighter and I fear the worst. All I know is that I am at a disadvantage, lying on the floor. The warrior kicks my supporting arm away from under me and my dagger falls from my grip. I am flat on my back and as useless as an upturned beetle. My assailant then places a knee on my stomach and pins me down. All I can do is flail my arms around uselessly.

'Lugh!' shouts the warrior, confident that his friend has made short work of a mere servant. 'I have the Queen. Fetch me the rope! She wriggles like an eel!'

But I can see Ferehar. He must have overcome the other warrior somehow, and has worked his way silently behind my assailant who is ignorant of his presence. Ferehar raises his dagger high above his head and is about to plunge it downwards but something in my eyes must have alerted the warrior for he dodges the blow, causing Ferehar's blade to nearly strike me where I lie. Ferehar is unbalanced by his downward action and now the warrior has the advantage. Standing quickly, he brings his knife down swiftly and expertly. Ferehar's skull makes a grinding noise, followed by a squelch as the blade connects with the softness of his brain.

He falls to the ground, but he has bought me the time I need. The warrior's blade is not so easily freed from Ferehar's skull and while he struggles to regain his weapon, I am on my feet, my knife once more in my hand. Then I see my chance. As the warrior bends over my faithful servant, his leather waistcoat rides up, exposing his back. Using all the strength I possess, I sink my dagger into his torso, as close to his spine as I can manage.

His entire body begins to judder. Then his legs buckle beneath him. He shakes so violently that he loses his grip on the blade that still protrudes from Ferehar's skull. He tumbles to the ground, twisting to look at me in disbelief. I return his gaze and without taking my eyes from his, lift his head by his hair and slice across his throat, absently licking away the blood that splatters my own face.

TWENTY FOUR

Ravensroost

Fionn

I have decided to tell Brendan everything, for I cannot see how we can possibly escape without his help. I know what I must do now. My leg has not yet healed but it will have to do; I cannot waste any more time and I will just have to put up with the pain. Once I am on horseback I will be alright, I am sure. I will head straight for Vipers' Fort and if Chela is still bent on reaching the Atres at Awelfryn, she can deliver my message to Irven. I feel sure that once the King knows who is behind Kendra's abduction, he will call off his plans to attack the Durotriges.

The Brothers who tend the dying King have not yet realised who I am and I appreciate it is my employment as a smith that has saved me, for it is a skill that takes many years to learn. They are probably looking out for a warrior. I keep out of their sight, however, for I know they have spies everywhere. News of my disappearance must have reached them by now and it is only a matter of time before my presence raises suspicion. I see how friendly the brothers are with the Vellani and I am sure they would not hesitate to reveal my identity to Doran.

It has been raining and the earth smells sweet from the summer shower. Using my stick, I make my way along the muddy track towards Brendan's home. Cooking smells greet me as I approach. I enter the porch and use my stick to bang on the great door.

'What brings you here, No-name,' asks Brendan, gesturing for me to enter. 'Would you care to sup with us? My sisters have prepared a mutton stew as good as any I have tasted.'

'Thank you, but no,' I say, indicating with a jerk of my head that I want to talk to him privately. 'Let us walk together.'

We sit side by side on a boulder close to the inner bank of Ravensroost's defences, out of earshot of Brendan's family and anyone who might be passing by. People will jeer, seeing us sitting closely together, but I do not care. Let them think what they will. I know also that Brendan is grateful that I am not ashamed to be seen at his side.

The rain has stopped but the boulder is wet and soaks through our britches.

'Did your grandmother not warn you about sitting on wet rocks?'
Brendan grumbles. 'It causes untold problems!'

I ignore his complaint.

'I need you to help me escape, Brendan.'

'I'll tell you one thing, No-name, you don't waste any time on preamble. Get to the point, why don't you!'

'You can call me by my name now. I am Fionn, son of Caradwg of the House of Morffryn, noble of the Atres.'

Brendan whistles in amazement.

'You jest. No, I can see, you do not jest. Well, upon my word, you render me speechless.'

'Speechless! I can barely get a word in edgeways,' I laugh.

'I had guessed you were of noble birth anyway,' says Brendan.

'How so?'

'Soft hands, that's how,' he laughs in reply. 'So, the healing woman brought your memory back, eh?'

'In a manner of speaking,' I say. I don't want to have to tell him that I've been lying all along although he probably already knows. 'Her name is Chela, by the way.'

I tell him everything, stopping short of disclosing what I know of Doran's involvement.

'There is something more, is there not?' asks Brendan, perceptive as ever. 'Something you haven't told me.'

I sigh. Brendan deserves more than this.

'Yes. But you won't like what I am about to tell you. It is the man of whom I have heard you speak, the one you call Lann, who kidnapped Kendra, and I believe it was on Doran's command.'

Brendan is silent for a moment, as he digests the information.

'Well that explains why Doran is getting all this weaponry ready, does it not? He is turning one tribe against the next in order to profit from the chaos. Once he has finished with the Trinovantes, he will probably set his sights on the other tribes.'

I shrug. His guess is as good as mine as to what the Vellani Lord is planning, but more importantly, do I have the right to put Brendan in this uncomfortable position? Should I have confided in him? We sit in silence. I do not want to rush him, for I know what I ask of him. Once it is discovered he has helped us escape, he will be hunted down and killed. Finally he speaks.

'I will help you, Fionn, but you must help me in return.'

'Brendan, you saved my life and have been my friend. Just say what you want and if it is within my power, I will help you. But before you give me your answer, know there is yet more that I ask of you.'

'Go on.'

'Chela comes with us. And Cederin.'

'Cederin? The slave?' Brendan's eyes open wide in disbelief. 'Have all your wits deserted you? What can you possibly gain by freeing, nay *stealing*, one of Doran's slaves?'

'I have grown to like the lad. I said I would help him.'

Brendan runs his hands through his hair in exasperation.

'It is going to be hard enough smuggling you and the healer out of Ravensroost, but a third, and a slave at that! Do you think I can command magic?'

I let him rant on for a while. Finally, he calms down enough for me to speak.

'What is it you require of me, Brendan?' I ask.

He takes a deep breath.

'You know that once Bryn dies and Doran is proclaimed King, the Kingship ceremonies will go ahead, don't you?'

'Ye.. yes?'

'Mylor will be thrice killed and buried in the ground to reinforce the Kingship boundaries.'

'Yes, that is the way.'

'I will help you, and Chela, *and* that worthless slave escape and I will come with you, but I need you to promise that when you have done whatever you need to do, you will come with me to the Isle of Lynd and help me free Mylor - before the ceremonies begin.'

I look long and hard at my friend's face and see the look of pleading in his eyes. I do not know even if such a thing can be achieved, for the Isle of Lynd is said to be impenetrable, but I owe it to Brendan to at least try.

'Very well,' I say, and as I speak, I grasp Brendan's shoulder. 'You have my word on it.'

TWENTY FIVE

The Isle of Lynd

Lann

My small boat, manned by two of Doran's slaves, rides the incoming tide. A hundred thousand birds rise up from the mudflats and soar into the afternoon sky, a curtain of swooping shimmering wings, dancing as one body. The spectacle fills me with something approaching joy. Too long have I had to live amongst those whom I detest and their base natures are beginning to chip at my very being.

There are those who dislike the relentless flatness that surrounds the Isle of Lynd, but not I. This place was once my home and I love the landscape, with its vast open skies, as though it were a part of me. The Isle, itself, rises out of the tidal estuary beyond which lies an endless stretch of marshland. On calm days, the mist gathers at the island's base, so that it appears to float on air.

I was seven summers old when Bryn sent me to Lynd to learn the Druids' lore. It was hard leaving my mother, for she had no man to call her own, but I knew Bryn would look after her, just as he looked after me.

Each year, at Beltane, I would return to my mother's hearth and stay at Ravensroost until Lamas but the rest of the year was spent amongst the Druids. They taught me how to fight using only my body; they taught me to recite the names of the stars and to observe how they move in the heavens. They taught me plant lore, and the mysteries of the soul. I was sure I was fated to join their ranks but when I was sixteen summers old, I was told that my education was complete. I was not destined to become a Brother, but instead I was to serve the Vellani. Although I was sad to leave the Druids of Lynd, I love Bryn as a father and pledged to serve him and his kin unto my death. And so when the Lord Doran returned from Rome and took me into his confidence, I saw the means by which I could serve the Vellani whilst avenging my mother for the horrors visited upon her by both the Durotriges and the Atres.

Deryn himself meets me at the jetty. He has aged since I last set eyes on him, but his gaze is as keen as ever. He embraces me as one would a son, and I feel my throat constricting with emotion. He leads me through a coppiced wood which, I remember, is full of bluebells in the spring. In the heart of the wood is the Nemeton, where we learned

171

to dismember slaves and read their entrails. I enjoyed the butchery, for it demands a certain skill with a knife, but the divination always did elude me.

The wood opens out into fields of shimmering wheat, and we cross the rickety old bridge over the Faram, a stream fed by a sacred spring, whose waters sustain the small settlement of priests.

I am shown to my quarters, a corner of a roundhouse which I am to share with some of the lay Brothers. Even though I have become used to my own company, I do not mind sharing, for I understand these men. I stifle a pang of regret for the life I could have led here, and smother the rising of a long-buried doubt: that I did not quite measure up to the Druids' exacting demands. Then I remind myself that mine is a different path.

A young priest by the name of Bari offers me refreshment. I learn that it is he who is in charge of Mylor, readying him for the Kingship Ceremony. I hope I will be able to attend his killing, for to partake in such ceremonies confers power on those who witness them.

When I have rested, I seek out Deryn once more, presenting him with Doran's gifts of gold and silver, before delivering my message. We are alone, for Deryn, as Chief Druid of the Isle of Lynd, is accorded his own abode. The elderly priest offers me a drinking horn full of wine which I accept gratefully.

'What news of Bryn?' he asks.

I tell him that my master is close to death, yet clings on to life.

'Bryn has been a good King,' says Deryn. 'He and my predecessor were like brothers and he is much loved by the Druids of this land. But he was never as ambitious as Doran. I believe that once he relinquishes his hold on this world, and Doran is proclaimed King, we Brothers, together with the Vellani, will achieve great things for this land.'

I know that Doran and Deryn think along the same lines and I am sure Bryn harbours the same ambitions, even if he cannot communicate them. He was always one to side with the Brothers. Deryn became the Chief Druid of Lynd around the time my King was stricken with his illness and since then, the Brothers have become even more active in the politics of this land. Some call it meddling, but I, for one, believe the Druids are the wisest men of all.

'Everything is proceeding as planned,' I say. 'Doran wishes you to know that he is ready for war. Just as soon as Bryn dies, he will act'.

'Tell Doran not to hasten his father's death. Bryn will die only when the time is right for his rebirth, which will be the right time for the Vellani to make their move.'

I am surprised, for I cannot believe Doran would ever consider hastening his own father's death.

'You did well,' continues Deryn. 'in taking the Atres girl.'

I feel as I did when I was a boy, basking in the Druid's praise.

'She is at Viper's Fort. She will give us no trouble, I guarantee, until all this is over.'

Deryn smiles.

'Tell Doran,' he says, 'that I have given my permission for the Atres to wage war on the Durotriges, and that the Canti and Regni are planning to take the Durotriges unawares from the east. Tell him also that I now have Caradwg, of the House of Morffryn on my side. When Irven joins battle with the Durotriges, Caradwg and four other Atres clans will hold back, so that their King is left undefended.'

I realise my eyebrows have shot upwards, despite my attempts to look in control.

'And what have you promised Caradwg in return?' I ask. Doran will be interested in this new turn of events.

Deryn laughs.

'Caradwg thinks he will be King of the Atres.'

It is my turn to smile, for I sense that Deryn has other plans for the House of Morffryn. Doran has been promised unopposed rule of the southern tribes. The lands of the Durotriges, Atres, Regni and Canti will fall under his domain.

'What of Caradwg's heir?' I ask. 'I have heard he went in search of the Atres girl?'

'Perished, as far as we can tell. There is no news of him. As you know, my brothers have ears and eyes everywhere. I doubt he will be able to find the Atres girl now, even if he is still alive.'

There is a question I wish to broach, but I must take care with my words, for I do not wish to anger my host. I take a sip of wine first.

'And Druce?' I enquire.

Deryn's face clouds over. I hope I have not upset him. Druce is the Chief Druid of the entire land, above even Deryn, dwelling in the Isle of Mona, beyond the great mountain, Ynys Mon, in the far west. He favours the old ways and does not approve of the Priesthood involving themselves in the politics of the land. He and Deryn do not see eye to eye.

'We have broken away from the Druids of Mona,' says Deryn. His voice is thick with anger. 'They weaken, while we grow strong.'

I digest the news but say nothing. My loyalty is to Lynd, but I know that Druce still commands much authority.

Before I take my leave, Deryn invites me to attend a divination. The means of augury is to be none other than the half-man, Mylor. I am curious to see how Mylor is faring and so I accompany the young priest, Bari, who has been told bring him to the ritual hut.

As we walk through the settlement, I glean from our conversation that Bari has struck up a friendship with Mylor. He has been commanded to keep Mylor company and to educate him in the ways of the Druids, but it seems their friendship has blossomed. I am surprised Deryn allows it, even if there is nothing in it. As we walk, I ask how Mylor is getting on with learning the Druid's lore. The wisdom of the Brothers is committed to memory by means of rhymes and riddles so dense that ordinary folk cannot fathom their meaning. Only through much questioning and listening can one make any sense of the conundrums. I avoided Mylor as much as possible at Ravensroost so I do not have the measure of him. All I know is that he and Brendan share the same perversion. They are an insult to nature.

'He is doing very well,' says Bari sadly. 'He would have made a great Druid.'

I find this difficult to believe. It is not that easy to become a Druid and Mylor, surely, is too stupid. I wonder if Bari has been corrupted.

Before long a dwelling, painted ochre and red, looms into view. I am not surprised to find that the entire place is at Mylor's disposal, full of every luxury a man could desire. Under normal circumstances a roundhouse this size would house at least ten souls, but Mylor is 'special'. He is being prepared to meet the gods and the priests are 'fattening him up' in readiness. He is free to roam the Island, but escape from Lynd itself is impossible.

We enter through the open doorway and I see Mylor sitting on the earthen floor, his eyes shut. I know what he is doing. He is trying to empty his mind of all thoughts. I used to find this exercise difficult, for just as soon as you banish one thought, another takes its place. I never did master it, and I am somewhat irritated to see that Mylor is so deep, he does not even realise we are watching him. It is only when Bari clears his throat, that he opens his eyes.

'You are doing well,' says the priest.

Mylor rubs his eyes and smiles. 'Yes, sometimes it works, other times it eludes me.'

Then he notices me.

'Lann!' he says, getting to his feet. 'What brings you here? The King..?'

'Is still alive,' I say. Mylor's relief is palpable. He may have mastered the emptying of the mind, but he obviously has not come to terms with his certain death, just yet.

'Have you any news from Brendan? Is he well?' he asks.

'I am sorry, but I have not seen anything of Brendan and he knows not that I am here.'

I am amused to see that he looks crestfallen. Just who does he think he is, asking me all these questions, as though I were a friend of his. The very thought!

'I have come to fetch you,' says Bari. 'Deryn wants you to attend the ritual hut.'

Mylor eyes widen in alarm.

'Do not worry, your time is not yet come,' says Bari, quickly.

'Then what?'

'There is a special ceremony tonight. As you are one whose death hovers around him, you are considered a link between this world and the next.'

Mylor begins to look worried again. 'What will be required of me?'

'You will see. Remember what I have taught you. Keep your breathing in mind at all times to steady your heart and you will be alright.'

Mylor and I follow Bari through the settlement. I am intrigued. During my time at Lynd, the ritual hut was out of bounds to anyone but the higher Druids. I recall that sometimes screams and shouts would be heard emanating from the roundhouse. I feel privileged to be invited this evening.

As we duck through the entrance, a blast of heat hits us in the face. There are three hearths, all of which have been stoked up to produce a suffocating atmosphere. Smoke from the fires makes my eyes water and catches the back of my throat. Then I notice that all the priests have stripped themselves of their white robes and sit around the hut, naked to their waists, and in the firelight, their torsos glisten with sweat. Mylor tries to back out of the hut, but Deryn is behind him, preventing his retreat. The old priest smiles a strange twisted smile, and even I feel uncomfortable.

'Disrobe, my friends, and join us,' he commands. His raven eyes are piercing and brook no argument. Bari and I remove our tunics and take our place in the circle of priests. Mylor moves to where Deryn indicates and removes his loose over-garment, baring his chest. He places his clothing on the floor and sits on the bundle, cross-legged.

The room is filled with smoke and I cannot see very much, but enough to notice that one of the priests holds a bowl of burning herbs that he wafts around the hut, adding to the already murky atmosphere. The herbs soon begin to have a strange effect on me. All at once the room seems large, then small. Deryn strides around, shaking a seed rattle, and as the herbs begin to work on my mind, it seems that the rattle whispers and sings.

A bowl is thrust into Mylor's hands and he is commanded to eat. I realise he has been given a large portion of dried mushrooms, small, with conical heads. I smile, because I know the effect they can have, especially on the unsuspecting.

'Eat!' commands Deryn, and as if to encourage the young man, takes a couple and stuffs them into his own mouth.

Mylor, is obviously terrified and does as he is told, finishing the entire bowl. I can tell he is fighting to keep the foul-tasting fungi down. Then each of us is offered a small handful of the same type of mushroom, but only one tenth the quantity Mylor has consumed.

The drumbeat reverberates throughout the roundhouse. It travels across the floor of the hut and works its way to my stomach where it hums and grows until it fills my entire being. It forms a pattern in my brain, swirling lines and interlaced animals speak to me in an elusive and symbolic tongue that I recognized from a life lived before my own birth. The beat takes over my thoughts and soon there is nothing but the drum, beating faster and faster until it comes to an abrupt stop.

I open my eyes. Mylor is writhing on the floor; specks of spittle are forming at the corners of his mouth. Deryn begins to speak and though it is his voice, it is as if an entity speaks through him.

'I am Dis,' says the voice. 'The very whispering of my name on the wind fills men's hearts with dread and causes the wheat to wither on its stem. I fly, dark as the night into the vast caverns of the thoughts of my people. There is no hidden sanctuary for those whose minds I search. I see. I know. I understand. The death throes of a slave, whose entrails squirm on the ground, the pattern of the clouds, the flight of birds, the scattering of stones - past, present, future, merge into one. Only I can make sense of the trail but with knowledge comes power, comes choice. The knowledge of all these possibilities, the ultimate vanity of choosing to rework the threads of time will be, has been, is my undoing. And yet I persist.'

Deryn's voice deepens.

'You are as free as the wind that howls through this miserable prison of flesh, blood and bone. Your mind is an unbounded ocean of time and space and though the shackles of mortality chaff your wrists and ankles and tether your body to this fragile world, you can spread your wings and fly, far over the three peaks, across the Llyn-y-Fan. What do you see, young Mylor, you who have stared at your very death? A purpose stronger than beaten iron courses through the earth and are you not born of this land?'

My heart is racing and I am in a lather of sweat. Deryn's voice becomes part of me, yet I cannot take my eyes off Mylor, who, I am sure, is about to expire. I can see the veins in his neck bulging. His face is red and his eyes stare in stark horror at his inner vision. I swear his hair is standing up from his scalp. Suddenly he lets out a scream so loud and piercing that I am forced to cover my ears. Then he laughs a laugh so deep that it chills me.

'What did you see?' demands Deryn, his voice a hoarse whisper.

Mylor giggles uncontrollably for a few moments then he begins to speak. He sounds to me as though he has lost his mind, and I wonder if Deryn has overdone the mushrooms.

'I was flying,' he says. 'My wings were those of an eagle and I hovered on a current of air.'

He pauses, remembering his flight. Deryn prods him savagely in the ribs.

'Below me were the dark waters of the sacred lake. I saw the purple clouds above mirrored on its surface, writhing with messages and omens. My feathers glistened in the sun. I flew down, closer to the source of the rhythm.'

He stops for a moment, a look of awe on his face, as though reliving his vision.

'Then the face of the Twilight God, Dis, appeared in the sky. His ancient mouth did open as though to shout but from the darkness of his throat issued a rope of gold at the end of which eight human heads were tethered. Then Dis cried out in torment and fell from the heavens, crashing to the ground, the eight anguished voices shouting all the while for help. Then a great cloud came rolling in from the east, smothering all in its wake.'

The room is deathly quiet, for surely this vision is one of the truest, and strangest. Mylor pauses, and when he begins to speak, his voice is full of awe and wonder.

'I was part of the essence of creation itself; past and future melded into one and for a brief moment in time, I understood all there is to know.'

He begins to weep. Deryn leaves him to cry for a little while, then urges him to continue.

'At the pinnacle of my understanding, I began to fall, the lake drawing me downwards, my wings paralysed. The waters approached, but before I entered the broiling mass, a blackness the like of which does not exist on this earth enveloped me, gnawing at my soul. I thought I was surely dying, but then I knew the death was not my own. A gentle hand stopped my fall and set me down on the lake's edge where the grass under my feet writhed to escape the oily waves that lapped the shore. When I looked at my hands they were those of a man, not a bird. At my feet was a raven, feathers glistening like anthracite, eyes obscured by death, a pool of crimson spreading from its open beak.'

As Mylor recounts his vision of the dead bird, Deryn pales and seems to shrink, his eyes wide. The acrid smell of fear rolls off his skin and begins to fill the room.

Mylor stops speaking. He turns to one side and vomits on the floor. The drumming has stopped, now the chanting of the priests reverberates around the roundhouse. Deryn squats in front of Mylor, his black eyes searching his face.

I realise that my mouth is dry and my lips are swollen with thirst. The heat in the room is almost unbearable, yet more wood is being piled on the fires. Sweat pours from my brow and my hands are wet and slippery.

Mylor faints and lands on the floor. I notice that Bari rushes to his side.

The chanting of the priests stops. The only noise is the crackling of the fires. The gathering waits for Deryn to speak but I can see that the priest is in a state of panic. He forces himself to address the gathering.

'The old god Dis is dying. The eight heads are the Great Tribes of the land whom he has in his thrall. A new power rolls in from the east to replace the old and we will be there to ride upon its wings.'

A murmur goes up from the priests. The death of Dis? A new order. I understand. He means the death of the old ways, the end of Druce and the rise of the Vellani in the east, who will rule the lands. And yet Deryn is terrified.'

And what of the dead raven?' enquires one of the elder Priests.

'The vision is incomplete,' says Deryn, his voice wretched, his lips trembling. He looks around the room. 'The ending is unclear. A veil hides the outcome, like a mist.'

'What will you do?' whispers one of the priests.

'Possibilities exist,' says Deryn, but he sounds unconvinced. 'No outcome is certain. It is up to us to choose the future.'

But as I listen to Deryn, a strange fear grips my stomach and I find I am trembling. The death of the bird is surely a bad omen and I believe Deryn knows its meaning. Then I remember my teachings and I realise that every priest in this room knows the same. Deryn's full name is Deryn Du and in the ancient tongue, it translates as 'The Black Bird'. The Raven. Then I realise why the aged Druid quakes in fear, for Mylor not only saw the death of our God, but also the death of Deryn Du himself.

TWENTY SIX

Viper's Fort

Kendra

'Girl, I need to borrow your clothing,' says Armelle, not bothering to use my name, though she knows it well enough. Why, by Esu, does she want my clothes? But it is not my place to question and so I bite down my anger and lower my eyes as I have been taught, and begin to disrobe.

'No! Don't you have anything clean?' demands Armelle, and I am irritated beyond measure to see that she is crinkling her nose. There was a time when I was attired in garments better than hers, my hair was soft and clean and my skin bathed with warm herb water so that it glowed.

I do not reply because I know I will sound insolent, but instead make my way to the corner of the royal women's roundhouse that I am allowed to call my own. It is no more than a cramped space behind a wattle partition with some furs to cover myself and the hard floor. I have no furniture, nor any possessions. My own clothes were taken away from me soon after I joined Armelle's household and exchanged for garments more befitting a slave. Chela, who took pity on me, gave me a set of spare clothing which in effect, amounts to everything I own. And now Armelle wants them. I present her with a loose robe and a long brown cape with a hood, fashioned from densely packed felt. As I hand over the birris, I wonder if I will ever see it again. Such capes are commonplace and so effective against the cold and wet that there is a demand for them even in Gaul.

'I need to leave Vipers' Fort,' says Armelle after I tie her hair back and cover it with the hood. I had guessed as much.

'You will say nothing about this, but I need you to come with me. I must get away from this place for a while but I don't want anyone to know, otherwise I will attract a whole party of followers. If you accompany me, the guards might think we are two common women from the farmsteads and leave us alone.'

I simply nod. Vipers' Fort is not a prison, yet it is a risky business, trying to leave undetected. If we are noticed, word will soon get back to Gowell's family that Armelle has gone walking in commoners' robes with her slave girl.

We walk together up the side of the hill overlooking the settlement. All I have to protect me from the rain is a woollen shawl Armelle flung at me, which I drape around my head. I think it belongs to Riana.

It is exposed and windy at the top of the hill but we soon find shelter under a stunted holly where we are able to observe the traffic as it comes in and out of Vipers' Fort.

After a while Armelle points to three wagons full of grain that are approaching the central gateway from the mainland.

'That will keep the guards occupied,' she says. 'Now's our chance.'

Sure enough, the guards are busy dealing with the new arrivals, and pay no attention to two women carrying baskets. Armelle's basket appears full but its contents are covered with a cloth, whereas mine is empty. As I follow Armelle, I realise she has given this 'walk' a great deal of thought.

I have not dared leave Vipers' Fort before, for fear of what Lann might do to my companions, but this is different. I am carrying out Armelle's wishes and Lann cannot punish me. Despite my misgivings about Armelle's motives, I feel a growing excitement at the prospect of leaving the hated Fort, even though I know I will have to return. Armelle swops baskets with me as soon as we are out of sight of the gateway and I am surprised at how heavy it feels.

Much of the terrain leading to Vipers' Fort is marshland, but the drove-way on which we walk is firm underfoot and before long the sodden ground on either side gives way to firmer land planted up with corn and barley. Ahead of us, looming large on the horizon, stands Mab Hill, the shape of a risen cob loaf. We head straight for it. Although the hill dominates the landscape and seems close, its distance is deceptive and it takes us the best part of the afternoon to reach its base.

As soon as I realise Armelle is planning to climb the hill, I begin to feel ill at ease. Mab Hill was once a place where people lived, full of houses and the laughter of children, but, so I have heard, it was deserted several decades ago as the people moved nearer the workshops and the navigable waters. It is truly bad to venture into an abandoned village. The closing rituals will have sealed the place and to enter now would allow the sorrow of desertion to spill out onto the surrounding land. The horror of our imminent transgression overcomes my fear of Armelle.

'Mistress,' I say. 'Don't you know what this place is?'

She gives me a withering look.

'Of course I do. Such qualms are for the ignorant, but then you would know no different, would you?'

I have no option but to keep quiet and follow. The hill fort's construction is similar to Awelfryn, with a bank and ditch encircling the entire area. At the top of the bank a palisade fence stands. At one time it must have been firm and strong, but now it is rotten and falling apart. The main gateway opens out at the hill's eastern end and though the great doors would have been firmly shut when the protective iron ingots were buried beneath them, the planking has rotted so badly that a shove from Armelle causes the gate to fall inwards.

It is a sorry sight that greets us. Roundhouses that were once people's homes stand empty, bereft of their hearths, and the thatch that must have at one time been so carefully tended, has fallen through the rafters, allowing rain to intrude and hasten the decay. Once sturdy doors are full of holes, and the daub on the walls has crumbled, revealing their wicker bones.

Despair seeps through me and out of the corner of my eye I see the flicker of ghosts, flitting this way and that. It is bad enough we have ventured into this godforsaken place, but what worries me most is the time of day. We have come a long distance by foot and if we want to return by dusk then we will need to start back soon. Armelle, however, seems to have a purpose. Before long she comes to a halt next to an old storage building, no more than a lean-to, but it retains something of its roof and provides a little shelter from the intermittent showers.

'Stay here,' she commands. 'I won't be long.'

'But Mistress, if we don't return soon, the darkness will be on us!'

She answers with a scowl. Clearly she does not fear the dark.

'Don't fret girl. There is nothing in the dark that will harm you.'

I have my doubts, but I keep quiet as I watch the Veneti princess take up the laden basket and disappear along the path that leads through Mab Hill. Then I notice that some of the buildings have been marked with chalk. These are fresh markings, not old, and they point in the direction Armelle has taken. It is obvious now that she is meeting someone. This tryst has been well planned. She is either brave or foolish. Either way, whoever she is meeting is important enough for her to risk being caught out in the dark.

As soon as Armelle rounds a corner, I jump to my feet, curiosity getting the better of me. If I am careful, she needn't know I am spying on her.

I ignore my unease and walk past the buildings that seem to have edged closer, pressing me in. I run from each chalk mark to the next until I reach the northern edge of the settlement.

Where was once a gate, there is now a gaping hole. I hug the outside of one of the houses nearest the gate and edge towards the exit, straining to listen. I am rewarded by the sound of muffled voices. I peer cautiously around the rotting fence and there in front of me, is a horse and cart, the type used by farmers to take their produce to market. But it is not the cart that makes me stop in my tracks, but the sight of Armelle, being helped onto the vehicle by none other than the bard, Keary.

My sheer amazement causes me to forget about caution and I move into the open, framed by the rotting gate posts. Keary says something to Armelle, who turns and smiles at me. Before I can utter a word, the Bard urges the horse onwards and the cart disappears down the track way, heading inland.

The enormity of the situation dawns on me and I realise that I may be held accountable for Armelle's disappearance. My only hope lies in Riana. Retracing my steps as quickly as I can, my fear is no longer centred on the spirits of the dark, but the wrath of those back at Vipers' Fort and most especially, the punishment that Lann will mete when he returns from his wanderings.

I run as fast as I can, leaving sinister Mab Hill behind me, sprinting as though those lonely spirits are after my soul. Stopping only to catch my breath, I run until my lungs are close to bursting and after what seems an eternity of anxiety, I reach the familiar gateway of Vipers' Fort. It is dark by the time I arrive at the settlement and without traffic; the guard has no-one to distract him. He stands to interrogate me, but I manage to duck under his arm. He does not bother to follow, for he knows I, a mere slave, am no threat to him, nor to Vipers' Fort.

TWENTY SEVEN

The Woods of Rhiw

Fionn

I lie on my side, facing Chela, on the hard floor of Brendan's cart, under a pile of cloth secured in place by a leather tarpaulin. Behind me is Cederin and I can feel his breath on the back of my neck. I am glad I am facing Chela, not Cederin for I can taste her breath, which is sweet, and warm, and can feel the rise and fall of her bosom against my forearm.

'Ow! You're on my hair!' she whispers.

'And your knee is in my groin,' I say, flashing her a grin. I feel elated, somehow, despite our predicament. I shift my weight so that Chela's hair is freed and she relocates her knee to a safer position.

'Hush now,' says Brendan. 'We approach the gates. I, for one, do not yearn to have my head displayed on Ravensroost's ramparts!'

We fall silent, and I notice how clammy my hands have become. We still have the guards to deal with, and if I look over Chela's shoulder I can just make out the gateway through the gaps in the planking that form the sides of the cart.

'By Esu,' curses Brendan in a low voice. 'It's Carod and Taral on duty. Comedians of the highest calibre.'

Brendan brings the cart to a halt and waits to be let through.

'Well if it isn't our own sweet Brendan,' says Carod to his companion.

Though the sound is muffled, I can hear the guards well enough and know they are looking down at the cart from atop the gatehouse.

'And what have you in your cart today, young lady?' asks Taral. 'Something exotic to tempt the men at the workshops, perhaps?'

'Woven cloth,' says Brendan, sounding bored.

'So you have been busy at the loom, eh?' asks Carod. I can hear the two men sniggering.

Brendan sighs. 'You know well enough that my sisters and my mother do the weaving. I am simply taking the fruits of their labours to the market. Now, may I pass?'

I hear Taral climbing down to open the gate and now I can see him through the planking, a big man with a round belly. Walking around the cart, he pats the cargo through the leather cover. The three of us remain perfectly still and hold our breath. We needn't have worried, however. Taral is more concerned with baiting Brendan.

'How about a kiss, sweetheart?' he mocks, puckering his lips together to make a smacking noise. 'A kiss for a brave warrior?'

Carod, who remains above the gateway, roars with laughter.

'So predictable,' says Brendan. 'Don't you know another tune? Come here then. Close your eyes and let me taste your sweet lips, if that's what you want.'

'Be careful, Taral,' says Carod, in an agony of mirth, 'or they will start talking about you!'

I watch as Taral minces around the cart in a parody of femininity. After what seems an age, he finally opens the gate and ushers Brendan through. Before the wagon is clear of the defences, however, a shower of urine cascades onto the cart, splattering Brendan and bouncing off the tarpaulin.

'A present to take with you, my love,' shouts Carod as the cart makes its way down the hillside. 'Lest you forget me!'

I can hear Brendan cursing as the wagon gains speed.

'Animals,' he says when he is clear of the defences. We can still hear the two guards laughing and hurling insults. 'Now be still and don't move until I say so. It will be a while until we are out of sight. At least the canvas stopped you from sharing Carod's present.'

Brendan sounds bitter, and I am not surprised, but before I can say anything, Chela speaks, raising her voice so as to be heard through the tarpaulin.

'Hey, Brendan,' she says. 'You did well. You outwitted those imbecile guards and it is they who will look foolish when our absence is discovered.'

By way of reply, Brendan, keeping his voice low, begins to hum a bawdy ballad. It has not taken long for his cheerful nature to reassert itself and under the dim light of our confinement, I exchange a smile with Chela.

'Are you alright Cederin?' I ask, and receive a grunt by way of an answer. I hope I have done the right thing, bringing the slave with us, but I wanted him to know that not all of the Tribes of the South uphold slavery.

As I inhale Chela's scented hair, my proximity to the young woman sets up a stirring inside me that I am not altogether comfortable with. I should be thinking in such a way about Kendra, not her older sister, yet here I am, wanting to kiss this woman whom I have grown to like in the time we have spent together. I try to master my body's desire.

'Brendan,' I say. 'Can we not break cover? We can hardly breathe down here.'

'Not long now, and we will be amongst the trees. Then you can come out of hiding.'

Although I know it was my promise to rescue Mylor that was the deciding factor, Brendan nevertheless acted swiftly once he had committed himself to helping us escape, and I find myself yet again indebted to my friend. Brendan took three horses from his family's own drove yesterday, on the pretence of taking them to new pastures. He took them deep into the forest and tethered them in one of his sturdier shelters, built of timbers and wattle. He left Gwilym and Chela's steed, Tanog, at Ravensroost, lest their disappearance arouse suspicion.

As soon as we are under cover of the trees, Brendan stops the wagon and undoes the canvas. We spring up, glad to breathe some fresh air. Cederin sneezes and looks about him suspiciously.

'I cannot thank you enough,' I say, as we dismount.

'It's not over yet,' says Brendan. We have to make haste while we can.'

He leads us towards the shelter where, to everyone's relief, the three chestnut mares stand placidly munching on the oats Brendan had left for them. We work quickly to transfer what goods we have from the wagon to the horses. We have not brought much. Water skins, saddle-bags and some food to tide us over, though Chela has managed to bring some of her precious seeds and a handful of small earthenware jars containing her salves and potions. Brendan disengages the wagon from his own horse and readies the stallion to take his weight instead. We will leave the wagon behind. Perhaps it will be found, perhaps not. Either way, it does not matter, for Brendan can no longer return home.

I glance at my friend. I feel guilty at what I have asked him to relinquish but if Brendan is upset, he does not show it.

'What will you do, Cederin,' I ask, turning to the boy, who has remained silent. 'You are free to choose. If you wish to accompany Chela to Awelfryn, you will be made welcome, for the Atres do not make use of slaves. I, for one, am heading first to the south, to the lands of the Durotriges, thence north east, towards Lynd, with Brendan.'

'I wish to travel to my homeland,' says Cederin. 'But I have no means of repaying the Lord Brendan for his horse.'

'I do not require payment,' says Brendan quickly. 'But this I ask. When you reach the Isle of Mona, seek out the Chief Druid, Druce, and tell him what the brothers of Lynd are doing, and how they corrupt the true way of the Brotherhood.'

'Thank you,' says Cederin, and I can see he is near to tears. 'I will do as you ask.'

As Brendan busies himself helping Cederin with his supplies and giving him directions, I turn to help Chela lift her pack onto her horse's back, and in so doing, noticed a glint at her wrist.

'So, you got your bracelet back,' I say. 'How did you manage that?'

Chela grins. 'I promised Doran I would aid him to kill off his father.'

'And?' I cannot hide my surprise.

'Don't be silly. I'm a healer! I could no more kill a helpless old man, than my own grandfather, if I have one.'

'Doran let you have the bracelet in good faith?'

'I gave the old man some herbs to make him sleep a little better, that's all. Doran thinks he is going to drop dead any minute. Though of course, he could,' she adds. 'But his death would not be of my making, I promise you that.'

'I have no desire to see Bryn dead,' says Brendan, scouring the trees nervously. 'The longer he lives, the longer Mylor lives. Come on, let's be on our way.'

Briona

Immediately after the killings, I waited in the darkness, too frightened to breathe properly, listening for any noise that might indicate the presence of other warriors in the forest. The fire died, the blackness enveloped me and the night dragged achingly on, filled with the sounds of nocturnal beasts stalking their prey.

Eventually I disentangled myself from the dead bodies that merged with my own. I was covered in blood, some from Ferehar, and some from the warrior whose life I took. The blood had cooled and congealed and my skin felt tight. It still does, and I long to wash myself properly in warm water.

After a while my mind began to work. At least the horses had not bolted in fright and I thanked Ferehar's departed soul that I have food for them and for myself, as well as water. I used some of the water to clean myself up as best I could, hoping all the while that wolves were not roving the woods. And so now I wait for dawn, until I can get my bearings and then move on.

I surprise myself as a sob wracks my body. Though Ferehar was a simple man, a servant, he laid his life down for me. I feel my resolve crumbling and let my tears fall freely. I cry not only for Ferehar, but for my loneliness and all that I have lost. My marriage, my children, all gone. It is the bleakest night of my life, but even at my lowest ebb when I am forced to acknowledge the darkness pervading my soul, I feel a hope begin to kindle, for I know that if I can survive this, I will spit in the face of death.

As the pale dawn filters through the woodland, I cover Ferehar's body with soft leaves, then say a prayer to the gods of the next world. The animals will tear his flesh from his bones so that eventually his spirit will be free to join his ancestors. I wish him a good journey. I do not bother to pray over the two warriors. I know them of course, they are two of Irven's best men, Lugh and Deri, and I have watched them grow from children into boys and then men. But I feel nothing for them.

By the time I am ready to leave, the sun is well over the horizon. I must make haste now, for the warriors will be expected back at Awelfryn, their tardiness a cause for concern. I wonder if Irven had commanded them to kill me. Or did he want me back, to face public humiliation before he executes me? Whatever his intention, I am in danger from the very man whose children I have borne.

I mutter a final prayer; mount my horse and leading Ferehar's horse by its reins, head south, using the sun to find my bearings. I know not where Lugh and Deri's horses have gone, and I do not have the time to search for them. I decide to stay under cover of the trees, where I am less likely to be seen. After spending the night alone, the woods no longer frighten me.

It is almost noon by the time I ride into a clearing where I decide to stop for a rest. Dismounting, I tether the horses to a branch and take in my surroundings. The ground is littered with bones. There is something wrong with this place. The trees encircling the clearing are too perfect and the stench of death too strong to have been caused by animals. To my horror, I realise I have stumbled upon the Druids' sacred Nemeton. I must leave straightaway. It is then that I see the new-born infant, lying dead on the ground, at the centre of the clearing. Its throat has been cut.

The memory, unwanted, and as sharp as a blade, slices through my already fragile mind.

I recoil, falling backwards, only to find myself caught in the grip of a bramble. The bloody carnage of the night, and now this. It is as though I have no control over my actions and even though I know I should be silent, I find myself screaming as I struggle to tear myself free. The thorns stick fast to my clothing and the sharp barbs gouge fresh blood from my hands. Droplets of crimson trickle to the ground. The earth here is thirsting for blood.

It is all too much. Exhausted from my ordeal, I find myself falling to the ground, and as I fall, it is as though I travel through a long passageway of darkness. It is welcoming and comforting, and it envelopes me entirely.

Chela

The noise is sharp and piercing. Unmistakable.

'Did you hear a scream?' I ask.

'Sounded like a woman,' says Fionn.

'It might be the Brothers,' says Brendan. 'Better not to interfere.'

'We cannot simply ignore whoever it was,' I say as firmly as I can. I find it hard to believe Brendan is thinking of just walking way. Cederin has already left and I am certain the scream was not from him. It was definitely a woman.

Brendan looks to Fionn for support but Fionn shrugs his shoulders.

'Chela is right,' he says. 'We must at least try. We can approach slowly and if it is the Brothers, we can retreat. But if it isn't..'

I smile my gratitude at Fionn. I can sense Brendan's annoyance, but my instincts tell me that I cannot let the matter rest. Brendan lets out a deep sigh then leads us in the direction of the scream. Just outside the circle of trees, we dismount and tether our horses before creeping towards the clearing.

'It is one of the Brothers' nemetons,' whispers Brendan. 'Be careful.'

We advance cautiously. There is no sign of the Brothers and so Brendan waves us on. As I enter the clearing, I see all at once, the woman lying on the ground, the dead baby and the two horses. The stench of death makes the hair on my arms tingle.

190

The extra horse suggests the woman has a companion, but she appears to be alone. Fionn is the first to act. He runs over to the woman and kneeling down, takes her hands in his and chaffs them briskly. I watch him, fascinated to see how gentle and concerned he is with the fate of a stranger. In only takes a moment, though, for me to realise that Fionn knows her.

'My Lady?' he asks, and the concern in his voice is obvious.

The woman opens her eyes and an expression of astonishment crosses her face.

'Fionn!'

I turn and look at Brendan, who is standing behind me. He merely shrugs.

'My lady,' says Fionn, incredulity causing his voice to break. 'What brings you to this?'

'It's a long story, Fionn, but, by Esu, you are alive! Is my daughter with you? I thought for a moment..' As she struggles to a seated position, she glances at me then shakes her head.

'I have not seen her yet,' says Fionn, 'but she is safe. What happened to you?'

'Safe, you say? Esu be praised!' The woman smiles and then grimaces as she looks down at her own torn clothes. 'I am running away. My husband is no longer the man I knew,' she says, tears springing from her eyes. 'I'm on my way to the Durotriges.'

Fionn, whose tongue appears to have been stolen, stands up and helps the stranger to her feet. I take in her dishevelled state. She appears uninjured, even though she is caked in blood. Her garments speak of wealth. I offer her a water skin and as she drinks, she stares at me. I begin to feel uncomfortable and turn to Fionn, waiting for him to speak.

'Chela,' he says, slowly and deliberately, 'this is Briona, Queen of the Atres, and mother of Kendra, whom you of course, know.'

I look at the woman incredulously. So this is my mother.

The woman lifts her hand as though to stroke my cheek, but stops herself, a look of surprise on her face.

'You know my daughter? Where is she?'

Briona, Queen of the Atres, *my mother*, is standing in front of me. I try hard not to stare at her, but I am hungry to take in every detail. I notice her earlobes are the same shape as mine and she wears the same nose. I did not get my hair from my mother though, for she is fair. Perhaps Kendra and I take after Irven in that respect. The thought comforts me for I do not want to think that I might be Hanu's child and my relationship with Gowell an unspeakable transgression.

The time is not right to reveal my identity, and I can see my mother wants to know what news there is of Kendra, and so I push my bracelet as far up my arm as it will go, so that she cannot see it. As I busy myself tending her cuts and bruises, rubbing on a salve made from Coltsfoot and Celandine, I tell her what I know about her daughter. *My sister!* After a while I fall silent as I realise Fionn is waiting to speak. He talks fast, appraising Briona of Kendra's kidnappers and Doran's meddling.

'The Vellani? But surely Bryn would not permit such a thing!'

'Bryn cannot speak, let alone govern. It is Doran who is behind all of this,' says Fionn, rubbing his hands together briskly as if to rid himself of a layer of dirt. The action makes him seem older.

Brendan, who has been waiting patiently, speaks up.

'I am sorry to interrupt this reunion,' he says, 'but we must be on our way. This is a Nemeton, and not a place to linger. Don't forget the Brothers are on good terms with the Vellani.'

Fionn introduces Brendan before speaking his mind.

'My first thought was to rescue Kendra, but now I know that I must warn Irven of Doran's part in all of this, and prevent the war with the Durotriges.'

Briona lets out a small, tired laugh and I am taken aback at the bitterness therein.

'I doubt he will listen,' she says. 'He is bent on war with Hanu and has already taken promises of aid from the Regni and Canti. They have their own reasons wanting to crush the Durotriges.'

'I must at least try,' says Fionn. 'and you must continue you journey to Vipers' Fort to rescue Kendra and tell Hanu what's going on. Chela will you accompany her?'

I nod. Where else can I go? I have found my mother. The woman is standing next to me and in effect my journey is over. I do not relish the prospect of returning to the Durotriges so soon after my leave-taking, but it is my only option, especially as my new-found mother is apparently estranged from my own father.

'Brendan, will you protect the women?'

'Fionn, we have an agreement, remember?' says Brendan. He sounds anxious. 'You have not forgotten, have you? If you have your own plans, then I will journey to Lynd myself. I fear Bryn will die at any moment and Mylor will be in grave danger.'

Fionn touches Brendan's shoulder. I notice how square and solid his hand is.

'Of course I have not forgotten. My word is my bond. But I cannot be in three places at once.'

'Don't worry about us,' I say. I can feel myself reddening. Do they think me totally without guile? 'We are not helpless and quite frankly it is an insult to suggest we are. I can wield a sword and dagger as well as any warrior.'

'I too,' says the Queen, who seems stronger than before. 'You know I am an expert rider, Fionn! Chela and I - we will be fine. We do not need an escort.'

Fionn ignores us.

'Brendan, listen to me,' he says. 'If Bryn dies, it will be one moon's journey at least before the Kingship ceremony. Witnesses will have to be summoned. Everyone will know about it and, I promise you, we will have enough time to rescue Mylor once all of this is sorted out.'

I am about to protest, but then hold myself in check, for although I do not require the protection of a man, I am well aware that Brendan knows the forest better than any of us. I decide not to press the point.

Brendan looks down at the ground but says nothing, and I feel my heart going out to him. He has sacrificed much to help us.

'I now know why they have taken Kendra,' says Fionn. 'It was to bring about this war. Once the battle is joined, Lann will have no more use for her and he will kill her. Please, Brendan. Chela and the Queen must reach Kendra before anything happens, and you are their swiftest means to Vipers' Fort.'

'You ask me to trust you, Fionn, and though you change your plans like a confused squirrel, I do trust you. Very well, I will do as you say, but when you have fulfilled this task, I will hold you to your promise.'

'Good man,' says Fionn. 'Brendan, I owe you my life and I will help you rescue Mylor, if it is the last thing I do.'

I scrutinise Fionn, trying to get the measure of him. He has surprised me. He is so young, just a boy, and yet he has something about him that sets him apart from the rest. Is it his presence, or the way he uses his words? I cannot say, except that he is destined to be a leader of men, of that I am certain.

I watch as he meets Brendan's gaze, sincerity etched on his face, then I turn away. This moment is theirs; I have no part in it.

It is Brendan who eventually breaks the silence.

'Come,' he says, smiling at Briona and I. 'We must make haste.'

TWENTY EIGHT

The Lands of the Atres

Fionn

The gods must be on our side, for not long after I leave the others, I come across two stallions, and judging by their accoutrements, they belonged to the dead warriors who were pursuing Briona. I am already leading one spare horse, but these two must be a gift from the gods. I strip them of their terrets and decorations which I hide under a pile of branches and leaves. Then I tether the three horses together and lead them out of the forest. Fortunately I do not have far to go before I am free of the trees, for with three horses in tow, my progress is slow and tortuous.

As I leave the lands of the Vellani behind and cross into my own familiar territory, the sun warms my back, and the sweet smell of early summer fills my nostrils. It is perfect riding weather, yet I cannot relax. On reaching the open moors, I set the spare horses free, slapping them hard on their rumps to send them off at a gallop at right-angles to my own trajectory. It is a shame to lose three good horses, but they are a price I am willing to pay in order to confuse those who follow my tracks. As soon as I am rid of the horses, I spur my own stead onwards, gripping the horse's flanks with my knees and as we break into a gallop, I revel in the familiar sensation of flying through the air. I am one with the horse and though my mended leg aches, the discomfort is bearable. Brendan has done well and the horse is strong and swift.

My thoughts turn to Kendra and I wonder whether the existence of her older sister might change matters back home. With the King's blessing, I courted Kendra with the express purpose of marrying her for the Atres throne, but now I find myself cooling to the prospect of such a union. I am fond of her, but in the brief time I have been in Chela's company, I have been struck by her beauty and strength. I wonder what she makes of me, and whether she might feel the same way.

By late afternoon I am at Broch Hill. I pause at the summit and looking back, I spy my pursuers in the distance, five tiny specks of dark against the brown sedge that covers the moors. I cannot help but smile. I am very nearly home now. They have no chance of catching me and once I have descended the hill, I will be well into Atres territory. No-one would dare pursue me so far into my own kin's territory in broad daylight. It is pleasing to know also, that I have led

Doran's men away from the others, giving them a fighting chance, at least. Sure enough, my pursuers, nervous of being in Atres country, do not follow.

As I look in the direction of Awelfryn, I see a group of six riders coming my way. Irven's men, at a guess, riding to find out what became of the warriors who went after Briona. The Queen had identified them as Deri and Lugh, two of Irven's finest men and I knew them well.

My first thought is to protect my friends, for I know that the search party will capture and possibly kill Briona, before disposing of Chela and Brendan. Once I have spoken to Irven and averted the battle, the Queen's betrayal will be meaningless in military terms in any case. Despite my regard for Irven, it does not take me long to decide where my loyalties lie. The riding party draws nearer and soon I am within hailing distance. I know all of these men and they recognise me straight away.

'My Lord Fionn,' says their leader, a warrior who goes by the name of Rawdon, displaying his full tattoos for all to see. 'We had thought you dead. It is good to see you.'

'As you see, I am alive and well, and heading for Awelfryn. I have news for the King regarding the fate of his Queen.'

'Oh? We are searching for her ourselves. And for the two warriors who went after her. What can you tell us?'

'She is dead,' I say, hanging my head. 'Her servant, Ferehar, too. I came upon Deri and Lugh who told me how our Queen first killed Ferehar and then herself rather than be captured. I could scarce believe my ears. Is it true? Was her life forfeit?'

Rawdon lets out a frustrated hiss of air.

'They were meant to bring her back! Alive.' Then he shrugs. 'Perhaps it is for the best,' he continues. 'She was well loved, and a public execution...??'

He raises his eyebrows to the sky.

'Deri told me she turned traitor. A sorry business,' I say. 'To think such things have come to pass whilst I have been away, but if she turned against the King, then she deserves no better. Lugh said she was fleeing to the Durotriges!'

'Where are they now, Deri and Lugh?' asks Rawdon. He is a conscientious man, keen to fulfil his duties.

'Deri wished to visit his kin near the southern Atres border and Lugh went with him. Seeing I was headed for Awelfryn, they asked that I break the news to Irven. I expect they did not relish the thought of telling the King of her death.'

'They should know better, the disobedient, cowardly fools. The King will not be best pleased with them, and they know it! Irven wanted a proper Accusation, with the Brothers overseeing it, so *they* could command her death, not he. Now there will be nothing but rumours that he put her to death unlawfully. Anyway, what of her body? Where does she lie?'

'They buried her in the Woods of Rhiw, rather than bring her back to Awelfryn.'

Rawdon looks at me for a long moment and I know he is sizing me up, wondering whether to take my words at face value. My lies up to now have been credible, but I realise that this part of my tale sounds weak. I hold my breath and after a moment he nods and turns to his men.

'Fionn, as we know, is the King's man,' he says. 'Chosen by Irven to rule after him. His word on the matter is good enough for me and without Deri and Lugh, we cannot hope to even guess where they have buried the Queen. Let us ride home with him.'

As we journey, I enquire after the King. Rawdon looks uncomfortable, evading my questions, and I wonder what I am riding towards.

'You will see for yourself, my Lord,' he says, before lapsing into silence.

It is early evening by the time the familiar chalk-white banks of Awelfryn come into view, its defences bristling with guards. The war footing has galvanized the Atres into action and they have limed their hair in anticipation of the battles to come. As I ride up to the gate, I am recognised and before long a throng of curious villagers follow my horse, calling my name and shouting questions. Smiling at the familiar faces in the crowd, I say nothing and, handing my horse to one of Irven's grooms, head straight for the King's roundhouse.

When I first set eyes on Irven, I have the greatest difficulty controlling my surprise. The King is sitting in his usual leather hammock-seat, a horn half filled with wine in his hand, but it is his face that sends a shiver down my spine. The man has aged ten summers since I last set eyes on him. Even in the dim light of the hearth's fire, his colour is grey though his cheeks and nose are red, and the lines on his face have gouged deep crevices where before there were furrows.

'Fionn,' says the King. 'I had feared you dead.'

'As you see, I am flesh and blood,' I reply, trying to sound positive. 'Kendra, your daughter, is alive also.'

Irven smiles but his smile does not reach his eyes.

'The gods be praised then. Where is she?'

'She is with the Durotriges, but they are unaware of her identity.'

Irven snorts in derision. He clearly does not believe in Hanu's innocence. I sit where he gestures and drink from the horn that has been thrust into my hand by the waiting attendant. I wait for him to ask after his daughter, but to my surprise, he shows no concern whatsoever. I compose myself, then break the news of Briona's death, repeating the story I told the warriors. To make the King believe me all the more, I express my sorrow at her passing. I know that lying to the King is dangerous, but when it comes to light that Briona is still alive, I will blame Deri and Lugh for the lies. They are hardly in a position to argue.

I watch as a flicker of sorrow crosses Irven's face, but it is soon replaced with a bitter smile. It seems Irven has nothing to say concerning the passing of his wife of twenty years and I begin to feel increasingly uncomfortable as our meeting takes on an unreal quality.

I tell Irven the rest of my news; that it is the Vellani who have been stirring trouble, setting one tribe against the next and finally, Doran's plan to march on the Trinovantes.

'It is Doran who is your enemy,' I conclude. 'Not Hanu. You must call off the battle.'

Irven does not reply immediately. He drinks even more deeply of his wine and when he fixes his gaze on me, his eyes are bloodshot and cold and his voice slurred as he speaks.

'Do not presume, young Fionn,' he says, 'to tell me what to do.'

'But..,' I begin to speak, but falter under his gaze. Such a look speaks of madness.

'The quarrel between myself and Hanu will never be resolved by peaceful means,' he says. 'And if it is true that the Vellani have orchestrated this entire scenario, then it will work to my advantage. It is not just about the Atres now, Fionn. I have secured promises from the Canti and Regni. Do you think they would have joined me in this because they backed my own personal quarrel?' His snarl brooks no answer. I keep my eyes averted from the King's manic gaze.

'You are young and stupid, Fionn. Both the Canti and Regni are sick of the Durotriges stranglehold on the Veneti traders, as are we. They want their fair share.'

'Yes my Lord,' I say. All I want to do is get out of the King's sight before Irven's wrath is turned on me. But despite myself, I voice the concern that has been eating away at me.

'My Lord,' I say, falteringly, before firming up my voice. 'What of Kendra? What of our agreement?'

Irven laughs but there is no mirth whatsoever behind his hollow cackle.

'I have other plans now, young Fionn. If I were you, I would return to your father's side and prepare the Clan of Morffryn for war. Your father, Caradwg, promises to ride at my right hand. He knows I am his master and has sworn his loyalty. If I were you,' says the King again as he leans forward, 'I would put Kendra out of your mind, and concentrate on helping me make the Atres great once more.'

'Do you not care about your daughter?' I am shaking, but cannot stop myself from speaking.

'Ha!' replies Irven. 'The Queen turned her against me when she was a mere babe. Like her mother, she is stupid and wilful. I will beget a daughter I can be proud of, as well as a new heir for my Kingdom. Go Fionn! Be gone! Get out of my sight!'

I watch, fascinated, as a dribble of wine escapes down Irven's chin. Briona was right. The King has changed beyond all recognition. As I back out of Irven's house, my mind reels. Had the King not promised me, and Kendra, the Atres throne? As my hopes drain away, I realise, perhaps for the first time, how much I truly wanted to rule.

Without stopping to rest, I grab myself a fresh horse from Irven's pound and leave Awelfryn, heading for Buzzardstone, my father's abode. I care not that it is night, nor that I have been riding all day. A gibbous moon hangs low in the sky to light my way, and I will be home before dawn. As I ride through the Atres gates, I glance behind me. For the first time in my life I fear the King, a man I had grown to respect above my own flesh and blood.

When I reach Buzzardstone, I head straight for the roundhouse where the warriors sleep. I will not disturb my father's household just yet and my news can wait until I have caught up with some much needed sleep. The only person who is astir is the servant, Anfaran, who guards the entrance to the roundhouse. Yawning, the boy points me in the direction of a pile of furs in a vacant corner of the room. I disrobe as quietly as I can and almost as soon as my head touches the soft skins, I fall asleep.

By the time I awake, the morning is well advanced and the hill fort is buzzing with activity. I am the only warrior left indoors, everyone else having risen long ago to set about their tasks.

A stack of warm buttered flat bread and cheese has been left for me next to the hearth. As I eat, I listen to the familiar sounds of home. The barking of dogs and the cackling of geese are to be expected, but a more urgent sound can be heard and it seems that from every direction there is a hammering of metal as blacksmiths turn out weaponry, or the high pitched singing of blade on blade as the warriors hone their skills. Preparation for war is well advanced all over the Atres lands, it appears.

The servant, Anfaran, comes in through the doorway, leading a grey hound by its leash. I recognise Pedwar immediately, and break into a grin.

'Well, well,' I say, ruffling the dog's shaggy coat. 'How did he get here?'

'Howell nursed him until he recovered and then sent him to await your return,' says Anfaran. 'He has been with me since.'

The dog no longer knows me and has formed a bond with the servant and so I decide to leave matters as they are, until I can reunite Pedwar with his mistress. My grin vanishes, however, as I realised that such a reunion is now nigh on impossible.

My eyes feel heavy from sleep and so I splash cold water on my face from the wooden butt that leans against the outside wall. Feeling a little more alert, I limp towards my father's roundhouse. The long ride has taken its toll.

Caradwg is in the middle of a discussion with three of his Elders. The news of my return has already reached him and so he does not react when he sees me. I am greeted with a smile, and I cannot help but notice that like Irven's the night before, my father's smile has a coldness about it. Our relationship has never been one of open affection.

'Fionn, I am gladdened to see you are alive and well!' he says, though to me it seems his greeting lacks conviction.

'Father. It is good to be home.' I am not lying. My encounter with the King has narrowed my options and Buzzardstone, my only refuge.

Caradwg dismisses the Elders so that we are alone. I notice a difference in my father. Caradwg appears more alive and in direct proportion, it seems, to the King's decline, he has grown in stature and confidence.

'Have you been to the King?' he asks, without preamble.

'I have indeed,' I say, meeting his piercing gaze. 'He is in a bad way. I fear his mind is taken.'

I tell my father about my talk with Irven the night before and how it seems that the King no longer has any need of the House of Morffryn. With Kendra's disappearance, we have lost the opportunity to rule. My father, however, appears unconcerned and his eyes are alive with excitement.

'Father, this war with the Durotriges is madness,' I say. 'You must use your influence to stop Irven before he brings ruin upon us.'

'Do you seriously believe the King will listen to me?' asks Caradwg. I cannot answer and so he continues. 'He has committed the Canti and the Regni to this fight. They have not entered into it for Irven's sake alone, but to smash Hanu's power in the south.'

'What chance to you really think we have?' I ask. 'I simply cannot believe that even the combined forces of the Atres, Canti and Regni will ever be enough to defeat the might of the Durotriges. Then there are the Vellani - they are scheming against the Trinovantes, but I suspect they wish to weaken us all so they can take the power for themselves.'

Caradwg inhales deeply and I realise my father is considering whether to trust me or not. I feel my anger rising, but before I can utter a single word, Caradwg speaks.

'Are you Irven's man, or will you be loyal to the House of Morffryn?' he demands. 'This I must know.'

I am taken aback by the question, not knowing where it leads, but I can only answer honestly.

'Irven has made it plain that I am no longer part of his plan,' I say. 'I am your kin, father, through and through. You may depend on me.'

'Good,' says Caradwg. 'Now listen. Irven is not the man he was. He sits in his house, brooding, drinking wine from morning till noon. He forgets how to rule.'

I say nothing. I have been told to listen and so that is what I will do.

'He fails his people. He takes their dues but offers no protection from the cattle raiders. And recently he has increased the taxes on the farmers. The Brothers sent an envoy to speak to me.'

I cannot hide my surprise.

'You say the Brothers? From Lynd? What is it they propose?'

'As we know, Irven has been less than, shall we say, 'co-operative' with them for some years now.'

I nod. My mouth is dry.

'You were our last hope, Fionn. It was believed that once you were made King and the house of Morffryn joined that of Irven's, matters would improve. Our clan has always sided with the Brothers. But with the young princess taken, those hopes have been dashed.'

'It was the Vellani who took her,' I say, but Caradwg silences me with his hand.

'Let me finish. I have learned as much, but that is of no import now. Matters have moved on. It now plays to our advantage that Irven's daughter has been taken.'

My head feels light. I cannot believe what I am hearing. He is talking about Kendra as though she were a stranger!

'Irven wants this war, and nothing will stop him now, not even the return of his daughter. And through this very war, he will play into our hands.'

'But the Durotriges must know what is afoot,' I protest. My voice sounds feeble to my own ears.

'Yes, the Durotriges did not get where they are without some guile. Hanu does know what Irven intends, but views him as a minor irritation. Alone, Irven is no threat to Hanu but as far as we can glean, Hanu has no knowledge of the Canti and Regni's pledge to join the Atres and therein lies his weakness. As we all know, Hanu is no better disposed towards the Brothers than is Irven. The Brothers *want* this battle. The Durotriges grow too strong. They make the Brothers nervous.'

'I see,' I reply, but my inner sight is far from clear. My mind is reeling with the information, and my own deadly secret. I have not mentioned Briona, nor that she is on her way to warn Hanu of the Canti and Regni's involvement. I wonder how my father would react if he knew I had aided her, and that she was about to scupper his plans? I play for time, trying to decide what to do for the best.

'So the Brothers are making use of the aggression to further their own ambition,' I say, trying to make my voice bland.

'You could say that,' says Caradwg. 'They want to know that whosoever is in power will be sympathetic to their cause. If Irven is defeated, the Brothers will raise me to be King of the Atres.'

'King of nothing but ashes!' I have found my voice. 'Is there something I am missing, here? The Durotriges are quite capable of smashing the Atres, even with the Canti and Regni against them.'

'Doran of the Vellani will march on the Durotriges when they are weakened by battle. If we do as the Brothers ask, those clans of the Atres who rally to the Vellani's side will survive and the lands of the south will be divided equally amongst us. I will be King and you, Fionn, will rule after me.'

Caradwg reaches for his drinking horn. He drinks deeply and wipes his mouth before continuing. For one fleeting moment, he reminds me of Irven.

'The Vellani will receive the lands of the Canti and Regni,' he says.

'So this will be a double treachery?' I retort, before I can stop myself. 'Does Doran intend to wipe out the Canti and Regni tribes too?'

'Fionn. It is time you became a man and faced the realities of life. We of the House of Morffryn are being offered not only the Kingship of the Atres, but the lands of the Durotriges and all that entails. The south and east will be ruled by two Kingdoms, those of the Atres and the Vellani, both of whom will be loyal to the Priesthood.'

'So what is it we must do?' I ask.

'We are to leave Irven and his supporters unprotected when battle is joined. We already have the agreement of four of the Atres clans in the south of the Kingdom in this matter and I am in the process of persuading some of the other clans to join us. I know, Fionn, that this is a risky venture and will mean splitting the Atres people down the middle. If it miscarries, it will be my head that will decorate Irven's ramparts. But you know as well as I that many of the clan leaders are unhappy with Irven. It should not be too difficult to persuade them to join us. We can then take our rightful place, ruling the Atres as is ordained, and if it means the Brothers play a larger part in our politics, so be it.'

As Caradwg finishes talking, I feel my blood run cold. Whereas Irven is drunk on wine and bitter hatred, my father is drunk on the promise of power, and his yearning has distorted his judgment. The tribes of Britain have always been true to their word but all that has changed.

I leave my father's roundhouse in a daze and return to the warriors' abode, at a loss to know what to do for the best. Pedwar is still there, and I call the hound to me, stroking his muzzle as I marshal my thoughts.

If Briona reaches Hanu and warns him of the Canti and Regni's plans, Caradwg's ambitions will be thwarted, as well as Irven's. I have just sworn allegiance to my father, and I know I ought to tell Caradwg, yet I cannot bring myself to betray Briona, Brendan and especially Chela, whom I now realise I love beyond all doubt. And the longer I stall, the more untrustworthy I will appear to my father.

My thoughts turn to Kendra, and I am suffused with guilt, not only for the feelings I carry for her sister, but because I know that she too will be killed by the madness that stalks the land. I put my head in my hands and weep, the hot tears spilling unchecked down my face, for I know there will be no victors in this war, only death and ruination for us all.

TWENTY NINE

Viper's Fort

Kendra

As I feared, Armelle's disappearance some eight days ago caused uproar. Gowell questioned me every day, often two or three times a day, about what had happened, each time trying to wring out a bit more information until Riana stepped in and stopped him haranguing me any further.

I was grateful for her intervention and apart from Gowell's interrogations since Armelle left, my life has begun to improve. Riana speaks to me gently, and though I am still a slave, I no longer have to suffer Armelle's temper. Lann has been away for some time and although the ever-present threat of Huw guarantees my continued silence, the absence of Lann makes me feel lighter, somehow. I have even managed a couple of visits to Malvina and Cator, as Riana took it upon herself to obtain Huw's permission. I was worried about how Huw would treat Malvina, but it seems that for the most part, he ignores her, which is good. It is a few days since I last saw them and so, emboldened by my new mistress' kindly disposition, I decide to ask if I might visit them again.

'I'm sure that will be alright,' says Riana. 'I will mention it to Lann.'

I feel myself shrinking inside.

'He's back then?'

'Yes, I believe he returned yesterday,' she says, completely oblivious to the effect her words are having on me.

No sooner has Riana finished speaking, than Lann turns up, his ugliness filling the doorway like a black cloud.

'Might I borrow your slave girl to help in the workshops,' he asks, sly as ever. 'We are short of hands.'

The burn scars have stiffened the side of his face so that his smile, superficial as ever, manifests now as an evil leer.

'Of course,' says Riana. 'I was about to ask a favour for Kendra in any case. She wishes to visit her friends. Perhaps when she has finished her work?'

'I will arrange it,' says Lann. He turns and speaks directly to me, and a shiver travels up my spine. 'Come by my house after the evening meal. The forge needs cleaning. After that you can see your friends.'

I am at a loss to know what to do. I know Lann is up to no good, but I had asked to visit my friends, and Riana has arranged it. I do not dare change my mind.

'Go,' says Riana, when I have completed my chores. 'And don't worry about rushing back.'

Every step I take in the direction of Lann's house is leaden with dread. What can he want now, I wonder. I have been good, I have not uttered a word out of place, and Riana seems pleased with me. Besides, it is early evening, a strange time to be cleaning the forge, but Riana had not thought to question him.

As I enter Lann's roundhouse my stomach churns to see that Cator is there as well as Malvina, who looks deathly pale. I dare for a moment, entertain the thought that Lann is simply doing as he had promised, allowing me to see my friends, but the look on the man's face soon dispels that hope. Lann is leaning against one of the timber uprights, casually holding on to Malvina, one hand cupped almost tenderly under the little girl's chin. In his other hand, he holds a knife. Cator is sitting stiffly next to the hearth, and despite the apparent normality of the tableau, I know we are in grave danger by the look of panic in Cator's eyes.

Lann points to a pile of rusty metal on the floor. As I look at it, the jumble of iron begins to coalesce into a set of slave shackles. I look at Lann in disbelief, causing him to smile.

'Put them on,' he says as he caresses Malvina's face with his dagger.

We obey without argument, and my hands shake as I handle the cruel metal. Only when he is satisfied that they are on properly, does Lann release Malvina. Cator and I wear a metal collar each to which a length of chain is attached, linking us together. A longer piece of chain trails from Cator's neck ring, designed, no doubt, for the slave driver to hold as though it were a dog's leash. Walking would be difficult enough, escape nigh on impossible.

Freed from Lann's grip, Malvina, whose feet have not entirely healed, limps into my arms and buries her head in my bosom. As I hold her close, I notice that she is shivering and from time to time splutters with a dry, cough. I decide to speak up.

'Lann,' I say, as politely as I can, 'Malvina here is unwell. Please, I implore you; let me take her to the women.'

'Do you think I was born yesterday?' says Lann, his fingers toying with the burn scar on his face. 'I have your measure by now, young woman and know how you plot your escape. There will be no healer. One move from either of you and your young friend will feel the sharpness of my blade. Understand?'

We understand. I know what Lann is capable of and fall silent as Cator, who must have sensed my distress, draws me close and holds me tight. The three of us huddle together across the hearth from Lann, who simply ignores us, whittling a piece of wood into an unrecognisable shape. I find myself wondering, not for the first time, at the hatred that emanates from him. What could have caused the man to be so bitter?

After what seems an eternity, Lann throws the stick into the dying fire in disgust and stands up. He slings a basket onto his back then prises Malvina away from me and throws her over his shoulder. With his free hand he grabs the chain and tugs it so that Cator and I have no option but to follow.

It is dark by the time we leave Vipers' Fort. The guards on duty nod at Lann. I know they will not question him – he is a noble and if he wants to take his slaves out at night-time, that is his business. They probably think he is heading for the workshops.

We stumble through the countryside, Cator and I walking ten paces in front of Lann, who carries Malvina. My fear mounts as the land rises higher and I realise we are at the cliff-top, with the unmistakeable sound of the sea crashing on the rocks below.

'We must try to overpower him,' whispers Cator. 'What have we to lose? If we are to die, we may as well go out fighting.'

'No, Cator, we must be patient. He has not finished with us yet. He still needs us for something, I am sure, and we cannot endanger Malvina's life.'

'Quiet!' says Lann

We lapse into silence, lurching along the well-worn cliff-top path. Though it is a cloudy night devoid of moonlight, the exposed chalk under our feet gleams in the darkness, guiding us. We continue in silence, the only noise, the clank-clank of our chains.

After what seems a very long walk, we begin a treacherous descent down the cliff face. There is a trail of sorts, but the loose screed causes us to stumble, narrowly missing falling onto the jagged rocks that wait below. My legs feel weak from the effort and I think I might faint, but Cator's strength stops me falling. I can feel my will ebbing and want nothing more than to stop fighting and be looked after. Tears prick my eyes but I dash them away with my hand. *Not now, do not weaken now, I tell myself, it's not over yet.*

With a prayer of thanks to the Great Mother, I begin to notice that the path has become shallower until at last we stand on a rocky beach, the tall cliff face looming over us. The sea crashes on the rocks and then slides back, slurping at the pebbles as it recedes.

Lann leads us along the base of the cliff until he stops at the mouth of a dark hole, its blackness emanating a fearful evil. Though I instinctively recoil, I have no choice but to enter the cave, feeling for the damp walls to guide me, muttering a prayer to appease the spirit of the cave. We climb a little, and at the end of the chamber the rocky floor turns to dry sand. I fall onto my knees, dragging Cator down with me. Lann drops Malvina into my lap and I wrap my arms around her, noting how hot she feels.

It is pitch black in the cave but my ears compensate for my lack of sight. I hear Lann fumble with the basket and dump it on the ground. I hear him striking a flint stone and building a small fire, and I am relieved that we will have some light after all. I notice two large earthenware water pitchers and a large sack stacked against the cold cave wall – whatever he is up to has been well thought out, that much is clear. Fed by dry seaweed and stranded driftwood, the fire takes, and throws shadows against the cave wall which glistens like a thousand stars. I look at Cator. He shrugs, and his simple gesture tells me that he cannot fathom Lann's actions either. Our gaoler then grabs the end of the chain and begins hammering, the sound of metal on metal so loud that I have to cover my ears. He is securing the chain to something, but to what, I cannot tell. Finally the noise stops and only silence rings in my ears. To my dismay, as soon as he has finished his task, he stamps the fire out and covers it with sand. My heart sinks.

'Wait here for me,' he says. 'I will be gone some days. There is food in the sack and water in the basket. Make it last.'

Then he leaves, and the darkness envelopes us.

THIRTY

The Woods of Rhiw

Chela

Brendan, who knows this forest, has decided that we would be better staying under cover of the trees. I fear we will be pursued by both the Atres and Vellani, and so I cannot fault his plan.

'Our progress will be slow, but I know this place,' he says, and he sounds confident enough.

'How long?' asks Briona. I can hear the weariness in her voice.

'It will take the best part of two days for us to cross the forest but the third day will see us clear.'

'With any luck, Doran will have sent his warriors after Fionn,' I say, then bite my lip as I realise the danger he has taken upon himself.

'He will have a better chance of escape on his own,' says Brendan who, I know, is trying to reassure me. I have grown to like Fionn in the short time we have been together. I hope he will be safe.

Even though the day is warm and the trees provide a dappled shade, we are ill at ease. I am worried about disturbing another of the Druids' nemetons, but Brendan reassures me, claiming he knows where the sacred groves lie and will give them a wide berth. I like Brendan and trust him, yet I cannot relax.

When the path allows us to ride next to each other, Briona and I talk in low voices about Kendra until the Queen has gleaned what she can about her young daughter.

'Why did she not tell anyone who she was?' she asks. 'Hanu would have helped her immediately had he known she was my daughter.'

'I think the man who captured her swore her to secrecy under some threat of punishment. In any case, she never denied she was from the Silures and did not speak a single word about her origins.'

'Then she must have had good reason,' says Briona, sighing. 'She is not one to keep quiet, believe me!'

'I think she may have been protecting her companions,' I say, mentally kicking myself for not getting to the truth.

'That comes as no surprise. It matters not to her that her friends are commoners, for she would not desert them. I should have looked after her better, kept her on a tighter rein.'

'I too could have helped her,' I say. 'I liked her a great deal, but I am afraid I didn't treat her as well as I might have done in the end. I thought she lied to me, but I was stupid not to see beyond my own problems.'

'Don't blame yourself. If Kendra chose to remain silent, you could not have known. Now, tell me about yourself,' she says after a pause, conscious that the subject of Kendra has dominated our conversation.

'When we stop,' I say, 'I will tell you everything.'

Though we pause to eat a hurried lunch and to water and feed the horses, we do not rest until it is too dark to continue without fear of getting lost. Brendan leads us to a stream with steep mossy banks and a flattish grassy area off to one side, dotted with ferns, where we can sleep. No fire will be lit tonight and so after we eat a meal of cold meat and leathery dried rosehips, Briona and I, little more than strangers to each other, huddle close under a blanket whilst Brendan wraps himself in his own and settles down to rest.

'You were going to tell me your story,' says Briona in a gentle voice. 'I am waiting.'

I do not reply. Instead I take off my golden bracelet and place it in Briona's hand. The Queen handles the cool metal. I realise she cannot see it.

'What is this?' she asks. 'It feels familiar.'

I swallow hard before replying.

'It has the figure of the Owl of the Durotriges inscribed on the inside.'

Briona sits upright. I can feel her tense.

'Where did you come by this?' she demands. 'Did Fionn give it to you?'

'No,' I reply. 'I have owned it since I was a babe.'

Briona lets out a small cry, startling Brendan, who has been dozing.

'What is it?' he says, his sword at the ready.

'Sorry, Brendan. It is nothing,' I say, biting my lip. 'Go back to sleep.'

'Do you want us found? Keep your voices down!'

'Tell me,' says Briona, ignoring Brendan. She keeps her voice to a whisper, but her words are charged with emotion.

In a soft voice, I tell the Queen what Elanor had said the morning before she died.

Briona is crying. When I finish speaking, she raises her hands and holds my face in front of hers, before enfolding me in an embrace.

'Then you are my very own daughter,' she says, through her tears.

The embrace feels like an intrusion. I bear it for a moment but then pull away. This woman might be my own mother, but we are still unknown to one another.

'When I found that Fionn and I shared the same bracelet,' I say, 'and he told me who had given him his, I knew you had to be my mother and Kendra my sister.'

'I should have known the moment I set eyes on you,' says Briona. 'You look so much like her.'

'Why? Why did you give me away?' I finally voice the question that has been plaguing me for such a long time and it feels strange releasing the words.

'To prevent your death. It was the Brother, Deryn, who filled Irven's mind with notions of power. He persuaded your father that if he handed over his first-born, he would be like a god who walked on land. They told him he would be invulnerable, super-human, even. Elanor's betrothed, Kelwin, knew all about it. He mentioned it to Elanor and she came to warn me. We switched you with another infant, then Elanor fled with you to the Durotriges.'

I digest the information, realising that Elanor had given up the chance of love and marriage to save me. Tears well up and spill down my face. Eventually I compose myself sufficiently to ask another question, one that has been forming in my mind since Briona's revelation.

'The mother whose babe you switched, what became of her?'

I hear Briona sigh. When she answers, her voice sounds tired.

'I have carried the guilt of what I did all these years in here,' she says, grabbing my hand and clutching it to her breast. 'And if I could make it up to the woman, I would.'

'What happened to her?' As I speak, I draw my hand away.

'Elanor arranged it all. The girl was a commoner of the Atres, an orphan who had lost her kin to the illness that scoured the land. She had no-one to turn to and had gone to Elanor for help saying she had been raped by a Durotriges noble, a man who went by the name of Lughaid. Elanor could do nothing to stop the pregnancy and when the woman's time came, she helped her give birth to twins, one boy and one girl.'

'At the same time that I was born, then?'

'Within a day. At first Elanor tried to persuade the woman to give up the girl, but she would not. Then we tried to bribe her, but she refused to part with the infant.'

Briona stops talking and I fear she will not continue, but after a long pause, she starts again.

'I am ashamed of what I did, but how can I continue to regret my actions when you are here in front of me?' she pleads.

'What happened to the woman?' I press the point, because I know that I live only because another died. I need to know, even though my mother is finding it painful to speak.

'We took the babe by force and banished the woman from Awelfryn, saying she had brought shame upon the Atres and would have to fend for herself.'

I cringe to hear of the unfairness and cruelty meted out to the woman and find it hard to believe Elanor would be party to such a crime, but I say nothing, wanting the Queen to continue.

'I know not where she went, but I understand she took her little boy Lann with her.'

'Lann? Are you sure?'

'Yes. The name of the boy has stuck with me. Why, do you know him?'

'I certainly do! He is the man who brought Kendra to the Durotriges, claiming he captured her from the Silures!'

'Then it is I who set this in motion over twenty years ago. It cannot be mere coincidence - this Lann must be the other twin,' cries Briona, causing Brendan to sit up once again..

'For the love of Esu!' he says in a stage whisper. 'How many times…?'

'Sorry!' I whisper, cringing like a five-year-old. Brendan however, realises that we are upset and speaks in a gentler tone.

'What of Lann?' he asks.

'Of course, you must know him well,' I say.

'Yes, I do. A strange fellow. He's from Ravensroost. Well, at least he is now.'

'Tell me about him,' says Briona. 'I must know everything.'

'I do not know from whence he originated,' says Brendan. I can see he is beginning to enjoy the attention he is receiving. 'but his mother turned up one day many years ago and asked for sanctuary. Lann was a mere babe.'

'Go on,' says Briona, who clutches at my hand, her grasp clammy and desperate. My feelings towards my mother are confused. To be capable of such ruthlessness! Then I think of Elanor, and the guilt she carried all those years.

'Well,' says Brendan. 'Bryn took pity on them and took them in, and grew fond of the boy. In fact, he near enough adopted him as his own. He sent him off to be educated by the Brothers until the age of sixteen, when he returned to Bryn's side. The Druids taught him well and he was practiced in their arts.'

'Which arts?' I ask.

'Tracking, hand to hand combat, that sort of thing. I remember watching him once in a fight. You could barely see him move, he was so fast, and he floored his opponent in a trice. Anyway, he was sent to the Durotriges when Doran returned from Rome, for Hanu to be his nutritor.'

Briona nods. 'Hanu was fostered in the same way to the Atres for a while. That was how he and Irven became the best of friends. Tell me Brendan, what became of his mother?'

'Oh, Cerid still lives with the Vellani. She has taken on the role of nursemaid in Bryn's household. But she is a strange woman.'

'How so?'

'It is hard to say. Bitter, I suppose would be the best way to describe her. Like a crab-apple'

It is obvious Brendan did not hear our earlier conversation.

'I know him too, of course, from Hanu's court,' I say. 'Hanu trusts him but I fear he is working up a storm, setting Atres against Durotriges.'

'Not that Irven needs much encouraging to engage in battle with Hanu,' says Briona.

'Lann would do nothing without Bryn, or Doran's blessing,' says Brendan. 'He loves Bryn as his own father, and by the same token, extends his loyalty to Doran. Believe me when I say that whatever Lann has done, he has done with Doran's full knowledge.'

'It's a complicated web, no doubt about that,' I say.

'Why is Irven so set against Hanu?' asks Brendan.

'It is a long story, over something that happened a long time ago, Brendan,' replies Briona, obviously reluctant to take the young man into her confidence. 'But we must try to get some sleep; we have another long day ahead of us.'

213

As we settle down together I wonder whether to ask Briona the final question that has been troubling me. Was Gowell my brother? Have I transgressed against nature's very laws? My mouth begins to form the words, but I stop myself. It is too intimate a question, and too soon to ask it. The matter can wait. Instead I ask about Irven.

'What occurred between my father and Hanu, to cause such enmity?'

Briona sighs before answering.

'Irven found us together. We were kissing.'

'What happened?'

'Hanu silenced me before I could say anything. Rather than dishonour my name, he let Irven think he had forced himself upon me.'

'Did Irven believe him?'

'At first perhaps, but he always had his doubts. I should have said something, at the time, but I always believed they would get over their differences. I was foolish and naive. Irven's jealousy and suspicion festered over the years and he grew to hate Hanu with a passion. He always regretted not killing him on the spot.'

'And you? How was he to you?' I want to find out more about my father.

'He did love me, very deeply, but he never truly believed I loved him after that. His love turned to hatred.'

'And did you? Love him, I mean?'

Briona says nothing for a long while and I think she must have fallen asleep. Then she speaks.

'I did love him. I really did. But all that changed. And it was not just Hanu who changed it. We could have put that behind us. Your father did not know Elanor had made the switch and it seemed to me that he did not care overly much that his first born was going to meet her certain death. I am sorry, Chela, I do not mean to turn you against your own father, but you asked the question and I am done with lies.'

I squeeze this strange woman's hand. I do not know what else to do.

'And it was at that moment, Chela, that I stopped loving him,' she says.

214

THIRTY ONE

Buzzardstone

Fionn

I am atop the gate of my father's hill fort and I cannot stay still. I find myself either pacing the ramparts like a demented cat or stopping to gaze over the thick wooden barrier that surrounds the settlement. The defences were designed to discourage enemies, but there are no attackers at the gate this evening. Hah! Just who is my enemy, I wonder, and curse my ambivalence, for if my passions are not true in battle, death with its slavering teeth will surely seek me out for the fool I am, and devour me at the first opportunity.

I can barely believe the audacity of Caradwg's plans, but I have to concede that my hopes must lie in the actions of my father, even if the deceit and treachery does leave a bad taste in my mouth. According to Caradwg, the House of Morffryn now has four clans who will rally to our side, and even though it is plain that Irven is clearly mad and unfit to lead, I cannot shake off the feeling of doom that permeates my being. A desire for power has coursed through my veins for a long while now, nurtured by Irven and Briona, causing my own father to be jealous, but this evening I am sickened by it all and find myself longing for the quiet life of a smith I experienced so briefly at Ravensroost.

The settlement beneath me sizzles with excitement. The warriors are ready, waiting for the sign, thirsting for glory and bragging to anyone who cares to listen, of their feats of bravery in past skirmishes. Most of the younger warriors, myself included, have yet to experience warfare on such a scale and it is only those whose beards are grey who remember the full-scale battles of their youth. Weapons have been sharpened to a razor's edge, the ceremonial shields shine and gleam from constant polishing, whilst the leather and hide battle shields are oiled and readied. Daggers are sheathed and unsheathed and the throwing spears examined time and time again to ensure their line is straight and true. The youngest warriors pack slingshot into their leather pouches and test their aim against the granary walls.

Horses are dressed and the light war chariots, built with speed and manoeuvrability in mind, are readied. The bronze semi-circular trumpets, whose mouths are fashioned in the likeness of dragon heads, are cleaned so that their noise will ring out loud and true, instilling fear into our mortal enemies.

Those unmarried women who choose to fight alongside their brothers plaster their long hair with lime, and their tresses stand out as fierce emblems of aggression. They too polish their swords until they slide easily in and out of the scabbards they wear at their backs. The men apply dye to their faces and torsos, the patterns of victory squirming on their muscles in the firelight. Those women who would stay behind to tend the livestock, the children and the old and infirm, prepare amulets and charms for their loved ones to wear in battle. There is no-one to prepare such charms for me, and I cannot summon the enthusiasm to join in with the men, nor to paint my body or lime my hair. The Atres wasted no time in my absence, preparing for war and I feel as though I have entered a world I no longer recognise.

I scan the horizon and the distant hills for the hundredth time. It will be dusk soon and if all goes according to plan, the beacons will be lit one by one, until they travel the length and breadth of the Atres Kingdom. It will be the sign we all have all been waiting for. Then I see a glimmer on the horizon which grows in stature until there is no doubt to its nature as it spreads its message. The cry goes up and the command is given. At Buzzardstone's highest point, a torch is put to Caradwg's beacon. The carefully laid bonfire springs to life, and soon it relays its message to the neighbouring hill forts, just one link in a shining network of fireflies, glowing in the dark, and speaking of war.

THIRTY TWO

Viper's Fort

Chela

Once we leave the southern end of the Great Forest, we begin to feel safe for the first time from pursuit by Atres or Vellani alike. On the third day, we exit the Woods of Rhiw, and enter the agricultural lands of the Durotriges where barley, rye and emmer wheat grow in the fields. We journey now on the main drove-way and the dry-baked mud, disturbed by our horses' hooves, hangs as an ochre mist in the air, clogging our skin and irritating our lungs.

The region becomes increasingly populated and we begin to meet other travellers on the road. At one point we meet a party of Durotriges warriors who ask for any sign of a fair-haired woman and a young man travelling together. I answer them honestly and we are allowed to continue on our way.

Eventually we reach Vipers' Fort's massive gateway, with its towering ramparts. My home, and although I left under a cloud, I am glad to be back. I know the guard well, for I helped heal his son last summer, and so he waves us through the huge wooden gate with a smile. Immediately we are surrounded by a throng of children and curious on-lookers who have come to gawp at us, travel weary and dusty from the road as we are. New arrivals, who are obviously not traders, are a constant source of interest to those who live within the settlement. The children all know me, of course, and sing out their greetings. I grab one little urchin and tell him to run and warn Hanu's household that an important visitor awaits audience, so that no time will be lost as we recover from our journey.

I head straight to my house. There is no sign of Grypsos; no doubt he is working on his ship, if he has not left already. I let myself and my companions in, and whilst I light the fire, Briona washes the grime off her face and Brendan tends to the horses.

I survey my home. I have not been away all that long and although the spiders have invaded and left a number of fresh webs in the rafters, it still feels like home and as soon as the hearth is ablaze, the welcome is complete. Grypsos has filled the water pitcher and as the dried herbs I left behind have not been disturbed, I am able to prepare a restorative brew for myself and my companions.

'I must see Kendra, then we should see Hanu straightaway,' says Briona and though she is tired, she looks excited.

Almost before she has finished speaking, there is a knock at the door and Ivor's familiar head, wreathed in a broad smile, pokes itself around the door lintel.

'I knew you would not be long coming!' I am so pleased to see him and rush to embrace my old friend. 'Let me introduce you. This is Briona, Queen of the Atres. Briona, this is Ivor, second son of Hanu.'

I cannot help but laugh as I see disbelief followed by sheer amazement cross Ivor's face.

'You leave us, vowing never to return, and then come back with the Queen of the Atres!' Then turning to the Queen, Ivor bows. 'My house is your house, my Lady, but may I be so bold as to enquire the purpose of your unannounced visit?'

'Don't be so stuffy, Ivor,' I say. 'The Queen has come to collect her daughter, then we must speak with Hanu.'

'You are full of surprises, Chela, yet you have not introduced me to this patient warrior who sits quietly at your side.'

I introduce Brendan, who nods at Ivor.

'Chela, my dear,' says the Queen, 'may I get a word in edgeways?'

I grin at Ivor. He must be wondering why the Queen and I are on such familiar terms.

'Young Ivor. I am delighted to meet you and any kin of Hanu, who is an old friend of mine. But first, do you know the whereabouts of the girl who goes by the name of Kendra?'

'Armelle's slave girl?'

'Yes,' says Briona. 'She is my daughter.'

The news is clearly too much for Ivor. He shoots me a mystified look and sits himself down.

'Kendra! A Princess of the Atres? By Esu, why did she not speak up? Had we known, we would have returned her to you at once! We knew Irven accused us of harbouring his daughter, but we sent word to him that we did not have her! We had no idea the slave girl was of royal birth.'

He looks sheepish to me. There is clearly more to come.

'Irven didn't tell me that the Durotriges had been in contact,' says Briona, anxiety edging her voice. 'He is set on revenge. But all that can wait. I must see Kendra now.'

'I'm afraid we don't know where she is,' says Ivor, looking down at the ground. 'Gowell wanted to question her further about the

218

disappearance of her mistress, but no-one has seen her for five days. I am so sorry, my lady.'

'Where could she have gone?' I ask.

'We think Lann, the man who brought her here, must have taken her to be sold to the Veneti, but we cannot find him either.'

Briona lets out a cry.

'Oh, no, no, no,' she says. 'We can't have missed her!'

'I'll scour the harbour,' says Ivor. 'It may be that the slave ships have not left yet! In the meantime, I'll let Hanu know you're here.'

And with that he rises to his feet and dashes out of my house, barking orders to his attendant who stand outside. Now it is my turn to be stunned. Did Ivor really say Armelle had disappeared? What in the name of the Great Goddess has happened? I am burning with curiosity, but bite down my need to know. Kendra's welfare is more important, and although I know Riana will have the answer, I will wait with my mother and Brendan until there is news of my sister. Sister, mother. The words are strange to me. I glance at Brendan, who seems at a loss to know what to do and is sitting quietly cleaning his nails. What on earth am I going to do with him?

After what seems an interminable wait, Ivor returns.

'No boat carrying slaves has left in the last six days,' he says 'and every boat in the harbour has been searched. They are not on their way to Rome.' He looks relieved.

'That means Lann is in hiding with her nearby somewhere,' I say.

Ivor nodded.

'Why, I cannot begin to understand, but I have commanded our warriors to begin a search in all the farmsteads in the valley and every house and granary in the nearby hill forts. We will also send a search party to Saramis. There is no more we can do at present and I am sure he has not travelled far or we would have known. Gowell has had his scouts searching for Armelle, and with the Atres preparing to march on us, there are spies all over the place.'

Briona nods at Ivor, indicating that she is satisfied that they are doing their utmost to find Kendra.

'I see you already know of Irven's plans,' she says, looking Ivor in the eye.

'Of course we know. We are not entirely without guile!'

Briona is about to reply, but I interrupt.

'Tell me, what is this I hear of Armelle?' I ask, unable to contain myself any longer. 'What do you mean by her 'disappearance'? Could Kendra be with her?'

'Armelle left fourteen days ago, but we know Kendra was here, with Riana, some five days ago,' says Ivor. He fixes me with his gaze. 'Armelle ran off with that scoundrel of a bard, Keary.'

I am speechless. Armelle, Gowell's betrothed, run off with another! I surprise myself at my own reaction, which is not one of elation or vindication, but of pity for Gowell. But there are more pressing matters to consider and so I put Armelle out of my mind.

'The Queen wishes to speak with Hanu, Ivor. Can you take us to him?'

Just then Hanu's personal servant is seen hovering at the doorway. I beckon him in and without preamble, he asks that Briona, Queen of the Atres, attend Hanu at his house. I do not move to accompany the Queen, sensing that this is one encounter where Briona needs some privacy. As my mother stands, I squeeze her hand. Briona smiles at me and then at Brendan, before turning and following the servant out of the roundhouse.

'Now,' says Ivor, including Brendan in his smile. 'Tell me absolutely everything, and be sure to start from the very beginning!'

THIRTY THREE

Ravensroost

Lann

My Lord, Doran and I wait patiently in the cramped area outside Bryn's chamber. Hidden from view, the old man's laboured breathing can be heard through the wattle partition. The rest of the royal dwelling is full of priests and the crying of the women is getting on Doran's nerves. Bryn's end is imminent, so we have been told. Could it really be happening at last? The old man has clung on for months now in the twilight world of half life, half death. Is he truly about to relinquish his hold on this reality?

I am glad I am here, to witness his end. The girl, Kendra, and the others will be secure enough in that cave. I did not dare leave them at Viper's Fort, for my continued absence might have made her bold, and Huw is not a quick thinker. Better to hide them away for the time being. No-one will worry about them, mere slaves. They will think I have sold them on. I cannot tarry too long here, however. I have left enough food in the cave to last them ten days or so, and I do not wish the little one to starve to death – I want her as a present for my mother. Besides, Doran has told me to keep the Atres girl safe until all of this is over. Not long now.

The Veneti woman and the Bard, Keary, are here. Keary confounded Gowell by turning his cart around and effecting Armelle's escape by boat. Gowell would have thought the bard too poor to hire a boat and did not think to look to the sea, and instead deployed his warriors to search the land. What a joke! He is a true idiot, and does not for one moment suspect Doran. I too came by sea and it only took me three days.

One other thing I have learned since coming here is that the healer, Chela, was captured and was Doran's prisoner for a while. She escaped, it seems, with a strange smith who did not know his own name, and they were helped by Brendan, of all people! Who would have thought he had it in him! Doran tells me that he cares not that Chela escaped, for he doubts she poses any sort of threat to his plans. From what Armelle has told him, Chela is no longer welcome at Vipers' Fort in any case, and it is unlikely she would return to Gowell. The smith's disappearance, however, disturbs my lord for he tells me that there was more to the young man than met the eye and he should have got to the bottom of it. As for Brendan, he had not thought him capable of treachery, despite what happened to his lover.

I know that Doran, despite loving his father, is tired of waiting for Bryn to die. He needs to get on with his plans, unimpeded by protocol and the constraints imposed on him by the tribal Elders. Although in effect he has ruled his father's Kingdom since the old man fell ill, the Elders would object to Doran engaging the Vellani in war whilst the King is still alive but I know that what truly irks the Elders is the way Doran ignores them, deferring instead to the Druids of Lynd.

Word from the Atres is encouraging. They have started their march towards the northern Durotriges border. We have also received word that the Canti and Regni are readying to march on their eastern border. Strong as the Durotriges are, they will be weakened by attack on two fronts. The treachery amongst the Atres will ensure the death of their own leader and all that remains is for Doran to mop up the weakened forces. Whether Bryn dies this day or not, Doran will have to take his chance soon, with or without the blessing of the Vellani Elders.

So engrossed am I in my thoughts that I barely notice the Druid emerging from Bryn's chamber. The Brother beckons Doran in. I hesitate for a moment and then follow. Doran, thankfully, seems oblivious to my presence. Bryn was like a father to me, too, and I deserve to be with him to witness his last breath. The Priest does not make me leave, and for that I am grateful. Bryn is gasping in an eerie death-rattle that reverberates around the whitewashed walls. His face is drawn, yellow skin clinging to his skull. Doran is standing next to his bed, his huge form towering over his frail father.

Suddenly Bryn wakens from his death-sleep. His emaciated arm shoots out from under the fur and in a movement of supernatural swiftness, he grabs his son's wrist. Doran recoils in horror, but his father, with a strength borrowed from the grave that awaits him, holds him fast. Turning his ghastly head around, he gazes at his son and heir.

'It is a black day, indeed,' hisses Bryn. 'A black day.'

And with that, the old King falls back onto his pillows and breathes his last, relinquishing his grip on Doran's wrist as he passes away.

A sob reaches from the pit of my stomach and I find that I am crying. Doran is pale and stands, gazing at his father, then as though emerging from a trance, pulls himself together and looks at the Brother who is beginning to intone a prayer to the underworld.

'It is done,' he says.

Turning on his heels, he pushes past me, and leaves his father's roundhouse, and almost before he is out the door, the keening of the women begins in earnest.

Trumpets sound throughout Ravensroost and a crowd begins to gather outside Bryn's house. I have been waiting with Doran all night and am surprised to see that it is still dark, the dawn a mere streak of purple on the horizon.

Later that morning, Doran emerges from his roundhouse and calls for a meeting.

Once the Elders, Nobles and Brothers have assembled, Doran speaks. I notice he has no trace of tiredness about him, and marvel at his strength. Bryn's death hurts me, but I take solace in the knowledge that he died when his time was right, at the moment of his own choosing.

'You will all know by now that my father Bryn has moved on to his next life,' says Doran.

A murmur ripples through the room.

'I will see to it that he will have a funeral worthy of his life. For three days and three nights we will observe the customs. We will burn beacons and there will be feasting all the while.'

The crowd mutter their approval. In the distance the sound of keening can be heard. The noise will not abate for several days. Sadly, I will not be here to witness the rituals as I must be away on the morrow.

'Then we have another business to deal with,' continues Doran. 'You know that I have been preparing our warriors to fight.'

The muttering in the crowd increases and ripples through the room until one of the Brothers bangs a drum for silence.

'Let the King speak!' he shouts.

Referring to Doran as 'King' so soon after his father's death stuns the room into silence. They behold their new leader, for good or for ill. I know that the Elders have spoken to Doran on a number of occasions, trying to tease out his plans. He merely hinted that he wished to take over the lands of the Trinovantes, but he kept silent on the matter for the most part and not one of the Elders could summon the courage to challenge him. I also know the Elders disapprove of him stealing Armelle away from the Durotriges, but I do not think he cares. Before he can speak, however, Doran is interrupted by the Elder, Glenwin.

'Whom do we fight, and for what reason, my lord?' he asks, not even trying to conceal his disapproval. I appraise Glenwin, recently elected to the Council of Elders, and laugh inwardly. If this is the only opposition the Elders can summon, Doran's way forward is easy.

'I have it on good authority that the Durotriges are planning to march on us,' says Doran.

But Glenwin has not finished speaking.

'Hardly surprising my lord, since you stole the Veneti woman from under their noses,' he says, casting his eyes around the room for support. Not one of the Elders meets his gaze.

Doran, seeing Glenwin's isolation, takes his chance and rounds on the man, freezing him to the spot with his glare.

'Hanu's plans were hatched a long time before I rescued Armelle from the Durotriges,' he hisses, asserting his power. 'I act for the good of the Vellani, remember that!'

Doran then proceeds to tell the assembly of the plans of the Atres, Canti and Regni, highlighting the advantages to be gleaned from a victory over the combined southern tribes. When he finishes talking, he looks around the room, assessing the mood. I can see the reaction is not entirely negative.

'Then we will be well placed, it seems,' says Glenwin, trying to regain the Court's favour, 'to forge an alliance with the Veneti.'

'Indeed we will,' says Doran, his eyes gleaming. 'Enough for now. Let me mourn my father in peace. We will meet again on the morrow.'

As the warriors, Elders and Brothers begin to disperse, Doran takes me to one side.

'The boy Annan,' he says.

'Yes my Lord?' I ask, but I already know where his words are leading and lick my lips in anticipation.

'Put him to death. Do it discreetly. Then return to Vipers' Fort and hold the girl until you hear of our victory.'

'Then I can kill her?'

'Yes. Or sell her. It's up to you.'

I nod and smile, stroking the scar on my face. I have already made my choice.

THIRTY FOUR

A cave on the Durotriges coast

Kendra

I have lost track of the days we have spent in this godforsaken cave. The only thing that marks the passing of day into night and night into day is the far distant glimmer at the cave's mouth. We are so deep within this hole that shouting for attention would be futile. We try of course, from time to time, but no-one hears us.

Lann has planned this well. There is enough food for us to live on for perhaps ten or so days, if we are careful, and there are two pitchers of water. The food is mainly cheeses with thick rinds, and bread that hardens by the day. There are also some leathery and bitter strips of dried rose hip for us to chew on and some dried fish. At least we will not die for want of food or water. A fire would cheer us up, but Lann has made sure we do not have that luxury. I know he will return, otherwise he would not have bothered with the provisions and it is this thought alone that stops me descending into despair.

Our chains mean we cannot move far and it is humiliating to have to defecate so close to each other, but it is surprising what one can get used to and even the smell our each other's waste no longer offends our nostrils.

Malvina worries me. At first her health seemed to improve a little but the darkness and the lack of air in this place has dragged her down. We sing to keep our spirits up but there is only so much singing we can do and most often we are caught up in our own fears, examining our inner souls in the pitch darkness. Cator tries again and again to free the chain from its anchor, but Lann has fastened it well; it will not budge.

Our conversation goes around in circles.

'We should try and escape,' says Cator. 'Perhaps Lann will not return, he has been gone a long while.'

My answer is usually the same.

'Oh Cator, even if we could free ourselves from the rock, how can we possibly climb back up that cliff, shackled as we are, with Malvina in the state she is in? And we cannot leave her alone.'

'I know,' says Cator. 'I just feel so useless.'

We have this conversation, or one just like it, every day, hoping that Malvina's health will improve enough for her to walk, so that we can send her out to find some living soul, to fetch help, but she seems to be getting weaker, her will to live ebbing away with each glimmer of dusk or dawn, I know not which.

We huddle close for comfort and sing children's songs, or tell stories of vengeful gods and beasts and faeries – familiar stories we were all taught at our mothers' hearths. And we sleep, of course, but our sleep is not good. Cator and I shout and cry out in our dreams. Malvina whimpers and the sound of her suffering makes me want to cover my ears.

She is sleeping now, and I lean against Cator's strong and wiry body while I explore the tender areas around my neck where the iron has rubbed the skin raw. I need honey for the wound, lest it fester. Honey! Such things speak of normality and sanity, not for the reality I inhabit right now. It is difficult to get comfortable, wearing these neck irons, but we speak together of happier times and plan what we will do when we get home.

'What will you do about Fionn?' asks Cator, as he traces a finger around my eye socket.

'I will tell him that I cannot marry him, betrothal or no betrothal,' I say. Cator's touch is tender and I feel a sudden and intense surge of love for him.

'Our liaison will not go down at all well,' says Cator, his fingers lingering on my lips. 'Me a commoner, you a future Queen.'

'After what we have been through, I'm sure we can weather that storm,' I say, kissing his fingers. 'I don't want to be a Queen, in any case. Not now.'

'Oh, what a pity, I would have made such a good King too!'

I find myself smiling at Cator's attempt at humour but the seriousness of our predicament reasserts itself. We lapse, once more, into a silence that is punctuated only by Malvina's laboured breathing.

THIRTY FIVE

Viper's Fort

Briona

I blink, trying to adjust to the gloomy interior of the roundhouse. I stand motionless in the doorway, until at last, I am able to make out Hanu's form in the shadows.

Then he is in front of me, taking my hands in his. I feel odd, as though I have become detached from my own body, watching everything unfold from behind a veil. Here is a face I have carried in my mind's eye for more than twenty summers. It is that face, yet it is not. Hanu has those same laughing grey eyes, and mad eyebrows that spring out in all directions. I remember their bushiness from my youth but twenty years on they have exceeded all expectations. His lips are still full and sensuous, as I remember. Then I recall his deep throaty laugh and wonder if he still carries it with him, or have forty bitter winters snatched it away? As he smiles I notice he has lost a few teeth, but that is not so unusual in a man his age. His neck is still strong and muscular and he carries himself well, though his belly does seem to round a little more than it ought. All of this I absorb in the instant before he raises my hands to his lips and kisses my fingertips. I feel confused and at a loss to know what to do, but I do not withdraw straightaway.

'Hanu,' I say. 'It is good to see you again.'

He does not reply but instead leads me to a leather seat. Sitting opposite me, he leans forward and holds my gaze as I sip his finest wine from an exotic goblet. It is made of glass! How exquisite!

'You are as beautiful and as strong as the day I met you,' he says finally, slicing through the awkwardness that has welled up between us. I can tell he regrets his words as soon as they have left his mouth, for they have a ring of hollowness about them. I too, wish he had not spoken, for something has been shattered, some dream I held.

'I am not here Hanu,' I say, surprised at the irritation in my own voice, 'to fish for compliments or to court your love! I have come to find my daughter before Irven, who has lost all reason, marches on your lands.'

Hanu sits back in his chair, and now there is a gulf between us. I wonder if my words were too harsh.

227

'I had no idea we harboured your daughter,' he says, his hand curling around the carved boars' head of his armrest as though to draw strength from its solidity.

'You really didn't know anything?' I ask, my voice softening.

'I never took your daughter,' says Hanu. 'And when I heard Irven's accusations, I instigated a search for the Atres princess throughout my land. She was nowhere to be found. I sent this message to your husband long ago, but it seems he preferred not to believe me. It did not occur to me for one moment it was the slave girl! When I spoke with her, she let me believe she was Silures, I swear!'

I appraise the man sitting opposite me. He is the most powerful leader in the land and though still charismatic, he appears small and insecure in his ignorance. How could he have failed to discover what was going on? Taking a deep breath, for I am committed now, I tell Hanu everything, how Kendra was kidnapped, the discovery of the Durotriges brooch, Lann's duplicity, and Irven's anger.

'As for Lann, I cannot begin to fathom his motives, for he was here in good faith, but as for Irven, why didn't he talk to me instead of leaping to such conclusions? I would have invited him to search if he didn't believe me.'

'I tried to tell him, but his hatred and bitterness had ripened fit to burst.'

'He hated me that much?'

'He suspected I always ..... had feelings for you and he knew deep down that you lied to save my honour,' I say. 'He hated you for it.'

'And did you?'

I look at him blankly.

'Did you always love me?'

I am lost for words. Had anyone asked me before I walked into Hanu's presence, I would have said yes, without a doubt. But now I am not so sure. This man in front of me is so different to the image I have been carrying inside myself all these years.

'I..I thought of you a great deal,' I say eventually, 'and Irven must have sensed that, but our marriage was never a happy one, and not just because of you.'

Before Hanu can reply, a noise is heard outside the hut. A guard knocks on the wooden porch-frame before poking his head around the entrance, announcing the arrival of two clan leaders from the east of the Durotriges lands. Hanu answers gruffly before turning towards me.

'We will talk again, soon,' he says. 'Thank you. Thank you for coming to see me.'

'There is something I must tell you,' I say. 'Though you probably know already.'

Hanu raises his eyebrows.

'The Regni and Canti have allied with the Atres and are amassing on your eastern borders as we speak.'

Hanu looks as though he has been struck by Taranis himself.

'What?' he shouts. 'This cannot be true! I would have known!'

'Irven has kept it a closely guarded secret. He plans to divide your forces.'

Hanu explodes into action. Shouting at his slave, he commands his sons to attend him. Gowell pokes his head around the door and Hanu orders him to arrange an urgent gathering at the Folk meet. The clan leaders are mostly already present, ready to take orders to deal with the threat from the north, but this is clearly a troubling new development.

Hanu sits down again, his head in his hands.

'How stupid I have been,' he says. 'I'm sorry, Briona, but there is much to be done. You will attend our Folk meet, of course. It will be on the morrow. I will send word when all are assembled.'

I stand to leave, but Hanu addresses me again.

'The matter of your daughter. We are scouring the area for Kendra. Rest assured we will find her.'

I shake my head. I cannot meet his eyes.

'Thank you, but I fear we may be too late. One good thing has come about though, but I will tell you another time.'

'Go on.'

'Chela, your healer. It turns out she is my eldest daughter. I have found one and lost another, it seems.'

Hanu smiles at me.

'You knew? Elanor told you?'

'She showed me Chela's bracelet. I remember Elanor turning up all those years ago with a tiny baby. She is a lovely girl, and I have seen to it personally that neither she nor Elanor ever went without. Irven was truly a monster. A man who would put his own child to death...'

'Irven was influenced by the Druid, Deryn. He is weak,' I say, and I realise I sound as though I am defending my husband. 'Thank you for looking after her, but I did not want to find one daughter only to lose another.'

'Don't worry. We will find Kendra. Will you stay with us?'

229

'I don't know, Hanu. My life is a mess, I cannot return to Irven, but I would like to stay until I know what has happened to Kendra.'

'So it was not for my sake that you came?' Hanu smiles. I wonder if he expects me to squirm under his gaze, but I look him in the eye.

'What passed between us was a long time ago,' I reply. 'You have had a wife and many children.'

'You did not ask me,' he says. 'Don't you want to know?'

I feel anxious all of a sudden and realise I am shaking. I know he is talking about our love. Perhaps some things are better left unsaid, but it is too late to undo what has been done. I wait for him to continue.

'I loved you then and I love you now,' he says. 'But it did not prevent me from also loving the woman who bore my children. It was different, but no less worthy.'

I return his smile, liking his honesty, but I have no words. It is too late for me and Hanu; I know that much in my heart.

'We will find Kendra, depend on it,' he says and as I move to leave, he places his warm hand on the bare skin of my arm, but my body does not respond. I feel nothing and I know that any dreams I harboured of our union were just the imaginings of a lonely woman.

THIRTY SIX

Chela

I scrutinise my mother's face, trying to gauge her emotions, but I do not ask how the reunion went, for my roundhouse is full of visitors. Grypsos has returned with Yarrow, whose care he has taken over whilst Ivor busies himself. The overjoyed hound keeps flinging himself at me, almost bowling me over each time.

'Down!' I shout. 'Out!' But Yarrow continues to disobey me, much to the amusement of my friends, and I cannot say I am altogether displeased for I have missed him too. Riana is here, as is Erea and Cinea, although Ivor has already left to join his father. Once Briona is introduced, she excuses herself to go and rest, whilst Grypsos and Brendan set off together to examine the Greek sailor's boat. We women are left alone and soon the conversation turns to Armelle and her 'disappearance'.

'I don't know what to tell Bearcban,' says Riana, who is worried about reprisals against her own kin back home.

'It's not your fault,' says Erea. 'Your role was simply to escort her. You could not have known how it would turn out.'

'She's right,' says Cinea. 'Don't worry. I'm sure you won't be blamed.'

'I knew she was fond of the bard, but I still can't believe she would have considered him worthy,' says Riana.

'Perhaps it was someone else,' I say, remembering Doran's interest in Armelle.

'You know something?' asks Cinea, quick as ever.

'Nothing definite, just a feeling,' I reply. Gowell should be the first to hear what I have to say.

'Well, she fooled us all,' says Riana, biting her lip.

'How is Gowell taking all of this?' I ask, trying to sound matter-of-fact.

'He was truly angry at first,' says Erea. 'And I believe he would have killed them both on the spot, but he has calmed down now.'

'He broods, and is quiet,' says Cinea. 'I think his pride has been badly bruised, but he'll get over it.'

'You should go and see him,' says Riana.

'Do you think he wants to see me? After all that happened?'

'I am sure of it,' says Riana. 'From what Ivor tells me, he is truly sorry for the way he treated you.'

'Well that's something,' I say and I flash Riana a smile. 'And you and Ivor, what news is there?'

Riana blushes crimson, much to the amusement of Cinea and Erea, who hoot with laughter.

'There is nothing to tell!' she protests.

'They are inseparable!' says Erea. 'And we are all delighted. I'm sure when all this is over, there will be an announcement.'

Erea's comment brings us back to the reality of our predicament and the imminent threat of war. We fall silent for a moment, contemplating the forthcoming battle.

'Will you bear arms Chela?' asks Cinea.

'I'm a healer, not a killer, though I can wield a sword as good as any man. I'd rather see to the sick, though, than kill, so I'll stay here and tend the wounded. After all, don't forget I am Atres by blood. And you? Will you fight?'

'Yes, of course, and so will Erea. We will stand alongside our brothers.'

'Then I wish you well,' says Riana. 'We Veneti women do not know how to fight, but I would stand by Ivor if I could.'

'We know you would, you are one of us now,' says Erea, squeezing Riana's arm. 'And Chela, Atres you may be by blood, but you are also my sister at heart.'

I am grateful to Erea for her words. I pat Yarrow's head and the dog licks my hand, wet and soft. It is good to be back amongst people who care for me. Regardless of my origins, this is, after all, my home.

It is not until the next day that I see Gowell. I am outside, fetching wood for the fire, when I see him striding towards me. As he approaches, I try to look aloof and disinterested, but as soon as I see his face, I realise the man suffers. Good. He deserves to, but despite my resolve, I cannot help but soften towards him.

'Chela,' he says. 'How goes it with you?'

'Well, Gowell. The mark on my neck has gone, at least.'

Gowell winces and is about to turn away when I catch his arm. I want him to suffer, but not to leave. Not just yet. Encouraged by this gesture, he raises his eyes and looks at me.

'I'm so sorry,' he says and I hear his voice catch in his throat. 'Come, will you walk with me?'

I nod and when he offers his arm, I tuck my hand in the crook of his elbow. The gesture is familiar. Before he set off to collect his Veneti bride we would often walk together thus. We pick our way through the settlement, avoiding the storage pits that dot the ground, those filled with corn seed have been sealed, but those no longer in use are filling up with offerings to the underworld. The stench of rotting carcasses occasionally hits our nostrils, food for the hungry goddess Ferana, who lurks beneath the ground.

Before long we reach the edge of Vipers' Fort's woodland. Still visible from the Folk meet, we are just out of earshot of anyone who would listen in on our conversation.

'I see you have found your mother,' he says. 'Who would have thought it, Chela, a princess of the Atres!'

'I am happy to have found her, and you are right, I would not have dreamt in a thousand seasons that I was of royal blood.'

'I should have known you were no commoner,' says Gowell, grinning at me. I feel myself melting. I could never resist his smile. 'All the trouble you gave me when we were growing up, you were way too haughty for a farmer's daughter!'

'It makes no difference now,' I say, looking away into the distance. 'My newfound Atres kin are about to throw their lives away in a futile war. I don't expect my father to prevail against Hanu. The Atres will be defeated, I am sure of it.'

'Hanu has no desire to see the Atres crushed,' says Gowell. 'This quarrel between our fathers goes back a long time. Perhaps there will be a chance to stop this madness.'

'Irven thinks Hanu stole his daughter,' I say. I do not mention Briona as I am not sure how much Gowell knows of the history between our respective parents. 'He refuses to believe the Durotriges are innocent in all of this.'

'Aye,' says Gowell. 'And therein lies the madness.'

We are silent for a little while, then Gowell speaks again.

'I did not drag you up here to talk politics,' he says, taking my hand in his. I do not pull away.

'I want to say that I am so sorry that I hurt you. I was angry and did not stop to think that Armelle could have caused the death of her unborn child herself. She did not love me, did not want me and now she has run off with a common minstrel, for all her airs and graces.'

I look at Gowell, and try to make my voice even.

'There is something you must know,' I say, taking a deep breath. 'I don't think it was Keary she went to be with. Yes, he helped her escape, but it was to Doran she fled.'

Gowell turns pale and his lower lip begins to twitch on one side, a tell-tale sign of his pent-up rage.

'The bastard son of a dog!' he says through clenched teeth. 'All that nonsense about wanting to see how we ran things around here! What a fool I have been.'

I try to think of something to say, but can think of nothing that will not sound banal. Gowell's hand feels heavy and clammy in mine. I ease myself from his grasp and cross my arms in front of my stomach. I am not ready for another display of Gowell's ill-temper, even though it would not be directed at me. Gowell struggles with himself awhile, then seems to calm.

'Don't worry, Chela, Armelle is nothing to me now. I see her for what she really is. What angers me most is that I have been played for such a fool.'

'Gowell,' I begin, but he silences me, placing a finger against my lips as he pulls me towards him, seeking out a kiss.

I pull away. I am not ready for this. Gowell must sense that he has been hasty and relaxes his hold, but seeks out my eyes. When he has my full attention, he speaks.

'Chela. I have treated you ill, but I see that you have it in your heart to forgive me.'

I nod, wondering what is coming.

'I should have listened to you before,' he continues. 'You and I were meant to be together. I was a fool.'

I am finding it difficult to breathe and feel light-headed.

'Chela, when all this fighting is over, will you marry me? Will you be my wife?'

I open my mouth to frame my words, but no sound comes out. I clear my throat and try again. I know what I want to say, but cannot seem to say it. Just as I am about to speak, there is a commotion from the vicinity of the Folk meet. People are shouting and a young lad is running towards us. Gowell stands to see what the fuss is about.

'Come quick! Hanu wants you now,' says the boy, gasping for air.

Gowell turns to look at me.

'I must go,' he says. 'But think on what I have asked.'

I watch my lover of old receding in the distance. A dozen different emotions jostle for supremacy somewhere between my chest and my navel. Not knowing what to do, I walk back to where Riana and the other women are gathered. The soothing motion of walking clears my head and by the time I reach the others, I have calmed myself sufficiently so as not to attract any questions from my well-meaning friends.

THIRTY SEVEN

Briona

I have been in the Folk meet all morning, listening to Hanu issuing orders, taking oaths from his clan leaders and ensuring that each and every one of them has their full quota of men to hand. He is in control, sober, and commands the respect of his clan leaders. I cannot help but compare him to Irven, who lost his way many years ago. I feel strange, sitting in what is, after all, the enemy camp. Then I remind myself that Irven ordered my death, and I am no longer welcome amongst my own people.

Hanu's scouts have told him the Atres army is a mere three days march away. The direction they are taking means they will be forced to traverse White Stone Valley where Hanu plans to greet them from the ridge overlooking the vale.

The Atres choice of route would have puzzled Hanu, had it not been for my information. The valley itself, whose dry floor is dotted with boulders, is hard to negotiate and Hanu would have the advantage, chopping Irven's army down before it could make any headway. But the Canti-Regni assault from the east makes sense of Irven's plans, effectively trapping the Durotriges warriors between two armies.

The warriors and elders have been in discussion for what seems an age and they are now having a brief but well-earned rest. Gowell has wandered off but I remain, for I do not wish to miss anything. Gowell and Ivor do not trust me, this much I can tell, and I do not blame them. I must work to earn their Trust.

Suddenly there is a commotion outside. Hanu looks up sharply as a young man, dishevelled and out of breath, barges in through the doorway.

'Annan! By Esu! What is the meaning of this?' says Hanu, rising to his feet.

It is clear that the young man has something important to say, otherwise his entrance would have been barred, and so he is ushered in. Without preamble, he blurts out his news. I watch as Hanu turns pale, clenching and unclenching his fists. The vein in his neck is throbbing. Ivor is already at his side. Hanu calls for Gowell, who comes running.

It is bad enough he has had to learn of his neighbours' duplicity from me, his enemy's wife, but when Annan arrives with the news of the Vellani's plans to annihilate the battle weary Durotriges, the Folk meet is thrown into uproar.

'How in the Great Mother's name could we have missed this?' Hanu roars at the assembly, all of whom remain silent, dumbstruck. The Durotriges' lack of intelligence is becoming an embarrassment, making them appear weak.

'Thank the Gods that young Annan here,' he says, slapping the young man on the shoulder, 'was able to reach us in time.'

'A fair wind sped me on my way, My Lord, but it could have been different. Doran wanted me dead. He is setting one tribe against the next. He plans to destroy all the tribes of the south and take control of us when we are all weakened.'

The young man is given refreshments and is allowed to tell his tale.

'It was the day after Bryn's death. I was grooming the late King's favourite mare, Onica, near the royal roundhouse when I heard the call for the meeting,' he says. 'Out of curiosity, I made my way to the Folk meet and stood just outside, behind one of the chicken houses. Not only did I hear all that was said, but I overheard Doran tell Lann to seek me out and put me to death! My blood ran cold, I can tell you, when I realised what was in store for me and for my kin back home.'

A murmur of accord ripples through the Folk meet. Encouraged, he proceeds with his story.

'I hid myself in the deep shadows behind the Vellani Folk meet until I was sure no-one was watching and then sneaked back towards Bryn's house. I saw Lann stride off towards Canogus' house, where I was lodging, and I knew I did not have much time. I made straight to where Onica was tethered and mounted her, urging her through the settlement, towards the western gateway. No-one paid me any attention. I was a familiar sight, remember, exercising the King's mare, and the news of Bryn's death was the only topic on people's minds. The battle plans had yet to reach the wider populace of Ravensroost.'

'I had only the clothes in which I stood and both myself and Onica would need provisions. I knew that riding overland through the Woods of Rhiw would be hard and slow. The alternative land routes, through the Canti and Regni territories would put me in grave danger and consume too much time. It would be safer and a great deal quicker for me to head for the coast and travel by sea.'

The Elders and Hanu nod their heads in agreement. I realise that as they listen to young Annan, each of them is wondering how the

Durotriges could have missed the signs of such deep treachery. Half listening to Annan's story, I mull over Bryn's passing. He was a good man, true to his word, but by all accounts his son is of a different mould.

'There is a farmstead on the borders of the Vellani and Trinovanti lands,' continues Annan, 'where an aunt of my lives with a Trinovanti farmer. I had not seen them in many months and as far as I am aware, no-one at Ravensroost knew of my kinship to her. Her name was Lilia and although she has a face as leathery as a water skin and her stomach hangs to her knees, she is pleasant enough.'

I can tell that Annan is enjoying telling his tale and the gathering indulge him, laughing at his description of his aunt, for he has risked much to bring his news. He takes a drink of wine before continuing.

'More importantly,' he says, 'Lilia lives close to the estuary of the Great River from whence I was able to pay using six sheep and a horse, borrowed from my aunt, for a boat and small crew to bring me here. She lives half a day's ride in the opposite direction to where the Vellani would expect me to flee and I was with her by suppertime.'

'And your pursuer?' enquires Ivor. 'Did Lann catch up with you?'

Annan grins broadly. He is clearly pleased with himself.

'He followed hard on my heels. He was not so easily duped, for he has clever mind, trained by the Brothers, but fortunately he was alone. I reached a boggy area and thought of a means of throwing him off my track. I dived into the bog, pretending I had fallen from my horse, and went under, but what Lann did not know, is that I used a reed to help me breath. A long cold time was I in that bog, with my eyes closed and my nostrils held tight, using just the reed for air, until I could stand it no more. I emerged from the bog, looking like a sacrifice come to life. I swear I would have frightened the bravest warrior! Anyway, Lann was nowhere to be seen. He must have given up, believing I had drowned.'

Annan is thanked and told to go and rest. I, along with everyone else at the Folk meet, marvel at the youth's bravery. I can understand why his pursuer did not follow him into the bog, for such places belong to Eluna, where the sacrifices are left for her to devour. A man risks his very life when he enters her dread waters.

'Take whatever treasures you wish, and make sure your aunt is recompensed tenfold,' says Hanu. 'You and she have earned them!'

Once Annan has gone, Gowell stands to address the Folk meet. Like his father, he is filled with rage.

'Doran has been meddling since he returned from Rome,' he says through gritted teeth. 'He cares not what he does, nor whom he offends. He will bring ruin on all of the land.'

'But at least we are warned and can do something,' says Ivor. 'And we learned much from Bearcban about the war tactics of the Romans when we were in Armorica, if you recall. No doubt Doran plans to try them out on us.'

Gowell, still standing, turns and points at me.

'Father, how can we trust the Atres Queen? She is Irven's wife after all. Could this not be a trap?' he asks.

I know he has been wanting to voice his suspicions all morning. As expected, the Folk meet voice their support. I try to hide my anxiety.

It is seldom that Hanu's sons experience their father's ire, but when Hanu turns his uncharacteristically icy gaze on Gowell, I am sure the young man's stomach must have churned.

'I, personally, will vouch for Briona's word,' he roars. 'I will hear no more on the subject.'

Gowell nods and exchanges a glance with Ivor. After a few moments Hanu calms himself sufficiently to continue.

'Gowell, I want you and Ivor to take the Clans of Rowan and Nared, Arth, Gefail and Coedgenau to the Golden Meadows. Leave as soon as you can. I will take the remaining clans to the north to meet the Atres.'

'How can we be sure of the Regni-Canti route?' asks Gowell.

'Fiacre and Neale, our kinsmen from the east, report suspicious troop movements just south of the Woods of Rhiw. Our enemy's only feasible route would be through the Golden Meadows. I am counting on you to take them by surprise and then march on to meet me at the Vale of the White Stones.'

'But if we are late, that would leave only seven clans to defend the White Stones against the Atres,' says Ivor. 'Will you have enough men?'

Hanu shrugs.

'They will have to be enough. With our army divided, on each front our forces and those of our enemy will be equal. Our victory is by no means guaranteed but I am counting on you both to rout the Canti-Regni alliance, for if you fail, I cannot hope to stand against the Vellani as well as the Atres with only seven clans. But let us not think of failure before we have even begun. Once you have vanquished our treacherous neighbours, you must join me at the White Stones so that at the very least, we will be able to meet the Vellani with a show of force.'

The speech is solemn and the entire room lapses into a silence. They Durotriges have been complacent, thinking they need not make too much effort to quash the Atres in the north, but things are different now.

'If only I had paid more attention to my neighbours,' Hanu says, berating himself. 'By the gods! I have taken my eye off the mark. What a fool I have been! I have squandered my attention on the Veneti and did not look to the land. I will not make that mistake again!'

'And Irven's posturing and talk of war hid the real threat,' says Gowell. 'We failed to see how Doran orchestrated all of this.'

'Aye, we did,' says Hanu. 'But let us not dwell on our mistakes. There is much to be done.'

And with that, the meeting disperses, each person sent to carry out his task, Gowell and Ivor heading north-eastwards, whilst Hanu himself prepares to face my husband, his old enemy, and a hatred that has been burning for a generation.

THIRTY EIGHT

Through the Lands of the Atres

Fionn

The horns reverberate across the land, their sonorous tones alerting the farmers to the army that marches their way. Even though I do not want this war, I find my pulse quickening.

As is the custom, Irven rides at the front, resplendent in his brightly painted war chariot, surrounded by his own clan, his ceremonial shield gleaming bright in the summer sunlight. Those of Irven's Elders who are fit enough to travel ride alongside the King, and I notice the mixture of expressions on their aged faces, for it is known some still oppose the war. Irven's massive stallion, Gelert, pulls the chariot across the rough ground and is likewise bedecked in finery. The thrice-polished bronze terrets, with their swirling designs, hang from the horse's harness, interwoven with bright cloth and feathers. On his back Irven carries his sword, sheathed in its scabbard, and in one hand he holds a lance, its iron tip yet unsullied by blood. Once the battle is joined, he will cast aside the ceremonial shield for one of toughened leather and wood and will ride on Gelert's back, but for now it is important for him to look the part of King. I have to concede that Irven does indeed look powerful, and for once, sober.

Following the royal clan come my kin, the House of Morffryn. I am mounted on my new white stallion, and ride alongside my father's chariot, too full of shame to look Caradwg in the eye. I recall how mellifluous my father's pledge sounded only yesterday and marvel at the depths of treachery my own kin can plumb. But I am in no position to condemn Caradwg, for my oath of loyalty to Irven is still sour upon my own tongue.

I count two hundred or so of Irven's household guard and clan, and I know that each of the other Atres clans can summon between one and two hundred warriors apiece. The army, in total, numbers around two thousand, five hundred souls, half that of the entire Durotriges forces. I know Irven is not worried. The King is confident in the Canti-Regni's ability to destroy part of Hanu's army, thereby evening the odds.

But I do not share the King's optimism and my secret rests heavily upon me. The closer the battle, the more agitated I become. Briona would have reached the Durotriges by now, in time to alert Hanu, who will deal swiftly with the Canti-Regni alliance before bringing his entire army to face us. Can I stand by and watch while my own kin are annihilated? And if the Vellani renege on their word and fail to come to the aid of the rebellious clans, we will all perish. Should I come clean and tell Caradwg of Briona's survival? Or Irven, even? I should have spoken up earlier, for my delay will be seen as treachery, and neither my father nor the King would hesitate in killing me where I stand. It is not cowardice that silences me. It is the knowledge that my death would be futile, for it will not avert the war.

Three days we march. By night the warriors camp and light small fires around which they play dice, tell stories and cook their suppers from food given freely by the local farmers. Those who have kin nearby are offered a bed whereas those without, make do with makeshift shelters of branches and hide. Once in Durotriges land matters will be different. The killing will start, as our warriors take by force what they need, slaying any who bar their way.

Each evening Irven rides amongst his troops, talking to the men, rousing their spirits and stirring a hatred towards the Durotriges who are now blamed for every cattle raid we have suffered over the last twenty years. Even the spates of bad harvest and poor trade are somehow linked to our enemy. In the hearts of most of the Atres army, there is now no doubt that the Durotriges must be crushed.

For those who have been won over by Caradwg's persuasion, not only is there a promise of victory over the Durotriges and access to the much coveted trade with the Veneti, but a new leader for our tribe, one who will look out for all their needs and who does not drown himself senseless with wine at every available opportunity.

It is the second night and I am sitting at my father's dying campfire, my head in my hands. Caradwg and the Elders of my clan are asleep and only the sentries are about, keeping their eyes peeled in case of a surprise attack. I am tired, but sleep eludes me. What to do? I stand abruptly then begin to pace back and forth, looking to the horizon, in the direction of the enemy.

'Enemy? Hanu is not my enemy,' I mutter to myself.

Then, through the fog of my thinking, an idea crystallises. An idea that has been there all along, simply waiting to be recognised. I know what I must do. It is risky, but I have no choice.

Relief floods through me and as I look at the sky, a gentle breeze stirs, seeming to blow away my confusion.

THIRTY NINE

Viper's Fort

Chela

I am standing with Riana on the ramparts of Vipers' Fort, watching Hanu's army leave, heading north and west.

Gowell and Ivor left yesterday and I cried to see my friends go to war. The brothers rode at the front, flanked on either side by their sisters, whose long limed hair rose like the fabled lion's mane from their foreheads, sweeping backwards into spikes half way down their backs. The men were also limed and had adorned themselves with blue war paint, crushed from azurite to a fine powder, mixed with goose grease, then smeared over their bodies. Those mounted on horses carried a sword at their back, a dagger at their belt and a spear in one hand. They looked so brave, and yet, as they receded into the distance, small and vulnerable.

And today, as we wave off Hanu's army, Viper's Fort wears a cloak of silence and feels heavy and oppressive.

'Where is Briona?' asks Riana.

'She is with Hanu,' I say. 'He has given the order that not a hair on her head is to be touched, on pain of death.'

'Then I am glad,' says Riana. 'I pray she will be safe.'

I look at my companion and cannot help but smile. If we two had not become friends, I would have thought all Veneti women were like Armelle.

I turn my attention back to the army and wave one last time.

'You British women are so strong,' says Riana, whose tears are flowing freely. 'I can hardly believe that Cinea and Erea have gone to war alongside their brothers.'

'It is how we are raised,' I say, but I too am struggling to maintain my equilibrium. I put an arm around Riana's shoulders.

'I know it was hard for you, watching Ivor go to battle,' I say.

Riana sniffs.

'He asked me to marry him before he left,' she says. 'He was so modest. Can you believe he actually thought I might turn him down?' She laughs through her tears.

'I am pleased for you,' I say. 'He will return, I am sure of it.'

My thoughts turn to Gowell. The two brothers are so different. 'Modest' is not a word that could ever be used to describe Gowell, but nonetheless, he has his charms. I have not given him an answer and I know that when he returns, he will want to know my decision. If he returns. And then there is Fionn. I have grown fond of him. He is kind, generous and handsome, but so very young, and promised to Kendra. I wonder what he is doing, and whether he will be alright. Will he have to fight the Durotriges? I imagine Fionn and Gowell facing each other, swords drawn. One would have to die, but I cannot decide which one.

As my thoughts turn towards death, I shiver, despite the early morning heat. The army have disappeared out of sight and so Riana and I walk back into the heart of Vipers' Fort, clinging onto each other for comfort.

There is much to be done. Cloth will have to be cut into strips to bandage the wounded, salves made to stop wounds festering, and pokers cleaned in readiness to cauterise those wounds that will not stop bleeding. Elanor taught me well. I know what to do and I order young children and slaves alike to fetch water and fuel for the fires and straw for bedding-down the injured. Broths of pork and barley simmer in every hearth, and herbs to dull pain will be gathered and infused in the imported olive oil or water.

Riana and I work for two whole days and often well into the night, chatting by the light of the small pottery lamps that hang around the large roundhouse. I often speak of Kendra; wondering if my sister is still alive. Part of me wants to go in search of her, but every corner of the Durotriges land has already been turned, and I realise the futility of such action. Besides, I am needed here.

When we have done as much as we can, we try to rest, but to each of us sleep comes only fitfully and when at last the dawn of the third day arrives, Riana and I both know that our loved ones are preparing to face their death.

FORTY

The Vale of the White Stones

Fionn

I sit astride my horse, struggling to see the Durotriges army through the dawn mist that lingers in Vale of the White Stones. I rub my injured leg. It is stiff from the nights spent in the open and I wonder if it will ever stop aching.

I declined Caradwg's offer to lead and now I feel keenly my insignificance, my individuality eaten up by the Atres army whose men form a line across the northern end of the valley. At the front are the sling-shotters, followed by foot soldiers. Behind them range the horsemen and at the rear, the chariots. We are a good twenty men deep. In the middle of the Atres line, at the front, I can see Irven standing on his war chariot, surrounded by his warriors. Taking up the rear, at Irven's right flank, stands the House of Morffryn, where I now wait, and on Irven's left, the Atres clans who remain ignorant of Caradwg's scheming.

Directly across the valley floor, the Durotriges warriors wait. They too must have marched through the day and night on the open roads and tracks, until they reached the Vale. A river must have at one time wound its way at its base, now all that can be seen are boulders and ferns, a perfect nesting sites for adders, but worthless in the eyes of the local farmers. I notice that the Durotriges warriors are perhaps slightly less in number than the Atres, indicating two possibilities; the first that Briona reached Hanu in time to warn him of the Canti-Regni attack and he has sent half his army to deal with that threat; or that the Durotriges have been taken by surprise and the rest of Hanu's warriors are engaged in defending their rear.

Between our two armies the valley narrows as the escarpment rises up on either side. This part is the most dangerous and whosoever will be drawn there will be at a disadvantage. As I expected, Hanu's warriors also form a line, opposite us, although I see that some of Hanu's men have been kept back and can be seen lining the western ridge above. It is difficult to gauge Hanu's numbers but that does not matter. I still nurse a slim hope of averting the battle. If I succeed, numbers will be irrelevant.

The mist begins to clear, allowing the sun to glimmer through in patches and enabling me to pick out Hanu from amongst the warriors.

Like Irven, he is stood atop a shining chariot, his ceremonial shield gleaming in the morning light. Around his neck he wears a thick golden torc but otherwise he is naked from his britches up. His chest has been smeared with azurite and his hair and moustache limed so they stand out against his blue torso. He looks otherworldly, but I notice his round stomach, and feel a tinge of surprise. The Durotriges king looks soft.

Once the armies are within hailing distance the taunting begins.

'Your mother is a whore who sleeps with dogs,' comes a cry from my left.

The answer, though muffled, can still be heard.

'Your sisters are the progeny of pigs!'

A murmur ripples through the soldiers on both sides whilst ever more inventive insults are concocted.

I can feel my heart thumping in my chest. I need to act now, but my limbs are leaden. Doubt fills my mind and alternatives clamour to be considered. Perhaps Briona did not reach Hanu. Perhaps the Durotriges remain ignorant of the Canti-Regni alliance. Perhaps Caradwg's audacious plan might even work, and I will inherit the kingdom after my father. My plan was to ride to the enemy and tell Hanu about the Vellani, in the hope that Hanu will insist on thrashing the matter out with words, not weapons. But now my idea seems stupid, doomed to failure.

Then Chela and Brendan's faces swim into my mind and I know I want no part in a battle that means certain death for my friends. To my father's surprise and to the murmurings of my clan, I break away from the Atres army and urge my horse forward.

I ride alone towards the enemy, not daring to look back at my father nor my King, whom I know will be purpled-faced with rage, for if it is thought Irven has sent me to talk, the very act will be viewed as an admission of weakness.

The short distance between our two armies takes for ever to cover. I can feel the sweat trickling between my shoulder blades as the Durotriges warriors part to allow me access to their King, watching me carefully all the while. I am less than a spear's length away from Hanu. I hold my hand up in the sign of peace. To my relief, Hanu responds in kind. As is the custom, the Durotriges army lower their weapons, and so when a volley of sling-shots is let loose from the Atres side, the Durotriges are caught off guard.

'What lowly trick is this?' snarls Hanu, and without further ado, jabs me in the side with his sword. I fall off my horse and as I land on the ground, I crack my head on a boulder. I hear Hanu's war cry then the Durotriges army surge forward as one. They swarm over me as though I do not exist, trampling me underfoot. *They think I am dead.* Hanu's warriors thin as the first wave engage with the Atres, allowing me to get my bearings. I still have my sword, the Gods be thanked. I stand unsteadily, and realise that blood is flowing down my face, obscuring my vision. The world swims, and then goes black, but I still have awareness. I am on my hands and knees and a searing pain is slicing through my guts.

The battle is in full swing and all around me men face each other at close quarters. Wiping the blood from my face, I spy a small hillock to my left, on top of which grows a stunted hawthorn. I crawl towards it, in between the boulders, needing a vantage point. It is as though I am invisible. The Durotriges army are focussed entirely on the warriors they face and so, inch by inch, I gain access to the hillock. I slump against the tree, swimming in and out of consciousness.

In one of my more lucid moments I see Irven across the divide, urging his men to battle. Mounted warriors, wielding swords, force their horses in front of the sling-shotters, whilst the spear bearers run towards the battle in the wake of the horsemen. Irven's troops are now at the narrowest section of the valley floor. I watch helplessly as the Durotriges warriors who are stationed on the hill let go a shower of spears, killing a handful of the Atres infantrymen, before riding down the hillside to join the main fray.

My brain begins to clear, but each time I move, giddiness overcomes me and so I have no option but to observe, uselessly, as the battle rages around me. I watch as the Durotriges horsemen, led by Hanu, head straight for Irven. But Irven stands his ground, his clan and his own warriors forming a tightly-knit force around him and I feel a surge of pride at my King's valour. Irven shouts for the other clans to join him. But they do not, and I feel sick to the depths of my being, knowing that I was party to my own father's treachery. Those clans loyal to Caradwg hold back, exposing Irven on either side. Just then, the hillside comes alive with Durotriges warriors who must have been waiting out of sight beyond the ridge of the hilltops, swelling the ranks of their army until they are double the number of our men. The Canti-Regni Alliance have failed us. The Durotriges let go yet another flurry of spears, cutting down the Atres infantrymen where they stand.

I struggle to my feet. I am Atres, after all, and I cannot stand by whilst my own kin are being slaughtered. The noise is almost unbearable. The clash of metal, the screams of men and horses, the smell of blood, all serve to fuel my fury. I stagger towards my King. A Durotriges warrior who was bearing down on me feels my sword-thrust through his bare chest. A foot soldier taking aim with a spear is separated from his head with one clean arc of my sword. I am so close to Irven now, I can almost touch him, but the effort of reaching my King has been costly and I am spent. I have lost too much blood and collapse, sinking to my knees. I am only a few paces away from Irven, but can do nothing but watch as he faces his mortal enemy, Hanu, who is in front of him, astride his horse.

'Fight, you coward!' Irven screams.

I watch as Hanu looks down at Irven. All I see is pity in the Durotriges King's eyes, a pity that seems to fuel Irven's hatred all the more. My King grips his sword firmly in both hands, as Hanu dismounts. The two men face each other.

'I have no quarrel with you,' says Hanu, and his voice is calm.

'You destroyed my life,' screams Irven, and lifting his sword aims a blow at Hanu's side. Hanu moves quickly and Irven misses his mark, the momentum of the stroke causing him to lose balance. Now Hanu has the advantage. With a look of sorrow on his face, he raises his sword. But before he can strike, Irven buckles to his knees, looking in disbelief at the spear tip that protrudes from his chest. Although I am barely conscious now, I turn to see who has claimed my King's life and my eyes widen in disbelief, for standing behind Irven is Briona and I know, without any shadow of doubt, that it is she who let loose the spear.

Irven's sword falls out of his hands. He tries to speak, but his breath gurgles in his throat. Then a crimson torrent of blood sprays out of his mouth in an arc, splattering all those who are close. A cry goes up.

'The Atres King is dead! Irven is dead!'

The last thing I remember as I lose consciousness is a sight that will remain with me for the rest of my life. And that is of Briona, Queen of the Atres, cradling her dead husband's head in her hands, while a cry of mourning, supernatural in its intensity, escapes her mouth.

FORTY ONE

Saramis

Kendra

I am dreaming. Cator and I are back at Awelfryn and it is a warm spring morning. He is holding a tiny fledgling in his hand, a wren. I reach out to stroke its soft downy head, but when I touch it, it turns to bone. I wake up, feeling bereft, and look towards the cave entrance. There is a glimmer of light, another dawn. But there is something wrong. I cannot pinpoint exactly what it is, but then a sudden movement from Cator causes me to sit up, my heart racing in my chest. Cator is sitting upright, as though listening for something, his body taut.

'What is it?' I ask.

'Malvina.. she...'

Then I realise what Cator has noticed and I have not. The silence. I feel the blood drain from my being. I cannot move.

I watch, in the near-darkness, as Cator places his hand on Malvina's brow and then to the side of her neck to feel for the life pulse. I say nothing as Cator puts his ear to the little girl's frail chest to listen for a heartbeat. And it is only when he closes her half-open eyes do I acknowledge that Malvina is dead, and a dry sob, that originates from someplace deep inside, wracks my entire body as I give it voice.

Once I let loose my tears, all my pent-up emotions find expression in my grief. I feel Cator's comforting touch as he strokes my back and after a long while, my sobbing subsides and we sit in silence together, I holding Malvina's limp hand. Eventually Cator speaks and I hear him as though from afar.

'We must bury her,' he says, tugging my hand away from the cooling body until at last, I let go.

Cator removes Malvina's hag stone from her neck and places it around his own. He scoops out a shallow grave with his hands and although I know I should help, I still cannot move. As he places Malvina in the hollow I realise that he is crying.

'Help me cover her up, Kendra,' he says thickly, but I can do nothing and so Cator works alone, scooping the sand into the grave until Malvina is no longer visible.

'We should say a prayer,' he says. 'Can you remember one?'

I want to speak, but no words come. I want to tell Cator that I have not lost my mind, that I can still think, but that my body simply refuses to obey my commands. I close my eyes and summon my strength and at last I find my voice and though my words sound weak and strange to my own ears, I begin to recite a prayer for the dead. Cator joins in.

Just as we are finishing, footsteps are heard at the cave entrance and a burning torch wavers to and fro. By the time Lann reaches us, we are silent. Seeing only the two of us he searches the back of the cave with the lighted torch before speaking in a low voice.

'Where is she? What have you done with her?'

'She is dead,' says Cator, pointing at the grave.

Lann snorts and kneels down next to the disturbed sand.

'If this is some sort of trickery...' he begins, and as he speaks, he scoops away handfuls of sand from the grave, until Malvina's little face is visible in the torchlight.

A cry escapes me, but I cannot find the words I want.

'Can't you leave her alone, even in her death?' demands Cator.

'Be quiet.'

Lann scrutinises Malvina's face and touches her cheek. Satisfied that she is truly dead, he stands and walks back a few paces.

'Cover her up again, then come with me.'

I watch as Cator covers Malvina's face for the second time. His anger is a wall, solid and unyielding. I am engulfed by Cator's emotions and as we stand over the grave, a searing hatred towards Lann, the like of which I have not experienced before, surges through me. His time will come and I will have him. All I need to do is get out of these chains and I will annihilate him, this Malvina, I promise.

Chela

It is just after dawn and the sun barely a glimmer on the horizon. I have just managed to fall into a sleep of sorts when there is a banging on the sturdy doors of my roundhouse. The pounding is so urgent that my heart leaps to my throat. What could be happening here that is so important? It will be a while yet before the wounded are brought in. Bleary-eyed and with Riana standing behind me, I open the door to Grypsos.

'Thank the Gods,' he says. 'You must come, quick.'

'What is it Grypsos?'

'The girl Kendra, and the other boy, Cator, I have seen them.'

'Where?' I demand, as I duck behind the partition to put on my day tunic.

'A man, he loads them onto a rowing boat. Chained with each other.'

'By the Gods! Where?'

'The beach to the south.'

I waste no time. Dressed, I emerge from the alcove, pull on my doeskin boots and fasten my cloak to my shoulder.

'Riana,' I say, 'I need you to stay here and tell the others where I have gone.'

Riana nods. Her eyes widen as she watches me sling my scabbard over my back and tuck my dagger into the pocket of my tunic.

'Be careful,' she cries, as I run out of the roundhouse after Grypsos. Of course, I will be careful. I have no desire to be reckless.

We run most of the way, stopping only to catch our breath. Lann had not used the harbour, but the beach at the southern edge of the headland. By the time we reach the shingle, we are too late. The rowing boat is already at sea.

'Come, let us be quick,' says Grypsos. 'We use my ship to follow.'

I flash him a grateful look. Thanks be to Esu that he is still here. We run around the promontory until we reach the harbour. Grypsos' boat, the Niad, is a deep-keeled Roman Merchantman, a sea-going vessel with cloth sails and a covered hold under which nestle four tiny cabins and a spacious cargo basin. Her size means she moors in the deep waters off the wooden jetty. Grypsos' crew of four men are already awake, and jump to attention when their captain barks orders for them to set sail. I see Brendan amongst them and give him a quick wave. I have not seen him for some days and I feel sorry for him. All he wants to do is get to Lynd, to rescue his lover, now that the news of Bryn's death has reached us. But although he is not exactly a prisoner, Hanu has made it plain that he is not to leave Vipers' Fort. He is a Vellani after all, even if he has betrayed his own kind. Hopefully Doran is too busy waging war to worry about kingship ceremonies right now and Mylor will not be put to death just yet.

While the crew prepare to depart, I scan the horizon for the rowing boat and can just see it bobbing along in the current, heading in a south-easterly direction across the narrow strip of water that separates Saramis from the mainland. I will Grypsos' crew to hurry up. Brendan disembarks and helps push the boat away from the jetty with a pole, remaining ashore. There is no time for the usual rituals so I mutter a prayer to Eluna and promise the Goddess a coin.

Though the crew work hard to set the sails, by the time the wind catches them and we are on our way, the rowing boat, a tiny dot in the distance, can be seen disappearing round the southern edge of Saramis. As soon as we are out of the harbour, however, the Niad begins to pick up speed and the sailors, understanding the whims of the weather and the local currents like their own kin, soon have the Niad picking up speed in pursuit. Despite my worries about Kendra, I cannot help but feel the excitement of being on a vessel the size of the Niad. I spent a great deal of time sailing with Gowell and Ivor and am used to the sea, but the way the Niad slices the water and its sturdy roll against the waves sends a feeling of exhilaration through me. Not wanting to seem superfluous, I busy myself coiling ropes and making sure there are no obstacles lying around for the sailors to trip over. I help with the rigging and because I am strong, I make a difference, proving myself an able sailor. My actions earn me the respect of the crew who grin broadly and sometimes toothlessly at me.

As the Niad gets into her stride and we round the Isle, I spot our quarry and immediately my hopes are dashed.

'We can't possibly moor where they have,' I cry. 'The Niad is too big!'

'There is a harbour, is there not?'

'Yes, there is a small but deep, natural harbour, but it's on the eastern side of the isle, not where they are heading.'

'Then we may be too late,' says Grypsos.

'Wait!' I say, as a memory floods back. 'There is an inlet not too far from the settlement and just around the corner from where they have moored. It's a little rocky but with your skill and the good weather we may be able to land.'

'And we will be out of their sight?'

'Yes!'

'Good,' says Grypsos and proceeds to bark orders at the crew. I scour the shore but I have not voiced my main concern. If Lann spots us, he might kill Kendra and Cator rather than surrender them to his pursuers.

Kendra

Lann takes us straight from the cave to a small rowing boat beached on the pebbly shore, where Huw is waiting.

'Get in,' he commands and we obey without a murmur. Huw sits at the stern, oars at the ready, his fat belly spilling over his britches. I regard him with disgust. He must have been paid much gold to betray his own kind.

Cator and I are made to sit on a narrow seat in the bows. I am shivering and Cator puts his arm around me, but I pull away, not wanting Lann to know the depths of my feelings for Cator, lest he use them against me.

Lann grabs hold of the second set of oars and the men row in silence. Once we are out into the main channel, the current picks us up and speeds us on our way to Saramis.

I wonder what Lann has in store for us. The very fact that we are alive means we still play a part in his schemes. I try to marshal my thoughts, to devise a plan, but my mind is full of fog. I look at Cator, strong and handsome, sitting next to me, grim-faced, but in control. He is in better shape than I.

We head towards Saramis' southern shore where we negotiate some jagged rocks until we reach a stretch of beach. As we disembark, I look towards the horizon and for a moment, my hopes are raised only to be dashed just as quickly. A trading boat, of Mediterranean build, approaches the island but then disappears out of sight around the headland. It looks like the one owned by Grypsos, but I cannot be sure. Lann ignores it, seemingly unconcerned, and shoves us in front of him, indicating we should take the rough path that leads to the interior of the island.

Before long, three roundhouses clustered close to one another come into view. When we reach the first roundhouse, Lann pushes us inside and proceeds to undo the slave chain and collars. I realise that any attempt to flee is futile, for Huw stands nearby clutching a dagger. He looks thirsty for blood.

'Chain the boy to the pillar,' says Lann.

Huw loses no time in dragging Cator to one of the interior wooden supports and shackling him to the pole by his ankle. Cator struggles but is stopped by a blow to his head from Huw's fat fist. At least he did not use his knife. I shoot Cator a warning look before realising that Lann is looking at me, an evil smile on his lips. He points to a pile of logs and kindling stacked against the roundhouse wall.

'Make yourself useful,' he says, and then points to a low dresser on which earthenware pots have been placed. 'There's flour, butter and water over there. Light the fire and make some bread. And if you try anything, anything at all, your friend here will meet a very nasty death. Do I make myself clear?'

I nod but do not meet his eyes. As I begin to busy myself with the kindling, Lann and Huw exit the roundhouse, but stop just outside the porch. Their voices can be heard plainly enough.

'As soon as you hear of Doran's victory, come and get me,' says Lann.

'Don't worry, I will,' says Huw.

'And make sure you don't head straight for Vipers' Fort either.'

'Do you think me stupid?' Huw sounds annoyed. 'We've been over the plans a dozen times. I just wish you would trust me.'

Lann hesitates before answering.

'Of course I trust you. And when this is over, you will have untold wealth and power, I promise. And you can have the boy to do with as you wish.'

I hear Huw grunt and a shiver travels down my spine.

'Come,' says Lann, his voice receding into the distance. 'I'll help you push the boat out.'

They mean to kill Cator, and then me. We had better do as Lann says. I pick up a handful of logs, but my hands are shaking so badly that I drop them on the floor. I look up at Cator and realise he has been talking to me.

'Kendra,' he is saying. 'By the door. The metal bar, bring it to me.'

I feel as though I am dreaming. I look at Cator but do not see him. My eyes are brimming with tears and my head feels full of bog-cotton.

'Kendra, my love, please!'

Something in the tone of his voice reaches me. I look up at him and suddenly connect. Racing over to the doorway, I grab the iron bar that is propped up against the wall. Lann, fortunately, did not see it. I hand it to Cator.

'A rock,' he says. 'Something to hit it with!'

I look around. I can't see anything that would be suitable. I am rooted to the spot. I feel useless, unable to think.

'Outside, by the chicken-house,' says Cator. He sounds unnaturally calm and I realise I must be trying his patience. 'I saw some stones as we came in.' As he speaks, he hides the iron bar under his tunic.

I walk towards the doorway and peer out. There is no sign of Lann. I find the rocks exactly where Cator said, and choose one the size of my combined fists, but my movements seem mired in honey.

'Hurry, Kendra!' I can hear Cator again, and his voice spurs me into action. I run indoors and hand him the rock.

'Good,' he says and gives me a quick kiss on the lips. 'Now keep watch at the door.'

I do not move. I am rooted to the spot; terrified Lann will return and kill Cator in front of my eyes. Cator hits the metal bar with the rock. The noise, as it reverberates around the roundhouse is almost unbearable. I want him to stop. I squeeze my eyes shut and cover my ears.

'Keep watch!' says Cator, and his voice edges on the hysterical, before he smashes the rock down on the bar once more. 'It's beginning to give!'

Cator's words bring me to my senses at last. I run to stand by the doorway. No sign of Lann just yet. A wave of nausea comes from no-where and rolls over me. I begin to retch.

'Kendra.'

I turn to look at Cator. He is grinning, holding the broken chain in his hand. He is free. I am about to say something, but check myself, for striding up the path towards us is the man I hate more than anyone in the world.

'It's Lann,' I say. My voice escapes as a whimper.

'Get out of the way,' Cator whispers.

I make a dash for the porch but I am too late. Lann's bulk looms over me, a sack of provisions on his back. But I am not finished. I retch again and this time my stomach yields greenish bile that lands at Lann's feet. He slaps my face and pushes me away.

'Go fetch yourself some water,' he says, pointing outside. 'There's a stream over there.'

I obey. I move a few paces away then watch as Lann enters the roundhouse. My knees feel weak and I sink to the ground. This is it. Cator will be killed, and then Lann will come for me. I know it. I cannot just stand by and let Cator die. I grab a stone from the ground and follow Lann into the roundhouse.

My eyes take a few moments to adjust. I see Lann's bulk move through the doorway then Cator, as silent as a wraith, appears from above. He has climbed the wooden pillar and as Lann enters the roundhouse, jumps down on top of him. Lann, caught by surprise, loses his balance and falls to the floor. I know Cator must act quickly for he is no match for Lann, who is strong and well-nourished and is already rising from the ground.

I needn't have worried for Cator wastes no time. A primeval battle cry escapes his lips and with almost studied precision, he smashes the iron bar down onto Lann's skull. Metal connects with bone in a sickly crunch.

Lann falls to the floor. His eyes close for a moment and then snap open as he tries to struggle to his feet. Now he is on his knees, rising from the floor. I am in front of him, looking at my enemy in disbelief, fear driving me. How dare he get up! It is as though a spectre from Eluna's marshes is rising from the dead. We cannot afford to fail now.

Then I remember I hold a rock. Lifting it in both hands, I am about to bring it down onto Lann's forehead, when he shoots his hands up and grabs both my wrists, dragging me towards him.

I scream, but Cator still has hold of the iron bar. He raises it over his head and with all the strength he can summon, smashes it into the back of Lann's head.

To my utmost relief, Lann lets go of my wrists and crumples into a heap, but Cator's rage has been unleashed. He raises the bar again, but Lann somehow manages to move to one side and the blow lands on his arm.

'Hit him!'

I find that I am screaming at Cator. I am terrified that Lann will get up and grab one of us again. Cator needs no prompting; the next blow is to the back of Lann's neck, causing him to fall forward onto his stomach.

All of a sudden it is as though the roundhouse is full of people and although I register the fact, I see them only through a mist of anger. Lann is lying there in front of me, his skull intact. He is motionless, but I want him dead. One more blow to the back of his head should do it. I want to see his brain flowing onto the ground, want his blood to stain the white chalky floor, and want to look into his glazed dead eyes. I look at Cator and he understands. He lifts the iron bar.

To my disbelief, a man, small but strong, grabs the crowbar out of Cator's hands. It takes me a few moments to realise the man is Grypsos, and behind him stands Chela. Grypsos leans over Lann and feels for a pulse before examining the rest of his body.

'Is he dead?' asks Cator. His voice is hoarse.

'No, he still lives,' says Grypsos. 'Though you have broken his arm and, I think, cracked his skull.'

'Let me finish him off,' says Cator through his teeth.

Grypsos shrugs and looks at Chela.

'No,' says Chela. 'He must come before the Elders and the Brothers. He has caused much sorrow. They must know the truth.'

I know that Cator, like myself, want above all else to see Lann dead, but our bloodlust is dissipating.

'And when he wakes up?' I ask. 'What then?'

'You no worry,' says Grypsos. 'He is too damaged to do any harm, and I will bind him well.'

I turn to Cator. He looks so tired. I run towards him and fling my arms around his neck, and my tears mingle with his. We walk outside into the sunshine, clinging to each other, leaving Grypsos to deal with Lann.

Grypsos, true to his word, finds a rope and secures Lann's arms behind his back, not caring that his prisoner, who has regained consciousness, cries out when he twists his broken arm. Grypsos then half drags him, half pushes him in front of us onto the Niad and commands one of his crew to guard him at all times. It soon becomes obvious to me that Lann is in no condition to run. Once we are at sea, I tear myself away from Cator and stand in front of my enemy.

As Lann raises his eyes to meet my gaze, I spit into his face, noting with satisfaction that he is unable to wipe the spittle away. But I am not entirely satisfied, and grabbing a heavy wooden broom from the deck, and seeing a broken shard of bone protruding from Lann's upper arm, I slam the broom into his wound so that he screams in pain.

'That is for Malvina,'

I raise the broom again, but Chela comes up behind me and prises my weapon away from me.

'Come, my sister,' she says. 'That's enough. I know he has treated you ill, but there will be a just revenge, don't worry. He is too injured to escape and Grypsos will see to it personally that he is taken straight to Vipers' Fort where he will be chained up and secured. He can do you no more harm.'

I look at Chela, and realise that tears are running down my face.

'You called me your sister,' I say. 'So you have forgiven me?'

Chela hugs me close and after a long moment, she speaks.

'There is nothing to forgive,' she says. 'And I call you my sister, not only because I love you as my own, but because you are my own kin.'

I look at Chela in disbelief.

'It's true, and I was a fool not to have realised it long ago,' she says. 'And what's more, our mother has been looking for you.'

'She's at Vipers' Fort?' I ask. I can scarcely believe my own ears.

'She was,' says Chela, 'but she has had to go away for a short while.'

'Where?' I ask, not understanding.

Chela sighs before replying and I feel a familiar twisting in my gut, as I prepare myself for the worst.

'We are nearly at the harbour,' says Chela. 'Don't fret, it's not all bad. Let's get home and see that Lann is secured. Then I will tell you everything.'

FORTY TWO

Viper's Fort

Fionn

It does not strike me as strange, to be moving through the air, but natural, as though I have known how to fly all my life. Higher and higher I float, until I bump against the smoke-stained thatch. I smile at the sensation as I observe the scene below me.

There are at least a dozen makeshift beds radiating from the hearth, each occupied by an injured warrior. Some of the warriors sport bandages soaked in blood; others mutter or cry out in pain. Slaves and children scurry to and fro, carrying bowls of water or strips of linen. I recognise Brendan sitting next to one of the beds, looking bored. How amusing to be watching my friend from such a height, when he can't see me. Then Brendan speaks and I am just able to catch his words.

'I seem to be spending an inordinate amount of time watching this one sleep,' he says.

A woman comes into view, an auburn-haired beauty who I recognised as my betrothed. Am I right? She looks older than I remember.

'And now he is smiling,' remarks Brendan. 'That's a good sign. He must be having a nice dream. Come on, Fionn, my arse is quite numb sitting here waiting for you to wake up.'

I look down and see a pale reflection of myself lying on the bed, thin lipped with blue eyelids. How strange I look. I must be close to death. Or am I dead? No, Brendan would not waste his time talking to a corpse.

I watch as a young girl enters the roundhouse, holding hands with a lad around the same age as herself. She also has auburn hair and looks familiar. I try to recall her name. Kendra that's it. Kendra, heiress to the Atres Kingdom. Memories crash into my brain all at once and then I am falling, no longer able to float and as I tumble downwards into a tunnel of darkness, pain sears through me. I try hard to resist the downward pull, wanting more than anything to return to the rafters amongst the drying bundles of herbs, where there are no troubles and no pain, just amused detachment. But the pull of that black place is compelling and I cannot resist its draw.

I open my eyes. I am lying on my back looking into Brendan's concerned face.

'He is awake,' says Brendan, his familiar countenance creasing into a smile. In response to Brendan's comment, a sea of faces appears above me.

'Can he speak?' says one.

'Give him water,' says another and I recognise the mellifluous voice as belonging to the healer, Chela.

A gentle hand is placed at the nape of my neck and a cup of cool water brought to my lips. I drink then struggle to an upright position. A pillow appears as if by magic at my back and I sink down again into the soft goose down.

'Do...you... know... who... I... am?' asks Brendan.

'Brendan, there is no need to talk to me as though I have lost my wits,' I reply. I had intended my riposte to be lively but my voice emerges as a croak. 'How long have I been here?'

Brendan laughs. 'I see you haven't lost your sense of humour at least. Welcome back! You were brought here two days ago and have been idling in this bed ever since.'

I try to raise myself, but find I cannot move. I look around and my eyes lock with Kendra's.

'You are safe!' I say. 'Thank goodness.'

Kendra blushes. She has let go of the lad's hand and stands looking at me.

'Yes, I am safe, Fionn. It is good to see you. Much has happened since I saw you last.'

'It certainly looks that way,' I say, causing Kendra to blush again. I remember now. This emaciated girl is my betrothed, not the beautiful angel with the gentle voice. I give the lad a sidelong glance. He is not to know I saw them hand in hand when I was floating above them all.

'Cator? I remember you. You were taken with Kendra.'

Cator nods. He looks awkward.

'Shh, let him rest,' says Chela, coming into view again, this time carrying a bowl of warm water. 'I need to see to his wound. There will be plenty of time to talk later.'

Kendra and Cator go together. My eyes follow them as they leave the roundhouse. You would have to be blind not to notice that they are in love, but I feel no rancour.

Chela pulls back the woollen blanket to reveal the angry gash on my left side, just below my ribcage. It has been expertly stitched.

'Good,' says Chela as she washes the wound. It's beginning to heal.'

The salty water stings me but I do not complain.

'Chela,' I say. 'It is so good to see you again. Can you stay with me a while and tell me what happened? I remember up to the point of Irven's death, but no more.'

'I need to tend to the others. Brendan will tell you everything,' she says and then drifts away.

Although Brendan did not witness the battle, the story has been recounted a number of times and so he tells me of all that has passed since the Atres and Durotriges faced each other at the White Stones.

'How did I survive?' I ask. 'I remember Irven being killed and Briona weeping over him, but after that, my memory is a blank.'

'Where have I heard you say that before?' asks Brendan.

I shrug, then wince in pain at the movement.

'I'm sorry I lied to you, Brendan.'

Brendan looks at me, and then breaks into a smile.

'I understand why you did so. Anyway, let me tell the story. Once Irven met his end, the Atres began to flounder.'

'My father?'

'Dead, I'm afraid, but he died a warrior's death.'

I fall silent. There was never a great deal of love between us, but the reality of Caradwg's end stirs up conflicting emotions within me. Guilt vies with sorrow but above all there is the realisation that I will never get to know the man who was my father. When I speak, my voice is thick.

'How did he die? Tell me.'

Brendan takes a deep breath.

'I will start from the beginning. You recall Annan? The youth who gabbles too much? Well he turned out to be a hero, can you believe! He discovered that the Vellani were behind everything and was able to warn Hanu in time.'

I nod, glad that everything is out in the open and although I am tired, I tell Brendan of my time at Buzzardstone and of my father's treachery.

'Yes,' says Brendan. 'Caradwg's plans came to light after the battle, but your father had a change of heart once he witnessed Irven's death. He must have realised that the Vellani had no intention of helping him and that he had been duped. Seeing the error of his ways, he urged those who were with him into the fight, even though it soon became obvious that his allies in the east had failed, for no sooner had the battle been joined than it was realised that the Durotriges had their full quota of men, and more.'

I close my eyes, remembering how the Durotriges had swarmed down the hillside to meet the Atres.

'No-one realised until well after the battle was over that Caradwg had held back deliberately,' continued Brendan. 'They put it down to the confusion of war and so, faced with the Durotriges, what remained of the Atres warriors rallied around your father and fought as one.'

I breathe out, releasing the tension I had been holding. At least my father had showed courage.

'When Hanu realised that the Atres fought with a new vigour, he ordered some of his warriors to peel off at the ends of the line and take the Atres from either side, driving them back down the valley into the section of the White Stones that was the most difficult to negotiate because of the boulders.'

'I recall those rocks,' I say. 'A bad place to do battle on horseback.'

'It was where Caradwg fell. A spear to the throat.'

Brendan pauses, but I urge him to continue.

'After Caradwg's death, the Atres began to flee before the Durotriges who were pursuing them, mowing them down like so much barley under a scythe. It was Briona who pleaded for mercy otherwise they would have been annihilated. They thought you dead, but after the battle, Briona found that you were still alive and sent you here to be tended.'

'How many of my people are dead?' I ask, not really wanting the answer.

'Around four hundred warriors, I am told.'

'And the Durotriges?'

'Fifty of those who fought at the White Stones lie dead; ten died at Golden Meadows, amongst them one of Hanu's children.'

Four hundred Atres! By Esu! A wave of nausea courses through me. Our losses are high, but I cannot rail against the Durotriges for it was my people who insisted on this stupid war.

'And the battle in the east?'

'The Durotriges routed the Alliance, taking them by surprise. Engus was run through with a spear in front of his men and so a deal was negotiated with Berris of the Regni, who suddenly lost his appetite for war! He was offered trading rights with the Veneti in return for his support against Doran. They all marched as one and reached the White Stones in time to defeat the Atres. I am sorry.'

'So am I. For everyone.' I realise how hoarse I sound and reach for the tumbler of water next to my bed. A sharp pain slices through me.

'Anyway, Briona was magnificent,' continues Brendan, pretending not to notice me wince. 'She took charge of the Atres as though she was born to lead. Once the meddling of the Vellani was made plain for all to see, the remaining Atres warriors agreed to join with the Durotriges and face Doran's army who, as we speak, march south.'

'And so all the southern tribes are united against the Vellani? That puts you in a difficult position, my friend.'

'It does indeed. The Durotriges have been good to me since I arrived here, but I am not allowed to leave. In any case, I have no stomach for Doran's fight. And Briona has vouched for me. I just hope Mylor is still alive, for as soon as I can leave, I will.'

'And I will come with you. I made you a promise I intend to keep.'

'If you are well enough, my friend, I will hold you to your word.'

'When do the armies face the Vellani?' I ask.

A shadow passes over Brendan's face. He swallows hard, for even though he has turned his back on his own people, they are still his kin. He looks me straight in the eye and for a brief instant, I glimpse his inner world.

'They fight on the morrow.'

FORTY THREE

The Vale of the White Stones

Briona

My intervention in the Vale of the White Stones saved the Atres from certain annihilation and now the clans look to me for leadership, for they know I am on good terms with the Durotriges and will obtain the best terms for our surrender. I take pledges of loyalty from each clan leader and when the full truth of Caradwg's scheming surfaces, I mark out those who plotted to betray Irven and although I have granted them clemency, they know I will watch them carefully in the future, their loyalty forever in doubt.

Kelwin, whom I have discovered was instrumental in fermenting the treachery against Irven, I single out, as an example to those who might think me weak. I have him brought in front of me and make him kneel. I do not speak to him; neither do I allow him to plead for his life. My stomach churns as I remember that he was once Elanor's betrothed, all those years ago, but I do not dare waver for the eyes of the Atres warriors are upon me. As two strong warriors hold him still, I thrust my sword through his heart in one fatal lunge. A cheer goes up and I know I have made my mark.

Hanu does not question my right to command the Atres, and while he rallies his own men, I arrange for the battle dead to be taken out of the Vale of White stones to an adjacent valley, where a gentle river flows into a large, deep lake. Close to four hundred dead! By Esu, it will take a long time to recover from this battle. Trees are felled from which platforms are erected, so that the souls of the dead will be carried to the heavens by ravens. Their weaponry is deposited into the lake amid much ceremony, as an offering to Eluna.

Most of the injured die soon after the battle and those who are close to death are slain by their own kin. Only a handful are considered strong enough to be worth saving and I ask Hanu if they can be taken to Vipers' Fort, where I know Chela will tend them, rather than to Awelfryn where there are no skilled healers. He does not object. When I eventually find Fionn, pale and still, I think him dead but a faint pulse throbs in his neck. Instead of ending his life, I make sure every care is taken to transport him to the Durotriges homeland.

Once I have seen to my men and have appointed those I trust to take charge, I seek out Hanu to thrash out the final details of our combined battle plan. I am no longer a powerless by-stander for now I have men at my command.

When Hanu heard the news of his daughter, Erea's, death, he wept openly. I watched him grieve and I cannot help but compare Hanu's emotions with Irven's coldness. If only my husband had shown such compassion; things could have been very different.

I find Hanu surrounded by his clan, his sons close at hand. They are beginning to trust me a little.

'What is there to learn?' I ask as I sit myself down on a boulder. A wooden tankard full of wine is thrust at me, but I wave it away. I want to keep a clear head. Hanu looks as though he has aged in the past few days but he still commands unstinting loyalty from his men, something Irven obviously failed to do. Poor Irven. I surprised myself in the end, with the grief I displayed at his death, but I had no choice. I had to kill him. Ours could have been a good marriage, a strong alliance, but he made too many bad decisions. He was weak. In the end it was him or me, kill or be killed.

'The Vellani have crossed the Great River at the western edge of Rhiw,' says Hanu and even though he is preoccupied with the imminent battle, he finds a smile for me.

'The Canti-Regni Alliance?'

'Ready and willing.'

'It will be expensive,' I remark, knowing that it will cost him his monopoly in trade with the Veneti but I also realise Hanu has no choice in the matter.

'It will indeed,' says Hanu. 'But I have erred badly. I hear Rome is flexing her muscles. Perhaps it would be a good thing for the tribes of this isle to work together for once.'

He looks and me, with his head inclined to one side and I know what he is thinking. What could be better than a union between our two tribes? I know he wants me and to my irritation, the knowledge makes me feel flustered. I had thought myself beyond such girlish frivolities and I am annoyed with myself for revealing my discomfiture. There will be no union, not for myself and Hanu, at any rate, but I have entertained the thought recently that there might be political advantage in a marriage between Chela and Gowell. They were once lovers, I am given to believe. I scrutinise Gowell. He is good-looking and not very intelligent; he will be an easy son-in-law to manipulate.

This is not the time to broach the subject and so instead we talk of the forthcoming battle and the trap we plan to set for Doran.

'He is a clever schemer, by all accounts,' I say.

'Then we must hope to outwit him,' is Hanu's dry response.

'Fortunately our losses at both battles were scant and the combined alliance of the southern tribes means we are easily twice the number of the Vellani. Our victory is assured.'

'You are right, of course, father,' says Gowell. 'But our armies are weary whilst those of the Vellani are fresh.'

'I never said it would be easy, my son. Rest now and worry about the morrow when it comes.'

I watch Hanu as he talks with his sons and I am filled with a sudden inexplicable sorrow, a deep loneliness of the soul. I bite back my tears and return to my warriors, who salute me and look upon me with respect. I do not sleep, but withdraw into myself and in the depths of the night I finally connect with my true feelings. The grey dawn finds me standing tall and proud atop my war chariot. My strength has returned. I killed my own husband, the Atres King, and the experience has shaken me to the core, but now I feel free to choose my own destiny. I am ready to lead and I know beyond all doubt that I need no man to tell me how to order my life.

Directly in front of me lies the Vale of the White Stones. I can just see the Vellani approaching in the distance, tiny, antlike, swarming into the wide mouth of the valley. It is time for me to position my men. I swap my chariot for a grey mare. Splitting the Atres warriors into two, I take charge of one section and lead them up the eastern side of the valley whilst ordering the second phalanx to the western ridge. They are to wait, out of sight beyond the ridges, for my command. They obey without question.

I am unused to fighting, but the Atres understand my importance as a figurehead. Five of my clan warriors surround me, ready to protect me to the death. I dismount and lie flat on the ground, surveying the valley below, waiting for Hanu to begin his assault. The waiting is interminable, but as the sun rises in the sky, the cry goes up from the Durotriges. I hold my men back, observing Hanu as he and his warriors surge towards the Vellani, meeting on the wide valley floor in a melee of blood and clashing metal.

I watch the battle unfold from my vantage point and feel only scorn for Doran whom I can see leading his men astride a black stallion. Although he wears the britches and cloak of his people, he has not limed his hair, neither has he painted his skin. Annan warned us that Doran had been studying Roman war tactics. I am curious to learn what that might mean.

It does not take long for me to find out. Doran commands his infantrymen to raise their shields above their heads and in front of them to form an impenetrable barrier so that the hails of slingshot and spears simply bounce off. They inch forwards bit by bit and whilst their opposite number reload their slings and reach for fresh spears the Vellani spearmen attack, causing heavy losses to the alliance at the front line. In this way the Vellani are able to advance, taking many lives but suffering few casualties themselves.

I turn to see Hanu urging his men on, in an attempt to crush his enemy through sheer weight of numbers but the losses he is sustaining cause his warriors to begin to waver in their resolve. The sun rises higher in the sky as the battle wears on.

Doran's men look to be gaining the advantage, but still I wait. Only when the entire Vellani army is in the Vale of the White Stones, do I make my move. I spring up onto my horse and wave my banner. My warriors surge down the hillsides surprising the Vellani from the rear and forcing them into the narrowest section of the valley.

Lacking the discipline of the Roman troops, Doran's men hesitate and their carapace of shields begins to fall apart. My warriors, seeing their chance, attack, slicing and killing as they go, driving the Vellani into Hanu's hands. Hanu now has them where he wants them, and attacks from the front, whilst shower after shower of spears hail down upon them from the warriors under Gowell and Ivor's command, who have been waiting on the ridges overlooking the narrowest part of the valley. The Vellani are now being attacked from the north, the south and from above.

I sit astride my horse, searching for any sign of Doran in the confusion. I lost sight of him moments earlier. Has he been killed? The fighting continues for a while until Doran's absence becomes apparent to his warriors, and they lose heart, their fighting dissolving into chaos.

I let out a whoop of sheer joy and ride down to the valley floor to join my men, and as I approach the battle scene, I hear the sweet sound of the Horn of Surrender. The Vellani are defeated. They have no option but to sue for peace. Hanu gives the order for the fighting to cease and gradually the clashing of metal begins to lessen until it stops altogether.

The Vale of the White Stones is yet again littered with dead, and the metallic stench of blood permeates the air. An eerie stillness has begun to descend on the valley, the quiet broken only by the whimpering of the dying or the sound of ravens, cawing in excitement at the feast before them, pecking out the eyes of the dead and watching the injured with beady black eyes. But when I reach the Atres warriors, they break the silence with a cheer. I go about my men, commending them for their bravery. They in turn, remark on my cunning and my tactics. I am pleased, and a fierce joy, the like of which I have never before experienced, surges through me. It is as though I have found my true destiny.

'There will be gold and honours for all those who have fought today!' I say. 'And together we will restore the pride and glory of the Atres people.'

The Atres warriors look at me in adoration and Irven is completely forgotten.

Only after I have taken further oaths from the clan leaders, and arranged for the Atres dead to be found and placed to one side, do I join Hanu and his sons.

'Doran?' I enquire. 'Has his body been found?'

It is Gowell who answers, his face black as a thundercloud.

'Our men have searched the battlefield, but the Roman cannot be found amongst the dead nor the injured. They must have hidden his body.'

A man is seen to come forward alone, indicating that he wants to talk.

'That is Canogus,' says Annan, who sits astride his horse, next to Gowell. 'He is a good man.'

Gowell snorts in derision.

'We should kill the lot of them,' he says. 'Then move on to sack Ravensroost. Or take them for slaves. We could turn a decent profit.'

'Hold still, my son,' says Hanu. 'Bryn was a friend of mine. The Vellani were not always so evil.'

I watch as the man Canogus approaches. The defeated warrior winds his horse through the dead, who number as many as the white boulders littering the valley floor, until he stands in front of the Durotriges leader.

'I ask that you spare my people,' he says.

Hanu nods. 'We will require reparations from you, as is the custom, but first we demand that you hand over your leader, the one who thinks himself a Roman.'

'He is not amongst us,' Canogus says. 'He must still be lying on the battlefield.'

'He is not there,' says Gowell, his words clipped. 'We have searched.'

Canogus shrugs. 'I assure you, he is not with what remains of our army.'

'If this is some kind of trickery?' Gowell, reaching for his sword, is ready to strike Canogus down.

Hanu stays his hand before replying.

'We will search amongst your men, Canogus, until we have found him. Annan here speaks well of you and we know this foolishness was not of your doing. I am willing to spare what remains of your army, but the Vellani will pay dearly for this, believe me. Firstly you will surrender your weapons and your horses. Then you can go home.'

Hanu looks at me for approval and I am gratified to be consulted. I nod in acquiescence.

'Our dead,' says Canogus, looking Hanu in the eye as he speaks. 'Will you allow us to build platforms and honour them?'

'No,' I say. It is my turn to speak. 'Let them rot into the ground. Let their bleached bones remain in this accursed valley as a lesson to those who think they can take what they want, when they want.'

Hanu raises his eyebrows but if he thinks me harsh, he does not say so. Together we watch the Vellani leader return to his men. Under the supervision of Hanu's warriors, the vanquished pile their weaponry in a heap in the middle of the valley, turn their horses loose, and taking whatever supplies they can carry, begin to walk homewards, the jeers and taunts of the victorious ringing in their ears. Gowell and his warriors go amongst them, scouring the retreating army for any sign of their leader, but none is to be found. The Roman has vanished.

FORTY FOUR

Viper's Fort

Kendra

I stand atop the ramparts, straining to see who is approaching Vipers' Fort. Above me, Huw's glazed eyes, rotting in his impaled head, study the horizon, following my own gaze. In the distance I can just make out a grey mass that seems to crawl across the land, slowly covering the distance to the Fort.

We are all still grieving the loss of Erea and I know that it is Cinea, who brought her sister's body back from the battleground, who feels it the most. Although it is a victorious army that marches towards us, their arrival is nonetheless tinged with sorrow.

'Do you think she's coming?' I ask Chela. I am referring to my mother. I have asked the same question several times, and know I must be annoying my sister, but I cannot help myself. I want to see her for I have it in my mind that only she can restore my life to what it was before I was taken; before Lann. Deep down, however, I realise that nothing can ever be the same, and the innocence I once enjoyed has gone. My father is dead; killed by my own mother, so I am told. He had his faults, but I loved him, just as I love my mother. In this world of uncertainties, I am finding it difficult to reconcile my mother's actions with my memory of her; in my mind's eye it is as though she has transformed herself into a strange and fabulous monster.

'Perhaps she has gone straight home,' I say.

'I am sure she will come here,' says Chela. 'She doesn't yet know you are safe and swore she wouldn't rest until she found you. Besides which, Hanu sent word ahead for his best accommodation to be made available for his visitor. It must be her.'

Cator stands next to me, his arm around my waist. I realise his excitement is also tinged with anxiety, for he has no idea how the Queen will take to the idea that we are in love. Yesterday he went to see Fionn alone, to ask that he relinquish his betrothal. Fionn was very good about the whole matter, but I believe he had an ulterior motive for I notice how he looks at Chela. *Good. Each of us may yet find their heart's desire in all of this.*

Before long I am able to make out the features of those who approach. Hanu, Gowell, Ivor and Briona ride together leading the procession and as I spy my mother astride her stallion, I let go of

273

Cator's hand and run through the gateway to greet her. Briona sees me and with a cry she is off her horse, running towards me until we collide in a massive embrace.

I lead my mother to her quarters, where a feast of cold meats, a warm stew, bread, dried fruit and honey await her, together with a cauldron of Hanu's finest wine. I realise I am gabbling, but cannot help myself as I tell my mother everything that has befallen me since I was taken. She listens intently until the story is told. She in turn, tells me her tale and we both cry when she tells me of my own father's disinterest in saving me, and finally of his death at her own hands. I hide this information deep inside, to examine it later.

'And so it is just you and Cator left alive,' she says when we have calmed ourselves sufficiently to talk once more. 'The others all dead! And where is the one whom you say saved your life?'

'I will go and get him,' I say, running to the door. I stop just short of the entrance and turn to face my mother.

'We are in love. Fionn has said he does not mind.'

I notice my mother's expression change. She says nothing and though she smiles, I know her smile is false.

'Go fetch him,' she says after a moment.

I run from the roundhouse to find Cator.

Chela

Riana disappeared with Ivor the moment they set eyes on each other and I am left alone to watch the rest of the warriors march through the gate. Gowell is at his father's side but as soon as he sees me, he dismounts, handing his horse over to one of the children who line the track.

'Chela. It's good to see you.'

'And you, Gowell. I am pleased to see you are unhurt.'

'You look well too. Are you enjoying being back at Vipers' Fort?'

I nod. Our exchange seems so formal and awkward and after a brief pause, I find my tongue.

'You do not seem happy, Gowell, for one who has just been victorious in battle. Does something ail you?'

'Perceptive as ever, my Chela.' Gowell's laugh is too loud and echoes around him. 'If you must know, I searched high and low for that vile cur Doran, but it seems he has eluded us.'

'Oh,' I say. 'I see. But surely he is no longer a danger to anyone?'

'I want his head to fly from Vipers' Fort's ramparts,' says Gowell and though he looks at me, it is obvious his mind's eye is elsewhere. 'I will hunt him down, do not fear. He made a fool of me and he will get what he deserves.'

'Perhaps you should let it be, Gowell, and look to the future.'

Gowell's face darkens and I know he will not, nay, cannot let the matter rest. He composes himself and smiles.

'Let us not talk of it now. I am home, and you are here, as beautiful as ever. Will you come and see me later?'

'Of course.'

He leans down and kisses me full on the lips. My body responds, as though it has a will of its own.

'That's better,' he says and with that, he walks off towards his father's roundhouse, weary, and, I note, a little dejected. Armelle's betrayal still rankles, that much is obvious. He has asked me to marry him, and though I think I still love him, despite all he has done, I cannot help but compare our reunion to that of Ivor and Riana, or the way that Kendra and Cator cling to each other. There is something missing. I wander back to my home where Fionn lies on his bed, Brendan as ever, at his side. Seeing the two of them together makes me smile. They have been good company of late and have often made me laugh as they parry their wits against each other. The rest of the injured have returned home until only Fionn remains and he will be up and about soon. We have spent a great deal of time together, telling stories or talking of our lives and I have grown fond of him.

Before long Brendan stands to leave.

'I promised Grypsos some help with his boat,' he says.

Fionn and I sit alone together in a companionable silence until he finally speaks.

'Chela,' he says. 'You have treated me far better than I deserve over the past few days and have saved my life. You are a healer beyond compare.'

'I have done no more than I would for any other friend. And I am fortunate in the herbs that Grypsos brings me. Think nothing of it.'

'But I do. And do you really mean it when you call me your friend?'

'Of course I do. You and I have been through a great deal together.'

'That's strange; those were the same words Cator used when he talked to me of his love for Kendra. He told me they were friends first and foremost but that the recent experiences they shared turned their friendship to love.'

'You have behaved very well, over that,' I say as I pass Fionn a cup of ale. 'You showed me what a generous person you are.'

'Oh, I realised some time ago that I did not love her in the way a man should love his betrothed. Even more so after I met you.'

'Fionn, you are such a charmer,' I say. I am flustered but Fionn does not seem to notice.

'Anyway, do you want to know what I said to Cator?'

'Go on.'

'I said that friendship was the best basis for a marriage.'

I give Fionn a sidelong glance, knowing where the conversation is leading. Fionn puts down the beaker and takes my hand, cradling it in his own. His square palm makes my hand look tiny. I am fond of him, but he is young and his body retains the slenderness of youth, yet his touch makes me tingle.

'Chela, will you be my wife?'

I am confused, for earlier this same day Gowell kissed me and I felt the same stirrings. It all feels wrong, somehow.

'Gowell has asked me,' I say after the silence begins to grow a little uncomfortable. Fionn looks concerned rather than angry. He is trying to understand my mind.

'And?'

'I think he still loves Armelle.'

'And you, do you love him?'

'I don't know.'

'Well, this conversation is not going the way I had hoped at all, but at least you haven't hit me around the head and called for help!'

I find myself grinning. It is generous of him to lighten the moment and I no longer feel awkward.

'Oh Fionn!' I laugh. 'So much has happened recently, that I don't know my own mind.'

'In that case I will wait until you do,' he says, squeezing my hand. 'But can I just have one kiss to tide me over?'

I know he is disappointed, yet he makes me feel at ease even at such a moment and I am grateful to him. I lean over to kiss him, aware that Gowell's touch still lingers on my lips. Our mouths are just about to meet when there is a loud knocking at my door.

'Who is there?'

A young boy's face peers around the doorway.

276

'It's the Lord Gowell,' says the boy. 'He has asked me to fetch you. He would like to speak with you, if you do not mind.'

Briona

Though I yearn to back at Awelfryn, I realise I must stay for as long as it takes to secure new trading rights with the Veneti. Hanu has promised me access to the southern ports and I believe he will honour his word. I intend to restore the Atres to their former glory and an alliance with the Durotriges will go a long way to realising my ambitions.

I am not happy with Kendra's choice in Cator. I would prefer her to marry Fionn, who is of noble birth and whom I trust implicitly but if she persists in her foolishness, she will have to relinquish her claim to the Atres throne. I cannot have a swineherd as King!

There is one further issue that troubles me these days and robs me of a sound night's sleep and that is presence of Lann, who languishes chained up in an unused granary.

A guard is on permanent duty outside his prison and all visitors barred, except for Chela who is allowed to tend his wounds. The man, by all accounts, is in a sorry state. His arm has become infected so badly that Chela at one point thought he would die. He suffered a fever that raged for three days, but Chela nursed him well and brought his temperature down so that after the third day he began to recover. She told me that she used up many of her most precious herbs imported from the east, including the strong foreign poppy juice that relieved his pain but caused him to ramble and talk of strange matters.

'He calls for his mother,' Chela told me and when I heard this, I decided that I must speak with him.

Though the guard is reluctant to allow Lann any visitors, he wavers when he hears my commanding voice and allows me access, providing the door remains ajar. I climb up the wooden ladder that leads to the granary and ease myself in through the narrow doorway. Lann wakes with a start and looks up at me as I enter. I kneel on the straw-covered floor, making sure my back is straight and look him in the eye.

'I am told you speak of your mother in your sleep. You must love her a great deal.'

'What would you know about love,' he replies, rattling his chains in an effort to stand.

He is filthy and in the cramped quarters of the granary I can smell his fetid breath, the breath of the sick.

'I am sorry.'

Lann gives out a bitter laugh.

'And what good is 'sorry'?' he asks. 'You killed my twin and turned my mother out to die. And now you are sorry. What a joke!'

'I did what I could to protect my own,' I say. 'And yes, what I did to your mother is inexcusable.'

'And so why are you here? To rub salt into my wounds? Go ahead.'

'I have come to offer whatever support your mother requires,' I say, still holding Lann's gaze. 'Her own farmstead, one hundred head of cattle, gold, wine, oil, whatever she wants. She can name her price.'

Lann screws up his face in a sneer.

'Bryn was kind to her, to us. She has all the material comforts she wants and she would spit in your face so much as take one little thing from you. All she would ask for is my freedom,' says Lann. 'Are you willing to grant that much?'

I find I can no longer hold Lann's stare, his hatred is boring into my soul. To my dismay, a sob escapes me and I begin to cry.

'And so the great Queen Briona is broken,' says Lann.

'If it's any consolation, my life has not been a happy one.'

'How dare you compare your trivial problems to my mother's starvation? Her homelessness? Her status as an outcast? What's more, you had choices. What choices did my mother have?'

I have no answer and so I stand to leave. This has been a humiliating waste of time.

'Wait,' says Lann. 'There is something you can do. Two things, actually.'

I can only look at him.

'I wish to see my mother one more time, before I am condemned to death.'

'I can grant that.'

'And I want your daughter to tend to whatever ails my mother.'

'That, I cannot promise.'

Lann looks at me then averts his eyes in disgust.

'Then this visit was a sham, was it not?'

Chela

I do not take long to decide on my course of action, despite my mother's doubts. I am relieved that at least something can be done to make amends for the errors of the past.

'Of course I will go,' I say, when Briona tells me of Lann's request, but I can see she is appalled at the idea.

'You will do no such thing, Chela. Your place is by my side now. We can forget the past. You had no part in what happened.'

'Mother, I would not be alive if it were not for yours and Elanor's actions. I am in debt as well.'

'No, you were innocent in all of this!'

'But still I live because another died. And anyway, all he wants is for me to look at his mother and administer some medicines. And we can journey directly from Ravensroost on to Awelfryn.'

My mother lets out a deep sigh.

'Very well. I cannot see what harm will be done and it may even do some good.'

When the plans for our sea journey are made known, the travelling party begins to grow in size. Gowell will join us, acting on behalf of Hanu in organising the reparations due from the Vellani. Fionn, who is up and about, also decides to take the opportunity to travel northwards with Brendan and make good his promise to accompany his friend to Lynd. I am worried that the journey will be awkward, with both Gowell and Fionn on board, until I learn that Hanu is to send us in two of his finest and largest vessels, one of which has a covered cabin where we women can shelter, thereby segregating the sexes. I can avoid both my suitors. Kendra and Cator will also join the party and will travel with us on to Awelfryn. Then of course there is Lann, who will journey with the men, chained and well-guarded.

And so, three days after my mother's conversation with Lann, we are ready to depart. I have managed to persuade the crew that Yarrow must come with me and the dog is overjoyed, wagging his tail and barking at the activities. I hope I do not regret my decision to take him, but having been separated from him once; I do not wish to repeat the experience.

Just before we are due to leave, I run off to the docks where the merchant boats are moored. I scour the quayside for Grypsos and then I see him, shouting orders to the workmen as they load the Niad with silver and tin. I tried to spend as much time with him as I could these

279

last couple of days, avoiding Gowell and Fionn and also my mother, and I found myself confiding in him about the choices laid out before me.

I cannot help smiling at his familiar face. As we chat, I look around the Niad. I love the smell of the salt on the wooden hull and its exotic Greek design.

'When do you sail, Grypsos?'

'Tomorrow,' he replies. 'I see you are ready for your voyage, also.'

'Not as exciting as yours, my friend!'

'I am here far longer than I should intend,' he says. 'It has been good to be with you, my thanks to your kindness, as ever.'

'You will return next year?' I ask, and I am unable to keep the anxiety out of my voice. Now that Elanor is no longer here, Grypsos might not be so keen to come back.

'Of course! On that you can count. Next summer, same place, without doubts.'

As he speaks, he encircles me with his strong arms and gives me a hug. His voice is gruff when he releases me.

'Now go, my Little Daughter. Until next year. But one thing to remember.'

'What's that?'

'Know your heart, and happiness will be with you.'

'But how?'

'Do not search for this thing. How you say? Yes, *engage* with life and the truth, it makes itself known.'

I run off towards the boats that await me and after a few moments we are underway. I will miss Grypsos, but he will be back, I am sure, with his big smile, his stories and exotic goods. No matter where I might be living next summer, I will seek him out.

From the prow of Hanu's boat, I wave to Grypsos until he is out of sight. When I can no longer see him, I turn and look at my travelling companions. Next to me stands Briona, and in the adjacent vessel, Gowell and Fionn, all three representing a different path down which the rest of my life could take.

'Know your own heart.' I repeat Grypsos' words over and over to myself. The problem is, I have no idea what my heart is telling me.

FORTY FIVE

Ravensroost

Chela

I had to hide my surprise when I saw Cerid for the first time. Although Lann's mother is younger than mine, she looks twice her age. She lives comfortably enough, sharing a roundhouse with Bryn's extended family, acting as a surrogate grandmother to the progeny of the royal household. But her face and body speak of disappointment and illness. Her grey hair is scraped over her scalp and her teeth are all missing, lending her face a sunken countenance. He eyes are rheumy with yellow flecks and her skin sallow and thick with lines.

I spend most of my time tending Cerid and am able to ease some of her pain with massages and potions. When I am not administering directly to my patient, I wait quietly in the corner, out of the way, in case I might be needed. Lann, who is allowed to spend as much time with his mother as he wants, treats me as though I do not exist and I am glad he does not speak to me. Briona has seen to it that he is not chained so that he can maintain a modicum of dignity in front of his mother, but a guard is posted outside the door, lest he try to escape.

Lann and his mother talk at great length and Cerid can occasionally be heard wailing and crying in the knowledge that her son will soon meet his death. But Cerid has a sickness that is eating her body, and eventually it will consume her altogether. This I know instinctively and the best I can hope for is to leave behind a quantity of my own medicines so that the Vellani herbalists might treat Cerid when I am gone.

Cator and Kendra spend their time with Fionn and Brendan, getting to know Brendan's family, whilst Gowell and Briona negotiate with Canogus for the Vellani reparations. On the second day, I manage to snatch a rare moment away from Cerid and find Fionn in the forge, occupying himself with a tiny abstract beeswax carving of a horse. I am eager to hear how the negotiations are progressing, and keen to be away from my patient for a little while.

'That's lovely,' I say as I scrutinise his work. 'I will look forward to seeing it finished.'

Fionn grins at my compliment and I realise how much I like him. I feel bad about not letting him, or Gowell for that matter, have my final answer and I know that Elanor would have told me quite bluntly to stop 'stringing them along'. I am not toying with them, thought it might seem as though I am. It's just that I feel so confused and under pressure to make a decision, and the more I am pressed to decide, the more my feelings on the matter elude me.

'What news is there?' I ask after a while.

'Briona and Gowell are demanding at least two thirds of the goods the Vellani receive from across the water,' says Fionn.

'For how long?' I ask. Although the Vellani do not deal with the Veneti, I am aware they conduct a roaring trade with the middle-men from Gaul.

'Five summers,' says Fionn. 'I believe Canogus counts himself lucky. It could have been a great deal worse for the Vellani. His family are unhurt and Ravensroost remains intact.'

'Canogus is to be king then?' I like Canogus, and believe him to be a good man.

'Yes. The elders have agreed. All he wants to do now is build up the oppida and the farming, making the Vellani self-sufficient.'

'He is wise,' I say, noting how easily he uses the Roman word, 'Oppida'. Times are changing and we cannot ignore the influence of Rome.

'Anyway,' says Fionn. 'Once they have sworn oaths of honesty, fidelity and peace, Canogus plans to journey to Lynd for the Kingship Ceremony. He will take Lann with him to be sacrificed instead of Mylor.'

'You will go with them?'

Fionn nods.

'Brendan and I, both, so that I can fulfil my promise, although now it is hardly a rescue, more a reunion.'

'Any news of Doran?'

'No sign of him,' says Fionn. 'But it is thought that when he saw the battle turn against him, he took the shield from a fallen Atres warrior, and used it to hide his face, which is how he escaped undetected from the Vale of White Stones. His woman, apparently, was in a safe house not far from the battle ground. He collected her then they managed to catch a boat across the water, so I hear.'

'He is half way to Rome by now, I shouldn't wonder.'

'Quite probably. I doubt we will see him again.'

Just then Brendan turns up. The three of us sit together and the men tell me bawdy jokes until tears run down my face.

'Now it's my turn,' I say. 'Three warriors walked into a settlement...'

'Which warriors?' asks Brendan.

'It doesn't matter. Alright, Dobunni. Three Dobunni warriors walked into a settlement...'

'I've heard it,' teases Fionn.

'No you haven't. Are you going to let me tell this joke or not?'

Fionn grins and I slap him lightly about his head.

'Three....'

Just then Gowell pokes his head around the forge entrance and we all fall silent.

'Chela,' he says, smiling at my discomfiture. 'I have come to say farewell. Will you walk with me a while?'

Fionn shoots Gowell a dark look, but says nothing.

Gowell leads me out of Ravensroost to a small spinney that affords us some privacy. We find a fallen tree trunk and he brushes away an earwig before inviting me to sit next to him. He curls his arm around my waist and draws me to him, looking into my eyes. Despite myself, I feel the familiar stirrings.

'Are you ready to give me an answer,' he asks, without any preamble.

I look at him blankly.

'My proposal,' he says, a little crossly, loosening his hold of my waist and crossing his arms over his chest. 'It would be a good marriage, joining Atres with Durotriges.'

I look at him as though from a distance and I can feel his mounting irritation. After too long a pause, I speak.

'Gowell. You know I have always loved you. You were my sweetheart from the age of five when you first asked me to be your wife. Do you remember?'

Gowell laughs, his ire evaporating.

'You carry the memory with you, after all these years? How amusing!'

'But you have been sorely hurt by Armelle, whom I know you loved,' I say, speaking slowly and deliberately.

'She is gone. Think no more of her.'

'It would be easier for me to forget her than for you, I think.'

'Are you saying no?' Gowell sounds incredulous. Clearly, he was not expecting a refusal.

'No, I am not saying no, exactly,' I say. 'But I would rather wait a little while longer before giving you my answer.'

'How long?'

'I do not know. Can you be patient? I need to know that you truly love me, and that when you kiss me, you are not thinking of another.'

I realise that I am not being entirely honest, for I have not spoken of my own feelings. But then, again, he has not asked me how I feel.

'Chela!' Gowell begins to protest, but then changes his mind. 'Very well. But do not make me wait too long, my love.'

'I will be fair to you Gowell and if you love me as you say you do, then a little longer will not make any difference.'

Gowell draws me to him and kisses me on the lips. His hands begin to caress my breasts and explore my clothing, seeking entry, but I withdraw from him and kiss him affectionately on the nose.

'Another time, Gowell,' I say and stand, offering him my hand. 'Let us return. You have your farewells to make, and I must see that Cerid is comfortable.'

And with that, we stroll back to Ravensroost, my arm tucked into the crook of his elbow, almost the way we were before Armelle came between us.

Briona

I am looking forward to returning home, but I still have some unfinished business to attend. Once the negotiations are concluded, I ask to be escorted to Cerid's dwelling. I am not sure what I will gain by seeing Lann's mother, but I feel compelled to seek out the woman who has been in my mind for over twenty summers. Perhaps seeing her and apologising might slay the ghost of my conscience once and for all. The guard announces my presence and I stride through the roundhouse door, my shoulders held back, and my head proud. Chela is following behind me and I am glad she is here. As soon as I set eyes on Cerid, however, I am lost for words and it is Lann's mother who speaks first.

'Well, if it isn't the mighty Briona, come to gloat,' she says in a thin and weak voice. Its bitterness takes my breath away. 'Have you come to see how I spend my last days with my son?'

I swallow hard to steady myself. Even then my voice wavers.

'Sorry seems a word too trivial for what I did. If there is anything you want, ask, and I will grant it you if it is in my power to do so. Anything but Lann's life, for that is not mine to give.'

'You had my baby killed.'

'I loved my own. I wanted to save her.'

'Oh how like a noblewoman to think thus. Did you think me too coarse, to lowly to be capable of love?'

I cannot meet her gaze for there is more than a grain of truth in what she says.

'You had a son left. I would have had nothing. You filled his mind with bitterness,' I say, but those are not the words I want to utter. I came to absolve myself of guilt, not open old wounds.

Cerid turns away as though she has no more to say, then snaps her eyes on me.

'There is something you can give me,' she says and I detect an edge of cunning in the woman's voice.

'What?'

'Your daughter, the healer. She will stay with me here, as mine own, for four whole seasons, or until I am dead, whichever comes first.'

'No,' I say. 'I cannot permit that!'

'I told you, mother, she is not true to her word,' says Lann, his eyes gleaming with hatred.

'I fulfilled my promise to you Lann; I let you see your mother before you are condemned to death.'

Lann shrugs and looks at Chela, waiting for her to speak.

'It's not a problem,' says my daughter. 'I will gladly look after you, Cerid.'

'I cannot allow it,' I say. I cannot believe what Chela has just said. 'You will be Queen after I am gone. This is no work for an Atres noblewoman!'

Chela looks me in the eye and I see the rebellion therein. I must be stronger and command her more forcibly, but I have underestimated my own daughter, whom, if the truth be known, is a stranger to me. I am not ready for her retort.

'I am not sure I want the Atres throne, mother. I was not raised with such expectations, unlike Kendra, who was,' she says, the colour rising to her face. 'Kendra was in line to rule before you and I found each other.'

'She has chosen a different path.'

285

Chela looks at me. I can see she is horrified and feel uncomfortable under her scrutiny.

'Because she has chosen to marry a commoner?' she asks.

All I can do is nod. Lann sniggers and Cerid cackles, delighting in the altercation between Chela and myself. I signal for my daughter to be quiet, but she will not be silenced.

'Mother, Kendra is far better suited to the task than I, and Cator is still young. There is plenty of time to teach him the ways of a King.'

'But you are my eldest, it's only right,' I say. I realise how transparent I must appear and I am furious at Chela for making an exhibition of herself, not to mention shaming me in public. 'We will discuss this another time. Come, let us go.'

'No,' says Chela. 'I stay. And do not worry; I'm not doing this for you.'

'But..'

'For Elanor, who carried the guilt of what she did all her life. I know in here,' she says, pointing to her chest, 'that she would gladly trade places with me if she could, but she cannot and she died without making amends. I do this for her.'

'Chela!'

'Please don't worry,' says Chela. She softens her tone, trying to appease me, but it is too late, I see her for what she is now; a headstrong, sentimental fool.

'I want to do this,' she continues. 'Once I am done here I will come and find you and we will be mother and daughter again.'

I struggle to find the right words. There is nothing I can do to stop her, for she is old enough to decide her own destiny. I take deep breaths and manage to control myself, startled at the depths of my anger.

'You will always be welcome at my hearth, my daughter,' I say, but I know my tone is icy, even to my own ears. By Esu! What have I done to deserve such wilful daughters? I know now that I will never be able to meld Chela to my purpose. I have no option but to concentrate on Kendra and Fionn once more. I am sure that once I have Kendra back at Awelfryn she will see the error of her ways. Especially if I can rid her of the swineherd.

As I leave the roundhouse, all I can hear is the sound of Cerid and Lann laughing. By Esu, let them die a painful death and may their souls linger in the twilight world. May they never find peace.

Chela

I am at the quayside standing next to Fionn and Brendan, and watch as my mother, Kendra, and Cator, accompanied by a dozen warriors, begin their journey down the tributary to join the Great River itself, from whence they will travel upstream to the lands of the Atres. Gowell has already left for Vipers' Fort and in some ways I am relieved he has gone.

Despite my quarrel with Briona yesterday, or perhaps because of it, as I watch my family disappear out of sight, I begin to cry and soon my whole body is wracked with sobs. It is Kendra whom I will miss, more than anyone. Even though Fionn and Brendan try to console me, it is a long time before my crying stops.

As we walk back towards Ravensroost, I begin to resign myself to my new life. Fionn and Brendan will be travelling to Lynd later today with Canogus and Lann, and although I have been here before, I nevertheless feel as though I am amongst strangers. I will have to bear in mind that mine is the conquering tribe and living here will bring its own problems, as bitterness at the reparations festers amongst the Vellani.

I conjure up the image of Elanor in my mind's eye and draw comfort from the memory of that familiar, loving face. Her presence around me is strong and I know I am doing the right thing.

I say goodbye to Brendan and Fionn and make my way back to Cerid's dwelling, my hand digging into the fur on Yarrow's neck for comfort, wondering what the next phase of my life has in store for me.

FORTY SIX

The Isle of Lynd

Fionn

The journey takes longer than expected, a good seven days, the northerly wind pushing us back, so that the two crew members have to constantly work the sails in order to make any progress. Lann spends his days shackled to the central mast and his nights under cover of the hide that is stretched across the bows to protect the cargo. No-one pays him any attention, save to give him water and food, and to empty the pot into which he defecates. He is not allowed to relieve himself overboard, lest he throw himself into the churning waters. Lann does not seem bothered at the lack of communication. He turns his mind's eye inwards and spends most of the journey asleep. Though his wound is no longer suppurating, he is still weak from his injury.

The other passengers and crew take it in turns to sleep under the cover and although the accommodation is dry, it is cramped and we are forced to search for a space to stretch out amongst the precious cargo. Some of what we carry is for trade but the majority of the goods are destined as gifts for the Brothers. In their straightened circumstances the clans of the Vellani have been forced to dig deep to find worthy enough gifts for the Druids, but they all agree as one that Canogus should be their leader and do not begrudge their contribution. Canogus accepted their support graciously and in a manner befitting a future King, but he has withdrawn into himself, a taut expression on his face, and his eyes as grey and fathomless as the sea on which we journey. He stands often most at the prow, gazing at the shore that is always just within sight, or looking straight ahead at the white crested waves. He says little and eventually I ask Brendan what ails him.

'He is readying himself for the rituals. Fasting, purging, sweating. You name it. Then there are the mushrooms. I'm surprised you don't already know all of this, having been groomed to be King yourself.'

'Well, I know as much as most people,' I say. 'But Irven never divulged the details. I expect he would have done so in good time, but things are different now. And I don't think Briona need go through any rituals. As Irven's widow she can just assume power.'

'True. But you could still be King after her, you know, if Chela agrees to marry you, that is,' says Brendan.

At the mention of Chela I feel a sadness begin to creep over me for I know, in my heart, that she does not love me in the same way that I love her. I do know, however, that I could make her happier than that idiot Gowell and so I must not give in to gloom.

'I have not lost hope. But tell me more about the mushrooms. Are they the same ones we swallow?'

'The very same, but massive amounts. In such quantities that can turn a man's mind, so I have heard.'

Most people, including myself and Brendan, have tried the mushrooms at one time or another, especially at Samhain when the dead are honoured and the division between this world and the next is blurred. In small doses, they enhanced the colours and play with time in a strange way, or give insights of wisdom. If taken with ale, they caused one to giggle uncontrollably for some hours. But there are casualties too. Those who over-indulge suffer nightmarish visions. Some never recover.

'Sounds dangerous to me.'

'Apparently under the guidance of the Brothers, a King can see the destiny of his people unfold before his eyes.'

'And Lann, of course,' I say, lowering my voice, 'will take Mylor's place as the sacrifice.'

'That is what has been agreed,' says Brendan, his eyes shining. 'I can hardly wait to see Mylor's face when he beholds me.'

It is late afternoon when we reach the estuary. The place has a strange hush about it. Our arrival has, however, been noted and before we have even docked, a number of white-clad priests are seen running down the track to meet us. News of recent events has, of course, reached Lynd and the welcoming party are not surprised to see that it is Canogus who arrives instead of Doran. Before setting foot on the sacred isle, Canogus gives thanks to Eluna for a safe journey. As he does so, he flings a sword into the deep water. I try to see where it goes; hoping for a glimpse of Eluna but the briny darkness devours the offering before it has even sunk the length of a man's body.

Canogus does not recognise the brothers who have come to meet us and after the brief formalities have been concluded and our weapons surrendered, he asked after Deryn.

'He is in the middle of a ritual,' says the Druids' spokesman, a plump balding man of around forty summers who goes by the name of Nolen. He looks nervous, worrying the stained hem of his white sleeve with his thumb and forefinger.

'Our prisoner here,' says Canogus, 'is the sacrifice I bring. He is not to be trusted, so I ask that you guard him well.'

It occurs to me that Lann was partly raised on this Isle and probably knows his guards. I hope he will not escape, for I am sure he is capable of much evil, even in his sorry state, but I do not voice my concerns, for it is not my place to do so and Canogus has already spoken. As Lann is escorted towards the western side of the Isle, Nolen leads us towards our quarters. Brendan, however, cannot contain himself any longer.

'The one who was brought here by Doran. Mylor is his name. Where is he?'

Nolen looks even more worried than before and exchanges a look with another of the brothers at his side. The blood drains from Brendan's face. There is something amiss, that much is clear. He looks at Canogus pleadingly.'

'Take us to Mylor, now,' says Canogus. His voice is strong and brooks no argument.

Nolen, clearly unused to assuming responsibility, looks relieved to be told what to do and quickening his step almost to a run, takes us along the path, not towards the settlement as expected, but to the woods that crest the highest part of the isle.

'Come quick then,' he says. 'You may be in time.'

We run towards a ring of ancient oaks, dark against the orange sky which is thick with circling ravens. Though the smell of carrion reaches our nostrils even before we enter the wood, we are still unprepared for what we encounter when we reach the clearing. The nemeton, a dark treeless patch of ground at the centre of the wood, is strewn with the entrails of all manner of beast and fowl. The area is ringed by trees and some of the remains that hang from their branches are recognisably human. Here is an arm, green and soft with decay. There, propped up against the trunk of another oak is a leg, whilst skulls of both animals and humans in various stages of decomposition litter the ground at the edge of the clearing. No grass grows at the centre, just flattened dark earth, stained with blood and compacted into a hard, slick floor and there, at the core of the nemeton stands a wooden altar. A chopping block to be precise, drenched in blood, some of which is black with age, some ruddier and ominously fresh. All of this we take in in one horrified glance, but it is the two figures at the centre of the tableau who command our attention. A white-robed priest, eyes wild, hair and beard askew, is raising a dagger into the air, ready to rip apart the belly of the naked man who lies across the altar.

The man's hands are tied together, as are his ankles. His arms flop backwards past his head and the only part of his body that is in contact with the sacrificial block is the small of his back. Time itself takes on an elastic quality as I see that his torso has been painted with intricate blue designs. The sacrifice is smiling at no-one in particular, seemingly unaware of the fate that is about to befall him.

Brendan surges into the centre of the clearing and stands in front of the priest, who is clearly in a demented state, as white flecks of spittle have formed at the corners of his mouth. His eyes narrow at the interruption, and he lowers his blade, focussing on the intruder.

'Who dares enter the nemeton?'

His voice carries throughout the woodland, reverberating off the trees. The sky has darkened and the orange has deepened into an unholy purple behind the trees. There is no wind and an unnatural stillness settles over the scene.

'Put down the dagger, Deryn,' says Brendan. His voice is calm and cold and I suddenly realise who he is addressing. It is none other than Deryn, himself, Chief Druid of Lynd. The man on the altar can only be Mylor.

Deryn laughs. Mylor giggles, not recognising his friend.

He has been drugged.

'What have you done to him?' Brendan asks.

'Stand back,' says Deryn, lifting the dagger to strike. 'The Gods demand it.'

Brendan, weaponless, can only rush at the priest, but Deryn still holds his knife and instead of ripping into Mylor's stomach, he turns and slashes at his assailant. Brendan manages to dodge the worst of the blow but slithers on a piece of slippery intestine and loses his balance, falling to the floor. The blade gouges a shallow cut on his cheek. I, and the rest of our party it would appear, are too stunned to move, but as Deryn raises his knife to strike Brendan again, I force myself to act. Before I can cover the small distance towards where my friend lies, a voice bellows out from the edge of the clearing. It is a voice like no other, deep and resonant, echoing through the forest, speaking an ancient tongue lost to all but the most learned of Brothers.

The words mean nothing to me, but Deryn freezes to the spot, his eyes wide, panic writ on his face. The voice is terrifying but what is even more immobilising is the strange language, older even than the ground on which we stand, resonant of the magic of creation itself. Deryn drops the knife and falls to his knees, then puts his forehead to the ground, rather than look at the source of the voice.

Brendan, conversely, stands up. He is covered in dark blood and purple entrails, but he does not care and peers in the direction of his rescuer. Though Nolen and the other brothers have thrown themselves prostrate on the ground, Canogus joins me at Brendan's side. The three of us stare at the trees, not daring to breathe. Then something stirs.

Whether by divine orchestration or coincidence, the purple clouds part to allow a golden shaft of dying sunlight to pierce the circle of trees, casting a halo around the figure emerging from the gloom. Though there is little light left, what I see will remain with me for the rest of my days. An enormous white stag shimmers in the shadows, its antlers bright against the darkness behind. Though I have never seen him before, I know instinctively that I am looking at the Nameless One, the god of all forms. I swear the beast looks directly at me before melting into the shadows, his antlers merging with the branches until he dissolves into the trees themselves. Where the beast stood now appears a man, a mere mortal in a white robe, speaking the ancient tongue. Behind him stand half a dozen white-robed brothers. Their leader hands his headdress to one of the brothers, then two others stride into the nemeton and yank Deryn to his feet.

'Druce!' whispers Brendan, but the Chief Druid from the Isle of Mona pays him no heed. His attention is fully on Deryn.

'I understand,' says Druce through gritted teeth, 'that you have been causing trouble, my friend.'

Deryn says nothing. His spirit broken, he is led away from the scene, all but one of the brothers following. The remaining priest rushes towards Mylor in a flurry of concern.

'Mylor!' he shouts. 'Are you alright?'

He withdraws a dagger from his sleeve and cuts the ropes that bind Mylor's wrists and ankles. Lifting him off the sacrificial block, he lays him on the floor and holds his face close to his own, examining Mylor's eyes, a worried look on his face.

'Quick! Help me,' he says. 'We must make him sick.'

Brendan rushes to help. The young priest flips Mylor over his knees as one would a choking child and with Brendan's help, sticks a finger into the back of Mylor's throat. We hear Mylor gag and then a torrent of vomit floods out onto the ground. Once Mylor starts to vomit, his body takes over until there is nothing left in his stomach.

'Good,' says the priest. 'Now help me get him to bed. He needs water and to be kept warm.'

Brendan takes one arm and the brother the other. Together they support Mylor who stumbles along, his teeth chattering. Canogus and I follow, too stunned for words in the aftermath of the evening's drama. As they carry Mylor away from the woods, I hear Brendan speak.

'And who, might I ask, are you?' he says, addressing the brother.

'I am Bari. I am Mylor's true friend. And you?'

'Brendan,' he says, his voice flat. 'My name is Brendan. Did Mylor mention me at all?'

The same dark purple clouds that had provided such a dramatic sunset proceed to cover the night sky in a choking veil before emptying their burden over the Isle in a torrent so dense that it is hard to catch one's breath. The rain comes down in vertical lines, battering the dried ground, bubbling down the walkways and paths until Lynd resembles no more than a lake of mud. By the time we reach the roundhouse, we are drenched to the skin, the painted designs on Mylor's stomach dissolving into a mesh of blue, the patterns lost for eternity.

Bari flings a piece of cloth at Brendan who dries his friend before putting him to bed under a thick covering of furs. A glimmer of recognition crosses Mylor's face before he slides into unconsciousness.

'Wake him up,' says Bari. 'We must make him drink.'

Brendan shakes Mylor awake and puts a vessel of water to his mouth.

'Here,' he says.

Mylor's eyes flutter open and he looks at his old friend.

'Brendan,' he whispers. 'Is that really you?'

We stay on the Isle for five days. Canogus is taken away to a secret place where he undergoes his purifications under the watchful eye of Druce and does not emerge until it is time to leave.

Mylor begins to recover from the herbs he had been given and is soon on his feet. He and Brendan spend a great deal of time together, whilst Bari, a pensive expression on his face, tends to Lann's needs. I find myself alone for the most part. I try to engage Bari in conversation but he seems ill at ease, and though pleasant, somewhat preoccupied with his own thoughts.

Lann is fed sumptuous food and wine, but in view of his violent past, remains shackled by one ankle to the central post of the roundhouse which he inhabits alone. After two days he is taken away and although no more is heard of him, it is known that he has been ceremonially killed and dismembered. His head remains at Lynd, but his torso will be buried at Ravensroost and his limbs carried by the brothers to the four cardinal points of the Vellani Kingdom, to be buried in the ground, a potent blessing of the tribal borders. He is not as powerful a sacrifice as Mylor would have been, but adequate for the rituals. The usual festivities accompanying a Kingship ceremony, where the leaders of the land come to witness the coronation, will be waived. The Vellani cannot summon the resources to mount such a feast.

On the day of our departure Canogus emerges from his confinement. He is changed man. He has a certain look about his eyes and though his countenance is grave, he gives the impression of one who has a clear idea of his own destiny, untroubled by doubt, strong and commanding in his stature. As I study my friend, I experience a tinge of self-doubt. Canogus looks so regal, so befitting his new role. Would I be able to command such awe, if I were to become King of the Atres?

Putting away such thoughts, I greet Canogus as a friend, and he in turn, greets me warmly. Together we board the vessel, ready to leave the Isle and impatient to get on with our lives. We are waiting for Brendan and Mylor and I pace up and down, wondering what is taking so long. My plan is to return to Ravensroost to see Chela one more time before heading westwards and home, to step into Caradwg's role as leader of the House of Morffryn.

Druce comes to bid us a good journey and to bless the wooden chest that contains Lann's dismembered body. Before he leaves us, I ask after Cederin. The slave, it transpires, was true to his word. He made it to the Isle of Mona in one piece and was able to warn Druce of Deryn's meddling.

'And how is he?' I ask.

'He is well. He works amongst us, a free man; a shepherd, and is planning to wed soon.'

My throat constricts at the news and I feel the sting of tears behind my eyelids. I look away from Druce's all-knowing gaze, lest I embarrass myself.

Four of the brothers of Lynd carry the chest onto the boat. They will journey with the sacrifice to ensure the ritual is carried out properly and then Canogus will be proclaimed King.

Before long, three figures are seen walking towards the boat.

'At last,' I say. 'I was beginning to think they weren't coming at all.'

As I watch, I notice Brendan looks sad, his eyes red, and it is not until I witness him grasp Mylor by the shoulders and then embrace him, that I realise he will be leaving his friend, nay his soul-mate, behind. Brendan, his shoulders heavy with emotion, climbs aboard and without a word to anyone, sits by the bows, his face expressionless. Canogus and I know better than to question him and leave him alone. He will find us when he is ready to talk.

As the Isle of Lynd recedes and the estuary opens up into the northern sea, the rain that has fallen in a constant stream for five days suddenly stops. Brendan turns for one last glimpse of the Isle where his true friend remains. He raises a hand in farewell, and as he does so, the clouds part to reveal an azure sky and a rainbow of startling clarity over Lynd. I look at Brendan and see him close his eyes and smile. I know what he is doing. He is making a wish.

FORTY SEVEN

The Lands of the Atres

Kendra

My reunion with Pedwar is noisy and joyful. As promised, as soon as Fionn returned to Buzzardstone he arranged for the hound to be sent to Awelfryn and I do not have long to wait for the goods wagon to arrive. Amongst the produce is Pedwar, eyes alert, tongue lolling, glad to be home. Once unleashed, he hurls himself at me, howling and whining in pleasure, knocking me to the ground at least twice. I cannot believe he remembers me, and I cry, burying my face in his grey mane, whilst Cator looks on, smiling, his eyes shining.

But our homecoming is not without its sadness and Cator and I have a sorrowful task ahead of us. Hand in hand we walk the distance to the dilapidated farmhouse at the far side of the valley below Awelfryn, trepidation in our hearts. The roundhouse is in dire need of repair, its thatch has fallen in places and the lime plaster on the exterior wall has decayed, revealing the wattle beneath, letting in the damp.

Cator pulls out the hag stone that was in his pocket and we look at it for a moment, as it lies at in the palm of his hand. He takes a deep breath then knocks on the door. Before long, a woman of middle years, a relative of his, appears. When she sees Cator, her eyes widen and she ushers us in, offering us food and drink, though it is obvious she can ill afford such hospitality. It would be an insult to refuse and so we accept her meagre offerings with thanks. Words are difficult. Cator places the hag stone in woman's hand, his touch lingering a moment, as though to comfort her.

The woman breaks down in tears, and I put my arm around her. After a while, we speak and the story of Huel and Malvina is heard. We take it in turns to tell the tale, leaving out the cruellest details until at last it is told. We make much of Huel's bravery and Malvina's resilience.

'We could not save them, alas, but their tormentor lies cold, in the ground,' says Cator at last. 'Not for him the joys of rebirth.'

Malvina and Huel's mother thanks us, crying all the while until we finally leave to visit Morvyn's folk, to repeat our sorrowful task.

It is a difficult day, but we cling together, glad of each other's company as we head home, not back to Awelfryn but to the farmstead wherein Cator's family dwell. They have made me welcome and it is with them I reside.

My mother was firm in her resolve. She made it plain that if I were to marry "the swineherd" as she insists on referring to Cator, that is my choice, but amongst Cator's folk I must live. I know she believes I will "see sense" and tire of my new life, but what she does not realise is how much I have changed. Does she really believe that after what I have been through, living in a farmstead is a hardship? Well, perhaps at last, I have grown up, a fact that my mother, who now seems unstoppable in her power, has failed to notice.

FORTY EIGHT

Ravensroost

Chela

Though my time at Ravensroost passes slowly, it is not all bad and the fact that I am away from the demands of my mother, Gowell and Fionn comes as something of a relief. I am yet to know my own heart and I hope that my servitude at Ravensroost will give me the time I need to think.

Lann's mother gives me a hard time. As far as she is concerned, it is my fault that her own daughter was murdered and it is also my fault that Lann's body lies buried at the heart of the settlement and his limbs have been scattered to the four corners of the tribal lands. Not for him, the knowledge of rebirth. His penance will be to guard the Vellani borders for all eternity.

Most days Cerid hurls abuse at me and sometimes she tries to beat me with her walking stick. What enables me to withstand her ravings is an image of Elanor in my mind's eye, and knowing that I live because another died. Deep down, I understand the woman and I bear her no rancour. I will be free in the fullness of time, to live my life as I choose; the woman I serve was not given the luxury of such choices.

At other times Cerid speaks softly to me, calling me by another name, Etain, that of her long dead daughter. Every day I massage Cerid's aching limbs and administer pain-killing herbs. The woman's demise is slow but sure, the illness inside her devouring her from the inside. Her skin is becoming sallower and more papery, her fingernails milky and ridged and her eyes cloudy, yet still she clings on to life. Lamas comes and goes, when the abundance of the earth goddess, Anwyn, is celebrated with much feasting and drinking. Then comes the late autumn festival of Samhain when we honour the dead. I make an offering in memory of Elanor and Erea and two others; my father Irven whom I never met, and Etain. In the early spring at the festival of Imbolc, I help herd the cattle through the ring of fire, to purify them in readiness for the summer. Beltane comes and goes with its life-affirming festivities and still Cerid lingers on death's threshold, weakening by the day but clinging on to her remaining fragments of life.

Three full seasons have passed since Canogus' return from Lynd to take up the mantle of Kingship. He and his wife cried openly when their little son was taken away to be raised amongst the Druids, as is the custom, and I empathise with their sorrow. Canogus' ceremony was witnessed by the Elders of each tribe, but in view of the Vellani's recent humiliation and straightened circumstances, he declined to host the full-blown celebrations that normally accompany a coronation. He and his wife are kind to me but they are caught up in the affairs of the Court and, because of my status as a daughter of the Atres ruler, they keep me at arms' length. The Vellani defeat is still a raw wound and the Atres' Queen, my mother, an unknown quantity.

I wonder how Fionn is faring, stepping into his father's shoes. Brendan returned to Ravensroost with Fionn, heartbroken and sad, but instead of staying with his own kin, decided to live at Buzzardstone, where Fionn guaranteed he would suffer no torment, to start a new life amongst the Atres.

When I am not seeing to Cerid's needs, I help Liam, the resident healer at Ravensroost, with the ailing and sick who come from afar. It seems my reputation as a healer has grown and I was amazed when Liam told me that my name is spoken throughout the land as one who can ease any pain or cure most ailments. It is not I, of course, but the powerful foreign herbs that do the work. Nonetheless, I must confess to being just a bit gratified by such news. Liam is a gentle and retiring man, of later years, and instead of being jealous of me, he is keen to learn all he can. I let him have as many seeds as I can spare and help him plant them out in the late spring, when there is no more danger of frosts. The delicate foreign plants thrive under his care but our relationship is by no means one-sided. Liam has many years' experience as a healer and he is a keen observer. He was taught by the Brothers themselves and knows the best moon times for different tasks as well as the correct prayers to say when creating a concoction. All this he teaches me and he is keen to impart his knowledge of the local herbs, and together we while away the time companionably, Yarrow, as ever, keeps close to me at all times.

I occasionally hear snippets of news from the boatmen who travel up and down the river. The Durotriges, true to their word, opened up access to the Veneti traders. All the tribes of the south and east are beginning to benefit from the additional trade, though the trickle of slaves from the north and west has now turned into a steady flow, the demand from Rome continuing unabated. I learn that Bearcban has forgiven the Durotriges for losing his daughter so carelessly and bears no grudges. Nothing further has been heard of Armelle and Doran and it is assumed they fled to the continent to start a new life in Rome. The meddling Druid, Deryn has been exiled to Gaul.

It is Riana and Cinea whom I miss most, and whenever a Durotriges sailor comes to Ravensroost I seek him out, wanting the latest gossip. It is midsummer when one such sailor, complaining of a persistent cough, comes to find me. Whilst I ply him with medicines, I interrogate him for the latest news. It seems that everyone is thriving at Vipers' Fort, but the juiciest bit of news is of a forthcoming royal marriage. I feel my stomach tighten.

'Who is to marry?' I ask. 'And when?'

The sailor shrugs. He is not from Viper's Fort itself and does not know the ins and outs of court gossip.

'One of Hanu's sons. I know nothing more,' he says.

I realise I cannot glean any more information from him, but just as he is leaving, I decide to ask one more question. He is, after all, a sailor and would know if a boat such as that owned by Grypsos had recently docked at Vipers' Fort.

'What of the foreign traders? Have any arrived recently?'

He looks thoughtful, rubbing his stubbly chin.

'Why yes, come to think of it. A Roman merchantman vessel. The Niad, I believe. Yes, I did see it. It's still at Viper's Fort harbour. In fact I do believe the owner was planning to travel the Great River. You may even see the ship. A fine specimen. More than I could ever aspire to,' he says morosely, before taking his leave.

I can barely contain my excitement. I believe the forthcoming wedding must be between Ivor and Riana, but I cannot dispel the tiniest suspicion that it might be Gowell. Perhaps he has tired of waiting for me to give my answer. Different emotions battle for supremacy until I shrug them off. It is useless to conjecture. The best news of all is that Grypsos is back in the country. Then I remember my duties and for a moment I feel sorely constrained by my promise. But I have given my word, and I will not leave Cerid now. I will have to bide my time until Lann's mother departs this earthly domain.

I do not need to wait very long. Around Cerid there develops a certain odour, sickly and sweet. I have smelled something similar before and know it for the smell of death. The ailing woman barely speaks these days and she is too tired to be abusive or violent towards me. She has taken to her bed and I spend long hours sitting next to her, carving toys for the local children out of soft green oak or stitching leather garments.

It is only a few days since I spoke with the sailor, when I notice Cerid's breathing has become more and more laboured until it is obvious she is breathing her last. I call for the women to come and attend, and a song is raised on which Cerid is borne to the next world.

I find myself crying for the wretched life Cerid lived and hope I have done something to alleviate her suffering. But even as I mourn, my excitement is growing, I have done my duty, for myself, for Elanor and Briona, and I am free at last.

It is always something of a mystery, is it not, that when one has made the proper sacrifices, how the Goddesses step in to lend a hand and smooth the way. As if by magic, three days after Cerid is placed on her platform and carried off to the heavens, a Roman merchantman is seen travelling up the river towards the quayside that services Ravensroost. Word spreads like wildfire and as soon as I hear the news, I take a horse from the pound and ride as fast as I dare to meet the boat.

'Grypsos!' I shout repeatedly, even before the boat is within hailing distance.

Before long I am able to discern the individual features of the crew members, and standing at the prow, grinning from ear to ear, is Grypsos, my dear old friend.

The boat docks and amidst a flurry of hugs, we make our way on foot to the Ravensroost, I leading the horse by its reins.

'It's so good to see you!' I say, and I know I am babbling, but cannot stop myself.

'What are your plans?' I ask, once we have sat down in Liam's house, tucking into a hearty pork and pea stew. Bundles of drying herbs hang from every post and the worktop is strewn with potions in various stages of completion. Liam hovers around for a while before leaving us to talk in peace.

'Once I have my fine goods from the Vellani, I plan to spend a little time with you, Little Daughter, before my return to Vipers' Fort. Then home,' he says. 'But, you, I had to see, though I suspect you would be already wed by now?'

I laugh, evading his non-too-delicately phrased question. Since Grypsos told me the wedding is to be between Ivor and Riana, I have not stopped grinning. 'Well, I am free now, and had hoped you will let me travel with you to Vipers' Fort.'

Grypsos is more than happy to oblige. After his business is concluded, I bid farewell to Liam and the others I have got to know at

Ravensroost. As we board the vessel, Yarrow at my heels as ever, I appraise the boat.

'This is not the Niad,' I say.

'It is Niad Two' says Grypsos proudly. 'My old vessel, it fell to pieces! The Goddess, she smiled on us, for we made it back without loss.'

'She is a beautiful boat,' I say, admiring the neatly turned woodwork. 'And strong.'

Grypsos beams, clearly proud of his newest acquisition.

The journey progresses without incident, and I use the time to acquaint myself with the boat, making myself useful as both sailor and cook. Grypsos retained his old crew and they welcome me and Yarrow aboard, regaling me with their ribald humour. It is said the Greeks hold women in disdain, but Grypsos and his crew are from Alexandria, where I am told, as in Britain, the women are strong, can own property and have rights under the law.

I love the way the boat lists underneath me, the fresh salty smell and the way the wind whips my hair into a frenzy. I feel part of the elements as I stand at the prow; no need here to stand on ceremony or worry that my hair is all of a tangle. Grypsos and I talk often and I ask him again and again to tell me about the huge beasts called elephants, or another animal, twice as large as a horse with a hump on its back. I half wonder if he is making up the stories to amuse me, nonetheless I enjoy listening to him, just as I did as a child.

Grypsos also talks of more serious matters, explaining how the Romans have taken control of the Mediterranean lands and how they fight amongst themselves constantly.

'The merchants, they are uneasy these days. Bad for trade,' he says, stroking his chin. 'And I think perhaps Rome grows to enjoy to fight. It is not good.'

We also talk about Elanor, whom Grypsos truly loved, and eventually the conversation centres on me and as my words tumble out in the presence of my old friend, who makes no demands and simply listens, I realise at last, what I must do.

FORTY NINE

Viper's Fort

Chela

On the third day, Vipers' Fort's familiar crescent-shaped harbour hoves into view. It is busier than ever, full of cargoes of grain, metal and slaves ready to be despatched in return for the ubiquitous amphorae of wine. As I behold the sullen slaves chained together at the quayside, snatched from goodness knows which tribe, I feel glad that Grypsos refuses to deal in human cargo.

'The Niad, it is not suitable,' he says but I believe that like me, he abhors the trafficking of people and the misery it brings. Instead he will load his hold up as far as he dares with the precious tin and silver from the south west, and the iron ore local to Vipers' Fort, as well as the cereal grains and cloaks that he will sell on route. But it is the metal that earns him his living. He has expert knowledge of the market and where to sell for the best profit.

As we dock at the quayside, I scan the crowds for a familiar face. None of my friends at Vipers' Fort are expecting me and I feel my excitement mounting. But I have something I must do before I see my friends.

'Grypsos,' I say, 'will you come with me to Elanor's resting place?'

We walk together until we reached the place of the dead, Yarrow racing ahead of us, knowing where we are heading. We climb the wooden frame until we reach the platform; it is windy up here, yet there is a stillness about the place. I see there are more recent burials, but I know which one is Elanor. On the morrow, Grypsos and I will bury her bones, quietly and without ceremony, for we know her soul has long gone, and my work for her is done. After a moment's silence, we make our way down to the ground.

'I came to the nemeton, below us in the woods, before Elanor died,' I say, 'to make an offering, and to ask for something in return.'

'And it was given?' asks Grypsos, sitting on a boulder and gesturing for me to join him.

'Yes. But at the time I felt my offering unworthy, and so it was. I did not understand the nature of sacrifice.'

'And now you do? Your time with Cerid?'

I nod.

'I thought I was doing it to atone for Elanor's part in Cerid's destruction, but in giving, I reached understanding.'

'Your heart? You came to know it?'

I grin at Grypsos.

'I did. Just as you promised.'

Grypsos and I walk together to the main settlement and I am greeted with warm hugs and excited chatter. After I have given an account of my year, the talk turns to the wedding.

'Only three days to go,' says Riana. 'I am so nervous, but oh, so glad you will be here to witness it!'

'Fionn and Brendan are coming, and Briona,' says Cinea. 'As Hanu's guests of honour. They will be arriving any day now!'

I receive the news gladly. Before long, Ivor and Gowell arrive. Ivor crushes me in a brotherly hug, whilst Gowell hangs back, no doubt gauging my reaction to him, but when I fling my arms around his neck and give him a warm kiss, a broad grin creases his face.

'It is good to see you again, Gowell,' I say, and find that I mean it.

Though Gowell wants to speak to me alone, the excitement and preparations for the wedding mean that he does not get the opportunity. The next day Briona turns up, accompanied by Fionn and Brendan and her greeting is warmer than I expected.

'I was so sorry to have to leave you at Ravensroost,' she says. 'But I thank you for making things right with Cerid in the end.'

'It wasn't so bad, after all,' I say, 'But tell me, where are Kendra and Cator?'

'Back home. They had no desire to return here.'

'Of course,' I say and I know my disappointment is plain to behold.

'You will be able to see them when we go home,' says Briona. 'I have much to show you, and you must learn the ways of the Atres.'

The words I want to say to Briona will have to wait until after the wedding, lest they spoil the joyous atmosphere.

It is obvious Fionn is anxious to talk to me and although I am pleased to see both he and Brendan, I manage to avoid our inevitable conversation until the time is right. I have noticed, however, that he has lost all trace of his boyishness and he has his full tribal tattoos. His shoulders and chest have broadened and his arms and neck are strong. He has a look about him that speaks of wisdom, but the humour in his eyes is still there. His presence makes me feel flustered, for I know he still seeks an answer from me but he has the good grace to leave me alone until I am ready to speak with him. I have a good excuse after all. It is customary for the bride's friends to stay close to her in the days leading up to her wedding, to wash and perfume her hair and body, to manicure her nails and to remove any unwanted body hair with soft warm wax and to tell her stories of love and honour. Riana's mother and father arrived yesterday in one of Bearcban's ships, bringing with them Riana's dowry and though it cannot compare to Armelle's, it is nonetheless perfectly adequate, a large portion comprising some of the finest Italian wines.

The wedding day comes amidst a flurry of excitement, the sky without a cloud and a warm summer breeze whispering through the trees. We women are up at dawn, helping to dress the bride, and when we have finished, she looks stunning. Riana's dark hair has been woven with summer flowers and she wears a light linen dress imported from the southern lands, embroidered with the geometric designs beloved of the Greeks and fastened at the waist by a finely engraved golden belt. She carries in her hands a solid gold torc, engraved with the Durotriges Owl, as a gift for her husband.

Ivor emerges from his father's roundhouse, blurry-eyed from the night's drinking with his warrior friends, but excited and happy. He too carries a gold torc, to present to Riana.

Druce, the Chief Druid from Mona has also arrived in good time with a handful of white-robed brothers, one of whom turns out to be the bard, Keary. When Gowell sets eyes on the musician, he reaches for his sword, but Hanu stops him.

'Not on your brother's wedding day,' he says, and his look brooks no argument.

The wedding, carried out in the open air, goes without a hitch. Prayers are raised, vows exchanged, blessings given and offerings buried at the entrance of Ivor and Riana's freshly constructed roundhouse. Keary sings his best, and when he stops singing, plays on his kithera. Each time he rests the guests roar and stamp their feet for more, until he is so hoarse he can no longer sing and his fingers almost bleed. It is then that the bards take over with their story-telling and their poetry. Wine flows like water from a spring and there is roast beef, roast pork and roast mutton to be had as well as honey-cakes and summer fruit.

As the day wears on into evening and the merriment grows, I take the opportunity to talk to the people I love. The first person I seek out is Hanu, who stands listening to one of the bards telling a long and well-known tale of love and romance. Next to him are Riana's parents. I draw Hanu to one side where we cannot be overheard and speak with him at length, until he kisses me on both cheeks. I am aware of Gowell watching from across the bonfire.

The next is Briona.

'Will you come and walk with me a while, mother?' I ask.

'What is it, my dear, that can't wait until after the celebrations?'

Briona is listening to the story and is not altogether pleased to be interrupted. Nevertheless, she follows me to my roundhouse and looking a little disdainfully at the plain furniture, sits down and waits for me to speak.

'There is something I must know,' I say, gathering my courage to ask.

'What is it, my daughter?'

'You told me that there was once something between yourself and Hanu... I must know, am I Hanu's child?'

Briona smiles. She knows Gowell and I were once close and I can see how her mind is working.

'No,' she says. 'You are Irven's daughter, without a doubt. Though Hanu and I loved each other, we were never lovers. Oh, I would have lain with him in an instant, but he was too loyal a friend to Irven.'

Relief floods through me as I realize I have not transgressed natures' very laws.

'Now, my dear, if there is nothing else...'

'Mother, there is one more thing. I am not coming with you.'

'Don't talk such nonsense my dear!'

'Hear me out. It was one of my happiest days when I found you, but I have no place amongst the Atres. I have no desire to rule, nor to follow in your footsteps. It is Kendra who is the one worthy to be your successor, not I.'

'Let us hear no more of this. If you are worried about causing a rift between yourself and your sister, Kendra understands full well what she has done and bears you no ill.'

'It isn't that, mother,' I say. 'I simply don't want to come with you.'

'But what are you going to do? Oh, I see,' she says, a smile breaking out across her face. 'I understand....'

I know what she is about to say and put my hand up to stop her.

'No, mother, it's not that. Kendra is the right person to rule. I cannot understand your aversion to Cator. I have said this much before. He is strong and brave and honest and it would not take long to teach him the ways of the court.'

'My dear, I'll hear no more of this nonsense. He is a swineherd, the lowest of the low. It is unthinkable that he could be King. You, on the other hand, are of noble birth and between us we can make the Atres great again. If you want to marry Gowell, then all well and good, I am not one to stand in the way of true love. I will simply have to rid us of Cator and make Kendra see sense and then she will rule. You see, my dear, if you marry Gowell, the alliance will be strengthened but if you go on to inherit the throne, the Atres would be ruled by the Durotriges and I could not allow that. Especially as I know I can make us great once more. Hanu has sworn to help me start up our own slave trade – Rome pays a handsome price for manpower.'

I look at my mother in horror.

'You wish to profit from the misery of others?'

Briona shrugs.

'It is the way of the world. Irven was foolish when he refused such trade.'

'Then my mind is made up. I want no part of it.'

Briona remains quiet for what seems a long time, struggling with something inside. Eventually she speaks and her voice is cold.

'I am sorry to lose you so soon, but whatever you decide to do, I wish you well. Just remember,' she says, squaring her shoulders, 'should you change your mind, there is always a home for you at Awelfryn.'

I watch my mother leave. My blood kin have not turned out quite as I had hoped, except for Kendra of course, who has shown courage and integrity. My own father wanted me dead, and years of bitterness has soured my mother's soul. It is Elanor who raised me as her own; Elanor my true mother, Elanor who has left me for all eternity. I look around my familiar home and it feels empty. *Nearly there. I am nearly there.*

Fionn proves harder to locate. He, Annan and Brendan have snuck off and are inside the Durotriges' main forge. They dragged an amphora of wine with them and are making a good job of polishing it off when I find them.

'There you are!' I say. 'Brendan, Annan, may I have a few quiet words with Fionn here?'

'Of course,' says Brendan, rising to his feet. He is a little unsteady, but still manages a broad wink at Fionn before leaving us alone. Annan, who I do not think is capable of speech, staggers after him.

I am relieved to see that Fionn is a great deal more sober than Brendan.

'I have come to give my answer,' I say.

'I thought you had, but I know it already.'

'And how is that?' I ask.

'I have seen how you look at Gowell,' he says. 'It's perfectly clear to me which one of us you have chosen. I wish you well.'

A small burp escapes as he finishes talking, causing me to giggle, despite the seriousness of the moment.

'Oh Fionn! You are such a wonderful person. And you are right about one thing, my answer is no, and I thank you for being so good and patient about it.'

'I wanted so much to be King of the Atres,' he says. 'But after I met you, I realised that my betrothal to Kendra was wrong, for many reasons. After I got to know you, though part of me still wanted to be King, I want you to know that's not why I asked you to marry me.'

'I know, Fionn, I know, and I thank you for that.'

'Hey, you never did finish that joke.'

I smile.

'Alright. Three Dobunni warriors walk into a settlement....'

We talk for a while longer and as we make a substantial dent in the wine, I tell him of my dreams and desires. As we re-join the party together, I see that Gowell is watching us closely.

He approaches and I gulp hard, the old familiar feelings are stirring, and the wine is making me feel mellow and warm. The festivities have gone on all day and well into the night. Guests are beginning to head towards their beds, and though the story-telling and poetry has stopped, Keary picks up his kithera again and begins to strum a soothing melody.

'Gowell,' I say before he can speak. 'You want your answer. Come with me.'

I take his hand and lead him to my house. As soon as we are inside, Gowell takes me in his arms and kisses me on the mouth. Though my body yearns for him, and the wine works to weaken my resolve, I withdraw and stand firm. Gowell smiles down at me, confident that I am, at last, his.

'Now, my Atres Princess,' he says. 'Will you be my wife?'

I give him my answer but he just smiles indulgently and shakes his head. He draws me down to lie next to him on the furs. He talks, and I listen. I used to think his ability to share his feelings set him apart from other men, and I loved him for it, but today his words fail to move me. Propped up on one elbow, I study his face as he plays with a strand of my hair. I know he is trying to win back my love, but as the grey light of dawn filters through the doorway, I notice the hardness around his mouth and a cold cruelty in his eyes. He asks me again, to change my mind, but I withdraw and he realises, finally, that I mean what I say. Before taking his leave, he unpins a brooch from his tunic and presses it hard into my palm.

'It carries the mark of the Owl,' he says, a sourness edging his voice. 'Do not forget its meaning.'

'Which meaning?' I ask 'There are two.'

Gowell does not answer, but I know which he has in mind. He shakes his head, turns his back on me and strides out of the roundhouse.

I look around my home, the place where I grew up, full of memories, both good and bad, but mainly good. I walk around its familiar circle. As I do so, I gather up those items that are precious to me; the square of silk from Ivor, the bracelet given to me as a child; a string of shale beads that once belonged to Elanor, a gold brooch with the image of an Atres horse Fionn made especially for me and a leash and collar for Yarrow to wear; a present from Kendra. Gowell's gift, I place on the flagstone next to the hearth where it will be found. Then I pack my spare clothing and a handful of the seeds, herbs and potions I consider indispensable.

As I turn to face the gentle dawn, a familiar shape looms in the doorway.

'Are you ready?' asks Grypsos.

'We are,' I say, stroking Yarrow's head.

'Then the Niad awaits.'

THE END

311

Author's note

I started writing The Owl of the Durotriges in 2008 after completing a degree in archaeology at Canterbury University. My dissertation was on the deposition of votive objects on boundaries and thresholds in Iron Age Britain, but the more I discovered about the era, the more fascinated I became with all aspects of Iron Age life.

I decided to write the story in the first person as I felt it in keeping with the oral traditions of the time. Some of the folktales that have survived to this day, especially the Irish and Welsh stories, may have their origins in Celtic Britain, but it is impossible to be certain, and the absence of any written record means we have to rely on archaeology and later scholarly scribbling, to inform us of the period.

Much credit is given to the Romans for their civilising influence, but there is growing evidence to suggest that Britain was creating her own towns well before Caesar, whilst conducting a roaring trade with the continent, not only via Gaul, but also from Hengistbury Head in Dorset with the Veneti tribe of Amorica (modern day Brittany).

Even the much lauded Roman roads are now believed to follow earlier Iron Age tracks. Although Julius Caesar gives the impression that we were a backward bunch of barbarians, we must remember that he was writing from the point of view of the invader, much in the same way recent colonialism justified its actions by insisting that it was bringing enlightenment to so-called 'savages'.

The names given to the Iron Age tribes, perhaps loosely based on their Celtic equivalents, were bestowed by the Romans who divided the land into administrative districts, and as such we cannot be certain what the tribes were called in the Celtic language.

Similarly, we cannot be sure of the exact territories the pre-Roman era tribes controlled. Some archaeologists place the Belgae geographically between the Atrebates and the Durotriges, whereas others, such as Barry Cunliffe (1991, page 160) don't include them at all. H Furneaux, in his translation of Tacitus' The Agricola and Germania, omits the Durotriges, Atrebates and Catuvellauni altogether from his map. For the purposes of my story, I have left out the Belgae, preferring to incorporate them under the 'Durotriges' banner and for ease of reading, I have shortened the names of the Atrebates to Atres, the Cantiaci to Canti and the Catuvellauni (who may or may not have even existed as a discrete entity at that time) to Vellani.

Archaeology can provide a wealth of detail about the everyday lives of ancient peoples, but the absence of a written record means that as a novelist, I am free, within reason, to embellish the facts.

I have, perhaps, taken liberties in suggesting that a Roman Merchantman vessel might have graced the shores of Britain at that time. There is ample archaeological evidence by way of amphorae of wine, imported pottery, coinage and glass, to suggest that Hengistbury Head was an entreport in receipt of goods from the continent and the Roman world, but none to support the presence of Roman ships in the area. During Caesar's time it is documented that his men were reluctant to cross the Channel as they thought they were at the 'end of the known world'. There is, however, evidence to suggest that the much earlier Phoenicians traded for silver off the Cornish coast and so, in my opinion, it is not beyond the realms of possibility that a Roman trading ship might have made the journey to Hengistbury Head.

The herb I have named Silverweed did exist and was known as 'Silphium' by the Greeks. Both Dioscorides and Soranus mentioned its use as a contraceptive and abortive agent. It is believed that it was harvested to extinction in its native Libya and attempts to revive its cultivation were met with failure.

Burial practices in the late Iron Age are varied. In the Dorset region there are burials in pits; in shallow graves, with and without grave goods. Examination of certain bones suggest that bodies may have also been bound and then left on platforms at the mercy of the elements (a practice known as excarnation) only to be gathered and buried later.

A character in the story receives a gift of silk; again there is no archaeological evidence to support this, but we do know that silk was available in Rome during this period and so if Italian amphorae, glass and tableware were finding their way to our shores, why not more perishable goods?

I also suggest that some of the herbs we believe were introduced by the Romans, may have made their way to Britain a little earlier, again via the trade routes.

The Owl of the Durotriges is a novel, and although I have tried as far as possible to confine myself to what we know from archaeological discoveries, I hope the reader will join me in conjuring a society where contact with the continental mainland was a more frequent occurrence that we may have hitherto imagined.

314

Suggested reading:

Iron Age Britain by Barry Cunliffe 1995 and 2004, BT Batsford
Hengistbury Head by Barry Cunliffe 1978, Elek Books
Iron Age Communities in Britain by Barry Cunliffe 1991, 3rd edition, Routledge
Prehistoric Britain by Timothy Darvill 1987, reprinted in 2000, Routledge
The Search for the Durotriges by Martin Papworth 2011, The History Press
The Conquest of Gaul by Julius Caesar, translated by S.A. Handford 1951, Penguin
Agricola and The Germania by Tacitus translated by S.A. Handford 1970, Penguin

Yassmin Sanders
2012

Lightning Source UK Ltd.
Milton Keynes UK
UKOW02f1209301015

261735UK00001B/69/P